The Lammisters

Declan Burke

NO ALIBIS PRESS

First published in 2019
by No Alibis Press
Belfast

Printed and bound by TJ International, Padstow

A CIP record for this book
is available from the British Library

Hardback ISBN 978-1999882280
Trade Paperback ISBN 978-1999882273
Ebook ISBN 978-1999882266

2 4 6 8 10 9 7 5 3 1

THE LAMMISTERS

or, a Progress,
embarked upon
by a mixed company
of gunsels, loogans, molls and knights
from Hollywood to Tropico Springs
whereupon they fell into some broils,
and here related
with vim sufficient
for the purpose
of moral instruction.

by EDWARD 'BUGS' DOOLEY

For each man's sorrows he hadst a tear,
For each man's need, a shilling
– Sterne

for Boo

Chapter One

In which the chorus doll Adele Fitzhalligon discovers that Sir Archibald l'Estrange-B'stard is by no means a chevalier.

There is the Tabard Inn, of course, and the Black Bear, and the Admiral Benbow, and the Light Heart, and many, many more, for it is the privilege of tale-tellers to open their story at an inn, which free rendezvous, the immortal Scott assures us, allows each traveller to display his or her humour without ceremony or restraint. Thus it is that our tale begins in a Hollywood gin mill late on the afternoon of April 29th, 1923, with our hero, the Anglo-Irish aristocrat Sir Archibald l'Estrange-B'stard, standing not upon ceremony, nor restraint, but tossing out zingers as might cause all five Marx Brothers to plunge into a post-season funk, if vaudeville might be said to have an off-season, which it does not.

Alas, dear Reader, Sir Archie has a Cervantic propensity to spend under the name of liberality on those occasions when bathtub gin is made available to a select clientele, in consequence of which, and at the very peak of his powers, Archie suddenly discovers himself at something of a loss as to his whereabouts and motive for same.

'Bartleby?' says he. 'Ho, Bartleby there!'

'Sir?' says Bartley McGuffin, who, being Sir Archie's secretary, is generally to be discovered at a discreet remove from the fray.

'I discover myself at something of a loss, Bartleby,' says Archie in anxious timbre, 'as to my whereabouts. Be so kind as to shed some light.'

'Certainly, sir. Your bewilderment is largely the result of your consuming an entire pot of Musso's afternoon tea, which, despite being served in a teapot and drunk from teacups, is in fact blushful Hippocrene of the bootleg variety and likely derived from wood alcohol, in consequence of which you are suffering from aggravated jake-leg, which tends to result in an excess of perplexity as to one's whereabouts and motive for same.'

'I see. And said whereabouts, Bartleby. Any advance there?'

'Of course, sir. You are currently at large upon the terrace of the Musso & Frank Grill, an exclusive adjunct to the famous eatery which is available only to select patrons.'

'I see. And my motive?'

'The observing of chorus dolls and pipterinos of the first water, sir, for, the weather being unseasonably mild for April, the terrace is thronged with jazz vamps and *ingénues*, along with schnooks and molls, and saxophone players and guys who write songs, and blondes with pink poodles, some boxing managers and freemasons, and at least two guys recently acquitted on a technicality of breaching the Main Act dodge. Yonder sits the motion picture producer Joseph Bloekman,' continues Bartley, who is not only an avid peruser of the Hollywood social pages but prone to expositionary reverie, 'deep in conversation with the theatre director Brock Pemberson; there Manley Halliday, all alone and staring morosely into his teacup. Close by, Adela Rogers St. Johns regales Alla Nazimova and Norma Desmond with the juiciest of current indiscretions, much of which relates to the *affaires* of Vanessa Hopgood, it being bruited about Hollywood's speaks that Ms Hopgood is affianced to both the motion picture mogul Samuel L. Silverstein *and* the bootlegger Rusty McGrew, which complex domestic arrangement, or so Ms Rogers St. Johns avers, is causing Ms Hopgood all manner of disquietude.'

'Duly noted. Although ...'

'Sir?'

'It occurs to me to wonder, Bartleby, as to why, given my generalised perplexity, you see fit to further burden the old noodle with additional pettifog.'

'Such is susceptible to ready explanation, sir, for you recently announced your intention, this just prior to your temporary bewilderment, to deliver yourself of the three most beautiful words in the English language, or any other.'

Here Archie's companion at table, whom your humble narrator has neglected to mention to this point, but is in fact the chorus doll Adele Fitzhalligon – I say, Adele, unable to restrain herself any longer, breaks in upon the foregoing with a spirited, 'O Archie! I love you too!'

'Ah,' says Archie. 'Bartleby?'

'Sir?'

'Ms Fitzhalligon appears to be mistook as to the three most beautiful words in the English language. Be so kind as to clarify on my behalf.'

'Sir, I will. It is my sad duty to inform you, madam,' says Bartley, now addressing Adele, 'that your declaration of the old incurable is ill-conceived, it being the case that Sir Archibald is a devotee of the noble Scottish art, i.e., golf, and is thus firmly persuaded that the three most beautiful words in the English language, or any other, are *tap-in birdie*.'

'O me!' sings out Adele as she experiences the giddy sensation of her hopes plunging down in wild career, whereupon, Adele being struck dumb in consequence of same, your humble narrator discovers that our tale, having begun in sprightly fashion and promising much by way of penetrating insight into the human condition, now threatens to run aground, it being the case that a chorus doll rebuffed and goggling mutely at an Anglo-Irish knight whilst said *chevalier* fiddles with a menu lest he catch said chorus doll's eye is by no means a scenario the serious Reader considers the Platonic ideal of narrative progression.

Indeed, the Reader may at this point discover herself querying your humble n.'s assertion that Sir Archie is a *chevalier*, his behaviour to date being more akin to that of a theatre-frequenting bawd than a gentleman with ambitions to be considered *preux*. To which your

n. can only reply that if it truly be the case, as Polonius once averred, that *the apparel oft proclaims the man*, then Sir Archie is as true a gallant as e'er flâneured upon any Hollywood boulevard, for Archie currently sports suede shoes, white flannel bags and a coat of blue superfine, and has his hair brushed into the Brutus style made fashionable by Mr Brummell. Further, Sir Archie lives in mortal terror of garnering a reputation akin to Cervantes' innkeeper, who boasted of a career spent largely in doing wrongs in abundance, much of which involved soliciting widows, undoing damsels and bubbling young heirs, which is precisely why Sir Archie now glances around and about the terrace of the Musso & Frank Grill, for fear a single instance of encountering Adele's stricken gaze at this emotionally charged juncture might cause him to instinctively respond to Adele's declaration of the old incurable by commencing to hum Mendelssohn's *Wedding March*, thus causing Adele to believe that he trembles on the brink of pledging his troth when said shot is not, in fact, on the board.

'Say it ain't so, Archie,' says Adele in plaintive register.

'Alas, old daffodil, it's as true as any trivet,' says Archie, albeit in kindly timbre, Archie being possessed of a heart as tender as his liver is cast iron.

Thus it is that Adele Fitzhalligon discovers herself possessed of *an uncouth pain tormenting her grievèd soul* (*cf.* Marlowe), which gloomy state of affairs is by no means ameliorated when Sir Archie, glancing around and about as per memo, claps peepers on the recently foreshadowed Vanessa Hopgood sashaying onto the terrace of the Musso & Frank Grill, and subsequently observes that *that* – i.e., Vanessa – is composed of such stuff as would take an awful lot to kill a man, which clumsy syntax persuades Bartley that Sir Archie might have been better advised to plunder the oeuvres of existing poets rather than attempt to coin an original phrase.[1]

1 Here Bartley McGuffin appears to be inadvertently prefiguring the immortal E.V. Rieu, who states as follows in his magisterial Introduction to *The Iliad* (1950): 'Now I think it is generally admitted that Homer did not invent the Story of Troy; also that it was the practice of ancient poets to build up their own edifice with the help of bricks taken from existing structures.'

'Who *zat*?' Archie now enquires in breathy tenor of Adele, which, e'en if we are to interpret Archie's words as a well-intentioned gambit designed to restore some vim to the repartee left languishing since his fateful deployment of the three most beautiful words in the English language, can only be considered an unpardonable *gaucherie*.

By now, of course, Adele Fitzhalligon has heard enough to choke a horse.

'Who, *that* tramp?' says she with no little asperity.

'Yon shimmering goddess?' says Archie in wild surmise. 'A tramp?'

'Notorious for it,' confirms Adele, before proceeding to descant in a manner not entirely advantageous to Ms Hopgood's reputation, for Adele is no slouch in the map department herself, being frequently compared to Olivia, the Vicar of Wakefield's daughter, who had that luxuriancy of beauty with which painters generally drew Hebe. To appreciate the depth of Adele's rancour, howe'er, we are now obliged to drift in wraithlike fashion back in time to the night before, and the moment when Adele stumbled out of the chorus line, pirouetted off the stage and toppled rump-first into Sir Archie's lap where he sat in the front row, which near-miraculous escape from harm was attributed by Adele to her rigorous training with the Royal Moscow Ballet and by her fellow dolls in the line to the fact that said improbable triumph of hope over physics was the third Adele had contrived in the past fortnight.

Adele, whose greatest trial in life has always been the petty jealousies of those less ambitious than herself, had risen above the vicious raillery with a dignified wrinkle of her delightfully freckled snub nose, instead noting with interest the small but intriguing bruise on her right thigh caused by the collision between Adele's taut flesh and the bulging wallet on Archie's hip.

What followed at the Beverly Hills Motel in the early hours of April 29th was as debauched a carnal coupling as might have plunged Caligula into a post-season funk, across which your humble n. now draws a veil lest the Reader be given the wrong impression of Archie and Adele, neither of whose *mentis* was entirely *compos* once they'd wrapped themselves around a Balthazar of the old fizzy shampoo.

Indeed, Adele's ability to match Archie posset for posset should have alerted our hero to her competitive nature. Alas, Archie, being a good three snifters below par, is so beguiled by *la* Hopgood that his instinct for self-preservation is currently hovering about three parasangs north of common sense, as the Reader will surely conceive when your n. reveals that Archie now breaks in upon Adele's spirited descanting with the observation that, in his considered opinion, Ms Hopgood might be deemed a latter-day Elizabeth of Bohemia, whom the immortal Wotton was pleased to consider *th' Eclypse and Glory of her Kind*.

Here Adele, realising that Archie has in common with the immortal Fitzgerald's Chevalier O'Keefe an enormous susceptibility to all sorts and conditions of women, gives a snort that wrinkles her snub nose in a most becoming fashion.

'She's already on the hook,' says Adele, perceiving herself in imminent peril of being trampled underfoot if she fails to head Archie off at the pass. 'To none other,' adds Adele, 'than Samuel L. Silverstein.' Adele being not only a veteran hoofer, as aforementioned, but so highly regarded as the oracle of all motion picture-related gossip, rumour and scuttlebutt as to be awarded the codename *Blavatsky* by the editors of Hollywood's blats, this on the basis of Adele's supernatural talent for winkling out scandal, calumny and slanderous tidings – I say, Adele now proceeds to confirm for Sir Archie that Samuel L. Silverstein is not merely the head of Silverstein Studios but the most enthusiastic trampoline artist of every casting couch therein, which fact, continues Adele, goes a long way towards explaining Vanessa Hopgood's scarcely plausible elevation to superstar of the silver screen. 'A girl can hardly open a magazine these days,' concludes she, 'without being transfixed by said cross-eyed witch glaring out draped in furs and pearls.'

'Zooks!' says Archie in breathy timbre, for Archie is himself feeling more than somewhat cross-eyed as he visualises said goddess clad only in furs and pearls.

Now Adele is an unusually perceptive young woman in affairs of the heart, as chorus dolls tend to be, but especially when she senses that the old boodle is about to rear up on its hind legs and bolt. Having winkled a few personal details out of Archie during those rare moments when their heads shared the same pillow, the most pertinent of which for the purpose of our narrative is the l'Estrange-B'stard antipathy to all things Iberian (more of which anon), Adele now lays a ranger across Archie's bow.

'Don't be fooled by the blonde hair. She's Mex.' Observing Archie's reaction, or, being scrupulously accurate, the complete absence of same, Adele goes all in. 'A Mexican,' says she, 'of Spanish origin.'

No dice. E'en Archie, cross-eyed, hungover and sniftered up the wazoo, could see Vanessa Hopgood was no Spaniard.

'Bartleby?' says Archie.

'Sir?'

'Take a memo, Bartleby.'[2]

'Sir, I will.'

Here Bartley McGuffin draws a writing pad from his inner pocket and jots down his Young Master's declaration of goodly woo, o'er which your humble n. now draws a discreet veil, for Archie's heliotropic prose has much in common with that of the unlucky Lady Lyndon, who had the knack of writing a great deal more than she meant.

'Got all that?' says Archie.

'Yes, sir.'

'Good man. Now cheese on over and deliver the goods.'

'Directly, sir,' says Bartley, and away he trots to make Vanessa sensible of Sir Archie's little necessities.

Here, alas, your humble n. encounters a narrative wrinkle which

2 Bartley McGuffin's position with Sir Archie encompasses a number of roles, including those of valet, *aide-de-camp*, caddy and confidante, although his official title is that of secretary, or *scrivener*, which frequently leads Sir Archie to refer to Bartley as *Bartleby*. For further details, see Chapter Eight.

will likely be familiar to any Reader who is also an author, which is that a character's departure, being necessary to advance the plot, has created something of a conversational *lacuna*, and especially when the scenario centres upon two formerly enamoured lovebirds struck so dumb as to call to mind the silence that befell stout Cortez and his men upon Darien peak.

Our tale thus threatening to slip into the dreaded *longueur*, your n. now avails of the opportunity to suggest that Adele offers the emotionally intelligent Reader a poignant variation on the immortal Austen's universally acknowledged truth, Adele being a veteran chorus doll and thus in dire need of a single man possessed of a good fortune, albeit Adele is by no means dogmatic in the matter of a future husband's current marital status. And yet, dear Reader, should we be swift to condemn Adele for being something of a revolutionary, by the immortal Austen's standards, in her bracingly modern moral flexibility? Your narrator contends otherwise, for a veteran chorus doll recently in receipt of goodly rummage is certainly entitled to seek assurances that said rummaging will not prove to be of the night-blooming cereus variety, and specifically that of the *Selenicereus grandiflorus*, which blooms only once a year, and for one night only, and that the rummager won't scratch the fixture just as soon as the rummagee wanders off to powder her delightfully freckled snub nose.

Having established Adele Fitzhalligon's most pressing concerns, and with Bartley McGuffin yet to return from Ms Hopgood's table, we now turn our gaze upon our spruce *chevalier*, Sir Archibald l'Estrange-B'stard, noting first that the bulging wallet which initially piqued Adele's interest represents only the tiniest fraction of Sir Archie's wealth. Indeed, were Archie to somehow contrive to lose his wallet, which possibility had vaulted to the very top of Adele's long list of ambitions in the immediate wake of their collision, Archie would, on discovering his loss, very likely respond with a 'Tut-tut!', or perhaps a more vigorous 'Blow!', before prevailing upon Bartley McGuffin to trundle on out to find him a new wallet and a camel-choking sufficiency of the old folding to cram inside. For Archie is the last remaining scion of the famed l'Estrange-B'stard dynasty of Knockfluck in the County Donegal in the Free State of Ireland, the fourth and youngest son of Sir Augustus 'Baffy' l'Estrange-B'stard IV, and thus the sole heir to *a fine family fortune* which requires the unstinting efforts of a Swiss accountancy firm with offices in six time-zones just to keep tabs on the compound interest.

That Archie is the sole heir is a matter of deep sorrow to the l'Estrange-B'stard firm. Percival, the eldest son, struck his colours on the Somme. Sylvain IX, the next in line and a pilot of rare promise, went down in a blaze of glory above the very same poppy-strewn meadows, his place in history secured as the seventh victim of that most dastardly Hun, the Red Baron. Finally, and long after peace had broken out all o'er, Caliban had succumbed to the Spanish 'Flu, a needless tragedy that further cemented the l'Estrange-B'stard antipathy to all things Iberian.

A painful litany, as the Reader will no doubt agree, although Archie is by no means the runt of the l'Estrange-B'stard litter. A magnificent specimen of testosterone made flesh, Archie gives on first meeting the impression that he wants only for an iron band confining his upper torso to perfect the Platonic ideal of oaken barrel bursting its seams. On his shoulders sits the proud round l'Estrange-B'stard head, and when Archie moves with intent – when dancing, say, or blasting yet another wayward drive out of knotty rough – grown men are moved to tremulously remark on Archie's uncanny similarity to a man-o'-war, sails full and humming with lethal menace. Indeed, Archie might well have been considered the very *sine qua non* of heirs to ancient dynasties were it not that his abilities in the realm of mathematics – crucial, alas, in a man of high finance – begin and end with the revolutionary new scoring system devised by Dr. Stableford for the noble Scottish art.[3]

3 Notwithstanding counter-claims on behalf of the Roman game of *paganica*, historians generally accept that the sport of golf originated in 15th-century Scotland. Along with whisky and the daubing of externals with blue woad to denote the taking of extreme umbrage, golf remains Scotland's premier export.

In a nutshell, then: Sir Archie is a healthy male specimen in possession of a considerable fortune who, as a consequence of his mother's lifelong devotion to the immortal Austen, is currently considered in want of a wife, said admirable maternal instinct being in large part responsible for Archie's recent absconding from Knockfluck in the County Donegal for the bright lights and chorus dolls of Hollywood. Which is why, acknowledging that the serious Reader demands a swiftly delivered narrative, we now return to the terrace of the Musso & Frank Grill, where we discover that Adele, having soothed her *grievèd soul* with yet another posset of bathtub hooch, has recovered to make a late rally.

'Archie?'

'Eh?' says Archie, whose eyes are lifted to the farthest horizon of the terrace.

'It's just …' Here Adele pauses to quiver. 'O Archie, my high-kick extension is on the fritz!'

'I was wondering what that might be,' says Archie, who has over the previous hour or so experienced frequent foot-shaped incursions into his loinal environs, a not unpleasant sensation given that said foot is encased in sheer silk. 'Was that fritz or frisk?'

'Fritz,' confirms Adele, which poignant syllable will undoubtedly alert the sensitive Reader to the fact that Adele had only two nights previously been in receipt of a second warning as to her high-kick extension and the rapidly deteriorating angle thereof, 90°N being considered the ideal and anything less than 70°NW a cause for instant dismissal. 'Alas,' says Adele with a heart-rending twitch of that delightfully freckled snub nose, 'I am currently operating at a maximum of 85°NW, owing to a combination of recurrent vapours and a touch of sciatica.'

'Still, where there's life there's hope, eh?'

'O Archie!' sings out Adele in a manner not entirely dissimilar to the immortal Burnet's *great Ocean rowling in the Air, without Bounds or Banks*, 'I am so desolate as to believe my American life will be possessed of no second act!', upon which, lashed unto the utmost verge of desperation, Adele embarks on what was afterwards considered one of the finest *grand jetés* e'er witnessed on the terrace of the Musso & Frank Grill, not least because it was executed from a sitting start and still managed to deliver Adele unto Archie's lap with pinpoint accuracy, whereupon Archie, being as true a flower of the chivalry of an ancient race as any of Maeonia's chosen warriors, commenced patting Adele upon the back and murmuring, 'That's it, old cauliflower. Better out than in, eh?'

Here, alas, we are obliged to take our leave of Adele and Archie, not from any want of sympathy for Adele's plight, nor to falsely create the illusion of narrative suspense by inserting a chapter ending where none might have been reasonably expected, but in order that the Reader might be furnished with a sufficiency of detail *vis-à-vis* Vanessa Hopgood's tempestuous relationship with Samuel L. Silverstein before Bartley finally arrives at Vanessa's table, which detail, being crucial to the Reader's understanding of our tale's philosophical proposition – i.e., *that the world might be a better place if only everyone would make a little more effort to get along* – will be revealed in Chapter Two.

Chapter Two

In which the motion picture mogul Samuel L. Silverstein states that the ideal motion picture photoplay boasts as many songs as it does writers, i.e., none.

Bartley McGuffin being recently bade by his Young Master to *cheese on over and deliver the goods* to Vanessa Hopgood, the Reader may now find herself wondering why Bartley has yet to arrive at his destination, for, e'en if we allow that the tables are so arranged on the terrace of the Musso & Frank Grill as to oblige a man to advance in zig-zag fashion, Bartley's journey is by no means conflatable with the Moor's arduous traverse o'er antres vast and deserts idle.

The matter, dear Reader, is susceptible to ready explanation, for Bartley, who variously serves as Sir Archie's scrivener, *aide-de-camp*, valet and caddy, is in the secret quiet of his conscience an aspiring author who has for some years now been secretly engaged upon his One True Work. Thus it is that Bartley, having earlier noted with some interest the theatre director Brock Pemberson and the famed motion picture producer Joseph Bloekman deep in conversation at a table nearby, has by no means proceeded directly to Vanessa's table with all the alacrity the verb *to cheese* might suggest, and has instead availed of Musso's seating arrangements to zig-zag off course and stroll past the table occupied by Brock Pemberson and Joseph Bloekman, whereupon Bartley, affecting to notice that his shoelace had come untied, got down on one knee to rectify same.

Alas for Bartley, he kneels down at the very moment when

Brock Pemberson rockets aloft from his seat, his demeanour very much that of Belinda on the occasion of a lock of her hair being snipped, albeit Brock proceeds to declaim in stentorian tenor that he is by no means the New York-based theatre director Brock Pemberton, which farcical case of mistaken identity might easily have been avoided had Samuel L. Silverstein e'er darkened the doors of a theatre for any other purpose than the wooing of impressionable chorus doll, which he has not.

Brock now storming off, in which endeavour he is somewhat constrained by being obliged to zig-zag rather more than a man might prefer when his ambition is to go and stand not upon the order of same – I say, Brock now departing the fray, your humble n. now confirms what the attentive Reader has likely already begun to conceive, which is that the famed motion picture producer previously identified as Joseph Bloekman is in fact the famed motion picture mogul Samuel L. Silverstein in disguise, Sammy being currently decked out in the pongee sports shirt, well-tailored jodhpurs and leather puttees currently favoured by Hollywood's more sartorially inclined motion picture producers.

'I did rather wonder,' says George P. Dangleberry III, whom your n. has previously neglected to mention is also present at the Silverstein table, and who, being possessed of a top hat and watches in both fobs of his pinstriped waistcoat, can now be identified as the financier Sammy is hoping will fund his latest motion picture wheeze – 'I say, I did rather wonder that Mr Brock Pemberton, on being summoned from New York at 2.15pm to attend a top secret conference at the Musso & Frank Grill in Hollywood, was agreeable to meeting at 4pm on the very same afternoon.'

'My understanding of same,' says Samuel L. Silverstein, in apologetic timbre, 'is that Brock Pemberton is something of a miracle-worker, and that traversing an entire continent in less than two hours would be child's play for a man who has somehow contrived to generate a smash-hit on the New York stage from a production that involves no songs and a mere six characters.'

'Think nothing of it,' says George P. 'In fact, it's *my*

understanding that farcical cases of mistaken identity are so common in Hollywood that you might as well roof the entire place and declare it a music hall.'

'Oh, absolutely,' says Sammy L. 'The fact is, you're no one in Hollywood these days until you've been mistaken for another citizen with a similar name, or whose physical characteristics so uncannily mirror your own as to be considered your *doppelgänger*.' Whereupon, having successfully reassured George P. that all is for the best in the best of all Panglossian worlds, Sammy rather spoils the effect by delivering himself of a sigh so piteous and profound that it seems to George a minor miracle that said *svengali* somehow fails, in so sighing, to shatter all his bulk and end his being.

'Mr Silverstein?'

'Yes?' says Sammy in doleful tenor.

'It seems to me, Mr Silverstein,' says George, 'that you are plunged into despair to a depth equivalent to full fathom five. Might you be persuaded to divulge the whys and wherefores of same?'

Sammy having first instructed Edward 'Bugs' Dooley to stick his fingers in his ears, Bugs being only now introduced as present on the basis that he is a photoplay reader in Sammy's employ and thus hardly worth mentioning in the same breath as such luminaries as the theatre director Brock Pemberson, the motion picture mogul Samuel L. Silverstein, and the financier George P. Dangleberry III – I say, having ensured that Bugs is by no means privy to the whys and wherefores of his plunging to such depths of despair as to cause sea-nymphs to hourly ring his knell, Sammy now informs George P. that he discovers himself inordinately disconsolate on foot of the strike.

'The strike?'

'The writers' strike, Mr Dangleberry, which commenced yesterday afternoon in the writers' pen at Silverstein Studios but quickly spread to every studio in the land, it being the case that writers, being offered the choice of writing or not writing, will invariably, and on the flimsiest of pretexts, plump for the latter. In consequence, Hollywood's photoplay scribes have to a man downed tools in pursuit of better working conditions, the most pressing of which include the demand *one writer, one chair* and the right to two bathroom breaks per day, not counting lunch.'

'Gadso!' says George P. with more than a touch of asperity, George being the manager of the Tropico Springs Savings & Loan and thus not instinctively inclined to sympathise with agitators, Wobblies and rabble-rousing radicals, whom George tends to conflate with the immortal Dickens' elderly female, who found in the lowest depths deeper still. 'One hopes you took the appropriate steps?'

'Oh, most certainly,' says Sammy. 'Studio-hired thugs have been dispatched to the vicinity of every speak in the greater Hollywood area, armed with cudgels and knobkerries and instructed to belabour anyone wearing spectacles or tweed with same, in consequence of which the scribes have been distracted from their initial grievances and are instead diverting their frustrated creativity into penning diatribes to the local blats denouncing the sub-standard quality of bootleg hooch being peddled of late in Hollywood's deadfalls, said liquor having fallen so far below par as to result in ferocious hangovers, the symptoms of which frequently include concussions, amnesia and visibly raised bumps upon the skull.'

'And am I to thus understand, sir,' says George P., 'that your interest in adapting Mr Pemberton's New York smash-hit play was largely rooted in the fact that his production is a non-singing, non-dancing affair boasting a mere six characters and – crucially – no writer?'

Here Sammy L. acknowledges the essential truth of George P.'s contention, and further reminds George that desperate times call for desperate measures, albeit Sammy neglects to mention that George P.'s presence at table is itself a measure of Sammy's desperation, Sammy at this point having so exhausted his potential sources of finance as to discover himself reduced to wooing the manager of a Savings & Loan located in a sleepy burg in the High Sierras.

'Taking your point,' says George P., 'the fact remains that you, sir, have lured me to Hollywood with the promise of a sure-fire smash-hit motion picture guaranteed to provide a return unparalleled in the annals of fiduciary history, only for said scheme to come a cropper due to a case of mistaken identity that would do credit to the more vivid imaginings of Messrs Gilbert and Sullivan. Worse,' continues George, 'there appears to be no alternative wheeze in place. This, sir, is shoddy stuff, and you may be sure that I will be informing the S&L's board of directors that Hollywood is no place to —Yes? Mr Dooley?'

Bugs having previously removed his forefinger from his right ear in order to raise his right hand, he now lowers same and enquires of Samuel L. Silverstein if this might be a good time to pitch his idea for a sure-fire smash-hit motion picture.

'It might,' says Sammy in despondent register, 'providing it's guaranteed to wow 'em in the aisles despite containing precisely no songs, it being the case that Silverstein Studios, in common with every other studio in Hollywood, has yet to master the technical difficulties involved in splicing sound and vision.'

'I can assure you, sir, that there are precisely no songs in *The Pilgrim's Progress*.'

'I see,' says Sammy. 'And might one dare hope that said *Progress* was composed by an anonymous scribe and might thus be considered, in the matter of remunerating same, possessed of no author?'

'Alas, sir, *The Pilgrim's Progress* has long been attributed to the immortal Bunyan.'

'I see. And the story?' says Sammy, whose knowledge of the classics is nowhere as comprehensive as the Reader might expect of a Hollywood motion picture mogul. 'Is our pilgrim's progress sufficiently interrupted by obstacle, unexpected revelation and reversal of fortune as to fill out the full hour of screen time now demanded by the more discerning motion picture devotee?'

'Absolutely, sir. Our pilgrim, called Christian, embarks on a journey from the City of Destruction to the Celestial City, whereupon he encounters much by way of demons, giants, dragons, harlots and angels.'

'Harlots, eh? Something of a rake, our Christian, I take it?'

'Not exactly, sir. Our hero suffering more than somewhat from nominative determinism, *The Pilgrim's Progress* is in fact a religious allegory framed as a dream sequence.'

'Hmmm. Sounds stodgy, Bugs.'

'Did I mention that it's out of copyright?'

'You did not.'

'Well, it is.'

'Speak on, young Dooley. Is there a treatment?'

Bugs, Sammy L. and George P. now huddling up, lest any idle scribe, director or producer get wind of a tale out of copyright, and, further, it being assumed that the serious Reader is fully abreast of every last nuance of the immortal Bunyan's epic, your n. now hastens to address the burning issue of whether Edward 'Bugs' Dooley is being entirely ethical in proposing to adapt *The Pilgrim's Progress* for the silver screen at a time when Hollywood's scribes are suffering such privation as to be reduced to writing advertising copy, moonlighting as cruciverbalists, or publishing slim volumes of poetry, as a consequence of which endeavour Bugs risks being denounced as a blackleg, scab or knobstick, or might well have been, had Hollywood's writers had the foresight to organise themselves into some kind of union or guild, which, alas, they have not.

Indeed, Edward 'Bugs' Dooley is as unwitting a strike-breaker as e'er crossed a theoretical picket-line, for our tale, which the Reader might believe to have commenced some minutes earlier with Sir Archie, Bartley McGuffin and Adele Fitzhalligon on the terrace of the Musso & Frank Grill, might properly be understood to have begun early on the previous afternoon, when the foundling Bugs Dooley, like so many photoplay readers before him, entered into said service having discovered that no advantageous place could be found either in possession, reversion, remainder or expectancy, and was no sooner set to work perusing a literary classic for the purpose of assessing same for motion picture photoplay when he was called into Samuel L. Silverstein's inner penetralium, whereupon Sammy, declaring himself unsatisfied with his brand new casting couch, prevailed upon Bugs to bounce around on same in order to locate the squeaky spring which was causing Sammy significant auditory distress.

Mission accomplished, Bugs returned to the writers' pen to discover the vast hall entirely bereft of scribes, editors and photoplay readers, at which point Bugs, presuming that it was someone's birthday, and that the veterans of the writers' pen had regrettably, but understandably, neglected to remember the newest addition to the team when departing early for celebratory possets of fizz – I say, Bugs, having shrugged, and smiled a wry, resigned smile, settled down again at his desk to peruse *The Pilgrim's Progress*, which yarn he had been handed first thing that morning, this according to the time-honoured practice of old sweats assigning the new guy an impossible task in order to break ~~his spirit~~ the ice, whereupon, having advanced with Christian as far as the Slough of Despond, Bugs began to experience something akin to the *many fears, and doubts, and discouraging apprehensions* suffered by Christian himself, at which point Bugs declared *The Pilgrim's Progress* an absolute frost for the purpose of entertaining the discerning motion picture devotee, and instead began wondering about the possibility of relocating said *Progress* from Merrie Olde England to Jazz Age California, 'which era,' says Bugs, concluding his admirably brief treatment, 'if we might date it from the title of Mr Scott Fitzgerald's seminal collection of short stories entitled *Tales of the Jazz Age*, is currently one whole year old.'

'Top hole,' says Sammy L. 'Bash me out a script, Bugs, and have it on the desk by nine tomorrow morning.'

'Sir, I will!'

'Now go, and let your haste commend your duty.'

'I go, I go, look how I go,' says Bugs, departing in some haste, 'swift as any arrow from Tartar's – Ow!'

The Reader easily conceiving that Bugs has contrived to bark his shin upon Bartley McGuffin's bonce where Bartley kneels in the aisle affecting to tie his shoelace, and that such impact is sufficient to remind Bartley of his obligation to proceed to Vanessa Hopgood's table with all the alacrity as might be achieved upon a terrace whereupon the tables are so arranged as to oblige e'en the most biddable of servitors to advance in zig-zag fashion, we now join Bartley as he sets out again for Vanessa's table, having first accepted Bugs Dooley's apologies in a gracious manner commensurate with our tale's philosophical proposition – i.e., *that the world might be a better place if only everyone would make a little more effort to get along* – the details of which, your humble n. hopes, will be revealed in Chapter Three.

Chapter Three

Concerning further particulars relating to Vanessa Hopgood's fractious disputation with Samuel L. Silverstein.

It being clear from the previous chapters that Vanessa Hopgood is to play such a significant part in our narrative as to be considered its heroine, your humble n. now offers a brief pen sketch of said mortal goddess. To wit:

Height:	5'7"
Hair:	Blonde
Eyes:	Wood-pallet blue
Aura:	Shimmering
Mood:	Bellicose

Naturally, any pen sketch, being necessarily brief, will fail to do justice to the latter-day Elizabeth of Bohemia that is Vanessa Hopgood, it being the case, to take but one example, that Vanessa's hair is not merely blonde, but fine-spun and bobbed like Irene Castle's, and is presently fluffed into curls. A more detailed account of Vanessa's beauty must be delayed for the nonce, howe'er, given that the emotionally intelligent Reader is very likely wondering aloud as to why Vanessa Hopgood, the most shimmering star in all of Hollywood's firmament, is currently to be discovered in Mood: Bellicose.

Your humble n. being at all times at the service of the Reader, we now employ the time-honoured literary conceit of eavesdropping upon characters conversing, having first drifted, in wraithlike fashion, to a vantage point behind Vanessa's table, the better to overhear the conversation Vanessa is currently conducting with Felicia Fortesque, a young woman who is ostensibly employed as Vanessa's secretary, but might more accurately be described as Vanessa's confidante, confessor and boon companion. The Reader is advised that a pen sketch of Felicia Fortesque will be made available during the next *longueur* to present itself for the purpose; for now, suffice to say that Felicia, whilst voted 'Most Winsome Smile (Senior Year) 1911' in Little Butte, Arkansas, is no Vanessa Hopgood, and especially in the business of shimmering.

It is a testament to Felicia's character, howe'er, that ne'er once in all her time in Vanessa's employ has Felicia experienced so much as an envious twinge at Vanessa's beauty, fame or wealth. Indeed, Felicia's first and every thought is invariably for Vanessa's comfort and happiness, as the Reader will readily conceive as we commence our eavesdropping, which, alas, due to the necessity of providing the Reader with the foregoing contextual detail, commences with Vanessa long since embarked upon tirade. To wit:

'... which was when *he* said to *me*, "You'll do it and like it, damn you!"'

'O Vanessa, the sheer *brute*,' says Felicia, employing a slim gold pencil to scribble shorthand notes, which she will later transcribe into Vanessa's diary, Vanessa being of the opinion that one can live or write, but one is unlikely to do both equally well, and especially when one has recently begun keeping a diary for the purpose of gathering sufficient material to generate a motion picture photoplay based on the tragical experience of a Hollywood *ingénue* so dedicated to pushing life to its Dionysian limits that she finds herself obliged to keep a diary in order to record the e'er-widening gulf between who she once was and the illusion she has become.

'Brute?' says Vanessa. '*I* should say so. So I says, "Silvers, baby, you can pop a cork in *that* barrel for starters. I'll do it if I like it, and the more you keep flapping your gums the less likely the liking gets."'

'Oh, I say – *touché*.'

'Thanks. Edith liked it too. So then Silvers goes, "But it's you I'm thinking of, V. Once the Gish does it, they'll *all* be doing it, and where will you be then?" So I says, "I'll tell you exactly where I'll be, my strike-busting chum – I'll be on the first tee at Hillcrest, limbering up for a long, straight drive down fairway the first. *That's* where I'll be."'

'You didn't dare.'

'Didn't I? Have you ever seen a haddock with its head pulled inside out?' Felicia, from her expression, hadn't. 'Well, order one now and you'll never have to wonder again. Oh, hullo – would you like me to sign that?'

This last, of course, is directed at Bartley McGuffin, who has been standing by for some moments now, proffering Sir Archie's missive whilst coughing discreetly into his fist, leading Vanessa to believe that Bartley is in the terminal stage of a lung ailment and anxious to fulfil his dying wish of securing her autograph before he expires entirely. Indeed, it is a matter of no little irritation to your n. that Bartley, having previously dallied in a manner that cannot be sufficiently deplored, subsequently availed of his experience of accompanying Sir Archie to St. Moritz the previous winter and commenced slaloming at speed through the terrace's zig-zagged table pattern, thus causing him to come to Vanessa's attention much earlier than your n. anticipated he might, with the unavoidable consequence of Vanessa and Felicia abruptly breaking off from the indiscreet discourse that would likely have revealed all *vis-à-vis* the fractious disputation between Vanessa and Samuel L. Silverstein.

Thus your n. discovers himself obliged to state the facts of the matter without further delay, this in anticipation of the Reader wondering aloud as to the nature of said contretemps, which furious storms – raised by the contending of Vanessa's wind and Sammy's water, respectively – are rooted in professional as opposed to personal concerns, the detail of which might be more vividly imagined were we to drift back in time to the late afternoon of the day previous, and Sammy's office on the Silverstein Studios lot, which is dominated by a desk that was once the poop deck of HMS *Inextinguishable*, behind which Samuel L. Silverstein is, as usual, not to be found.

Instead, Sammy is ensconced upon his brand new casting couch, which he is patting in encouraging fashion, as is his wont, whilst Vanessa, from the safe distance of the other side of the room, is shaking her head, which is her invariable wont when Sammy commences to caressing the japonica-red velvet.

'Just one tumble,' says Sammy in a tenor only half an octave below the volume of beseeching generally associated with frantic importunity.

'Nerts to you, buster,' says Vanessa.

'Madam, I urge you to reflect and consider.'

'Nay, nay,' says Vanessa, 'and thrice nay.'

The foregoing being only a short sample of an extended but rather monotonously repetitive dialogue, your humble n. here interpolates to clarify Adele Fitzhalligon's assertion that Samuel L. Silverstein is not only the CEO of Silverstein Studios but *the most enthusiastic trampoline artist of every casting couch therein* by noting that Sammy, hailing originally from a poverty-ridden *shtetl* in darkest Ukraine, grew up in a one-room shack lacking all furniture, and thus ignorant of that most simple of childish joys, i.e., bouncing up and down on a bed. Now sufficiently wealthy to indulge his every whim, and keen to make up for lost time, Sammy has a brand new couch installed in his office every Friday, with dire consequences for the dignity of anyone unlucky enough to be summoned to said hallowed precinct, Sammy being as persuasive as only a Hollywood producer can be when it comes to cajoling actors, actresses, associate producers, photoplay readers and key grips into performing unusually vaulting *pas de deux*.

On the afternoon under advisement, howe'er, Vanessa, being by no means in mid-season bobbish form, is loath to lower herself to such soaring heights, and thus invokes her immortal predecessor Fanny Goodwill in begging Sammy to restrain the impetuosity of his transports.

'Very well,' says Sammy, leaping from couch to desk in fair facsimile of Mr Douglas Fairbanks, who, having just now manoeuvred the *Black Terror* alongside, has descried a fair maiden lashed to the mast of the *Inextinguishable*. 'Let's get down to cases.'

Here Sammy outlines his proposal that Vanessa submit her larynx yet again to the surgeon's scalpel in order to rectify a chortle recently observed to stun an ox at sixty paces, to which Vanessa responds in the saltiest of Anglo-Saxon vernacular, the gist of her contention being that enough is entirely sufficient, this on the basis that Vanessa, if we might be so bold as to quote her directly, has already endured more blade-work than the Pietà.

To which Samuel L. Silverstein replies, as would any self-respecting *svengali*, 'And look how *that* turned out.'

Vanessa now commencing to rework old material – i.e., enquiring of Sammy if it is his intention to make of her a minstrel, before proceeding to veto said possibility without allowing Sammy the opportunity to reply, for Vanessa, despite being sored up more than somewhat, refuses to believe that it is truly Sammy's intention to transform his most shimmering star into a wandering musician – I say, your humble n. here avails of our latest *longueur* to reveal that the source of Vanessa's Mood: Bellicose might be traced to one Thomas Edison, a man whose ceaselessly inventive mind had already conjured into being several marvels of the Modern Age e'en before he began tinkering in the realms of audio recording and thus plunging our heroine into existential snit.

Indeed, it is no coincidence, dear Reader, that our story opens on April 29th, 1923, for only two weeks previously, in the Rivoli Theatre in New York, Mr Lee De Forest, adapting an innovation first proposed by Mr Edison, had broadcast the first ever moving picture with sound recording.

Which is to say that, as of April 15th in the Year of Our Lord 1923, anything was possible. Revolution, not to labour the point, was abroad and wreaking its mischief. Indeed, the *talkies*, as Sammy's fellow visionaries have dubbed the phenomenon, are already considered *such stuff as dreams are made on*, in consequence of which Samuel L. Silverstein has no desire to see his 14% market share of the American Dream Factory decline to an appreciable degree, for Sammy is a man who prides himself on Silverstein Studios' reputation for being in the vanguard of any profit-boosting innovation, if not actually leading the charge, it being Sammy's experience that pioneers get shot, and usually in the back.

Moreo'er, given that Vanessa Hopgood was recently anointed America's Darling™, and that much by way of time, effort and samolians had been invested in rendering her such, it was Sammy's fervent belief that Vanessa should grasp this once-in-a-lifetime opportunity with the light but firm grip for which she is renowned on those occasions when Vanessa takes up her trusty brassie and advances to the first tee.

At this point the intelligent Reader, anticipating yet more fame and fortune in Vanessa's future, and perhaps e'en experiencing a tender glow at Sammy L.'s faith in his prodigy, may wonder anew at Vanessa's froward disposition, for it is now that Vanessa and Sammy engage in the pelters previously referenced, wherein Sammy warns Vanessa that she is in grievous danger of losing ground to the Gish, and Vanessa announces her intention of hieing her way hence to the first tee at the Hillcrest Country Club, whereupon Vanessa's companion Edith gives vent to a rafter-shuddering 'Bravo, V!', which interpolation obliges your n. to belatedly note that Vanessa was accompanied to Sammy's office by none other than Edith Cummings, aka the Fairway Flapper, champion golfer and socialite *nonpareil*, Edith and Vanessa being firm friends who enjoy a remarkable mutual devotion, and not only to one another but to the noble Scottish art, i.e., golf, to the extent that Edith is rarely to be seen in public without a niblick in hand, and especially when accompanying Vanessa to Sammy's office, it being the case that a niblick makes for a very passable knobkerrie should the occasion demand same, i.e., on those occasions when Sammy so far forgets himself as to excessively press his suit in the matter of a little casting couch trampoline action.

Having so noted, your n. now returns to the burning issue of the Reader's wondering aloud as to Vanessa's froward disposition despite the promise of yet more fame and fortune accruing to America's Darling™ in the very near future. The confusion is in equal parts due to your humble n.'s failure to fully clarify Vanessa's predicament and to circumstance not providing him with the opportunity for same since first we encountered *la* Hopgood on the terrace of the Musso & Frank Grill, said circumstance being that, with Vanessa feeling every bit as *cuffed and buffeted through the world* as was the young Oliver Twist, and given that neither her secretary Felicia Fortesque nor the missive-brandishing Bartley McGuffin are comedians to rank alongside Messrs Chaplin, Keaton or Lloyd, Vanessa has to date had little inclination to laugh.

As to Vanessa's predicament, your n. is first obliged to provide the Reader with a *précis* of Vanessa's appeal to the motion picture audiences of America, which we begin by stating that Vanessa Hopgood does not merely *shimmer* on the silver screen, but *glitters* and *gleams* and *smoulders*, yea verily, like a Spanish sailor on shore leave in a port that is not Spanish. Indeed, Vanessa is possessed of that rarest of divinely inspired gifts, which is to cause men to wish to be more than God made them whilst simultaneously persuading women that God has provided them with more or less the same tools that Vanessa herself employs in bringing said men to heel.

All this Vanessa Hopgood does, and more. What she does not do is laugh. The Reader may hardly credit the proposition, but the fact remains: despite the acres of celluloid devoted to Vanessa's ineffable smiles and her concomitant, albeit inaudible, chuckles, giggles and (presumably) tinkling laughter, Vanessa Hopgood has not been heard to laugh aloud in public since the day she signed her first contract with Silverstein Studios.

Indeed, the embargo on Vanessa's laughter was handed down from on high, and by no less a personage than Samuel L. Silverstein himself, whose very marrow had curdled on the occasion of Vanessa giving vent to what she imagined was a silvery trill as she signed her contract. Alas, said silvery trilling, as Sammy later confided to his legal counsel, Abraham 'Abie' Cohen, was in fact the kind of noise Sammy imagined a set of bagpipes might achieve were it to be tortured upon the rack. It was, Sammy stressed, the kind of laugh that sneaks up on the old *joie de vivre* and cracks a sock full of wet sand across the back of its neck.

Thus is revealed the *fons et origo* of the fractious disputation between Vanessa Hopgood and Samuel L. Silverstein, with Vanessa understandably reluctant to undergo yet more corrective surgery on her larynx, e'en if such might prevent beasts of the field from starting like guilty things upon a fearful summons were Vanessa to so much as titter in appreciation of an unintended malapropism.

Is it any wonder, then, that on the date aforementioned, Vanessa Hopgood might be discovered upon the terrace of the Musso & Frank Grill so desolate at the prospect of Thomas Edison's mischief-wreaking revolution as to be plunged into existential snit?

'Felicia?' says Vanessa.

'Vanessa?'

'It occurs to me to wonder aloud, *apropos* the sinister progress of revolution, as to whether, if Lafayette comes, might Robespierre be far behind?'

'Ah,' says Felicia, 'there you have me. Eighteenth-century political theory isn't really my *forte*, I'm afraid.'

'Just as I suspected,' says Vanessa, turning away from her unimpeded view of Hollywood Boulevard lest she be assailed by visions of tumbrils rolling down the broad avenue; whereupon, having turned away, as aforesaid, Vanessa discovers herself gazing upon Bartley McGuffin, who, having recently declined Vanessa's kind offer of autograph, has been obliged to stand by whilst Vanessa engaged in antimonial reverie concerning her future prospects, but who now, having accidentally re-established eye contact, stands not upon the order of presenting Archie's declaration of woo, but immediately states as follows: 'Madam, please allow me to present the credentials of Sir Archibald l'Estrange-B'stard, a devoted admirer of your motion picture performances.'

Here, as the Reader will easily conceive, Bartley is coming it tolerably high, it being the case that Archie had breathily enquired

'Who *zat*?' of Adele Fitzhalligon on the occasion of his first clapping peepers on Vanessa, although any fair-minded Reader will also concede that Bartley, being a good and faithful servant, here makes up for his previous want of alacrity by observing the spirit if not the letter of Archie's particular veneration of Vanessa's rare endowments.

'Oh well, I *say*,' says Vanessa, thrilling to Bartley's mellifluous diction, Vanessa, in common with most Hollywood actresses, being accustomed to men presenting rather more than their credentials on first introduction. 'Absolutely, Sir Archibald,' says Vanessa, digging an elbow into Felicia's ribs in the universal gesture for shift-up-one. 'Always room for a lord at table, I always say.'

'I fear, madam, that I have failed to make myself sufficiently clear,' says Bartley. 'I merely present said credentials on behalf of Sir Archibald.' So saying, Bartley now executes a matador's pass, thus allowing Vanessa her first discreet glimpse of the magnificent specimen currently craning his neck to peer around Adele Fitzhalligon, who, having established herself in what might be considered pole position on Archie's lap, is loath to relinquish her advantage.

'The pumpkin-headed one?' says Vanessa.

It is with a murmur concerning Archie's aristocratic bearing that Bartley now confirms Vanessa's identification.

'And you're saying he's a lord?'

'Sir Archibald, madam, is a knight of the realm.'

'Is that better than a lord?'

'Not according to Debrett's, madam.'

'The Long Island Debretts?'

'Debrett's of London, madam.'

'Ah. Them I don't know. Felicia?'

Here Felicia states that she has, regrettably, yet to make the acquaintance of any Debretts, London-based or otherwise.

'But you're vouching for him?' enquires Vanessa of Bartley. 'He's on the level?'

'Very much so, madam.' Here Bartley flourishes Archie's missive.

'If I may present —'

Here Vanessa, who has a horror of being observed reading in public lest unemployed photoplay scribes commence leaping from shrubbery brandishing sheaves of double-spaced type, waves away the note. 'Play her as she lies,' says she, 'and whip the wrists through.'

'Madam, I will,' says Bartley, before reading aloud Archie's *billet doux*, which sets forth Archie's contention that Vanessa is *a maid to paragon all description and wild fame* in that *she excels the quirks of all the blazoning pens combined*, and, moreo'er, were the conversation e'er to turn to the subject of *th' essential vesture of creation*, would very likely prove *so inexhaustibly marvellous as to tire e'en the most stalwart ingener.*

'Not bad,' says Vanessa as Bartley draws to a close. 'Felicia?'

Here Felicia allows that Vanessa has previously entertained gentlemen with less promising prospects than Sir Archibald l'Estrange-B'stard, and further reminds her companion that she has, on occasion, o'erlooked far more obvious physical defects in her petitioners than pumpkin-shaped heads.

'True for you. Bartley?'

'Madam?'

'Pray tell his excellency Sir Archibald, post-haste and so forth, that his credentials have been received in the spirit in which they were conceived.'

'Very good, madam.'

Bartley now offering the ladies a full scrape and half a short bow, he pirouettes neatly around the table behind him and sets off in the slaloming style for the far side of the terrace and the table whereat Archie might be descried dampening down anxiety's flames with a stoup of bathtub hooch.

The scene thus set fair for a fresh outbreak of the old incurable on the terrace of the Musso & Frank Grill, your humble n. now urges any Reader keen to remain abreast of events pertaining to Vanessa and Archie to proceed directly to the next chapter but one, it being the case that the excerpt immediately following is concerned with one Rusty McGrew, a bootlegger, gangster and outlaw whose absolute contempt for those ridiculous distinctions of *meum* and *tuum* (i.e., mine and yours) best characterised by the immortal Fielding's robber chief Jonathan Wild will have a marked impact on the fortunes of those characters already introduced, and must thus, according to the immortal Aristotle's infallible *Poetics*, make an appearance sooner rather than later, lest he enter the narrative any later than Chapter Four and forever after be suspicioned a literary conceit akin to the dread *deus ex machina.*

And so we go.

Chapter Four

In which is introduced the item of mortality alluded to at the conclusion of our previous chapter, i.e., Rusty McGrew.

It being the custom on the stage in all good murderous melodramas, or so the immortal Dickens avers, to present the tragic and the comic scenes in as regular alternation as the layers of red and white in a side of streaky, well-cured bacon, your n. now proceeds directly to a disused warehouse located in the docklands area of Bay City, i.e., a venue some miles remote from the Musso & Frank Grill, it being the case that your humble n.'s facility for wraithlike drifting through space and time allows for the travelling of great distance faster than a reasonably erudite citizen might say *cat*.

Thus it is that, at the very moment Sir Archie first claps peepers on Vanessa Hopgood, we arrive in the Bay City warehouse to find ourselves in the presence of our narrative's anti-hero, who, being familiar to a variety of law enforcement agencies as Jasper Huxtable 'Rusty' McGrew, is considered the spiritual heir of the immortal Virgil's Cacus for thinking in the savagery of his heart not to leave any crime or treachery undared or unattempted. It being probable, then, that our tale will very soon erupt in broils and disventures, your humble n. takes this opportunity to provide the Reader with the obligatory pen sketch of Rusty McGrew. To wit:

Height: 6'3"
Hair: A big bushy head of curly red
Eyes: Iron grey

Features: Strangely reminiscent of Norman helmet
Mien: Piratical

Alas, we do not encounter Rusty at his most convivial, for Rusty is currently experiencing a degree of discomfort your humble n. will not scruple to describe as *the plaguy pip*, which is to say that Rusty, being a bootlegger awaiting the delivery of the latest batch of his *liquid assets*, is acutely aware that the disused warehouse wherein he beguiles the time belongs to another, and that the Californian judiciary takes a dim view of trespass, regardless of whether the property under advisement is disused, derelict or otherwise unoccupied.

It should further be noted, moreo'er, that the mood is e'en fraughter than it might have been, this in consequence of several of Rusty's most trusted associates being recently wafted aloft to a better world than this, without Rusty's permission and against his stated wishes, courtesy of lead poisoning administered at a velocity of roughly 1,450 feet per second, this on the orders of Rusty's most fearsome rival, Juan 'Lefty' Palomeque.

Or so Rusty suspicions. For lo! Rusty has so many rivals that an exhaustive list of potential foes would include every grown male for fifty miles in every direction (or, in the case of West, as far as the Catalinas), the notable exceptions to which list are Foxy, Redser and Carrots McGrew, all of whom, as the Reader may have already begun to suspect, are bound to Rusty by blood ties, albeit said ties are metaphorical rather than tangible, blood being a pitiably poor binding agent, as any Reader who has vainly attempted to staunch a punctured artery will no doubt attest.

In consequence, the warehouse bristles with a remarkable quantity of ordnance, being composed in the main of Tommy Guns, sticks of dynamite and an armour-plated Duesenberg furnished with a carriage-mounted M1895 Gatling Gun, which latter Rusty has recently purchased from an enterprising young quartermaster on the occasion of the US Army declaring the Gatling obsolete, Rusty independently coming to the same conclusion about the Gatling M1895 as did the immortal Keats with regard to *daisies, vermeil-rim'd and white*, i.e., that a thing of beauty is a joy for ever.

The *mise en scène* thus established, we now join Rusty & Co. as the Siblings McGrew, so bristled about with Tommy Guns, persuaders, Betseys and knobkerries as to resemble hedgehogs besieged, huddle together in the shelter of the armour-plated Duesenberg and enter conclave. To wit:

'Haul her wind,' says Redser. 'They're standing out in the offing with an eye to blockade.'

'Reef in, Mariner Two,' says Rusty. 'They'll be here.'

'It's all ahoo,' says Carrots.

'Four bells and all's well,' counters Rusty.

'Handsomely now!' sings out Foxy. 'Away aloft, trice up and lay out. Sheet home. Give her every stitch of canvas she'll bear. Belay there!'

Here your humble n. notes that the Siblings McGrew, being no one's fools, have adopted a secret code designed to discommode any agent of law enforcement *vis-à-vis* their nefarious intentions, said code employing maritime terminology derived from A. Basil Lubbock's magisterial tome, *Round the Horn Before the Mast* (1915, John Murray). Thus the foregoing dialogue excerpt alludes to the imminent arrival of a goodly number of desperadoes operating under the aegis of Juan 'Lefty' Palomeque, who, under the guise of delivering a batch of *liquid assets*, plans a reverse ambuscade designed to wreak what the immortal Homer was once pleased to describe as *doings beyond all remedy* on the unsuspecting Siblings McGrew, which strategy is fatally undermined by the fact that Rusty is not, in fact, e'en remotely unsuspecting, this in consequence of the double-agents Rusty has had the foresight to place in Lefty's camp.

'Fire as she bears, gentlemen,' says Rusty.

At least, such are the words that depart Rusty's lips, although it behoves your humble n. to report that they likely go unheard due to their utterance coinciding with an armoured truck crashing through the warehouse doors, upon which can be discerned masked citizens blazing away with weaponry of semi-automatic design, said unheralded arrival being largely the fault of Rusty's look-out, Frenchie 'The Rock' LaRoque, who, stationed high in the warehouse rafters, is in fact a triple-agent in the employ of Lefty Palomeque.

Here your humble n. pauses to note that contained in the foregoing is this narrative's main sub-theme, i.e., that perfidy will borrow perfidy, and blood wash blood, which sub-theme is employed to throw into sharp relief, and ultimately illustrate, by our tale's conclusion, the philosophical proposition that *the world might be a better place if only everyone would make a little more effort to get along*.

But now we return to the action, wherein erupts the previously advertised broils and disventures, the mayhem of which will be most comprehensively appreciated were your n. to employ several approximations of loud and discordantly abrasive noise, a gambit which will likely prove effective if the Reader might contrive to hear, with her mind's ear, said sounds occurring simultaneously. To wit:

Rat-a-tat-TAT! tinkle Chicago Pianos on all sides;

Pheee-ow! sings a bullet sizzling past Rusty's right temple;

Ba-doing! goes an errant round as it ricochets off the Duesenberg and shoots vertically aloft to bury itself in the left kidney of Frenchie LaRoque where he perches in the warehouse rafters;

Ka-BOOM! bruits a bundle of dynamite tossed by Carrots under the armoured truck;

Thunka-thunka-thunk! thunders the carriage-mounted M1895 Gatling as sundry trusted associates of Juan 'Lefty' Palomeque go stumbling about the warehouse in stunned imitation of decapitated fowl.

It being your humble n.'s responsibility to set the scene, and the Reader's obligation to exercise her imagination by embroidering, amplifying and otherwise embellishing the factual details so provided, your chronicler further reports that the warehouse is by now *choked with smoke*, *reeking of cordite*, and *populated by persons of a blackened visage such as might be envisaged by the immortal Bosch in a bid to illustrate the plight of those treacherous citizens doomed to languish for all eternity in the Ninth Circle of Hell.*

It is for the benefit of the more sensitive Reader, howe'er, that your n. draws a veil o'er the events now unfolding, it being the case that this narrative is by no means concerned with violence, carnage and gore *per se*, but with the consequences of violence, carnage and gore, said consequences being for the most part moral and philosophical, but on occasion emotional and psychological too. Thus, having employed for the sake of said sensitive Reader the cinematic convention of *panning away* from the action to gaze aloft, and there hold for a moment upon a single white dove rising and rapturously going towards the *holoughnesse of the eighthe spere* (*cf.* Chaucer), the better to provide an image rich in pathetic fallacy, we now return to the Siblings McGrew as they emerge from the sulphuric haze, with visages blackened and reeking of mephitic exhalations, to enter again into *pourparlers*. To wit:

'Raked 'em stem to stern!' exults Redser as he plucks cotton wadding from his ears.

'Left gaping holes 'twixt wind and water!' sings out Carrots.

'Avast there!' whoops Foxy, who has yet to pluck the cotton wadding from his ears.

Said jubilance and exultation continuing apace for some goodly few moments, it is eventually noted by his subalterns that Brother Mariner One is by no means exhibiting the bobbish mid-season form of a general who has recently engineered a comprehensive rout, but is instead staring blankly before him like a man who has just now had his letters returned by a chorus doll previously considered a three-star cast-iron plunger.

'What gives?' enquires Redser in the sombre tenor of a man who has gazed aloft in the hope of detecting larks upon the wing and numbered among his sightings only stormy petrels.

'Plan B,' says Rusty.

A mere two syllables, aye; but not since King Leonidas stood before the Three Hundred and declared *Στεκόμαστε!* have so few syllables sent such a frisson through the ranks. For lo! Rusty's Plan B is the very antithesis of *Στεκόμαστε!*; indeed, it is no exaggeration to state that said syllables render the Siblings McGrew so bemusedly disconcerted as to resemble Napoleon's troops on the outskirts of Moscow when the words *battre en retraite* came a-whispering like a poisonous frost.

'Run?' says Redser in blanching timbre.

'Cut out?' whispers Carrots.

'*Muss es sein*?' croaks Foxy.

'Aye,' says Rusty. '*Es muss sein.*'

And it is now that the Siblings McGrew fully grasp the gravity of the situation, for Rusty, being particularly devoted to Beethoven's later works, does not invoke The Master lightly. And one has only to glance around to glimpse, as best as one might through the pall of smoke, the reason why Rusty insists *it must be*, for the prone forms of the fallen lie around and about as far as the eye can see, albeit said range is confined to roughly five feet in any direction as a result of the optical blurring generally caused by an excess of cordite, smoke and mephitic exhalations.

E'en so, it is apparent to all that several dozen of Juan 'Lefty' Palomeque's most trusted associates now lie still upon the warehouse floor, so stunned by the deafening volume of the Gatling in the close confines of the warehouse as to be rendered insensible, and thus effortlessly bound and trussed, the better to be transported to the warehouse wherein Cecil B. DeMille houses his expendable extras, it being the case that Cecil is currently mulling o'er the possibilities of his long-gestating epic *Genghis Khan: The World Must Go*, while around them pool much of the bullet-shattered delivery of *liquid assets*, said pooling being responsible for the prone and horizontal forms of many of the McGrews' trusted associates, most of whom resemble beached fish as they adopt with gusto the thrifty principle of *waste not, want not*.

Alas, as the choking smoke slowly drifts aloft, the extent to which the warehouse has been sorely used becomes clear – its doors splintered and sagging upon hinge, its walls scorched and breached, its rafters so ahoo that e'en the most sympathetic judge would be hard-pressed to accept that the damage wrought was suffered during a shooting-party mishap, or in consequence of an accidental discharge during a routine inspection of weapons, and particularly when said weapons were illegally held Tommy Guns, loosely bundled sticks of dynamite, and a carriage-mounted M1895 Gatling.

'Only one thing for it, boys,' says Rusty. 'We burn it to the floor and go to ground until the heat dies down.'

'That could take a while,' says Redser. 'Yon stuff's ninety-eight per cent proof.'

'I speak,' says Rusty, 'literally *and* metaphorically.'

Here the Reader will easily conceive that Rusty's words elicit a collective gasp, and then an excited babble, o'er which Foxy can be heard to state that he discovers himself in imminent peril of being knocked down with a feather, which possibility is always something of a concern for Foxy due to his chronic case of acute pteronophobia. Such a trifle, howe'er, is precisely the quality of pettifog Rusty cannot afford to indulge: for Rusty, in crises as in matters of the heart, is very much a man of decisive action.

Plan B thus in train, Rusty stands not upon the order of his going, but delays only to issue orders pertaining to the salvage of what remains of his *liquid assets*, the loading of several dozen erstwhile nemeses onto a truck bound for the holding pens in Cecil B. DeMille's warehouse, and the marshalling of a horde of trusted associates so spifflicated on 98% proof bathtub hooch as to resemble a cadre of Spanish sailors on the prowl in a port that is not Spanish – I say, Rusty stands not upon the order of his going, but departs the warehouse forthwith.

His destination? Ah, and well may the curious Reader enquire in so tremulous a tone. For Rusty McGrew, our narrative's very own personification of Doom, hightails it away from the warehouse conflagration bound for Hollywood and the Blue Phalarope,[1] his trajectory as arrow-straight as Destiny itself, providing said allusion allows for Rusty's wearing and tacking as he zooms onward through the streets of Greater Los Angeles in the gathering dusk, said zig-zagging manoeuvres an entirely sensible precaution for an outlaw, gangster and bootlegger who has in the past hour achieved the status craved by many but reserved only for the truly dedicated few – *Public Enemy Number Nine!*

1 In our haste to introduce Rusty McGrew to the tale no later than Chapter Four, lest his belated entry be considered a narrative contrivance akin to a *deus ex machina*, we have, alas, neglected to mention that Archie, Vanessa, Adele and Bartley will at some future point depart the terrace of the Musso & Frank Grill, bound for dinner at the Blue Phalarope, a nightclub owned by Rusty McGrew (more of which anon).

Chapter Five

A belated Prologue. Archie and Vanessa finally meet.
A revelation which suggests that one of our characters is by no means the mild-mannered boon companion she professes to be.

With Rusty McGrew's credentials as *the scourge and wrath of God* (*cf.* Marlowe) firmly established, we now drift, wraithlike, back to the terrace of the Musso & Frank Grill, albeit in the salaaming manner, your n. being obliged to abase himself before the Reader, who, accustomed to the High Style, is likely outraged that your n. has to date neglected to provide a *Prologue*, wherein, according to the principles laid down in the *Poetics*, might be established our narrative's main theme. Thus it is that, begging the forgiveness of any Reader discommoded by the literary equivalent of a gaucherie suggestive of an unpardonable want of couth, your n. now belatedly delivers this tale's *Prologue*. To wit:

> *Prologue*
> The world of late being woven from tales and narratives and suchlike fictions as might persuade the Reader that we tremble on the very brink of a new Dark Age, notwithstanding that all ages are considered Dark by the citizens living through them, Good Times being generally the preserve of citizens dwelling in the Republic of Posterity, it being the case that any Age considered somewhat murky is by some strange alchemy rendered Golden once viewed through rose-tinted hindsight, or, if not exactly Golden, at the very least burnished sepia, a

fair example being Classical Athens, frequently ruled by tyrants and demagogues but ne'ertheless historically regarded, all things considered, a Golden Age – I say, for the benefit of any Reader who discovers herself cast down and emotionally discommoded by this *warlike, various and tragical age* (*cf.* Cowley) in which we live, with language debased and meaning askew, your humble narrator here recounts the progress, doings and sayings of a disparate group of pilgrims as they set out from Hollywood bound for Tropico Springs, proving, as they go, this narrative's thesis, i.e., the philosophical proposition that *the world might be a better place if only everyone would make a little more effort to get along.*

Our main theme thus officially instituted, we now arrive at Vanessa Hopgood's table on the terrace of the Musso & Frank Grill, where, as the attentive Reader will no doubt recall, we left America's Darling™ anticipating the imminent arrival of her freshly minted swain, Sir Archibald l'Estrange-B'stard, who currently hot-foots it towards Vanessa's table trailed by the ever-faithful Bartley McGuffin and a silently simmering Adele Fitzhalligon. It being thus only a matter of moments before Archie and Vanessa finally meet, your n. now hurries to clarify a number of references previously made by or about Ms Hopgood, i.e., '*Edith*', '*Hillcrest*' and '*took up her trusty brassie*'.

'*Edith*', of course, is self-explanatory, Edith Cummings being the Fairway Flapper, champion golfer and socialite *nonpareil*, Edith and Vanessa being, as previously attested, firm friends who enjoy a remarkable mutual devotion. '*Hillcrest*', meanwhile, refers to the Hillcrest Country Club located in Cheviot Hills, Los Angeles, and which was established in 1920 as a golf club with an exclusively Jewish membership, although it appears that Vanessa, being officially affianced to Samuel L. Silverstein, is frequently found to be navigating Hillcrest's fairways in no little style, said style being both sartorial and sporting. Finally, and first clarifying that a '*brassie*' is the wooden-headed club a golfer uses to strike his or her first shot off the tee, '*took up her trusty brassie*' confirms what the attentive Reader has likely long suspected, which is that Vanessa Hopgood is a dedicated practitioner of the noble Scottish art, i.e., golf.

Indeed, when as a child she first dared to dream, Vanessa discovered herself passionately aflame with the ambition of being crowned Champion Golfer (Ladies) of America, the most important consequence of which, for the purpose of our narrative, was that the young Vanessa was no more interested in becoming an actress than might, to quote the immortal Kipling, any toad beneath the harrow.

It is Samuel L. Silverstein's greatest sorrow that, fame and fortune notwithstanding, Vanessa's ambition has not wavered by so much as a starved quark during her rapid ascent to the status of the most shimmering star in all of Hollywood's firmament. For her part, it is Vanessa's contention that if Sammy's notoriously fine-printed contracts had delivered a fortune in proportion to her profit-generating fame, then Vanessa might well have sold her soul and embraced her creatively barren but lucrative destiny. Howe'er, the notable absence of any digressions on the subject of increased percentages during Sammy's haranguing of Vanessa to submit to repeated surgeries have left Vanessa with very little option but to invite Sammy to take a very long hike down a dogleg par five; and lo! who should enter, stage left upon the terrace of the Musso & Frank Grill itself, but Sir Archibald l'Estrange-B'stard, aristocratic heir to a fine family fortune who is, *pace* Austen, in want of a wife, and with a passion for the noble Scottish art to boot.

O Atropos! Is there no end to your mischief?[1]

'What ho!' halloos Archie as he finally arrives at journey's end, albeit his entrance is rendered rather more dramatical than he intended by Felicia Fortesque's improperly stowed diamante Dior clutch, which, left carelessly in the aisle, now works upon Archie

1 Atropos: one of the Three Fates, or *Moirai*, who, along with her sisters Clotho and Lachesis, constitute the ancient Greek world's personification of the concept of Fate and Destiny.

in much the same way as banana skin upon court jesters of yore and sends him flailing off at a tangent sufficient to plunge Harold Lloyd into an off-season blue. An inauspicious overture, or so the more sophisticated Reader might believe; but stay! That Archie comes to a screeching halt on his hands and knees under the table with his large round head in Vanessa's lap is in fact secretly regarded by both parties, if we might paraphrase the immortal Milton, as something of a sable cloud turning forth her silver lining on the night and casting a gleam o'er Vanessa's metaphorical tufted grove; indeed, both parties, were they to be more honest than first impressions generally allow, are battle-hardened veterans of the non-verbal head-in-lap introduction that tends to be frowned upon in more conservative social gatherings.

Thus it is that Archie, who might otherwise have found himself rendered speechless by Vanessa's radiant beauty, discovers himself spluttering his customary apologies by rote, while Vanessa puts very little back-lift into the right cross she lays almost tenderly on Archie's jaw, just below his left ear.

Vanessa being native to Wisconsin, howe'er, and having grown up spending a considerable portion of the Badger State's nine-month winters on the ice playing hockey with her half-dozen elder brothers, e'en very little back-lift is required to send Archie sprawling in reverse out into the aisle, where he finally slides to a halt at Adele Fitzhalligon's feet.

Your n. now advises those Readers championing Adele Fitzhalligon's cause to avert their eyes, for there is no merit to be gleaned from the vengeful stamp she addresses to Archie's groin, Adele reasoning – correctly, as it turns out – that Archie is so unseamed by his coming a purler on Cordelia's diamante clutch and Vanessa's subsequent pugilistic rebuff that all injuries incurred will be later credited to the Hopgood-Fortesque joint account.

The emotionally intelligent Reader will likely conceive at this point that the auguries are ill-fated for Archie, although here your humble n. reluctantly inserts himself into the narrative to caution against the leaping to any conclusions without first taking into consideration the stuff (stern) of which the l'Estrange-B'stards are made. As he lies in the aisle with head pounding, groin aflame and – if we might paraphrase the Bard – heart unseated and a-knocking about his ribs, Archie immediately identifies the symptoms as those generally associated with hangover, concussion, or love. With dignity a fond memory, and swiftly concluding that there is little to be lost by assuming the most favourable diagnosis (i.e., love), Archie leaps to his feet and commences persiflage forthwith.

'Ta-*da*!' sings out our hero, in the vain hope that Vanessa might believe his entrance rehearsed and his humiliation deliberately contrived solely for her amusement. Aye, and well may the Reader wince at the irony, for Archie abases himself in tragi-comical fashion before the one woman in Hollywood who is contractually bound not to emit so much as a girlish giggle in public, e'en if – and on this point the fine-printed contract is adamant – Charles Spencer Chaplin himself were to set about the back of her knees with an expertly directed peacock feather.

O Atropos, thou cruel minx, you excel yourself!

Vanessa thus rendering a fair facsimile of Buster Keaton impersonating a cigar-store Indian, and Felicia, as always, taking her cue from her boon companion, Archie has no option but to assume he is in receipt of a silent (but no less deafening) Bronx razoo. A lesser man might have crept away, and consoled himself with the quaffing of a Melchizedek of the old fizzy shampoo whilst lolling in the arms of Adele Fitzhalligon, said strategy, as it happens, being Adele's fervent hope, but Archie's stuff (stern) has a spine not unakin to the *Victory*'s beam, circa Trafalgar, as it broke the line between *Redoubtable* and *Bucentaure*. Rallying, as did the immortal Nelson, to let fly the proverbial treble-shotted broadside, Archie now ventures to suggest that the weather is tolerably mild for this time of year, what?

Detecting no potential for contract-voiding hilarity in this conversational gambit, Vanessa allows that the weather is indeed mild, although she has known it milder at this time of year, and then courteously invites Archie to take a pew and commence worship.

'Ra*ther*!' says Archie, plonking his broad behind down on the seat indicated. 'Pitching the old woo, eh?'

Alas, dear Reader, it grieves your n. to relate that while Archie's passion for Vanessa would compare favourably e'en were the metric employed that of the immortal Dante's for Beatrice, Archie's command of the English language is roughly that of his illustrious literary predecessor. Which is to say that, for the moment at least, albeit with the proviso that we shall return immediately to Vanessa and Archie should they broach a subject other than current and prospective climatic conditions, your n. has no choice but to cast his net upon uncharted waters for the lyrical cut-and-thrust of courtly *tête-à-tête*, *viz.*, the three-cornered *imbroglio* currently blooming in the favourably humid habitat indigenous to Bartley McGuffin, Adele Fitzhalligon and Felicia Fortesque.

The scenario is this: Adele, after studying the form and allowing that Bartley McGuffin might well place at decent odds in the Adele Fitzhalligon Golden Ticket Stakes, is watching Bartley like the proverbial hawk gazing hungrily on the fabled mouse upon a frog's back, i.e., unblinking and steely-eyed, while Bartley watches Felicia Fortesque like a rival hawk putting the glad eye on the very same frog-mounted mouse. Felicia, for her part, appears insensible of any and all raptor-ish staring, being instead consumed with the articulation of her thoughts as she scribbles with a slim gold pencil in the notebook in her lap.

'Bartley?' says Adele.

'Madam?'

'What's the scoop for later on?'

'Madam?'

'For Archie, I mean. What's the plan?'

'I'm afraid I am not privy to Sir Archibald's intentions, madam.'

'You're saying he hasn't even booked dinner yet?'

'Sir Archibald is something of a free spirit, madam. He prefers when possible not to commit to times and dates.'

'Absolutely. It's one of his most charming features, I find.'

'Indeed, madam.'

'But surely,' says Adele, with visions of her hoped-for nosebag wafting aloft on Pegasian wings, 'it couldn't do any harm to make a provisional booking.'

Sir Archie as a rule favouring the free-association approach to conversation, Bartley is at this point expert at appearing to engage in public discourse while his mind is busy elsewhere, and generally on his One True Work. Such had certainly been the case during the foregoing, when Bartley had been lending the lie to the immortal Austen's rhetorical query as to who can think of Miss Smith when Miss Woodhouse is near, precisely by thinking of Miss Smith (i.e., Felicia Fortesque) despite the adjacent presence of a shimmering Miss Woodhouse (i.e., Vanessa Hopgood). It now occurs to Bartley that were he to encourage Adele's suggestion in the matter of a provisional dinner booking, he might well secure a moment or two alone with Miss Smith, aka Ms Fortesque, an opportunity Bartley is loath to let pass.

'A capital idea, madam,' says Bartley. 'Shall I ask for a telephone to be brought to table?'

'Trouble yourself not,' says Adele, taking her cue from Bartley's linguistic stylings, 'for I must needs go inside, the better to powder my nose, forsooth.'

'Very well,' says Bartley as Adele takes to her heels. The reason for Adele's secrecy and haste will be revealed presently, but for now we remain with Bartley and Felicia, between whom a silence blissfully slumbers, disturbed only by the scratching of Felicia's slim gold pencil and Bartley's repeated clearing of his throat, at which extended detonation Felicia glances up with a vague smile and a querulously raised eyebrow, her expression a fair facsimile of the playfully contemptuous means by which Vanessa Hopgood regularly lays waste to a million libidos.

Bartley being a man like any other man, and the local climate tending towards the humid, even a fair facsimile of Vanessa Hopgood is sufficient to raise Bartley's temperature, get him damp around the collar, and absorb the moisture from where it does most good, i.e., between tongue and mouth's roof.

'Full many a flower is born to blush unseen,' begins Bartley gamely, before belatedly realising the surfeit of sibilance employed by the immortal Gray in this particular instance, 'and waste its fragrance on the desert air.'

'Pardon me?'

'What I mean to say,' croaks Bartley, 'is who can think of Miss Woodhouse when Miss Smith is by?'

'I'm sorry,' says Felicia, shifting forward on her seat. 'Are you having a stroke? Shall I call for assistance?'

Swiping the nearest bumper off the table, Bartley quaffs the lot. 'A compliment,' he gasps. 'I was trying to pay you a compliment.'

'Oh! To me? Really?' Here Felicia lays aside her notepad and slim gold pencil and clasps her hands together. '*Do* tell.'

'Well,' says Bartley, and proceeds to inform Felicia that, all things considered, and while acknowledging Miss Hopgood's beauty represents a *cri* of the absolute *dernier*, it would be a man of singularly myopic perspicacity who might fail to appreciate Felicia's comparative beauty *vis-à-vis* the ornament to her species that is Miss Hopgood.

'If I'm hearing you correctly,' says Felicia, after sifting through all this chaff in vain hope of locating a single grain, 'you're suggesting that men wearing spectacles might find me almost as attractive as Miss Hopgood.'

'Said myopia, madam, is wholly metaphorical.'

'I see,' says Felicia through lips your n. will not scruple to describe as compursioned. 'And this Miss Smith you reference, who appears happy to dally with a woodlouse?'

Bartley, delighted to be of service, now offers Felicia a *précis* of the immortal Austen's *Emma*, including brief character sketches of the vivacious Miss Woodhouse and the drab social-climber Miss Smith, by the end of which Felicia is scribbling so furiously that she snaps the lead point of her slim gold pencil.

'Pardon me,' says she, reaching under the table for the diamante clutch that has recently caused Archie to come so spectacularly a purler. Bartley believing Felicia to be searching for a replacement pencil, he discovers himself perturbed more than somewhat, and then some, when Felicia's hand emerges from the clutch wrapped around what appears to be a double-barrelled derringer, a Remington of the calibre .41 rimfire short colloquially known as a 'muff pistol', although Bartley would be the first to admit that he is no expert when it comes to ladies' firearms.

'I triple-double-dare you,' says Felicia, levelling the derringer at Bartley's groin, 'to breathe just one more syllable.'

With the foregoing as evidence, your n. believes that he betrays no confidence in informing the Reader that Bartley McGuffin's lack of expertise concerning ladies' firearms extends into the broader realm of femininity, for women, in Bartley's experience, are not quite another species but so exotically different, with their unique customs, culture and language, as to constitute a superior race. E'en so, and despite a penchant for literal interpretation that is the unfortunate but inevitable by-product of a minor degree in Anglo-Irish literature from the lesser Dublin university, Bartley immediately grasps the crux of the matter, which is that the tone of Felicia's voice – every bit as hard, blunt and iron-ish as the derringer's double muzzle – suggests that her dare (its multiple compound notwithstanding) is to be interpreted as encouragement to give any urge to speak the old miss-in-baulk for the foreseeable future, which is why Bartley now refrains from enquiring as to why Ms Fortesque might discover herself so provoked as to so precipitously out with a muff pistol, and instead falls back on the tried-and-tested formula of clearing his throat, which, alas, being softly delivered due to Bartley's understandable wish not to startle his freshly minted adversary, could very easily be construed by Felicia as an 'Um.'

Technically speaking, of course, an 'Um' constitutes a syllable, regardless of how softly it might be delivered and despite the tone in which it is couched (Bartley's timbre, in e'en so brief an utterance, combining elements of the quizzical, the deferential and the most perplexing torment of doubt), with the consequence that Felicia Fortesque, according to the parameters established, is well within her rights to plug Bartley McGuffin plumb spang where it might do him the least good, which she immediately proceeds not to do.

To understand why Felicia does not instinctively respond to Bartley's provocation by scratching what is most certainly a severe itch upon her trigger finger, we must here pause our narrative, the better to relate the expositionary reverie which will illuminate, and, by way of light's corollary, cast shadow upon, Felicia's history, character and motivation, which, being a complex and extensive history of treachery and subterfugial perfidy, warrants the commencing of an entirely new chapter, i.e., Chapter Seven, to which we now proceed gallop-post and sparing not the horses, pausing, indeed, only for so long as it might take to relate the events of Chapter Six, wherein will be discovered Samuel L. Silverstein rendered so low in spirits as to be mistaken for Irish by the immortal Dickens, said worthy being of the opinion, as any Reader who has read the serialised version of *Oliver Twist* will testify, that *the Irish are generally the lowest order of anything*.[2]

2 The reference, alas, was omitted in the edition first published in book form by Mr Richard Bentley (1839).

Chapter Six

In which Samuel L. Silverstein discovers himself the focus of an investigation into Hollywood's nascent Bolshevikism. A digression on the advisability of apostasy, e'en in the name of true love.

It is considered ill-judged by Hollywood's *cognoscenti* for a man to dally too long on the terrace of the Musso & Frank Grill, for such suggests a man is losing his touch when it comes to the striking of deals, the breaking of strikes, or the wooing of dames. Thus the Reader will appreciate that Samuel L. Silverstein has long since departed the Musso & Frank Grill, in consequence of which our latest chapter commences in a manner contradistinctive to that of Creusa fading from Aeneas' sight into the insubstantial air, by which is meant that we materialise from the aether at the corner of Wilshire and Irving, alighting upon the *lapis lazuli* tiles of Sammy's palatial white stucco mansion in the Moorish style before adopting the cinematic conceit of the *aerial pan* in swooping down from the roof onto a manicured lawn fringed by monkey-puzzle trees, upon which can be observed Sammy, Ethel Barrymore, George P. Dangleberry III, Mae Murray, Mrs Gloria Teasdale, the promising young tunesmith Cole Porter, and sundry other chums of Sammy, all of whom are engaged in croquet tourney, albeit one in which the result is unlikely to be logged by the United All England Croquet Association, for Sammy's variation on the sport involves our rotund *mogul* impersonating a croquet ball as he rolls himself, head o'er heels, through the legs of a clutch of swimsuit-clad starlets beguiled into believing they are auditioning for Sammy's latest wheeze, an epic stage musical entitled *Oh! My Wicked Wicket Ways*.

Thus the reader will easily conceive that all is well in Sammy's little corner of Eden, with snail upon thorn and fizz fairly foaming o'er the brim of capacious bumper. But stay! Mortal happiness is but a goad to the gods, those celestial sociopaths who first make mad those whom they wish to destroy; and, there being naught more likely to render Samuel L. Silverstein hopping mad than a good clean game of croquet interrupted, the reader may confidently anticipate an event which will disturb Sammy in his wicket endeavours.

And lo! as if by magick or summoned by alchemy there appears through the french windows of Sammy's Moorish mansion a citizen clutching an alligator-skin briefcase and possessed of the furtive demeanour all legal professionals have been obliged to adopt since the dark days when Dick the Butcher and his ilk loosed mere anarchy the length and breadth of the kingdom.

'Mr Silverstein?' booms our divinely dispatched goad. 'A word, if I may?'

'Ifacks!' sings out Sammy, who has in common with Hamlet's deceased father a distaste for being cut off in the blossom of his sins. 'Cohen? Is that you?'

'It is I,' confirms Abraham 'Abie' Cohen, motion picture studio lawyer and public notary, a man renowned for his fiercely partisan representations on behalf of those unlucky thespians who fall afoul of the notoriously rigid laws of the Californian legislature, which body of men are, in Abie's considered professional opinion, so pernickety about such trivialities as the driving of automobiles whilst squiffed and the accidental skewering of Filipino butler that they may as well have stepped off the *Mayflower* just the week before.

'Hell's teeth,' mutters Sammy, hauling himself vertical and sending a yearning glance in the direction of Gloria Larouche, the willowy *ingénue* he has long since identified as the ideal wicket through which to peg out. 'What is it *this* time?'

'The matter might be best discussed *in camera*, as it were.'

'How many times do I need to tell you, Abie?' says Sammy as he trudges across the manicured lawn towards the patio where Abie awaits. 'No cameras, no recordings, and no more on paper than a man might need to wipe his —'

'What I mean,' interjects Abie, 'is that we need to speak privately.'

'Ah. In that case, step into my inner penetralium.'

As Sammy leads Abie inside and down the corridor to his study, and we drift along wraithlike in their wake, your n. avails of said temporary narrative *lacuna* to belatedly provide a pen sketch of Samuel L. Silverstein, it being the case, apparently, that Sammy's role in our narrative is considerably more important than that of mere *provocateur* deployed to provoke Vanessa Hopgood into abandoning fame ~~and fortune~~ in preference for her childhood dream of becoming Champion Golfer (Ladies) of America. To wit:

Height: 5'8"
Hair: Absent
Stare: Penetrating
Shape: Egg-ish
Disposition: Libidinous

'Go to, Abie, and spare not the horseflesh,' says Sammy L. as he sinks into the leather chair behind his desk, puts flame to Havana and pours himself a jorum of Scotch, it being Sammy's firm belief that Scotch insufficient to drown a sack of kittens is not only a waste of effort but an insult to the Highland stalwarts and their craft. 'Time, tide and croquet wait for no man.'

'Alas,' intones Abie, situating himself in the wing-backed chair before Sammy's desk and positioning his briefcase on his lap, Abie having learned the hard way that a good alligator-skin briefcase makes for a stout shield, Sammy's self-control being rather less than it might be when tidings are such as to cause the Silverstein brow to knit – 'I say, alas, I am the bearer of bad news.'

'When a man's attorney shows up to a croquet tourney bearing before him an alligator-skin briefcase,' says Sammy in philosophical timbre, 'that man would be a fool to expect good news. Am I a fool?'

'No.'

'Is that briefcase encased in alligator skin?'

'It is.'

'Are you my attorney?'

'For now, yes.'

'For now?'

'I regret to inform you, Mr Silverstein, that I am by no means possessed of a licence to practise in the Ukraine. Nor, for that matter, in any of the newly created republics of the USSR.'

It is no exaggeration, dear Reader, to say that Sammy's brow now knits. Being entirely accurate: the brow knits, the nostrils flare, and the mouth flops open like unto Alpine tunnel for toy train.

'Say again?' says Sammy with a strange kind of hoarse squeak, this once he has recovered the power of speech, a process hastened by the dumping of a liquid ounce of Scotch down the hatch and hence to the engine room to oil the pistons.

'I am very much afraid, Mr Silverstein, that I was in receipt early this afternoon of a request from the Department of Labour for clarification of your status *vis-à-vis* American citizenship. If said clarification is not forthcoming in a timely manner, a deportation order will be issued.'

By now Sammy's expression is that of an infant giraffe instructed to segue, mid-totter, from Viennese waltz into Argentine tango. For this, in truth, is a pip sufficiently plaguy to set every hair standing like quills upon the nervy porpentine, had Sammy any hairs to set standing, which he does not. He does, howe'er, possess a soul, and it is no exaggeration to say that the bolt has entered therein.

'O!' says he. 'I am fortune's fool!'

'Further,' says Abie,[1] 'there is some concern that you are a

1 'Abraham 'Abie' Cohen' is in fact the *nom-de-guerre* of one Zsigmond Szabó, first-born son of second-generation Hungarian immigrants, who, after closing down three

Bolshevik subversive currently disseminating Communist propaganda through the medium of motion pictures.'

'Me?' squeaks Sammy, waving his Havana around in a manner not unakin to Toscanini spotting a bassoonist filching a violin bow for the purpose of scratching an itchy ankle midway through the overture to Beethoven's *Fifth*. '*Me* a Communist?'

'The evidence consists of photographs of you fraternising with a Mr Charles Chaplin at the Pickfair residence on March 23rd.'

'Chaplin? He was bumming a smoke!'

'Be that as it may,' says Abie, 'the evidence is that you were not only fraternising with, but providing succour to, known sympathisers with the socialist movement. The order for a thorough investigation has come down from on high.'

'Hoover?'

'Mr Hoover, indeed,' says Abie in pious register, it being not beyond the bounds of possibility, in Abie's opinion, that Sammy's home is by now tapped, wired and/or bugged, with any sound recordings thus derived to be played back in public session at some point in the future. 'It appears that the fearless and charismatic Deputy Head of the Bureau of Investigations has taken a personal interest in your case.'

'But why me, Abie? Why *me*?'

'It's the strike.'

'The writers' strike?'

'Correct.'

'But I'm a strike-*breaker*, Abie. You know that. I paid for those knobkerries out of my own pocket.'

'Cash in hand, I'm afraid. No actual record of same. As per your strict instructions, no more on paper than a man might need to wipe his —'

'By Juno!'

'And then, of course, there's the new script you secretly

consecutive attorney-at-law practices in Ohio, Minnesota and Texas, respectively, finally hit upon the wheeze of hanging out a shingle with a distinctly Hebraic flavour, with spectacular results.

commissioned not two hours ago upon the terrace of the Musso & Frank Grill.'

'But that's strike-breaking too!'

'Indubitably. However, it's more the subject matter than the intention that Mr Hoover finds disturbing.'

'Disturbing? It's a wholesome religious allegory of Merrie Olde England. A literary classic, and one out of copyright to boot.'

'Indubitably, sir. Howe'er, it's a little-known fact that Mr Hoover is something of a literary connoisseur, and as such believes that the immortal Bunyan's scathing critique of the Gomorrah-ish roystering, against which the heroic Christian rebels, might be interpreted by some commentators as an allegory for those conditions which pertain in virtually any Prohibition-era city you might care to mention, and which might, if adapted for a motion picture audience, prove unnecessarily incendiary in these turbulent times. Further, Mr Hoover has concerns about the book's sub-theme, which contrasts relativism with realism, although here, I believe, he has somehow contrived to confuse *The Pilgrim's Progress* with *The Canterbury Tales*. In short,' says Abie in concluding tenor, 'Mr Hoover has issued a *nolle prosequi* against any and all Hollywood adaptations of *The Pilgrim's Progress*, which edict we may as well apply, until further notice, to *The Canterbury Tales*.'

'Couldn't he just give us notes?'

'Notes, Mr Silverstein?'

'Notes, Abie. Suggestions of an advisory nature, designed to enhance a story's appeal for the broadest possible audience.'

'Are you suggesting, Mr Silverstein, that *The Pilgrim's Progress* might be successfully abridged?'

'Are you suggesting, as your peremptory tenor might lead one to believe, that it might not?'

Sammy's query now fomenting a heated debate on the necessity of remaining scrupulously true to the source material when adapting a literary masterpiece for the silver screen, we may for the moment leave our velitating pair to their dispute, the better to note the salient narrative detail Sammy must eventually consider once he has accepted Abie Cohen's double-edged contention that (i) 300 pages of Restoration religious allegory into a three-reel motion picture photoplay will not go, and (ii) the *sans-culottes* who comprise the greater part of the contemporary motion picture audience are as familiar with *The Pilgrim's Progress* as to notice the absence of any elided material only if Sammy were to roll it all together to form a caber to be ceremonially tossed before each showing – I say, the salient narrative detail is that Samuel L. Silverstein, having discovered he is about to be deported back to the Ukrainian *shtetl* from whence he came, finds himself in dire need of credentials sufficient to prove his unswerving commitment to Uncle Samuel.

'Well,' says Abie Cohen, on being warmly pressed for advice on how best to address the issue under advisement, 'the very first thing I would do is stop using the phrase *Uncle Samuel*.'

'Duly noted.'

'The second would be to hie thee to a church and marry.'

'Consider it done.'

'To a woman with a *bona fide* American passport.'

'Ah.'

'My recommendation for the blushing bride is Vanessa Hopgood, it being bruited about all over Christendom that you and she are not only a red-hot item but already affianced. Also, she's under contract, and thus in no position to refuse.'

'True for you.'

'You'll pardon me for saying so, Mr Silverstein,' says Abie, readjusting the position of the alligator-skin briefcase in anticipation of brow-knit rancour, 'but you appear sorely deficient in the ardour traditionally expected of the pre-nuptial swain.'

'Ah me,' says Sammy. 'Oh my.'

'There's a wrinkle in the scheme?'

'The wheeze, not to put to put too fine a point on it, is phlegmy.'

'I see.' Here Abie opens his briefcase and extracts a brown-spotted banana, Abie understanding that Sammy is about to bare his soul and that naught but a potassium-packed chunk of slow-release energy will set him up nicely for the rigours ahead. 'Have on.'

It is a reluctant but grateful Samuel L. Silverstein who proceeds to unburden himself *vis-à-vis* the current contretemps between he and the shimmering goddess known to mortals as Vanessa Hopgood, although your humble n. here draws a veil o'er Sammy's tale of woe, in part because the Reader is already *au fait* with the gist thereof, but largely because Sammy, having sluiced down kitten-drowning quantities of Scotch on top of the cataracts of fizzy shampoo already consumed, cuts rather a piteous figure as he quivers at the prospect of being banished to the outer darkness of a Ukrainian *shtetl*, and your humble n., with no other obvious villain to hand (Rusty McGrew, on the evidence to date, being more anti-hero than villain), cannot afford to allow for the possibility that the sensitive Reader may begin to sympathise with Sammy's plight lest our narrative be leached of the essential tension that exists between hero (or, as seems increasingly likely, heroine) and antagonist.

Here, as Sammy rambles on, your n. takes the opportunity to confirm what the Reader has no doubt readily conceived, which is that Sammy's latest woes have their roots in his ongoing contretemps with Vanessa Hopgood. Indeed, it gives your humble n. precisely no pleasure to relate that Vanessa, sored up at Sammy's insistence that she submit to the excision of roughly two-thirds of a perfectly healthy larynx, had that very morning dropped a dime on Sammy, informing the local immigration authorities about Sammy's illegal entry into the USA courtesy of his appropriation of a false identity at Ellis Island, and his subsequent seditious wheeze, as the head of a Bolshevik sleeper cell, of transforming the American Dream into the nightmarish scenario *of all for one and one for all* via the newly influential medium of motion pictures.

Indeed, it is with no little disappointment that your humble n. relates the foregoing, for until this moment Vanessa Hopgood has been our narrative's strongest contender for the plum role of damsel in distress. Now, alas, it must be reluctantly recorded that Vanessa Hopgood, America's Darling™ and previously a shimmering beacon of Truth, Hope and Innocence, is no longer *a wise virgin but a foolish one (cf.* Matthew 25.7), her wick untrimmed and flame guttering like unto a lantern untended, albeit Vanessa's shimmering remains undiminished, and further acknowledging that Vanessa's virginal status, wise or otherwise, has been metaphorical rather than actual since the long, hot summer of 1916.

'It would appear,' says Abie Cohen, having listened patiently to the foregoing, providing we exclude your n.'s digression on Vanessa Hopgood's wick – 'I say, it would appear, Mr Silverstein, that you are completely dished.'

'And?' says Sammy L., who has bared his soul more in hope of practical advice than pithy recap.

'How are you squared with the Swiss?'

'The Swiss?'

'More the banking fraternity than the populace in general. Good terms, I hope?'

'Spit it out, Abie.'

'I am simply suggesting that it might be prudent to consider squirrelling away a doubloon or two in a Swiss bank account as insurance against the worst coming to the worst, which, if the immortal Manley Hopkins is to be believed, is invariably the worst's wont.'

'You want me to flee?'

'My personal preference, Mr Silverstein, would be for you to remain *in situ* as a *bona fide* American citizen, with all the required documentation and proof of same to hand should it be necessary at some future point to confirm the legality of your status.'

'But?'

'Putting my personal and professional preferences to one side, I would be in breach of my position of trust if I did not advise you that, in the temporary absence of the previously referenced documentation and proof, it might be wise to take certain steps.'

Here, conscious of the likely presence of audio-recording equipment, Abie raises his eyebrows and engages in a finger-mime that mimics a man *taking certain steps*, i.e., ascending a staircase, the implication being that said staircase should lead directly into the fuselage of an aeroplane about to depart for parts unknown but preferably foreign. Then, noting Sammy's rather owlish glower, Abie extends his arms to either side and waggles them a tad.

'I see,' says Sammy.

'Shall I make the necessary arrangements?'

'Not just yet. There may be a knot or two to be disentangled first.'

'Given your precarious legal position, Mr Silverstein, I am obliged to press you to be specific. Knot singular or knots plural?

'Well, one. But it's Gordian.'

'Ah. A knot, then, composed of several knots.'

'Handsomely put, Abie.'

'Might I suggest you unsheathe your sword and, with one smooth swing, slice through said intractable bind?'

'Oh, I would, Abie. But it's Moxie.'

'Ah.'

'I can't leave Moxie.'

'No, well, that goes without saying. What man could? I don't suppose,' says Abie, having pondered the conundrum, 'she'd go with you?'

'*She* might. But I think her *abuela* has finally settled now. And her sister Consuela is due to be married in May.'

'*Mazel tov*,' murmurs Abie automatically. 'And may I inquire,' says he in delicate register, 'if it is only love's filaments that bind you and Madame La Roux so closely together?'

'There is no *only*,' says Sammy in haughteous register, 'when it's a matter of love's filaments.'

'No, of course not. I was simply —'

'What joy is joy,' enquires Sammy in hollow tenor, 'if Sylvia be not by?'

'It's a puzzler, surely,' says Abie.

'I feed upon the very shadow of her perfection.'

'An ambrosial feast, no doubt. But Mr Silverstein, if I may redirect you to the matter in —'

'Whither she goest,' says Sammy, 'I goest; wherever she lodgest, I will lodge; and her people will be my people, and her God my God.'

'Steady on,' says Abie. 'I thought she was Mex.'

'Pardon?'

'I mean to say, isn't Madame La Roux of Mexican ethnicity? And, in consequence, Catholic?'

'Love knows no dogma, Abie.'

'No, of course. But still.'

'Still?'

Here Abie Cohen, taking his cue from Don Juan's mother Donna Inez, *look'd a lecture, each eye a sermon, his brow a homily.* 'You're a *Jew*,' says Abie with the tremulous fervour only accessible to a second-generation Hungarian immigrant who is not Jewish but merely pretending to be when confronted by the horrific prospect of apostasy. 'You can't give up your *God*.'

'E'en if,' says Sammy in as melancholy, long and withdrawing a roar as might have inspired the immortal Arnold as said worthy gazed out upon Dover Beach, 'my God has given up on me?'

This being such heresy as to cause Sammy to be immediately rendered a pillar of salt with no recourse to appeal, Abie now discovers himself gazing upon his employer's resolutely fleshy features with unmixed horror, it being made clear to Abie, providing the absence of instantaneous divine retribution might be considered a reliable sign, that Samuel L. Silverstein *is no more Jewish than is Abie himself*, and is thus not only guilty of appropriating the identity of a Chosen Person upon his entry into the United States at Ellis Island, as is currently alleged by the local immigration authorities, but peccable to a fault in emulating certain stereotypes in order to enjoy those social and professional benefits enjoyed by Jewish gentlemen who have ascended to the rarefied heights of the motion picture industry.

Thus the Reader will easily conceive that there now follows a bitter theological wrangling e'en more antimonial than the debate attending that of significantly abridging *The Pilgrim's Progress* for the silver screen; and, two diametrically opposed opinions in the matter of religion tending to generate more heat than light, and the early evening being sultry enough without adding to the humidity unnecessarily, we now employ the cinematic convention of *panning across the room* to fix our gaze upon the doorway, through which will momentarily appear the aforementioned Sylvia, or Moxie La Roux, the delicately nurtured of Mexican ethnicity who has stolen the heart of Samuel L. Silverstein, it being your n.'s experience that, narratively speaking, frequent references to an absent character generally prefigure, and often precipitate, said character's entry into the fray.

Here, Moxie being unaccountably delayed, your n. avails of the opportunity to state that no fault accrues to the Reader should she discover herself possessed of a faint suspicion in the matter of Samuel L. Silverstein's devotion to his Sylvia, i.e., wondering if said constancy is in some way bound up with Sammy's financial prospects. For it is rare indeed in these turbulent times to encounter a Reader whose milk of human kindness has not been soured by the cynicism of the modern novel, their very soul's cream transmuted into a clotty yoghurt, or perhaps e'en a kind of cottage cheese, by the base shenanigans of villains so devious that they no longer sport the moustaches by which the emotionally intelligent Reader might once have instinctively identified them as Mr Hydes.

Indeed, it is no wonder, in these dark days, when *good men do bad things for the right reason*, that the sensitive Reader might discover the needle of her moral compass spinning wildly in search of true north; and, thus dizzied and disorientated, lapse into a post-season funk of believing that e'en the most innocent of motives may be tainted by self-preservation; or, worse still, that e'en the most malign of deceitful intentions may secretly harbour a virtue to recommend them.

Moxie being extravagantly late, as is both her personal wont and the privilege of all beautiful women, and the doorway thus remaining devoid of any and all arrivals resembling *femmes fatales*, for such is the role your n. anticipates Atropos has sketched in for the unsuspecting Moxie, e'en if Moxie is widely regarded a latter-day Lady Byron, i.e., a superior woman, if a little encumbered with virtue – I say, we now provide the obligatory pen sketch of Moxie La Roux, it becoming apparent that Moxie, being our tale's romantic foil, is to play a more significant role in our narrative than previously suspected. To wit:

Height:	5'2"
Eyes:	Flashing
Hair:	Curly
Shape:	Undulating
Demeanour:	Mercurial

Moxie, alas, standing significantly upon the order of her ingress, we are now reluctantly obliged to *pan across the room* again, Sammy and Abie having come to the conclusion of the bitter wrangle aforementioned, neither prepared to concede the other's point but both understanding that a compromise of sorts is required if they are to present a united resistance to the implacable advance of legal writ. To wit:

'It's not quite cricket, old boy,' says Abie.

'Not quite, no.'

'In fact, now that I think about it, the renunciation of religious belief is entirely unlike *any* sport requiring bat and ball for its successful execution.'

'Not e'en remotely,' agrees Sammy with a pang of regret that may have had something to do with his momentary apostasy but was more likely related to the tourney recently abandoned on his manicured rear lawn. 'Quick question, old legal eagle.'

'Fire away.'

'Do the Swiss go in for croquet at all, do you think?'

Alas, Abie's answer – which was, for the record, that such

information lay beyond his immediate remit, but that he would contact the Swiss Embassy in pursuit of same come daybreak on the morrow – I say, alas, Abie's answer is drowned out by a sound not unlike that which might have been made by the Vandal hordes pulling down the temples of Rome had said hordes had access to the portable chainsaws newly patented by Canadian millwright James Shand, by which we understand that the imminent arrival of Moxie La Roux is imminent no more, for the deafening whine of rapidly revolving steel teeth grinding marble to dust is almost precisely the noise generally made by Moxie when said latter-day Lady Byron discovers herself displeased, a good example of same being the case under preferment, in which Moxie arrived at Samuel L. Silverstein's palatial mansion in the Moorish style only to literally trip over one of the bevy of semi-garbed *ingénues* littering the back lawn, and her mood was in no way improved, as she cut a swathe through said bevy towards the french windows, by the fleeting if not particularly fond reminiscence that it was during such a croquet tourney that Moxie had first caught Sammy's eye.

'Sam-eeeeeeee!'

'In the study, dumpling-bear.'

And in sweeps Moxie La Roux giving it the full Susan B. Anthony, i.e., declaring that the bevy aforementioned is the absolute frozen limit, the volume and timbre of her declamation causing Abie to start like a guilty gazelle upon a fearful summons, as most people tend to do when Moxie gives it the treble-shotted verbal broadside, with the inevitable consequence of Moxie believing that everyone within earshot has something to hide, which in turn increases her anxiety and sends Moxie shooting up through the registers until her larynx emits a quality of white noise that causes dogs' brains to curdle in their skulls.

It being the case, then, that Moxie is for the nonce sufficiently distressed as to find herself incapable of articulating her displeasure with Samuel L. Silverstein beyond shrilly intimating that she discovers herself, like some ill-looking fellow of the immortal

Dickens' conceiving, *bound on no very well-disposed or harmless errand*, your humble n. now proposes a tactful withdrawal, thus allowing Moxie to catch her breath and marshal her thoughts in order that she might find herself in bobbish mid-season form when we return again to Sammy's palatial mansion in the Moorish style, thus allowing us to proceed directly to Chapter Seven, wherein, as previously promised, will be related the complex history of Felicia Fortesque's treachery and subterfugial perfidy.

And so we go.

Chapter Seven

In which Felicia Fortesque is revealed as a spy in the house of love. Sir Archie discovers himself wandering in the realms of modals past.

The history of Felicia Fortesque's subterfugial perfidy being both complex and extensive, your n. now commences our latest chapter with a pen sketch of Vanessa Hopgood's boon companion, as previously promised:

Height:	5'9"
Hair:	Auburn
Eyes:	Grey-blue, although more grey than blue
Facial shape:	Cordate
Role (presumed):	Miss Smith to Vanessa Hopgood's Miss Woodhouse
Role (actual):	Spy in the house of love

For lo! the persona of mild-mannered boon companion to Vanessa Hopgood is but a *masque* for Felicia Fortesque, who is in fact covertly employed by one Jasper Huxtable 'Rusty' McGrew, the terms of which employment consist of Felicia receiving a weekly stipend for reporting to Rusty the facts of Vanessa's conversing, carousing and otherwise dallying with men who are not Rusty McGrew, for Rusty, in contradistinction to Cervantes' infamously faithless Anselmo, is by no means desirous that his Camilla's virtue might pass through fiery trials of vigorous solicitations and addresses.

At this point the attentive Reader may be tempted to thumb

back through our narrative to Chapter One, wherein might be discovered the intelligence, delivered by Adele Fitzhalligon, that Vanessa Hopgood has pledged her troth to Samuel L. Silverstein. Desirous of sparing the Reader any unnecessary effort, your n. now confirms that Adele did in fact state the foregoing; moreo'er, it is important to state that Adele was not engaged in misrepresentation in so stating. Indeed, the engagement of Samuel L. Silverstein and Vanessa Hopgood is a matter of public record, being announced with the requisite fanfare in the trade sheets and gossip blats only three months ago, all courtesy of multiple dimes dropped by one *Madame Blavatsky*.

Here your humble n. hastens to reassure the Reader that the responsibility for any confusion arising from the peddling of false information can be laid at the feet (clay) of those most inveterate of dissemblers, Vanessa Hopgood and Samuel L. Silverstein. Indeed, it gives your n. no pleasure to relate the tawdry truth of the matter, which is that Vanessa and Sammy L. are bound not by the silvery filaments of young love's yearning, but rather by *an engagement of convenience*.

Yea, verily, and well may the Reader gasp aloud, and wonder if worse is to come. Indeed, any Reader possessed of a delicate disposition may prefer to leaf ahead to Chapter Eight, for your n. is about to confirm what the more emotionally evolved Reader has already begun to suspect: that Vanessa Hopgood is secretly stepping out with Jasper Huxtable 'Rusty' McGrew, this despite Adela Rogers St. Johns being fully persuaded that Rusty McGrew is a disreputable *arriviste* whose considerable personal wealth, being a fortune composed in the main of *liquid assets*, was as speedily and violently as it was recently amassed. In other words, and forsaking coy sesquipedalianism for plain Saxon nouns, Rusty McGrew is renowned among state and federal law enforcement agencies as crueller than that most notorious scorner of the gods, cruel Mezentius from Etruria, and is red-haired Irish to boot.

Thus the Reader will easily conceive that Rusty McGrew's is not a reputation Silverstein Studios wishes to have associated with its most shimmering star, with the result that Vanessa Hopgood, who adores Rusty for his wickedness, as Sycorax did Caliban, finds herself in need of a respectable beau upon whose arm she might lean whilst attending public events, it being common knowledge that all dolls, but especially motion picture goddesses, are prone to toppling over for the want of an upright gentleman to take the strain of her remaining vertical.

Enter, stage left, Samuel L. Silverstein, as respectable a beau as Hollywood has ever been able to lay claim to (which is, *ex confesso*, the faintest possible praise by which it is possible to damn a man without troubling those most hawk-eyed of raptors, the legal eagles), Sammy being successful, rich and single, and thus in want of a wife, albeit here your n. is obliged to state that Sammy is by no means the self-sacrificing *chevalier* his troth-pledging might suggest, for the corollary of said Austenian thesis is, of course, that if such a man should declare himself as *not* in want of a wife, then the public at large, prodded by the collective conscience of Hollywood's gossip columnists, may commence to wonder aloud as to why he might be so determined to confirm himself a bachelor.

The truth of that particular matter, as Adele Fitzhalligon would undoubtedly confirm were she not elsewise engaged in making a provisional dinner booking at the Blue Phalarope – I say, the simple truth behind Sammy L.'s reluctance to begin humming Purcell's *Trumpet Voluntary* is that Sammy walked barefoot out of a Ukrainian *shtetl* some two decades or so before our tale commenced, and has spent much of the intervening period elbowing his way upward into Hollywood's rarefied echelons by dint of a flagrant disregard for the laws of man and God alike. Thus it is that Sammy, being Ukrainian by birth and American by disposition, is doubly reluctant to expose his hard-earned fortune to the possibility that any future Mrs Silverstein, being ignorant of the immortal Balzac's dictum pertaining to great fortunes and great crimes, might at some point let slip a sliver of incriminating pettifog whilst in the presence of those impressively industrious employees of the IRS, the Bureau of Investigation, or the Monopolies Commission.

In a nutshell, then: the *engagement of convenience* allows Samuel L. Silverstein to present himself to the world as a respectable beau who is, for the nonce, and for so long as his engagement endures, no longer in want of a wife, while further delivering a fig-leaf of respectability behind which Vanessa and Rusty can dance the subterfugial hoochie-cooch to their hearts' content.

But if the three-cornered *imbroglio* consisting of Sammy, Vanessa and Rusty is pre-arranged and fully understood as a sham by all three principals involved, cries the Reader (or so your n. presumes), how is it that Rusty McGrew finds it necessary to deploy the tale-tattling Felicia Fortesque as Vanessa's secretary, confidante and boon companion?

Here, alas, your humble n. is obliged to report that, as is generally the case with a rhetorical question, the answer may be discovered within the query itself, for Rusty McGrew is so paranoiacally jealous that he once stormed out of a production of *Othello* threatening to sue the Bard for libel *and* racial slur. For her part, Vanessa Hopgood, being a woman of conventional appetites, is by no means immune to the slavish devotion of an attractive man, handsome being the first, and very often only, requirement of a surpassingly high proportion of Vanessa's co-stars. Meanwhile, Samuel L. Silverstein is reputed a swordsman to rival the great Douglas Fairbanks, one consequence of which is that Sammy is always likely to whip out the old *épée* at a moment's notice, and has e'en done so in Vanessa's presence, which ill-considered unsheathing prompted Vanessa to swear a sacred oath that she would only e'er touch Samuel L. Silverstein on the occasion of his being embalmed for a minimum of three days.

Thus, to paraphrase the immortal Burns, the best laid plans of mice and men *gang aft agley* (the Reader, of course, understanding that 'mice and men' is here deployed as poetical shorthand for a studio head, a bootlegger and a shimmering mortal goddess); hence Felicia Fortesque's role (actual) as a *spy in the house of love*, and the recently deployed derringer, or 'muff pistol', pointed unerringly at the loinage area of one Bartley McGuffin, the introduction of which, as the Reader has undoubtedly already begun to conceive, might be considered *foreshadowing*.

Said foreshadowing takes the form of two parts, the first consisting of the reason why Rusty McGrew saw fit to arm Felicia with a lethal weapon, which is not to provide Felicia with a means of self-defence should her cover be blown, but for any occasion when Felicia finds herself required to act in decisive fashion should a gentleman of Vanessa's casual acquaintance attempt to refine that familiarity into something rather more intimately intense, regardless of whether said amorous endeavour is embarked upon with or without Vanessa's explicit consent.

The second foreshadowing is framed as a literary reference, one implicitly understood by devotees of classical Russian theatre as *Чеховское ружьё*, or *Chekov's gun*, wherein the immortal Chekov states, as one of his principles of dramatic development, that if a blunderbuss or any suchlike implement of lethal ordnance hangs above the fireplace in Act One, it must be employed to extinguish the lights of some quasi-aristocratic bounder by the end of Act Three, this for fear an audience member, his hopes for a bit more pizzazz than classical Russian theatre generally delivers finally dashed, might rise up, yoink the frustratingly inert Roscoe from over the hearth, and blaze away until writer, director and at least three of the leading principals are no more flesh than grass.

The foreshadowing duly sketched in, and the required atmosphere of impending doom thus established, we now return to Bartley McGuffin, who remains frozen in that fateful moment immediately following the utterance of the offending syllable *Um*. Unaware of Felicia Fortesque's need to preserve her subterfuge, Bartley awaits what he believes to be the inevitable descent of Time's hammer, it being an *ironic twist* that Time and the Remington derringer both operate on the percussive principle, all the while trembling in anticipation of the imminent arrival of a groin-shredding .41 calibre rimfire short; and the mind, to paraphrase the immortal Milton, being of its own place, wherein can be devised a hell of heaven, and a heaven of hell, Bartley's thoughts now wander from his current predicament in a phenomenon that will be familiar to those Readers who have found themselves in immediate danger of going the way of a quasi-aristocratic bounder in a Chekhovian third act, i.e., *his life flashes before his eyes*.

Alas, your n. is obliged to report that said mental two-reeler proves a considerable disappointment to Bartley McGuffin, consisting as it does of a series of sliced drives, duffed niblicks and two-foot putts sent trickling downhill past the hole on the right-hand side. Ironically, the image that jerks Bartley out of his maudlin reverie is that of a ball driven straight and true the best part of two hundred and thirty yards down the fairway but which came to rest nestling in the shadowy recesses of a temporary drain the groundskeeper had neglected to mark GUR.[1] The blend of rage and despair that had accompanied Bartley's belated understanding that his was a pointless existence lived as a microscopic speck in what is at best a blindly indifferent and at worst mindlessly hostile universe returns now to enflame Bartley's instinctive fight-or-flight response as he raises his gaze from the derringer's pitiless muzzle to meet the equally merciless stare of Felicia Fortesque, and it is now that Bartley McGuffin digs deep, mining a hitherto unsuspected seam of courage, fortitude and grace under pressure, and there finds, just when he needs it most, the wherewithal to give vent to a provocatively defiant sniff.

'Sir?' says Bartley, his own fierce glare meeting Felicia's Gorgon-like stare at a ratio of roughly 2:1 (in favour of Felicia).

'Bartleby?'

'My apologies, sir, but I neglected to remind you of your tee reservation at San Gabriel tomorrow morning.'

'Ah. Very good, Bartleby. Most obliging.'

1 GUR – 'ground under repair'. Had the groundskeeper so marked the temporary drain, Bartley would have been entitled to drop his ball at the nearest point of relief, and thus proceed with no penalty. Alas, it was not to be; and Bartley squandered seven shots hacking out of the temporary drain, spattering his plus-fours with slimy mud in the process.

The genius of Bartley's gambit may have escaped the Reader for the nonce, but when your author reports that Vanessa Hopgood reacts to the words *tee reservation* by executing a creditable impression of the proverbial rocketing pheasant, the full extent of his strategy immediately becomes clear, Bartley being a keen peruser of the entertainment blats and thus fully cognisant of Vanessa's devotion to the noble Scottish art.

'You *golf*?' breathes Vanessa, her eyebrows shooting aloft, yea, like unto the tail feathers of the rocketing pheasant previously advertised. Emanating from Vanessa Hopgood, the combination of fluttering eyebrows, ragged breathing and unbridled admiration might well have melted a more sensitive man than Archie into something resembling a waxy puddle; but then, Archie's stuff is of the metaphorical *materiel* that broke the French line at Trafalgar without so much as a *Pardonnez-moi, m'sieur.*

'Golf? Ra*ther*. Oh, I say,' says Archie, belatedly cottoning on, 'you don't happen to play, what?'

'*I* should say so.'

'You should?'

'I *should*.'

'Yes, well,' says Archie, who is never entirely comfortable wandering in the realm of modals past, and especially when it comes to nailing one's colours to the mast in the matter of the noble Scottish art, 'you certainly should, old daffodil. What say you and I step it out at San Gabriel tomorrow morning?'

This suggestion being met with the kind of chaffering and cooing that generally attends a dovecot on the occasion of a weasel joining the ranks, Adele Fitzhalligon's arrival at the table with news of a provisional dinner reservation could not have been more timely or auspicious. For there are few things more likely, to continue the foregoing simile, to get the wings of young love-birds all a-flap than the discovery of a mutual interest; and when said interest is the noble Scottish art, then said doves – and here the simile really earns its corn – may well take wing and soar aloft on winged bliss, rapturously going towards the concavity of the eighth sphere, &c., one consequence of young love's first flush, of course, being the belief that God is in his heaven and all's right with the world, a philosophical purview that the Reader, whether by instinct or education, will surely recognise as more aspirational than pragmatic, there usually being something somewhere in the world, and generally in those post-colonial nations struggling to manage the expectations of a newly independent populace, that isn't quite tickety-boo.

Which is to say that, when Adele returns in timely fashion to announce that a dinner reservation (provisional) is *in situ*, neither Archie nor Vanessa, being otherwise engaged in gazing upon the other and being mutually dazzled, pause to enquire as to the venue wherein said reservation is made, while Bartley and Felicia are sufficiently occupied with their ongoing Mexican stand-off, albeit one conducted sitting down and composed of two people, only one of whom possesses a weapon, to abdicate all responsibility for the evening's arrangements to Adele.

Thus it is that our party abandons its table on the terrace of the Musso & Frank Grill in Hollywood, bound, as the attentive Reader will undoubtedly recall, for the Blue Phalarope, and thus unwittingly (with one notable exception) *sleepwalks into tragedy*, the italicised foregoing, your humble n. reluctantly reports, being the premeditated consequence of Adele Fitzhalligon's ambition to see Sir Archie or Vanessa Hopgood, and preferably both, laid low by a well-aimed teapot, the heart-breaking details of which will be revealed in chapter the next.

Chapter Eight

A chapter which some Readers will consider too long, and others too short, and yet others entirely unnecessary.

It being your humble n.'s most passionate desire to ne'er lead the Reader astray unless he do so deliberately and with malice aforethought – i.e., our narrative, finding itself in want of a *twist*, requiring the introduction of *red herring* – I say, notwithstanding his most fervent wishes, your n. is ne'ertheless obliged to postpone recounting the heart-breaking details of Adele Fitzhalligon's ambition to see Sir Archie or Vanessa Hopgood, and preferably both, laid low by a well-aimed teapot, it being the case that Bartley McGuffin will discover himself at the heart of said intrigue, in consequence of which he will very likely be referred to as *Bartleby* by Sir Archie, which persistent bloomer may well cause the Reader to conclude that your humble n. is in error, or else heedless of crucial detail, and in consequence come to wonder if said n. can be trusted to deliver the facts of our narrative with the accuracy and precision demanded of the conscientious narrator.

Thus it is that, in order to reassure the Reader of your humble n.'s *bona fides*, we are now obliged to draw back from our breathless tale, the better to engage in expositionary reverie pertaining to the l'Estrange-B'stard dynasty, and in particular its relationship with the written word. To wit:

In consolidating a fortune built, in order of progression, on pillage, blackmail and buccaneering by applying roughly the same principles to the boardrooms and stock exchanges of the modern world, the l'Estrange-B'stard firm has always found it more advantageous to focus on certain aspects of a young man's education at the expense of others.[1] Thus, for example, it was no surprise to anyone when, while reading English whilst up at Trinity, and taxed with skimming just one of the immortal Melville's tales in order to qualify for the academic credentials already purchased on his behalf, the young Archie opted for *Bartleby the Scrivener* o'er *Moby Dick*, and mainly for reasons that will not be lost on any Reader who has suffered the agonies of wading through interminable pages of close-printed prose that seem to meander gently when the quick dart might prove the lesser of two evils.

It is for the benefit of said Reader, then, that we cut to the chase with the astonishing revelation that in all the long and distinguished history of the l'Estrange-B'stard firm, not one man (or woman) of letters is to be found. No author, no playwright, nor cruciverbalist nor advertising copywriter; nay, not e'en a poet. There was some small hope cherished for Sylvain IX, who in addition to showing promise as a pilot had as a youth been discovered carving what was first presumed to be dirty words, but was subsequently discovered to be the first draft of a letter to the editor of the *Daily Mail*, into the door of the outdoor privy used by the scullery maids; but alas! what literary laurels might have subsequently accrued went up (and down) in flames in the fateful moment when the Red Baron fixed Sylvain's Sopwith Camel in his crosshairs.

Why this should matter can be laid squarely at the feet of the immortal Sassoon, whose *Memoirs of a Fox-Hunting Man* had piqued the interest of the l'Estrange-B'stard paterfamilias, Sir Augustus 'Baffy' l'Estrange-B'stard IV, largely in consequence of the words *fox* and *hunting* being intrinsic to the title of said bittersweet account of Edwardian idyll. Tucked into a tartan blanket in his bath chair as his nurse read aloud, the aged venerable listened with increasing agitation, frequently interrupting the flow to complain bitterly

1 For a detailed history of the l'Estrange-B'stard dynasty, see Appendix 1.

about the author's paltry efforts when compared with the dashing deeds of his own ancestors. Unknowingly, Sir Augustus was in the pupae stage from which every aspiring author emerges; and when, one morning, he gave vent to a frustrated 'Rot and vomit! The cat could do't better!', the transformation was complete.

Howe'er, and in common with all successful titans of commerce, Sir Augustus was acutely aware of his own limitations, and understood that he himself would appear very low down on a list of candidates considered ideal for the purpose of compiling the l'Estrange-B'stard chronicles, not least because rampant gout had rendered him incapable of pressing nib to paper with any degree of accuracy. Consequently, word went forth to the Republic of Letters that a young gentleman was required – young ladies being considered unsuitable due to some of the fruitier aspects of the yarn; Sir Augustus had *In Traditional Pirate Fashion* in mind for a working title – to write the great untold story of the l'Estrange-B'stard epic, remuneration commensurate on experience, *&c.*, bed and board included.

Enter, stage left, Bartley McGuffin, whom we now afford the pen sketch due every character likely to influence our narrative to any noticeable degree. To wit:

Height:	5'10"
Hair:	Brown
Golf handicap:	17
Education:	The lesser Dublin university
Prospects:	Remote

For lo! Bartley McGuffin was a freshly minted expert in Anglo-Irish literature from the lesser Dublin university, a qualification Bartley had belatedly discovered to be exactly as useless as his father, a publican and aspiring politician from Tubbercurry in the county of Sligo in the Irish Free State, had forewarned.

Thus it was more in hope than expectation that Bartley set out for the l'Estrange-B'stard seat at Knockfluck in County Donegal for the purpose of interview, unaware that Fate – or, to be precise, Atropos, who after four millennia of diligent spindling quite fancied a whirl as a muse, or even a dryad – I say, Atropos was that very morning feeling bored and fickle, and of a mind to stick her oar into human affairs just to annoy her sisters, who, after a heated debate the previous evening, were refusing to countenance e'en the possibility of change.

The contextual facts, as they apply, are as follows:

> Bartley was the first of seven applicants to be interviewed that morning;
> Sir Augustus, being that morning the worse of a small pot of port consumed the night before, had delegated responsibility for interviews to his only remaining son and heir, Sir Archibald;
> Bartley's meagre 2:2 in Anglo-Irish literature from the lesser Dublin university was in large part due to the number of hours spent hiking up and down the dunes adjacent to the fairways of the Portmarnock and Royal Dublin golf courses in vain pursuit of wayward balls;
> The thick mist that had enveloped Knockfluck and environs for the past month was showing signs of lifting, offering Archie the vague promise of a swift nine holes before it descended again;
> Due to his agitation and impatience, and his own literary endeavours at Trinity, Archie, glancing at the list of candidates, had read 'Bartley' as 'Bartleby'.

The facts thus established, we now proceed to the first fateful meeting of Sir Archie and Bartley McGuffin. Shown into Archie's study, Bartley found our *chevalier* practising three-foot putts into a tooth-mug propped against the wall, and was moved to voice his admiration of Archie's unorthodox grip when two putts in a row went rattling home. A mood of bonhomie thus established, the interview proceeded, with Archie leading the way.

'Know your stuff, do you?'

'Yes, sir.'

'A regular Melville, what?'

'Well, I wouldn't go so far as to say —'

'Bartleby, eh?'

'Sir?'

'He was a scrivener, you know. Bartleby.'

'Indubitably, sir.'

'And here you are!'

'Indeed, sir.'

'Well, there it is. Don't suppose you have time for a swift nine, eh?'

Thus it was that Bartley McGuffin passed into the employ of the l'Estrange-B'stard firm as Chief Scrivener. Officially, his role was that of chronicler of the l'Estrange-B'stard dynasty, and to his credit Bartley was not to be found wanting in the matter of hours spent perusing the dusty documents, ledgers and balance sheets that made up the bulk of the library at Knockfluck, at least on those rare occasions when his other duties allowed. For, Bartley being an accommodating chap with a flair for discretion and an endearing habit of ending every other sentence with the word 'sir', he soon discovered himself promoted to the position of Sir Archie's private secretary, a variation on the traditional gentleman's gentleman that required of Bartley a heretofore unsuspected talent when it came to writing up score cards, bankers' drafts, *billets-doux*, IOUs and travel itineraries.

Indeed, whene'er pen was required to be put to paper, Archie deferred on all counts to his scrivener, whom he invariably referred to as Bartleby, there being no one who thought it worth their while to correct him, least of all Bartley, who, if he had learned anything at all whilst attending the lesser university, or more precisely on those rare occasions when his ball found its way out of the dunes onto the fairways when he *should* have been attending the lesser university – I say, Bartley had learned the hard way that Fortune is, if we might paraphrase our old friend Tristram Shandy, *a notoriously ungracious duchess*, and not a lady to be unnecessarily taxed with whys and wherefores when at last she deigns to smile.

Howe'er, it would be a matter of great sorrow to your humble n. if the Reader, based on the foregoing, were to form a negative impression of the character of Bartley McGuffin, Esq., and conclude that Bartley is, in the common parlance, a sponge, a leech and a mooch. Indeed, those Readers who are also writers, current or prospective, as Readers often tend to be, may recognise in the preceding lines the broad outline of a young man with *an eye to the main chance*, which is to say a citizen on the lookout for a cushy billet where porter and pottage might be earned for a minimum of effort whilst he secretly labours o'er his One True Work.

All of which is correct and true, of course, although your humble n. begs the Reader to consider Bartley's mitigating circumstances. Firstly, and as previously noted, Bartley was born the son of a publican who aspired to public service, and as such, the *naturâ* being as *rerum* as ever it was and ever will be, Bartley may be understood to have had the desire for an easy life bred into him in the womb, and is thus blameless in this regard, it being the case that *the son shall not bear the iniquity of the father* (*Ezekiel 18:20*), the mother, as always, being entirely innocent in such matters, apart from contributing the womb, to which guilt accrues, as any reasonable Reader will undoubtedly agree, only insofar as a scabbard can be held accountable for the subsequent deeds of its blood-drenched dagger; which is to say, not at all.

Secondly, and more pertinently for the purpose of our narrative, Bartley's wanderings in the realms of Anglo-Irish literature whilst semi-attending the lesser Dublin university had instilled in him a particular affection for the work of the immortal Sterne, most notably that of *Tristram Shandy, Gentleman,* and specifically the paragraph wherein Sterne expands upon Uncle Toby's HOBBY-HORSE, which we here recount in full for the edification of the Reader:

> A man and his HOBBY-HORSE, tho' I cannot say that

> they act and re-act exactly after the same manner in which the soul and body do upon each other; Yet doubtless there is a communication between them of some kind, and my opinion rather is that there is something in it more of the manner of electrified bodies, — and that by means of the heated parts of the rider, which come immediately into contact with the back of the HOBBY-HORSE. — By long journeys and much friction, it so happens that the body of the rider is at length filled as full of HOBBY-HORSICAL matter as it can hold; — so that if you are able to give but a clear description of the nature of the one, you may form a pretty exact notion of the genius and character of the other.

Bartley being greatly taken by this literary diversion into philosophy's sylvan glades, it struck him with no little force that a contemporary novelist might well apply the HOBBY-HORSICAL theme to modern technology, and weave around the motif a tapestry illuminating the perils likely to befall an incautious humanity wedding its prospects to new-fangled inventions. A lesser, or more literal, mind might have conceived of a similar mode of transport – Mr Ford's motor-car, for example, or the locomotive steam engine, or even the humble bicycle – but it was Bartley's singular inspiration to lift his eyes to the furthest horizon and incorporate into the design his own private obsession, i.e., the noble Scottish art; or, in a word, golf.

To wit: Bartley found himself wondering if a man who played sufficient golf might discover, *by long journeys and much friction*, flesh and iron blending to form a new material, a substance unimagined by scientist and alchemist alike, such that a creature not unlike a monster of Doctor Frankenstein's invention, albeit benign, might ultimately emerge.[2]

2 Here Bartley appears to have overlooked the crucial matter of the golf club *grip*, which prevents the golfer's hands from coming into direct contact with the iron or wood of

All of which is to say that Bartley, tho' by no means spotless of conscience, may be forgiven his blemishes when we consider that his sin against the l'Estrange-B'stard clan – a sin of omission, moreo'er, rather than commission – is the consequence of Bartley's pursuit of Art, Morality and Higher Purpose in the modest hope of enlightening the generations to come.

Indeed, it is with similarly noble ambitions, and with an almost identical degree of modesty, that your humble n. now advises any Reader keen to penetrate the opaque details of Adele Fitzhalligon's scheme to see Sir Archie or Vanessa Hopgood, and preferably both, laid low by a well-aimed teapot, to now proceed to Chapter Ten, it being the case, alas, that Chapter Nine is largely concerned with pressing matters of woo as they pertain to Jasper Huxtable 'Rusty' McGrew.

the club shaft. The thesis remains intact; however, the hybrid creature who might emerge from such extensive HOBBY-HORSICAL friction would be composed of a blend of flesh and sheepskin, leather or rubber, depending on his or her particular taste in the matter of golf grip.

Chapter Nine

A short chapter of no great importance on its own merits,
but which is required to be read as a sequel to Chapter Four,
and as a key to a chapter which will follow in due course.

Our tale now returning to our narrative's antagonist and anti-hero, Jasper Huxtable 'Rusty' McGrew, of whom, as if he were the antithesis of the ideal Victorian child, much has been heard but very little seen since he departed the Bay City warehouse at the conclusion of Chapter Four, your humble n. now hastens to reassure any Reader who suspects that his unconscionable delay in revealing the details of Adele Fitzhalligon's nefarious plot is a base attempt to falsely contrive narrative suspense. Indeed, the current lull in proceedings is no more than a simple matter of physics, for the Blue Phalarope, on the corner of Sunset and Cahuenga, is situated so close to the Musso & Frank Grill on Hollywood Boulevard that the cabbie hailed to transport Archie, Vanessa, Adele, Felicia and Bartley hence was obliged to drive around the block three times to make the trip worth his while, whereas, by contrast, the disused warehouse in Bay City recently vacated by Rusty McGrew lies many miles remote from the Blue Phal, which distance, compounded by Rusty's tacking and wearing through the streets of greater Los Angeles in zig-zag fashion, causes Rusty to arrive at the Phal a little later than your humble n. might have wished, not least because Rusty, somewhat dishevelled after his exertions in vanquishing his foes, and trailing smoke, sulphur and more than a whiff of mephitic exhalations, is in no fit condition to immediately receive his guests.

Thus, whilst our Quintet mill about the lobby of the Blue Phal in a state of keen anticipation of concurring with Vanessa's assertion that *they do you awfully well at the Phal*, we now drift upstairs to the suite of apartments Rusty McGrew calls home, this in the hope of inserting an adjective or two which might chivvy along Rusty's dressing for dinner.

'Lor, sir!' says Bendix McGroarke as Rusty sweeps in trailing more than a whiff of mephitic exhalations. 'Been into the fireworks again, have we?'

'Evening dress and bracer, Bendix,' says Rusty, divesting himself of his smoke-blackened ulster, 'and not necessarily in that order.'

'Immediately, sir. And might sir be requiring a bath to rid himself of the cordite residue currently adhering?'

'A capital wheeze, Bendix. Make it so.'

'Right you be.'

There being very little e'en the most ingenious of narrators may achieve in the matter of inserting adjectives sufficiently dynamic to chivvy along a man at bath, your n. now cools his heels in the living area of Rusty's apartment suite and instead contents himself with confirming, for the benefit of the curious Reader, that the bootlegger Rusty McGrew maintains the Blue Phalarope nightclub merely as a *front*, which is to say a clearing house for the rinsing of filthy lucre derived from the retail of his *liquid assets*, Rusty opting for a nightclub over other establishments on the basis that absinthe makes the heart grow fonder, it being Rusty's experience that fond hearts are more likely to spend time and splosh in carousing and wassailing than hearts more inclined to *make sad mone* (*cf.* the immortal Hayman), said ingenious scheme, alas, being foxed to no little extent by the fact that every man, woman and child in the greater Los Angeles area understands the Blue Phalarope to be a *façade*, the piles of broken teapots carted away from the rear entrance every morning a telling clue that the Phal is in reality a *speak.*[1]

1 *Speak, speakeasy* (n.). An establishment purveying the psychoactive narcotic of alcohol, currently illegal under the relevant provision – Title II, section 3 – of the Volstead Act of 1919.

Indeed, no one is more aware of the charade than the federales, not least because virtually all senior members of the LAPD, and a considerable number of the lower ranks, are in monthly receipt of bulky brown envelopes from Rusty McGrew, a significant chunk of which generally finds their way back to Rusty via the bars and gaming tables of the Phal, which mutually beneficial arrangement is in real and present danger of being disrupted by an imminent raid led by that most incorruptible of police detectives, Aloysius 'Bumbles' McGee (more of which anon).

Blissfully ignorant of his impending doom, and now bathed and changed, his cravat loosely knotted in the Osbaldeston style, and with most of the cordite residue shaved from his angular jaw, Rusty McGrew hoists his brogans onto his mahogany desk and sets about climbing outside of Bendix's follow-up restorative. Here your n. is sorely tempted to let slip the words 'refreshed', 'galvanised' and 'bobbish mid-season form', the better to unconsciously prompt Rusty to rally around like all good men to the party downstairs; alas, Rusty is determined to savour this rare moment of peace, for Rusty, as is his habit most nights, will later descend the curved staircase to the nightclub below, there to glad-hand and back-slap the politicians, flappers, ward heelers, *ingénues*, gendarmes and freemasons who throng the Blue Phalarope six nights a week, said swarm drawn by the Phal's exotic range of entertainments, which include a jazz trio and string quintet, a chorus doll ensemble, nine forms of gambling in the back rooms, a bevy of torch singers, twin comedians from the Bronx, and the unscheduled but regular eruptions of drama that generally attend a jostling horde quaffing from teacups as if said chinaware contains the finest 98%-proof bathtub hooch this side of Beantown, which it generally does.

Indeed, this moment should be one for Rusty McGrew to relish, for recent events at the disused warehouse in Bay City have finally established Rusty as Hollywood's very own scourge and wrath of God and ninth overall in the pantheon of America's Most Wanted. The Reader being no doubt an upstanding moral pillar of her community, it may strike said Reader as somewhat repugnant, and perhaps e'en perverse, that said state of affairs might be a matter of some satisfaction for Rusty, in part because the Reader is very likely, either by instinct or education, fully agreed with Lord Henry Home Kames in the matter of *Subjects best suited to tragedy*.[2] To wit:

> The misfortunes of a wicked person ought not to be represented: such representation may be agreeable in some measure upon a principle of justice; but it will not move our pity, or any degree of terror, except in those of the same disposition with the person represented.

Such being the case, your n. is obliged to prostrate himself yet again, salaaming and strewing *mea culpas*, for neglecting to provide the Reader with the salient pettifog that will fully contextualise Rusty McGrew's apparent flouting of all that is considered sacred in any society that believes itself polite, civilised and progressive.

The situation is this: born and raised in an inner-city tenement on Dublin's Buckingham Street, Rusty McGrew was as a young man *thrown back on his own resources*, by which genteel allusion is meant that Rusty was from an early age introduced to that absolute contempt for those ridiculous distinctions of *meum* and *tuum* (i.e., mine and yours) best characterised by the immortal Fielding's robber chief Jonathan Wild. Due to some unpleasantness in early 1916, when Rusty's scheme to knock off Dublin's General Post Office over the traditionally quiet Easter weekend came something a purler, Rusty found himself obliged to abandon the land of his forefathers and make haste for the New World, whereupon, on landing in New York after working a three-year passage on a tramp steamer helmed by a captain who was rather more Odysseus than Palinurus in the matter of navigation, Rusty, being red-haired Irish, discovered it chiselled in the stars that he should become a longshoreman, politician or gendarme. Being as previously noted

2 Kames, Lord Henry Home, *Elements of Criticism* (1762).

a man of decisive action in love and crisis alike, Rusty immediately consulted with his faithful retainer Bendix McGroarke, who *looked into his heart* in similar fashion to the Lord working his wonders (Samuel 16:7), whereupon Bendix and Rusty struck upon a compromise: Rusty would give the bootlegging a whirl for so long as the Volstead Act remained on the books, and then, providing he was still sufficiently unpunctured, invest his hard-earned mazooma in running for public office, with the White House his ultimate goal.

Ne'ertheless, Jasper Huxtable 'Rusty' McGrew, as we observe him lounging in his armchair, swirling a posset of Bendix McGroarke's most invigorating restorative while a modest truncheon of Cuba's finest smoulders in the onyx ashtray, is nowhere as content as the Reader might expect of a man who has recently consigned a plurality of his most mortal foes to the holding pens in Cecil B. DeMille's warehouse, leapt into the pantheon of America's Most Wanted, and can also claim the heart of the world's most shimmering motion picture star for his own. No indeed, for deep in his heart Rusty understands exactly how the Macedonian felt when, apropos the immortal Hayman, *Great Alexander wept, and made sad mone, because there was but one World to be wonne.*

'Bendix?'

'Sir?'

'I am making sad mone, Bendix.'

'To the extent that you discover yourself in perfect understanding of the Bard's philosophical sentiment, *viz.*, into each life some slings and arrows must fall?'

'Precisely.'

'Would a balm of *fierabras* answer, squire?'

'Couldn't do any harm,' says Rusty, on consideration. Alas, when Bendix swoops in bearing said tincture on a silver salver, it is to a distinct absence of the old *gaieté de coeur* that generally heralds a sighting of Bendix's fabled variation on Sancho Panza's bracer.

Bendix being in the way of a minor character, and thus not

entitled to the traditional pen sketch, it nevertheless behoves your humble n. to inform the Reader that Bendix offers considerably more by way of service than the duties of a batman oblige him to render. For Bendix is not only Rusty's moral compass but his true (i.e., geodetic) north; moreo'er, ne'er was an ear more sympathetic or attentive than when attached to the cranium of one Bendix McGroarke, and in particular the right ear, the left being rather less attuned to the nuances of the human heart's foibles since the day, aged nine, Bendix had on a bet employed a ball-peen hammer to snugly wedge an alley taw marble against the tympanum of said auditory organ. In short, Bendix combines the roles of confidante, *consigliere*, sounding board and conscience, and can, on request, be depended upon, providing Rusty remembers to address the correct ear, to deliver insight, solution, comfort or critique.

'Yon sad mone,' says Bendix as he proffers the silver salver. 'Be it derived from torments spiritual, animal or mineral?'

'Maybe all of the above, Bendix,' says Rusty in gloomy tenor. 'And maybe none.'

'I see,' says Bendix. '*Quod petis, est nusquam*, perhaps?'

'In English, Bendix,' says Rusty in a timbre your humble n. will not scruple to describe as testy, for Rusty has, in common with the Bard, and providing the immortal Jonson might be believed, small Latin and less Greek.

'Begging your pardon, sir. What I mean to say is that you appear surprisingly discommoded this evening, especially in light of your considerable triumph this afternoon.'

'Aye, true enough,' says Rusty, with a sigh that ruffles Bendix's sideburns and sets them dancing like gnarled grey wheat in the breeze. 'But Bendix – what's it all *for*?'

'*For*, sir?'

'It's like this,' says Rusty. 'It feels ... Well, you know how it goes when a man, by which I mean a man I know well, a chum as it were, and he gets the sensation of ... Actually, now that I recall the conversation, the chap experiences not so much a sensation as the absence of same, if you see what I mean, more an ineffable sense that, all things being equal, there is no one thing more equal than the next, in a manner of speaking, and this being the case, well, there it is.'

'"Answer, and answer not, says Solomon,"' says Bendix. 'Pray continue.'

'Well,' says Rusty, illumination's torch flickering intermittently as he goes groping blindly through the labyrinthine passages of the mind, so that – not to labour the metaphor – he trips over a loose paving stone and pitches headlong between those stools labelled *mot juste* and *bon mot*, with the result that he only shrugs, and proceeds to gaze helplessly across the desk in the general direction of Bendix's right ear.

'Say no more,' says Bendix.

'You have it?'

'I believe so, sir,' says Bendix in a tone of such archly self-satisfied and yet hintingly secretive elusiveness as might be most accurately described as *knowing*.

'Then out with it.'

'Ennui,' says Bendix.

'No!'

'Funk,' says Bendix.

'You say so?'

'The moving finger writes,' says Bendix, 'and having writ, moves on.'

'But the writing, Bendix! What does it declare?'

'Ah,' says Bendix. 'Therein lies the rub.'

'Do you say?'

'Said I not so?' says Bendix, inadvertently quoting the immortal Herbert.

'You did. But the rub – any advance there?'

Here Bendix nods, conveying the quality of quiet fulfilment that will be familiar to those Readers who, whilst in service as confidante, *consigliere*, sounding board or conscience, has struck upon the very *bon mot juste*. 'A legacy,' says he.

'A legacy,' whispers Rusty, despite being struck dumb by the glory of Bendix's revelation but considering it impolite, given the gravity of the occasion, not to register some form of appreciation, hence the muted syllables previously recorded.

'A bairn,' clarifies Bendix.

'Singular?' importunes Rusty.

'Aye, well, one will likely do it,' allows Bendix, 'the essence of your angst being that you're richer than Croesus, Public Enemy Number Nine, and the only man who can claim the heart of the world's most shimmering motion picture star for your own, but with nary a soul to outlive your span of three-score and ten and thereafter bruit your glory to the world. Mind you,' cautions Bendix, 'once you get started, it's very hard to stop.'

'Oh?'

'I only know what I'm told,' says Bendix with that prim twist of the lips generally described by the French narrators as a *moue*, Bendix being Presbyterian by instinct and education and thus possessed of a lifelong distaste for matters carnal.

'Hmmm,' says Rusty.

'Indeed,' says Bendix.

It may be difficult for the Reader to understand, as Rusty contemplates the prospect *standing to attention in the service of Venus*, why his pen sketch, updated, would now include the observation that Rusty's current emotional state is Mood: Sombre. It is for the edification of said Reader that your n. here reluctantly interpolates in order to reveal that, notwithstanding his well-earned reputation as a Cacus-like bootie renowned for thinking in the savagery of his heart not to leave any crime or treachery undared or unattempted, Rusty McGrew is a man of uncommon noble virtue. Not to put too fine a point on it, Rusty McGrew, in all other ways a man of the world, is *a swordsman yet to clear scabbard*; which is to say that, whilst otherwise fully grown by dint of age and accomplishment, Rusty is, as previously advertised, red-haired Irish Catholic, and has thus yet to *make whoopee*, *play nug-a-nug*, *dance the Paphian jig*, or – apropos the Bard – *grope for trout in the peculiar river*.

'They say you can go blind,' says Rusty.

'So I'm led to believe,' says Bendix, whose Sunday School lessons had instilled in him an admirably cautious instinct against leaping to conclusions e'en when confronted with self-evident truths, for e'en though, as may be said, all men's sight in time grow dim, it was Bendix's private reflection that ocular degeneration afflicted fornicator and Presbyterian lectern-thumpers alike.

'It's a rum do, Bendix.'

'What can't be cured must be endured.'

'*Muss es sein*, Bendix?'

'Aye, squire. *Es muss sein*.'

For a moment or two, as Mood: Sombre descends into Mood: Solemn, Rusty and Bendix sit in a silence that might, but for the dictates of good taste, given Rusty's desire for an heir, be described as gravid. Nothing, they know, will ever be the same again. For these doughty warriors have campaigned long and hard together, inseparable as they trudged through metaphorical blazing deserts, scaled the proverbial mountainous heights, and sat out allusional freezing winters on the high bare slopes warmed only by fierce embers of burning ambition. And now? Would a wife – for Rusty, being a man of noble virtue, had no more thought of dancing the Paphian tango without first making honest the woman so intended than he would allow a Kerryman dress him for breakfast – I say, would a wifely woman, newly chatelaine, find room in her heart, or indeed by her hearth, for so devotedly partisan a menial as Bendix McGroarke?

Such are the despairing thoughts of Rusty McGrew; while, for his part, Bendix, believing his Young Master sufficiently burthened for the nonce, refrains from broaching the delicate topic of Rusty requiring Vanessa Hopgood's explicit permission before he e'en begins to think about nudging his allusional canoe upstream.

At last Rusty rouses himself from reverie. 'A bumper for the throttle, Bendix, and then it's time for all good men to rally round to the party.'

'That's the spirit, sir!'

The bumper being called for, it comes, and is quaffed. Suitably *refreshed*, and suddenly *galvanised* into *mid-season bobbish form*, Rusty rises from behind his desk, fluffs his Osbaldeston cravat and strides forth, only pausing at the door for a backwards glance to say, in a voice choked with pent emotion, 'See you in the funny papers, Bendix.'

And Bendix, drawing himself up to his full height (a smidge over five feet, due to pronounced spinal curvature resulting in severe kyphosis), salutes the departing Rusty, and declares, *apropos* the immortal Plutarch, 'Return with your shield, squire – *or on it*.'

Chapter Ten

Wherein Moxie La Roux discovers herself a woman scorned. Abie Cohen demands satisfaction from his employer on the occasion of the first misty dawn to present itself for the purpose.

Rusty McGrew's fancy now lightly turning to thoughts of Paphian jigs, the attentive Reader may well discover herself wondering aloud as to the fate of Moxie La Roux, who, being a doll of Mexican birth, is by no means possessed of the US citizenship required of Samuel L. Silverstein's future bride, e'en if Moxie is in fact Sammy's very own Sylvia, upon the shadow of whose perfection Sammy is wont to feast, *&c.* Your humble n. being, as always, entirely in the service of the Reader, we now return to the corner of Wilshire and Irving and Sammy's palatial mansion in the Moorish style, wherein Sammy has commenced explaining away the presence upon his back lawn of scantily-clad *ingénues* so numerous as to constitute *the full Ziegfeld.*

'We're casting that stage musical,' says Sammy in reassuring register, guiding his one true intended to a comfortable low chair and positioning the ottoman just so. 'Remember? The croquet epic *Oh! My Wicked Wicket Ways*. I believe it was you who suggested that young whippersnapper Cole Porter for the libretto. Ring a bell at all? Abie?'

Having thus skilfully aimed Moxie's ossifying glare in the general direction of his legal counsel Abie Cohen, Sammy skips around his desk and makes with the fizz, Moxie being as partial to a bumper of decent shampoo as any woman e'er born, Mexican or otherwise, all the while lavishing upon his one true beloved a smile of the purest pleasure, such as might be imagined wreathing the immortal Wordsworth's phiz as said worthy, gazing down from his vantage point o'erlooking a meadow of golden flowers, belatedly realised that, were he to crowbar in a touch of the old *vales and* first, *daffodils* might be made to rhyme with *hills*.

'I do *like* Cole Porter,' says Moxie, somewhat mollified in the wake of a restorative gulp or three, and now finger-tapping upon the armchair a *tumpity-tump* which the musically inclined Reader will identify as the melody to *Olga, Come Back to the Volga*. 'Although I can't say I recall any mention of croquet epics. A prospect, is it?'

'Well, imagine Valentino in *The Sheik*, only he's wearing plus-fours and wielding a mallet. Abie?'

'Yes? Ah, yes. Stands to reason.'

'And might there be a small but crucial role for a certain dumpling-bear?' enquires Moxie, who, having first rearranged her phiz to resemble a particularly froggy trout, has now adopted a coquettish timbre.

'I can't imagine why not,' says Sammy. 'Abie?'

'Judged on merit alone,' says Abie after two false starts interspersed with a fit of dry coughing, 'the question answers itself. Howe'er, given the, ah, complex structure of your finances, Mr Silverstein, it may be more profitable in the long term if Madame La Roux were to remain the silent partner in the arrangement, which I fear would prove an impossibility were Madame La Roux to e'er appear on a stage.'

'And why's that, Abie?'

'Well, the acclaim would be instantaneous, and public scrutiny unavoidable. I would go so far, Mr Silverstein, as to employ the word hysteria. The cost, alone, of the security issues to be managed in marshalling the photographers camped out night and day craving only a single glimpse of Madame La Roux would be astronomical.'

'I see. Moxie?'

'Well, one hates to cause a fuss if one can at all avoid it. Hysteria, you say?'

'A degree of nationwide frenzy to knock Valentino into a cocked tricorn, madam.'

'Coo!'

The attentive reader no doubt recalling the l'Estrange-B'stard antipathy to all things Iberian, including Iberian-derived, and thus anticipating a fractious encounter at some future juncture between Sir Archie and Moxie La Roux, we now draw back for the nonce from the Silverstein-Cohen-La Roux triptych as Abie lays it across Moxie with considerable vim ('Bigger than Jesus, dear heart, it stands to reason.') in order to refute the scuttlebutt being bruited in the less salubrious dens of Hollywood, the gist of which is that Sammy L. is prone to lark-ish rising at break of day to sing hymns at heaven's gate in praise of Moxie as a result of a singular appetite for chili-soaked *tamales*. A fearful calumny, a base slur, and an egregious misrepresentation of the facts: for while it is true that Moxie is a proud Mexican who can trace her roots all the way back to Cortez and his enthusiastic ravishers of the native population, and equally true that Sammy loves Moxie to distraction, albeit a distraction which is itself regularly interrupted by Sammy's veneration of the endowments of the chorus dolls, *ingénues* and cigarette girls to be discovered in Hollywood's speaks and deadfalls – I say, it is Sammy's fervent belief that he would have loved his most darling patootie with a love fair and true, the occasional croquet tourney notwithstanding, were she Esquimaux, Yahoo or Erin-born.

Thus it is with a heavy heart and an expression on his map akin to the head librarian at Alexandria as he watched a fortune in late return fines go up in smoke that Sammy breaks in upon Abie's Moxie-directed encomiums ('The classicists, madam, will in future be obliged to refer to the goddess as *Half*phrodite.') to announce that, in lately discovering himself a single man in possession of a good fortune, albeit one requiring temporary legal protection against said fortune's forfeit upon deportation, he finds himself in want of a wife.

'O Sammy!'

'Indeed. Abie?'

'Ah, well. I am very much afraid, Madame La Roux, that the matter is nowhere as limpid as, for example, your exquisite peepers. Hoover, you know. Issues of national security and so forth.'

'Sammy?'

'Abie? You might be better qualified to field this one.'

'Yes, of course. In a nutshell, madam, which is to say if we cut to the *sine qua non*, and therein find the nub nestling snugly in the bosom of the gist, as it were —'

'Abie?' says Moxie, and where a lesser chronicler might suggest that Moxie La Roux somehow squeezed into said twinned syllables the din attending the sack of Troy, the crackling of Ilium's topless towers (*cf.* Marlowe) included, your n. here contents himself with noting that Moxie's one-word query is wholly devoid of any stress or implication that might suggest her entire future hangs upon Abie's answer, which is in itself, as the emotionally intelligent Reader will undoubtedly agree, and particularly as Moxie's demeanour is not only mercurial but as fiery as might be expected of any self-respecting chili-fuelled *tamale*, a telling commentary upon the significance of said reply for one Moxie La Roux.

'Madam,' says Abie, having availed of the foregoing digression to gird his loinage sufficient unto the moment, 'it gives me no pleasure to bear the sad tidings that your one true intended, Samuel L. Silverstein, has no choice but to marry Vanessa Hopgood at said lady's earliest convenience.'

'I see,' says Moxie, confining herself for the nonce to the two-syllable conversational gambit, by which we understand that Moxie, whether or not she trusts to God, is keeping her powder dry. Now, history records that said tactic has met with mixed success, it being the case that the party of the first part requires the party of the second part to possess *a natural psychology*, which is to say a psychology that abhors a vacuum, and thus, when the dialogue lapses, find themselves bruiting forth all manner of information useful to the party of the first part. That Moxie is fully aware of Abie Cohen's weakness in this regard we may take for granted, for Moxie, being a woman, has ne'er found herself required to be especially intuitive in the matter of male flaws, the winkling out of which rarely entails anything more ingenious than confining herself to as few syllables as are necessary to maintain the conversational flow; howe'er, the particular circumstance here related is further enhanced to Moxie's benefit by her prior knowledge of Abie's secret passion for the immortal Chaucer, and in particular *The Canterbury Tales*, which passion a handsomely squiffed Abie sprung upon Moxie one night amidst tiki-lit revels when he announced that he believed himself the very reincarnation of *the verray parfit gentil knight*, who *loveth chivalrye, trouthe and curteisye*.

Thus it is that Abie, at this very moment simmering in a *jus* of self-recrimination for the part he is playing in crushing the hopes and desires of the fair maiden Moxie La Roux, now divests himself, in a chivalrous burst of curteisye, of the trouthe, the whole trouthe, and nothing but the trouthe.

'It's, ah, nothing personal,' says Abie. 'Simply a matter of squaring away a detail or two *vis-à-vis* citizenship and suchlike. Once the old knot is safely secured in sheepshank fashion, it'll be business as usual.'

'Oh yes?' says Moxie, who is by now playing a blinder with the two-syllable retort.

'Absolutely. Wouldn't you say so, Mr Silverstein?'

'Eh? What's that now?' says Sammy L., who had tuned out of the conversation when he found himself humming *Olga, Come Back to the Volga*, which melody raised all manner of unpleasant connotations given Sammy's terror of being exiled unto the badlands adjacent to said Volga by dint of Mr Hoover's patriotic excess, and further causing him to wonder why Cole Porter, being American-born and an alumni of Harvard *and* Yale, hadn't gone the extra mile and discovered an internal rhyme for the Mississippi or the Rio Grande, which cogitation has led Sammy to suspect that Cole Porter is, in fact, a Communist subversive disseminating coded messages to his fellow travellers through the medium of popular song, and thus something of a bargaining chip Sammy might bring to the table when J. Edgar commences *pourparlers*.

'I am reassuring Madame La Roux,' says Abie, 'as to the pain and anguish currently wringing her brow, and that thou art her ministering angel, and will remain always thus.'

'A fair point, Abie, and well made. Moxie?'

'*Quo bono*?' says Moxie, who, having broken through the two-syllable barrier with aplomb, now powers on, delivering herself of a tremulous speech in which she declares that she, and no one else, has stolen Samuel L. Silverstein's heart, albeit that said larceny occurred during a moment of post-coital weakness during which Sammy declared that he gave up the organ aforementioned with significantly more enthusiasm than he had the pound of flesh demanded by the Internal Revenue Service that very morning, by which means was Moxie, to her horror, given to understand that her prospective yokefellow was in the habit of paying tax, or had, in the best case scenario, previously paid tax on at least one occasion, a schoolboy error of such magnitude that Moxie was at first stunned into silence, which resulted in a conversational *lacuna* – Sammy having since dozed off in post-coital bliss – that allowed Moxie to devise a cunning wheeze by which Sammy would sign over power of attorney in the matter of his vast cash reserves to one Moxie La Roux, said recently arrived Mexican national being yet to formalise her relationship with Uncle Sam and thus something of an enigma wrapped in a mystery inscribed in invisible ink upon a *tabula rasa* to the upstanding public servants of the Internal Revenue Service.

Indeed, it was likely Moxie's stated antipathy to the IRS that first caused Sammy to experience the first faint tremors of love's awakening, with the consequence that Moxie now causes the very laws of geometry to bulge at the seams as she elbows her way into the already crowded love triangle previously composed of Samuel L. Silverstein, Vanessa Hopgood and Rusty McGrew, it being the case, as per memo, that Moxie is Sammy's one true intended, e'en if, by virtue of her Mexican birth, she is precluded by Article Four of the Silverstein Studio's Memorandum of Association from e'er marrying the studio's CEO, or any member of its board of executive directors.[1]

'And can you confirm that you actually signed this power of attorney, Mr Silverstein?' enquires Abie Cohen, this after allowing a respectful moment to elapse to indicate his heartfelt admiration for Moxie's chutzpah.

'Can I take the Fifth?' says Sammy.

'Not entirely apt in this context, old erstwhile Midas,' says Abie, who is beginning to understand why his stipend has recently begun to wither on the vine.

'In that case, yes.'

'I see,' says Abie, albeit in the subdued tone of a lawyer who perceives too late that his client has, if we might plunder the Aeschylean oeuvre, cast on his soil whetstones that sharpen souls to bloodshedding. 'And may I be so indelicate, Madame La Roux, as to cautiously probe your intentions as to Mr Silverstein's unknown millions in the wake of his proclaiming the Vanessa Hopgood-related banns?'

'Government bonds, I think,' says Moxie. 'Low-yield, of course, but steady as she goes.'

'Indeed.'

'Although, for giggles, I'll probably chuck a million or four into construction.'

'Your beauty is surpassed only by your wisdom, madam.'

'I don't suppose,' says Sammy, 'you could be persuaded to invest in a high-concept stage musical centring on a *risqué* croquet tourney, libretto by up-and-coming fifth columnist Cole Porter?'

'Send me the script, we'll set up a meeting. Who's starring?'

'That's, ah, yet to be decided.'

1 Generally speaking, a Memorandum of Association does not apply to the USA, which instead requires a company to state its Articles of Incorporation; here we must assume that Abie Cohen has advised Sammy L. to register Silverstein Studios in an off-shore jurisdiction, very likely the Bahamas.

'Vanessa Hopgood?'

'That coal-gargler? Certainly not.'

'I see.'

'Might you have someone else in mind, madam,' enquires Abie, 'for the life-changing role of the devastatingly attractive mallet-wielding Siren?'

'I might,' says Moxie. 'Or I might just look into a casino.'

'Stick it all on black, eh? *Victori sunt spolia* and so forth.'

'In a manner of speaking. I understand Count Nikolai Kuryakin is keen to divest himself of his Monte Carlo holdings due to some post-Bolshevik cashflow issues, and the old Louis Quinze Casino is going for a snip.'

'Top hole.'

'First, however, I intend to marry.'

There follows a joint Silverstein-Cohen intake of breath not unakin to that of Alexander's troops when, at Gaugamela, they first clapped peepers upon the elephant cavalry of Darius III, and the reader is advised to intuit no negative criticism of Sammy L.'s courage – for such, indeed, was the entirely understandable response of the peerless Macedonians in the van – when it is further revealed that an involuntary micturative spurt issues forth to dampen Sammy's inner thigh.

'Marry?' says Abie in tremulous tone, whose chutzpah-related admiration only goes so far, said destination being roughly where it bumps up against the prospect of his monthly stipend going the way of all flesh.

'Correct,' says Moxie, falling back upon the two-syllable retort like unto Darius III at Gaugamela when the Macedonians began treating his previously unconquerable pachyderms tolerably rough.

'A marriage of convenience?' says Sammy, who would have drawn himself up to his full height were it not for the tell-tale stain on his inner thigh, and is thus forced to attempt high dudgeon from a sitting position, which is never a good look.

'How *dare* you?' demands Moxie, her eyes flashing like unto the Koh-i-Noor (or pair of same) stuck in the navel (or navels) of

Salome sashaying through the dance of the seven veils. 'A Mexican woman marries only when moved by the finest of all feelings.'

'And may we enquire as to the identity of the gentleman,' says Abie, 'who will shortly discover himself blessed beyond all mortal reckoning?'

'I have admired Jasper since first we met,' declares Moxie. 'He is a man of dash and vim, of vision and vigour, and as generous as a tentful of Samaritans in the run-up to Mothering Sunday.'

'A catch, then?' says Abie.

'I'll put it like this, old legal eagle. I danced him the seven veils the very first time we met, and he begged me to hold off at veil the fifth lest my modesty be sacrificed on the ruined altar of his desire.'

'Bad show, that,' offers Sammy in peevish register, 'interrupting a professional mid-gig.'

'Be that as it may,' says Moxie, 'it remains an imperishable truth that Jasper Huxtable McGrew is a gentleman who stands head and shoulders above the puffed and reckless libertines of Hollywood, and a shining example to all the dawcocks of said Sodom-ish burg in the matter of how a lady likes to be treated.'

'Nerts to you, sister,' says Sammy.

'Madam,' says Abie, 'I trust you will not take offence at my desire for further clarification when I enquire as to whether the Jasper Huxtable McGrew to whom you refer is in fact the notorious outlaw, gangster and bootlegger Jasper Huxtable 'Rusty' McGrew, who was only this evening, due to his wilful destruction of public property and the consigning of several dozen captives to the living hell of Cecil B. DeMille's charnel house, declared Public Enemy Number Nine?'

'Yes and no,' says Moxie.

'Yes *and* no?'

Here Moxie informs Sammy and Abie that her first meeting with Jasper, previously alluded to, occurred when she interviewed for the position of in-house choreographer at the Blue Phalarope, Moxie, her convent education notwithstanding, being expert not only in the dance of the seven veils but burlesque in general, including several saucy variations on the conventional chorus doll routine. In consequence, Moxie now draws a distinction between the Rusty McGrew infamous for his Borgiastic penchant for sensual cruelty and the urbane nightclub manager Jasper Huxtable McGrew of Moxie's acquaintance. 'When he is with me,' says Moxie, 'he is Jasper, a man of such inflexibly upstanding moral rectitude as to be skeletally composed of a minimum of five of the seven pillars of wisdom.'

'An example to us all, no doubt,' says Abie. 'Can I take it he doesn't lug along his beloved carriage-mounted M1895 Gatling to your intimate rendezvous?'

'He does not.'

'The very soul of discretion, then. And his less, ah, morally rectitudinal activities when you are not in his immediate orbit, madam – they give you no pause for thought?'

'Am I my Jasper's keeper?'

'You will be,' scoffs Sammy, 'when they finally crowbar him into the zoo where he belongs.'

Here we draw a momentary veil o'er the scene, it being the case that Moxie La Roux is newly sick with the old incurable for Rusty McGrew and thus understandably intemperate in her response when said swain is denigrated by her beau's putative rival, and may in consequence be forgiven, or so your humble n. believes, for responding to Sammy L.'s scornful sally with a *prise de fer* so salty as to approximate the Dead Sea at high tide.[2]

'Nerts squared,' retorts Sammy.

'Very eloquent,' says Moxie. 'Perhaps you might like to deliver your *bon mots* in a speech at the wedding?'

'Consuela's wedding?'

'*My* wedding. To Jasper Huxtable McGrew.'

'*Entre nous*, sister, you might want to fix your sights a little lower.

2 Technically speaking, the Dead Sea does not experience significant tidal variations. It must be assumed that the reference employs exaggeration for the purpose of comic effect.

On Redser, maybe. Because as I understand it —'

It is at this point that Abie Cohen belatedly intervenes, partly because his finer sensibilities as an aspiring *parfit gentil knight* are sorely dented by Moxie's heretofore unsuspected verbal dexterity in the realms of the coarser Anglo-Saxon vernacular, but mainly because he realises Sammy is about to put a hitch in Moxie's giddy-up *vis-à-vis* her impending nuptials. Which is why Abie, lacking the conventional glove of the Russian poet brooding upon insult, now lays about Sammy's phiz with the brown-spotted banana skin.

'How *dare* you insult this woman's honour, sir?' bellows Abie as Sammy picks chunks of stringy phloem from his right ear. 'I have no choice but to demand satisfaction on her behalf. I will see you upon the misty heath at dawn, sir, or see us both damned!'

'O *Abie*,' breathes Moxie. 'What curteisye!'

'Madam,' says Abie, 'I am at your service. If I can be of any assistance whatsoever, e.g., in helping to track down the elusive Rusty McGrew should he prove for any reason less than amenable to meeting you at altar rail, I can recommend a reputable private investigation bureau manned by Twombley Bumppo, an ex-Pinkerton man who served under Captain Clovis E. Duhain himself.'

'Thank you, Abie, but that won't be necessary.'

'Alas, madam, I fear that, in consequence of his warehouse-related activities, and given the dim view the Californian judiciary takes of the destruction of public property, Rusty McGrew is on the lam as of late this afternoon, which is to say Rusty is in the wind, a veritable Scarlet Pimpernel. They seek him here, they seek him —'

'According to Ramon the Doorman, he's at the Blue Phal,' says Moxie. 'Pulled in an hour ago, reeking of mephitic exhalations.'

'Ah.'

'And the Californian judiciary,' says Moxie, 'can take a running jump. Where was the Californian judiciary, Abie, when Juan 'Lefty' Palomeque was terrorising the good citizens of Chavez Ravine, extorting tithes and ravishing fair maidens?'

'Is the query rhetorical, madam?'

'It is.'

'Very well. Have on.'

'Thank you. I say, "Nowhere, Abie," said *nowhere* being the answer to my rhetorical query as to the whereabouts of the Californian judiciary when Juan 'Lefty' Palomeque was terrorising the good citizens of Chavez Ravine, extorting tithes and ravishing fair maidens.'

'Just as I suspected,' says Abie.

'Which is why,' says Moxie, 'Jasper Huxtable McGrew is, as of late this afternoon, hoist into the pantheon of Chavez Ravine heroes for dispatching Juan 'Lefty' Palomeque and his *hermanos* to Cecil B. DeMille's holding-pen for expendable extras, and why I, Moxie La Roux, am on my way to the Blue Phal to pledge my troth to Rusty, just as soon as I have, in my capacity as said Phal's *coryphée*-in-chief, ironed out the last few wrinkles in tonight's ballet performance of a hot jazz riff on *The Rite of Spring*.'

'*Mazel tov*,' murmurs Abie automatically. 'But just to clarify.'

'Yes?'

'Might one assume, from the foregoing, that the scales have yet to fall from Rusty's eyes in the matter of young love's awakening?'

'The heart knows what the heart knows, Abie.'

'Indubitably. But has the heart taken a moment to sit down and compose a *billet-doux* to sundry other organs, most of which are crucial to the launching of what might be described by a finer poet than I as *love's frail craft*?'

Here Moxie can be observed to draw herself up to her full height (5'2", albeit Moxie is this evening sporting black T-straps with a moderate heel, and is thus a formidable 5'5"), her eyes flashing lightning like unto Belinda's on the occasion of a lock of her hair being snipped. 'Do you doubt, sir, that any man could resist Moxie La Roux?'

'Is the query rhetorical?'

'It is not.'

'In which case, madam,' says Abie, 'there is naught left to say other than to directly quote that Gentleman of Parson Adams' acquaintance in stating that *if I have any Wish it is for some blest Accident by which I may contribute with my Life to the least Augmentation of your Felicity*,' whereupon the magnificent Moxie La Roux, having nodded graciously at the noble sentiment thus expressed, disembogues with sails a-billow, leaving in her wake a prolonged disquietude during which Sammy glares at his perfidious legal counsel while Abie displays a heretofore unsuspected fascination with the ceiling coving.

'What the ruddy hell,' says Sammy, holding up the offending brown-spotted banana skin, 'was *that* all about?'

'It appeared to me, Mr Silverstein, that you were about to put Madame La Roux abreast of the scuttlebutt bruited abroad in the less salubrious taverns pertaining to Rusty McGrew's invariable response on those occasions when his opinion is besought in the matter of Vanessa Hopgood, which is that, if heaven would make Rusty another world of one entire and perfect chrysolite, he'd not have sold Vanessa for it.'

'Your point, Abie?'

'Said tittle might well have taken the bloom off Madame La Roux's boomps-a-daisy. It might e'en cause her to think twice about lavishing her considerable charms on Rusty McGrew.'

'Well, exactly.'

'Leaving aside the extent to which such spiteful revelation might redound poorly upon any gentleman who professes to play the sport of cricket, or e'en its more sedate cousin of croquet, not only within the rules but according to the spirit of the game – I say, informing Madame La Roux of the rumours pertaining to a McGrew-Hopgood alliance would hole us below the waterline.'

'Loose lips sink ships?'

'With the likelihood of all hands finding themselves lost,' confirms Abie.

'And if we *don't* divest ourselves of spiteful revelations spoken in haste due to a life-long habit of loving not wisely but too multivariously?'

'Ah,' says Abie. 'Therein lies the rub.'

'Pray tell, sage counsel, eschewing all verse and going straight to chorus.'

'The matter, Mr Silverstein, is susceptible to a ready explanation. If we paraphrase our dear departed Swan of Avon, and acknowledge that the course of true love rarely doth run —'

'No poetry, Abie. Get to the good stuff.'

'Very well,' says Abie. 'In a nutshell, we need Madame La Roux to marry Rusty McGrew.'

Here Sammy L. favours Abie Cohen with an old-fashioned gawp. 'Why so?'

'Because Rusty McGrew is a notorious outlaw, gangster and bootlegger, and currently Public Enemy Number Nine, and thus no more than a dropped dime away from finding himself buckled into Old Sparky, a tragedy to cast a pall o'er those who consider themselves Rusty's intimates, to be sure, but a pall that may in time reveal itself a cloud fringed with silver sable, i.e., the widowed Madame La Roux finding herself back on the shelf and chafing at the prospect of wearing naught but out of season black for the foreseeable future, with – and here I draw your attention to your current *imbroglio* with the authorities *vis-à-vis* immigration and citizenship – I say, the widow La Roux will emerge from what I can only imagine will be a miraculously brief period of mourning with a *bona fide* American passport stashed in her possibles.'[3]

'I see. I'll o'erlook the poetry this time, Abie, and bring you back to this dime of which you speak, which seems to me, if I am not succumbing to wishful thinking, to have taken on the dimensions of a sword that might be described by Biblical scholars as Damoclean.'

'Sir, it has.'

'Are you currently in possession of this dime of which you speak?'

3 Rusty McGrew being, as aforementioned, of Irish origin, the issue of his US citizenship will likely become hotly contested should our narrative conclude, as is entirely likely at this point, with Rusty frazzled to a crisp in Old Sparky, which wrinkle may well belatedly render Abie Cohen's cunning scheme undone.

'I am.'

'Then once more unto the breach, Abie. The game's afoot. Let not I dare not wait upon I might, but cry havoc, and let slip the dimes of war!'

'Consider it done, Mr Silverstein. In the meantime, howe'er, it being the case that the wheels of justice tend to take the scenic route as they go about their grinding exceedingly fine, may I suggest that you hie yourself hence to the Blue Phalarope with all due haste, the better to be on hand lest Rusty McGrew discover himself compelled to take a noble knee in the presence of Vanessa Hopgood, and thus be no more than a single bound away from administering a glove to the cheek of said interloping woo-pitcher, by which it might be understood by all present that you plan to demand satisfaction, or see you both damned, on the next misty dawn suitable for the purpose?'

'It is true that I will not,' says Sammy.

'No?'

'It strikes me as excessive, Abie, verging on the melodramatic.'

'Do you hesitate to extend your courage by your actions?' says Abie, inadvertently quoting the immortal Virgil.

'It's more the aesthetics of the thing,' says Sammy. 'Being possessed of an artist's soul, one hates to gild the lily unnecessarily, or deliver the grand gesture where no flourish is required, strictly speaking, or —'

'*Shtetl*,' says Abie.

'Then again,' says Sammy, 'on urging myself to reflect and consider, and belatedly alighting on the wise words of the immortal Cervantes, I recall that it is the brave man who carves out his fortune, and that every man is the son of his own works.'

'Bravo, Mr Silverstein! Faint heart ne'er won the fair lady.' At which Abie Cohen takes up his alligator-skin briefcase and sweeps out in hot pursuit of the recently departed Moxie La Roux, hoping to share her taxi cab into town, it being the case that Abie, his stipend withering on the vine, has recently been forced to economise, the dime clutched in his hand weighing upon his spirit like unto the fabled thirty pieces of silver as he prepares to betray not only Rusty McGrew but his own aspirations towards verray gentil knighthood, by way of which we touch upon yet another sub-theme of our narrative, which treats with *the law of unintended consequences*, it being the case that Vanessa Hopgood's dropping of the first fateful dime on Sammy L. *vis-à-vis* his immigration status has resulted in Sammy instigating a retaliatory dime-dropping manoeuvre designed to conclude with Rusty McGrew shipping voltage sufficient to light up Saigon for the duration of *Têt*, which eventuality would very likely crimp, constrain and otherwise forestall Vanessa's grand plan for white picket fences and apple pies cooling on kitchen windows, said sub-theme providing an ironic variation on to this narrative's philosophical proposition, i.e., *the world might be a better place if only everyone would make a little more effort not to go around dropping dimes willy-nilly,* the diligent pursuit of which would result not only in a kinder, fairer and more pleasant existence for all concerned but save everyone a small fortune in dimes to boot, albeit Pacific Bell would likely go broke in three months flat.

Alas! the modern narrator may dream in colour but must awake to shades of grey, which is to say your humble n.'s duty is not to yearn for prelapsarian idyll but report with steely-eyed rigour upon the flaws, failings and foibles of the modern world, all of which, and much worse, are to be observed in the Blue Phalarope on a nightly basis, to which venue your n. now hies himself hence, having first slipped, in wraithlike fashion, into the cab being shared by Abie Cohen and Moxie La Roux, the latter bound, as the attentive Reader will undoubtedly recall, for the venue aforesaid, the better to put the finishing touches to the choreography for tonight's hot jazz take on *The Rite of Spring* before launching herself at the unsuspecting Rusty McGrew, Rusty having neglected to place any double-agents in the camp of our tale's preeminent Mexican *ingénue*.

To the Phal, ho!

Chapter Eleven

In which Felicia Fortesque's true identity is revealed.

Rusty McGrew recently departing his apartment suite in a manner wholly incompatible with delay (i.e., 'strides forth'), and thus likely to descend the stairs to the Blue Phalarope at a pace commensurate with that of love-struck swain resolved to have the banns bruited throughout Christendom with all haste, your humble n., having drifted inside the Phal to take up position behind the banquette table whereat Vanessa, Archie & Co. are at revels, which is neatly situated adjacent to both dance floor and jazz trio orchestra, and further affords a view of the entrance door through which Rusty McGrew will eventually achieve ingress – I say, your n., anticipating Rusty's arrival at any moment, now cautions the Reader that our current chapter contains numerous instances of revelation, perfidy and subterfugial masquerade, any single example of which may cause a Reader more than usually sensitive to the ripe stuff to recoil in horror and consider our Quintet an assemblage of scrubs, perishers and sword-swallowing mountebanks – in short, a congeries of wrong gees.

Having issued said caution, howe'er, and lest the Reader feel obliged to rush to judgement on behalf of a society that believes itself polite, civilised and progressive, your n. further takes the liberty of reminding the Reader of what she already instinctively knows,[1] which is that the quality of mercy is not strained, but

1 In the immortal Austen's *Mansfield Park*, Mr Henry Crawford contends that Shakespeare is part of an Englishman's constitution, for the Bard's thoughts and beauties are so spread abroad that one is intimate with him by *instinct*. Thus, and providing we

instead droppeth as the gentle rain from heaven to bless twice and become the monarch better than his crown (or, depending on gender, tiara).

Rusty McGrew still notable by his absence, and your humble n. being loath to allow our tale lapse into *longueur* more often than is strictly necessary, we now sketch in the more notable citizenry of the Blue Phalarope's *dramatis personae*, which includes (albeit the list is by no means exhaustive) Nick the Greek, Eddie Cantor, some boxing managers and freemasons, Theda Bara, the shimmy-dancing Jane Mast, Titanic Thompson, Tom Mix, two of the three Talmadge sisters, the infamous blonde who caused a bishop to kick a hole in his stained-glass window, the UCLA football team, George von Elm, Benny Bunco, Gloria Swanson doing her Charlie Chaplin impression, Gilbert Roland wooing Pola Negri, and a sprinkling of off-duty chorus dolls quaffing such quantities of illicit hooch as might have caused Carrie Nation to reel away in search of the nearest fainting couch were she present, which she is not, it being the Blue Phal's motto that 'All Nations are Welcome except Carrie', this on account of Carrie's enthusiasm for attacking saloons, speaks and deadfalls with a hatchet.

Also present, lounging in a booth against the rear wall, is the rather less noteworthy but – for the purpose of our narrative, at least – potentially intriguing Edward 'Bugs' Dooley, the former photoplay reader recently commissioned by Samuel L. Silverstein to bash out a motion picture adaptation of *The Pilgrim's Progress* by nine o'clock tomorrow morning. Impressed by Bugs' work ethic, for it seems to your n. unlikely that any aspiring scenarist might pause in his endeavours for a restorative posset of fizz before his task is entirely complete, we now drift across to Bugs' booth, keeping a weather-eye upon the entrance doors lest Rusty McGrew appear, there to discover Bugs deep in conversation with

might make allowances for Mr Henry Crawford's gender bias, which is, alas, by no means untypical of e'en the most enlightened of Regency gentlemen, we can confidently assume that the Reader is sufficiently familiar with the Bard's works as to be considered *instinctively* intimate with same.

the cigarette girl Toots 'Fata' Morgana, who is generally to be discovered working the aisles at the Musso & Frank Grill, but who, as she informs Bugs just as we drift into eavesdropping range, has agreed to work a late shift at the Phal to cover for her firm friend Gladys 'Crikey' Riley, who, in consequence of one of the Phal's chorus dolls rushing off to a party thrown by Cecil B. DeMille to celebrate an entirely unexpected windfall of expendable extras, has been promoted to the chorus line to dance *The Rite of Spring*, her hopes of nailing down a permanent spot as soaring as her high-kick extension (last measured at 92° NE).

'Nice,' says Bugs, purchasing a pack of Chesterfields e'en though he doesn't actually smoke, for Bugs and Toots were foundlings together at the Cleveland Street Home for Cruelly Abandoned Mites, and Bugs is a citizen who is ne'er intentionally behindhand in the matter of supporting his fellow former mites. 'It so happens I've had something of a promotion myself.'

'Oh yah?' says Toots.

'Yah. Remember last night I was telling you how I'd secured a pew at Silverstein Studios as a photoplay reader?'

'Oh yah,' says Toots.

'Well, I'm a writer now.'

'Yiminy!' says Toots. 'You're writing a real actual motion picture photoplay?'

'Well,' says Bugs, who, for all his faults, is never less than scrupulously honest with those mites with whom he'd toiled in harness at Cleveland Street, 'I would find it much easier to agree with the foregoing were you to eschew the present tense continuous and content yourself with the knowledge that I have in the very recent past been commissioned to write a real actual motion picture photoplay.'

'Is there a part for me?'

'No,' says Bugs in scrupulously honest timbre.

'No?'

'Technically speaking,' says Bugs, 'there's no part for anyone just yet.'

'Because,' says Toots in belatedly dawning register, 'being a writer, you're out on strike. One out, all out, don't mourn, organize, each according to his needs and so forth.'

'It's not so much that,' says Bugs, 'as the old blank page producing such a blindingly white glare as might cause any passing Esquimaux curious enough to glance into my garret to coin yet another word for snow.'[2]

'I see,' says Toots. 'E'en so, there's an undeniable gleaming fringe to the sable cloud of said blindingly white glare.'

'Oh?' says Bugs, absentmindedly lighting a Chesterfield and popping a smoke-ring. 'And what might that be?'

'Well,' says Toots, 'I'm no expert in literary matters, of course, being naught but a lowly cigarette girl plying her trade in a nightclub purveying the psychoactive narcotic of alcohol in direct contravention of the Volstead Act of 1919, but it seems to me as if you're suffering from a touch of writer's block, which is as close to simultaneously working and being on strike as any mere mortal is likely to achieve in his three-score and ten.'

'A good point,' says Bugs, 'and elegantly made. Howe'er, should I fail to deliver a first draft of *The Pilgrim's Progress* to Mr Silverstein's desk by no later than nine a.m. tomorrow morning, my three-score and ten is likely to be considerably foreshortened, and not by the ten.'

'Coo! *The Pilgrim's Progress*, you say?'

'Said I not so?' says Bugs.

'You did.'

'May I take it you're familiar with said *Progress*?'

'You could say that,' says Toots.

'Assume I already did,' says Bugs, 'and take it from there.'

Being bade as aforesaid, Toots now recounts how Mrs Hurlothrumbo, being the beadle's pleasantly plump wife at the

2 Alas, the popular notion that the Esquimaux peoples have an abundance of words for snow is misguided, it being the case that Esquimaux languages are in fact similar to German in their fondness for compound words. Thus any Esquimaux glancing into Bugs' garret would likely state that there was stuck in his Underwood 'an-unusually-big-rectangular-flake-surprisingly-defaced-with-erotic-doodles'.

Cleveland Street Home for Cruelly Abandoned Mites, loved nothing more than to read her charges to sleep, and would frequently entertain the girls' dormitory with dramatically enacted passages from a variety of classical sources, a non-exhaustive list of which included *The Spanish Tragedy*, *Marius the Epicurean*, Book Two of *Paradise Lost* and – the Reader will no doubt be wholly unsurprised to learn – *The Pilgrim's Progress*.

'So it would be investing the truth with the bare minimum of stretchers,' says Bugs, 'to state that you are fully cognisant of the plot, narrative scheme and character motivations that has rendered Mr Bunyan's tale of allegorical peregrination a timeless classic?'

'Oh yah,' says Toots.

'And might you be persuaded, were I to purchase every last package of cigarettes on your tray, to dally awhile and share your thoughts on same?'

'It's a date!' sings out Toots, who, your n. now hastens to confirm, has long since harboured a romantic affection for Bugs Dooley to rank alongside that of the Venetian lady who would have walked barefoot to Palestine for a touch of Lodovico's nether lip.

'Yes, well,' says Bugs in havering tenor, 'first things first, eh?'

Bugs and Toots now huddling up o'er Bugs' notebook, which conclave, in concert with the tympanum-scorching volume of hot jazz emanating from the Hot Stomp Trio on the bandstand, renders your n.'s attempts to eavesdrop and lip-read entirely futile, we now turn again to gaze yearningly across the Blue Phal's dancefloor at the entrance door, it being the case that Rusty McGrew – or, being precise, our anti-hero's delayed arrival – is by now causing your humble n. no little concern for his well-being, i.e., to wonder if Rusty has not come a purler in descending the stairs as a consequence of an untied shoelace or a loosely knotted Osbaldeston cravat flapping aloft to obscure the visage at a crucial juncture.

Rusty thus bearing for the nonce a strong resemblance to the cat i' the adage in allowing *I would* wait upon *I dare not*, and it being further true that time, tide and Reader wait for no man, your n.

discovers himself with no choice but to proceed directly to the long-promised revelation and sketch in the heart-breaking details of Adele Fitzhalligon's subterfugial scheme. To wit:

Adele, scorned by Archie and thus *brewing hell's fury* (*cf.* Congreve), snuck away from the terrace of the Musso & Frank Grill to make a provisional dinner booking at the Blue Phalarope, which apparently thoughtful gesture was in fact embarked upon with *malice prepense*, i.e., in full possession of the knowledge that Rusty McGrew is the owner of said Phal, by dint of which revelation the Reader will readily conceive that Adele's provisional dinner booking is a perfidy predicated on the assumption that Rusty, being notorious for ravenous craving when transformed into green-eyed monster, would be holding court at the Phal and – all going to plan – discover himself sored up more than somewhat by Vanessa Hopgood's arrival in merry-making coalition with Archie, all of which would likely result in Rusty stating his considered opinion that said Vanessa is naught but a lewd minx, and, having commenced to foaming at the mouth, and by and by breaking out to savage madness, subsequently dispensing much by way of pummellings and multiple busts in the snoot with any knobkerries, teapots and suchlike instruments of chastisement that might come to hand, said havoc being focused on any gentlemen discovered in the immediate vicinity of America's Darling™, in the aftermath of which Adele Fitzhalligon would swoop down upon the fallen and bear away the stricken Archie on his metaphorical shield, the better to subsequently revive him in some private boudoir with the aid of a Balthazar of the old fizzy shampoo.

O Adele!

Alas, our potentially dramatical Donnybrook existing in a state of abeyance for the moment, as we await the entry of Hollywood's latter-day Clausus of the blood of the Sabines, who was a great army in himself, i.e., Rusty McGrew, your n. here contents himself with employing the cinematic convention of the *establishing shot*, by which is meant a description of the Quintet's table, which, as previously advertised, is a banquette situated adjacent to both the dance floor and the Hot Stomp Trio's bandstand, although not too close to either to risk auditory impairment or the unheralded arrival of a hoofer sent sprawling as a consequence of an excess of 'tea' and one too many left feet, and where a general air of bonhomie prevails, as may be gauged by the toasts being offered by Archie and Vanessa as they hoist their teacups aloft. To wit:

'What ho, old sport!' sings out Vanessa.

'What ho, old beldam!' halloos Archie.

Here your humble n. pauses to note, in order to satisfy the curiosity of any Reader wondering how, given the tympani-scorching volume of hot jazz currently being laid down by the Hot Stomp Trio, and the excited babble of an assemblage of citizens quaffing 98% bathtub hooch, and the thunderous drumming of many feet engaged in the hot-shoe shuffle – I say, any Reader wondering how said n. may assert with authority the foregoing dialogue can be fully reassured as to your n.'s *bona fides*, it being the case that any narrator worth his or her salt must be possessed not only of a good ear for the rhythms of speech but a talent for lip reading too, lest he or she find themselves obliged to faithfully record the conversations accruing when his or her subjects hie themselves to a nightclub, deadfall or speak wherein may be discovered hot jazz of such tympani-scorching volume as might render his or her characters' dialogue inaudible or indistinct.

It being likely that there remains a Reader or two unconvinced of your humble n.'s facility for accurate lip-reading, your n. hereby offers an example of same, it being further the case that the Reader has been promised Felicia Fortesque's ~~unmasqueing~~ unmasking, to which revelation we immediately proceed. The scene (within a scene) is this:

Felicia Fortesque sits quietly at the banquette aforesaid, this in contradistinction to wassailing citizens around and about, Felicia being instead engaged in scribbling notes with her replacement slim gold pencil, her quiet industry noted with some interest by Bartley McGuffin, whom the attentive Reader will recall is an aspiring novelist whose mind rarely strays far from his One True Work, e'en when he has been triple-double-dared to speak just one more syllable by a woman in possession of a double-barrelled Remington derringer of the calibre .41 rimfire short.

'I say,' says Bartley, directing his opening gambit at Felicia in the manner of, say, HMS *Inextinguishable* launching a ranger o'er the bows of the *Black Terror*. Gaining no purchase, he clears his throat. 'I say, "I say."'

'That,' murmurs Felicia without lifting her blue-grey eyes from her notebook, 'is six syllables, providing we discount the throat-clearing, which for the moment I do.'

'Yes, but —'

'Eight,' says Felicia, her hand already snaking toward the diamante Dior clutch wherein the foreshadowed muff pistol lies like an arquebus upon Chekhovian chimney breast.

Lesser men than Bartley McGuffin might have quailed at this point, but Bartley has not spent three years in the service of Sir Archie in vain, which is to say that his stuff, whilst not to be compared with the *Victory*'s keel as it broke the line between *Redoubtable* and *Bucentaure* at Trafalgar, is ne'ertheless sufficiently robust to ensure that Bartley's quail bent but did not break. Instead he clears his throat again, takes a deep breath, and speaks as follows: 'No woo, there is none.'

Your humble n.'s facility for lip reading also extending to dramatic respiratory effects, the Reader will readily conceive that the sharp intake of breath now executed by Felicia Fortesque suggests that her utmost astonishment has been excited by Bartley McGuffin's apparent pitching of woo. In so conceiving, howe'er, the Reader would be sadly mistook; for, properly rendered, and such being Felicia's understanding, Bartley's words were in fact *No Woo, There Is None*, said capitalised italicisation indicative of Bartley's quoting the title of a novel, play, poem or similarly significant cultural artefact, the mere mention of which is sufficient to cause Felicia Fortesque to inhale in the unexpectedly severe fashion previously described.

'Pardon me?' says she, having finally exhaled.

'*Suddenly One Bombay Springtime,*' says Bartley. '*A Man of Undeniable Boots.*'

'My good man,' says Felicia, 'you appear to be babbling. Shall I call for a physick?'

'Madam,' says Bartley, standing up in order that he might better bow low and extend a courtly leg, 'your most humble servant, and devoted admirer, at your service. Allow me, Ms de Havilland, to call for said physick.'

Here Felicia, upon being addressed as 'Ms de Havilland', can be observed to start as if upon a fearful summons bellowed in her ear whilst at bath, whereupon Felicia prevails mightily upon Bartley McGuffin to retract his courtly leg and make all haste in retaking his seat, lest she be obliged to employ her muff pistol to cool him off.

'Ah,' says Bartley as he retakes his seat as bade, 'but the double-barrelled Remington derringer is very rarely instantly lethal unless discharged into a vital organ at close quarters, which momentary delay in expiring would allow me some few dying words by which I might betray the true identity of the beazel who has left me so terminally punctured as to warrant me peppered for this world, a denouement bearing an uncanny similarity to the climax of the novel *Do Not Go Gently, Good Knight* by the bestselling and critically acclaimed author Cordelia de Havilland, who is admired by yours truly, Bartley McGuffin, as the twentieth century's finest exponent of the Flaubertian ideal of the novel as a book about nothing and depending upon nothing external, but which is held together by the internal strength of its style, said tome having no subject, or at least a subject which is to all intents and purposes invisible, if such a thing is indeed possible, which contentious proposal remains a matter of some heated conjecture in the more rarefied literary circles.'

'You wouldn't dare!' hisses Felicia / Cordelia, so furious at Bartley's threat of unmasking that the marked lack of sibilant syllables proves no impediment to her hissing.

'I might.'

'Such, sir, would be the act of a villain so base as to resemble a spaniel fawning. Art thou a villain?'

'Villain I am none,' says Bartley.

'Art too,' says Felicia.

'Art not,' says Bartley.

'Art so,' says Felicia.

The foregoing sketch, given the vehemence of both parties, promising to continue in similarly music hall vein for some time, and your humble n. having it on good authority that Rusty McGrew's staircase descent has gained the return, or, more precisely, *the point of no return*, your n. now interpolates to unmask Felicia Fortesque, as previously pledged.

But stay! sings out the Reader. Has Felicia not already been unmasked as a very viper upon the bosom of Vanessa Hopgood, who, to paraphrase the immortal Milton, *committed to such a viper her most sacred trust of secresie*, Felicia being not the confidante she pretends to be, but instead *a spy in the house of love*, charged by green-eyed Rusty McGrew with the reportage of intelligence pertaining to Vanessa's dalliances with any and all male specimens who are by no means Rusty McGrew?

Such, indeed, is most certainly the case; and yet, to the sensitive Reader's undoubted shock and dismay, your humble n. has it on good authority that the foregoing dissimulation accounts for a mere two-thirds of Felicia Fortesque's perfidy.[3] For, notwithstanding her duplicitous role as a double-agent, and furthermore compounding same, Felicia is in fact a triple-agent for the purpose of our narrative, being in truth, and as alleged by Bartley McGuffin, Cordelia de Havilland, the critically acclaimed and bestselling author of such tomes as *Tuesday Grace is Full of Child* and *A Pirate's Love is Booty True*, Cordelia being currently engaged

3 The Reader likely wondering, yet again, as to the narrator's *bona fides* in the matter of excavating closely held secrets, your n., whilst refusing in all instances to reveal his sources, refers the Reader to the narrative mode 'omniscient first-person', the practice of which requires any narrator worth his or her salt to master not only the skill of lip reading, but mind reading too.

in subterfugially researching her *magnum opus*, which tome Cordelia has conceived as a searing *exposé* of Volstead-defying Hollywood, or at least to the extent that the Flaubertian ideal will allow, and which features for its protagonist an ethically unconventional entrepreneur who goes by the name of Buster McTrew, which moniker will, Cordelia hopes, subtly convey to her audience the extent to which Buster is heroically proportioned in the department where it might do her readers' imaginations the most good.

O Cordelia!

Alas, your humble n. is here obliged to report that Cordelia de Havilland's peccability does not end there, it being the case that Cordelia's inspiration for her opus appears to be the immortal Cervantes' *The Trials of Persiles and Sigismunda*, this on the basis of Cordelia's working title (*The Trials of Buster and Sigismunda*) and the one-line synopsis she has already submitted to her agent, the redoubtable Baroness von Sacher-Masoch, *viz.*, "Led by the bootlegger Buster McTrew and his nuptially intended Sigismunda Beauchamp, a gang of palookas, want-wits and damnable jades of various nations experience a harrowing series of episodes both dangerous and chivalrously romantic, said gang united and ultimately bound together by their misfortunes and a mutual desire to refute the baseball columnist Damon Runyon's contention that all of life is 6 to 5 against."

Thus it transpires that Cordelia's betrayal of Vanessa Hopgood may be rendered mathematically as *betrayal*, for Cordelia is not only a Milton-ish viper nestling in Vanessa's *embonpoint*, but one who fully intends to reconfigure the information winkled out whilst masquerading as confidante and boon companion as a fictional *exposé*, it being the case that Cordelia's pen sketch for Sigismunda includes the lyrical descriptors 'shimmering', 'earth-bound goddess', and 'eyes of wood-pallet blue'.

Here your n. acknowledges that the intelligent Reader may be reserving judgement upon Cordelia de Havilland, it being true that your n. has yet to vouchsafe his sources, and especially as said n. is claiming to enjoy what appears to be unrestricted access to the notes and private correspondence of a bestselling and critically acclaimed author, which, if it be the case that Cordelia is, in fact —

'Hot diggity!' sings out Adele Fitzhalligon, who has been observing in ceaseless vigil the nightclub door, through which Rusty McGrew has just slouched with all the enthusiasm of the proverbial rough beast contemplating the road to some dusty Levantine hamlet, which entrance, despite being possessed of significantly less bounding, leaping and bursting forth than your n. might have preferred young love's ambassador to display, is ne'ertheless ideally timed to allow us conclude our current chapter, the better to whet the Reader's appetite, in cliff-hanging fashion, for the inevitable snoot-busting carnage to come.

Chapter Twelve

In which Rusty McGrew discovers himself trembling like the cat i' the adage, torn between his love of a good woman and a burning desire to cool off a knight of the realm.

'Coo-ee!' trills Adele, leaning in behind Vanessa and flapping a paw at Rusty McGrew who, having recently slouched through the nightclub door, now prowls and prowls around the balcony o'erlooking the dancefloor like a one-man Midian troop. 'O'er here!'

Now Rusty, as previously said, is a man of decisive action in love as in war; thus it is that, when his eyes finally penetrate Vanessa Hopgood's shimmering aura to discover the adjacent presence of a barrel-built woo-peddler, it is with Rusty the work of but a single bound to land himself ringside.

Alas, if Adele is disappointed by the dearth of knobkerries, yataghans and sundry suchlike tools of cranial despoilment to be observed about Rusty's person (and she is), such disenchantment is as naught compared to the anti-climax she now experiences when Rusty, rather than raking Archie stem-to-stern with a convenient teapot, draws himself up stiffly and gives a terse inclination of the head (hardly more than 18° from true) which he fully intends all at table to interpret as a respectful bow.

'Ladies,' says he. And then, having allowed the merest pause to convey the impression that he is dubious of his information, 'Gentlemen.'

'Rusty!' cries Vanessa, 'how very good of you to join us. Have you met Sir Archibald l'Estrange-B'stard?'

Rusty allowing that, had he previously encountered Sir Archibald l'Estrange-B'stard, he would be unlikely to have forgotten such a distinguished grandee, and Archie subsequently confirming said non-event, Vanessa now proceeds to introduce them formally, with the result that Archie, following suit, rises from his seat to mirror Rusty's terse 18° bow and deliver a muted 'What ho, what?', at which point Vanessa further introduces Bartley McGuffin and the glum Adele Fitzhalligon.

'And Felicia you already know,' says Vanessa, little knowing that Rusty knew Felicia before Vanessa knew Felicia, hence Rusty and Felicia's sharing of a subterfugial glance that might most accurately be described as *knowing*, albeit nowhere as *knowing* as the glance subsequently shared between Felicia-Cordelia and Bartley McGuffin on the occasion of Felicia-Cordelia – henceforth to be referred to only as Cordelia – I say, Cordelia de Havilland now *shoots a look* at Bartley which eloquently, if silently, reminds Bartley of the double-barrelled derringer's potential as Chekhovian arquebus were Bartley to err in bruiting abroad the truth of Cordelia's egregious abuse of Vanessa Hopgood's *most sacred trust of secresie.*

It being vanishingly rare that your humble n. might e'er find himself in flawless concord with any character, it being the case that the needs, wants and wishes of a character very rarely coincide with those of his or her narrator, said conflict being not only desirable but of absolute necessity in the construction of a tragical tale that requires said characters to undergo rough handling and emerge stronger, wiser and happy e'er after – I say, your n. is rarely to be discovered in untrammelled accord with his characters, but in the case under preferment, and given the explosive potential of a collision between Rusty McGrew and Sir Archie as they vie for Vanessa Hopgood's shimmering heart, it is difficult to disavow the glum Adele Fitzhalligon's muttered verdict on the foregoing as something of *a damp squid*, a judgement with which some Readers, fond of an occasional literary schmozzle, might well concur. In point of fact, your humble n. would go so far as to endorse the thwarted frustration currently being experienced by Adele, given that it was his stated intention, only a few short pages ago, to engineer an encounter between Archie and Rusty for the express purpose of enhancing our tale's tension, said narrative strain to be violently released in ructions, flailing limbs and the busting of multiple snoots – in short, the Donnybrook not only aforementioned but explicitly promised.

Indeed, it is with no little chagrin that your n. reports the growing conviction that his control o'er our narrative's characters is somewhat less than absolute. By way of illustration, your n. refers the Reader to the case of Rusty McGrew, who, or whom, only a few short pages ago, *strode forth* from his apartment suite bound for the nightclub downstairs with the firm intention of parping Clarke's *Trumpet Voluntary* (previously misattributed to Purcell) at Vanessa Hopgood. At which point, as the attentive Reader will no doubt recall, we left Rusty to his own devices, this on the assumption that a grown citizen, fictional or otherwise, is entirely capable of descending a flight of stairs without requiring assistance or audience, and went before him to join the Quintet at their dancefloor-adjacent table, Reader and n. alike keenly anticipating the ructions to follow once Rusty clapped peepers on Archie's interpolative pitching of woo.

But stay! therein lies the rub, if by *rub* we might be understood to mean the crucial absence of intelligence that led Reader and narrator alike to make an assumption now revealed as erroneous. For, while it may be correct to assume that a grown citizen may descend a flight of stairs without assistance or audience, it would be negligent to blithely assume said citizen's state of mind will be precisely the same at the foot of the stairs as it was at the top, or, indeed, at the return, if the staircase consists of more than one flight.

Thus, in acknowledging this negligence, your humble n. now proposes that the Reader join him in drifting, wraithlike, back in time to consider the facts:

Fact I: Rusty McGrew exits his office and slouches toward the top of the stairs humming a hymnal excerpt the more religiously musical Reader will recognise as *Awake, my soul, and with the sun thy daily stage of duty run*, the implication being that Rusty is invoking the Divine Ineffable as he goes forth to do his duty, i.e., bend the noble knee in the presence of Vanessa Hopgood.

Fact II: The musical cues notwithstanding, the expression flitting about Rusty's map as he reaches the top of the staircase is that of a man suffering a discommoding dose of the marthambles, which is to say his features have coalesced into a mask of pained restraint such as might be observed upon a bishop observing a blonde through a brother bishop's stained-glass window.

Fact III: Rusty McGrew, as previously noted, is a fully grown male specimen, and, as such, and in common with every man born of woman, is in the very throes, as he descends the stairs, of an almighty mute struggle to arrange the words 'you', 'me', 'marry' and 'will' in the correct consecutive order, particularly when convention demands that any and all grammatically correct arrangements of those most fateful of words (i.e., 'Will you marry me?', 'Marry me you will?', 'You will marry me?') are obliged, as the foregoing punctuation suggests, to conclude in the interrogative mode.

Fact IV: Rusty's almighty mute struggle has less to do with his being possessed since childhood of a sensitive soul which fears rejection more than hunger, bullets and oysters out of season, but is in fact the consequence of Rusty's impulsive decision to splice his destiny to that of Vanessa Hopgood, it being the case that Rusty, being at heart a true *chevalier*, is acutely aware that any suggestion of tying *the sacred knot which death alone can dissolve* (*cf.* Cervantes) must immediately be followed by the flourishing of a ring attached to a diamond no smaller than a camel's molar, in the matter of which last Rusty McGrew is well provided, Rusty being the proud possessor of more diamond rings than Jacques Cartier, albeit Rusty's diamond rings, being larcenously acquired, are for the nonce so hot as to require housing in an asbestos-lined safe, and thus unfit for the finger of e'en the most unprepossessing of prospective chatelaines, let alone a goddess recently catastarized by the Hollywood gossip mongers and so prone to shimmering she has been obliged to trademark the words *America's Darling*™.

Fact V: Thus, as Rusty McGrew reaches the bottom of the staircase, and thence enters the Blue Phal in the slouching style, our previously enraptured swain is the very exemplar of procrastination the Bard counselled against, which is to say, he trembles like the cat i' the adage, i.e., dallies on the very brink of *letting I dare not wait upon I would.*

Fact VI: Rusty McGrew is, as previously advertised, a man of decisive action, as attested by his requiring no more than a moment and a single bound to land himself ringside at the Quintet's dancefloor-adjacent table. Alas, a moment being an unsatisfyingly vague unit of measurement, and the mind, as the immortal Milton reminds us, being of its own place, wherein can be devised a hell of heaven, and a heaven of hell – I say, said moment was of sufficient duration for Rusty to realise that Archie's barrel-chested presence was a valid reason for letting *I would* go hang in favour of *I dare not*, Rusty – mid-bound – realising that the scragging of a woo-bruiting knight of the realm, albeit one taking place at a time and place remote from the place of business which serves as Rusty's *front*, would likely buy him all the time he might need to rush out and buy a diamond ring unlikely to singe the fair flesh of Vanessa Hopgood's finger.

Here endeth the facts of the matter.

Your humble n. proffers the foregoing not to gain the Reader's sympathy, nor to abdicate his responsibility, but simply to alert the Reader to the difficulties of maintaining narrative cohesion when a storyteller finds himself at the mercy of a character's whims and foibles, a matter of no little importance when said character, previously advertised as *a man of decisive action*, so cruelly illustrates the cautionary imperative of *caveat emptor* as to cause your n. to tremble on the very brink of plunging into a post-season funk.

The foregoing digression thus concluded, we now rejoin the narrative fray, drifting wraithlike into position to observe the dancefloor-adjacent Quintet (temporarily expanded to Sextet), pausing only to note, for the benefit of the Reader, that the foregoing digression as it relates to Rusty McGrew likely applies to all other members of the company, most of whom – as the attentive Reader will recall – are engaged in subterfugial masquerades.

And so we proceed:

'Rusty,' coos Vanessa in the direction of the swain reluctant, 'I have the most wonderful news!'

'You don't say.'

'I do. Archie,' says she, indicating said barrel-chested knight of the realm, 'golfs.'

'No!'

'Yes! Archie?'

'Too true, old virago!' pip-pips Archie.

'In fact,' Vanessa sings out, 'Archie owns his own golf course!'

'Do you say?'

'I do. Archie?'

'Correct and factual, old termagant!'

'Hell of a thing,' says Rusty, who had first encountered Vanessa Hopgood on the ninth fairway of the Old Mill course in Bay City, when Vanessa sent a rare slice from near the eleventh green into the pothole bunker Rusty was excavating as he attempted to hack out in the general direction of the ninth fairway from whence he came. Said encounter being precipitated by the coming together of Vanessa's ball and the parietal section of Rusty's skull, their introductory remarks were more than somewhat spiced with a distinctly salty tang; but once Rusty's vision finally cleared (Rusty's caddy, Foxy, confirming that any temporary ocular disorientation was in fact due to Vanessa's shimmering aura), a mutual attraction was quickly established, Rusty declaring that where once he had seen stars in consequence of ball-parietal collision, the only stars he now observed – those of the silver screen notwithstanding – were the celestial orbs of metaphorical planetary alignment, which is to say, continued the full and unabridged Rusty, that it was surely

Fate which caused him to hook his brassie and send him into the pothole bunker, there to intercept Vanessa's surprisingly wayward approach to the eleventh green.

Indeed, so passionately did Rusty invoke Atropos and her thread-spindling sisters that Vanessa, being immune to the lure of astrology in particular and the theory of predestination in general, ne'ertheless found herself yielding to Rusty's interpretation of events, Vanessa being otherwise at a loss to explain her slice, being at the time two under par for the round and as a rule considered faultless with niblick in hand.

Alas, the romance that subsequently blossomed had much in common with the night-blooming cereus, and specifically the *Selenicereus grandiflorus*, which blooms only once a year, it being the case that said romantic blossoming was a consequence of Vanessa's being, much like the night-blooming cereus, *kept in the dark* as to Rusty's true feelings *vis-à-vis* the noble Scottish art, for Vanessa so loved the noble art for the purity of its simple joy (i.e., whacking a small ball around a large field) that it never occurred to her that others – pertinently, one Rusty McGrew – might take up the baffy with malign intent.

For lo! it gives your humble n. no pleasure to reveal that Rusty McGrew is *a bogey golfer*, which is to say he plays off a handicap of 18, and that he is neither embarrassed to say so in public nor has e'er expressed any desire to lower that number to the mid-teens, for the truth of Rusty McGrew's belated conversion to golf lies in his pragmatic adoption of the mashie as an equally effective but decidedly more ergonomic tool of chastisement than the unwieldy baseball bat, the mashie providing considerably more whip and a wristier swing. Further, it is Rusty's experience that a gendarme, on requesting a motorist to pull over for a routine traffic stop, and subsequently discovering a full set of golf clubs in the trunk, is more likely to direct that motorist to the nearest country club (and possibly provide an escort) than if the trunk is packed to the gunwales with Louisville Sluggers. Finally, Rusty is of the opinion that the country club golf course is unparalleled in the opportunities it offers – in woodland, stream, dyke, old mill and pothole bunker – for the rapid concealment of recently deceased ex-associates, a good example of same, for the purpose of illustration, being a barrel-chested woo-pitching interloper with designs on Rusty's one true intended.

Your humble n. leaves it to the Reader to reckon the exact number of weather balloons Vanessa's high dudgeon might imperil were she to discover the extent of Rusty McGrew's duplicitous shenanigans *vis-à-vis* the noble Scottish art, your n. being for the nonce otherwise engaged in pointing out that Vanessa's conscience is by no means entitled to consider itself stainless at this juncture, unless we are prepared to turn the Tiresian eye to Vanessa's dalliance with Sir Archie, which we are not, in consequence of which your humble n. is obliged to confirm that Vanessa may be arraigned alongside Cresidye, whom the immortal Chaucer believed possessed of *a sliding heart*, e'en if, being conducted in brazen fashion, the Vanessa-Archie *affaire* hardly qualifies for the soubriquet *subterfugial*. Ne'ertheless, your humble n. is obliged to declare that, in carrying off her masque *in plain sight*, Vanessa's ploy may in fact count as doubly subterfugial, and, the conventional mathematics (wherein a double negative amounts to a positive) not prevailing in the realm of Love, Vanessa may thus be accounted the most egregiously treacherous of the citizenry gathered about the bandstand-adjacent banquette.

Thus we return to the temporary Sextet to discover that the conversation consists of Archie regaling the company with his boyhood adventures with the Goodrich pneumatic, said object being a golf ball with a compressed air core, a radical development akin to the Bounding Billy that would surely have revolutionised the sport were it not for its unfortunate tendency to explode; and yet, even as he guffaws in unison with the rest, Rusty McGrew is purposing in the secret quiet of his conscience to persuade Vanessa to allow he and Archie to embark upon a swift nine without the benefit of her shimmering presence, the better to finagle Archie into the old mill at Bay City's Old Mill Country Club and there cool him off with his (i.e., Archie's) own brassie.

And so, as our narrative comes panting hotfoot to the conclusion of Act One, with the imminent *raid* previously alluded to (for hark! the distant thunder of pounding flat feet can be discerned e'en above the ragtime revels of the Hot Stomp Trio), our temporary Sextet may be declared something of a perfidious conga, it being the case that the chorus doll Adele Fitzhalligon is planning to usurp the silver screen siren Vanessa Hopgood, who is scheming to betray the god-scorning Rusty McGrew, who is conspiring to cool off the knight errant Sir Archibald l'Estrange-B'stard, who is plotting to forsake his batman Bartley McGuffin,[1] who is conniving to grass up the bestselling and critically acclaimed author Cordelia de Havilland, who plots to betray all and sundry courtesy of her daring *exposé* of Volstead-defying Hollywood in *The Trials of Buster and Sigismunda*, all of which, alas, recalls the worst excesses of that Cacus who was renowned for thinking in the savagery of his heart not to leave any crime or treachery undared or unattempted, and, further, makes a mockery of this narrative's philosophical proposition, i.e., *the world might be a better place if only everyone would make a little more effort to get along.*

O humanity!

1 Archie being a true *chevalier*, he is entirely innocent of any taint in the matter of subterfugial perfidy, it being true that Archie's wooing of Vanessa Hopgood is conducted openly and honourably, Archie being so blootered on bathtub hooch as to entirely forget Adele Fitzhalligon's announcement of Vanessa's engagement of convenience to Samuel L. Silverstein and wholly ignorant, as is the rest of Vanessa's millions of admirers, of her private arrangement with Rusty McGrew. Further, the only citizen to believe Archie guilty of perfidy is Bartley McGuffin, who fears the loss of his cushy billet, mess of pottage, *&c.*, should Archie's suit prove successful; however, e'en if such should become the case, your humble n. is obliged to state that, in the matter of Bartley's cushy billet, Archie must be considered to be acting *at all times* without malice aforethought.

Chapter Thirteen

A raid on the Blue Phal. Rusty McGrew invokes the Lockean hypothesis enshrined in the Declaration of Independence.

Our latest chapter being devoted, as previously intimated, to a police raid on the Blue Phalarope, your humble n. now hastens to reassure any Reader concerned that our tale might discover itself abruptly foreshortened, with major and minor characters alike batoned into the back of Paddy Wagons, and consigned to cells to languish therein o'ernight, or e'en longer if their friends and family fail to raise sufficient splosh to go bail, or, as might well be the case with Rusty McGrew, transported directly to San Q and immediately strapped into Old Sparky – I say, your humble n., conscious as always of his Reader's concerns, hereby states that the imminent raid will by no means result in our tale's foreshortening, and is in fact contrived in order to invest our narrative with a degree of vim that has heretofore been sadly lacking, it being the case that our tale, despite repeated references to the immortal Bunyan's classic, has achieved remarkably little *progress* to date, the Quintet, for example, having advanced only a couple of blocks from the terrace of the Musso & Frank Grill to the Blue Phal on the corner of Sunset and Cahuenga, whilst Rusty, despite starting out strong by journeying all the way from Bay City to Hollywood, appears to have developed a rather disappointing flair for procrastination.

What renders this lack of progress all the more frustrating is that our tale's sluggish advance is largely due to circumstances beyond your humble n.'s control, which helplessness is vividly illustrated by the cameo now provided by Moxie La Roux and Abie Cohen, who have travelled by shared taxi cab all the way from Sammy's palatial mansion on the corner of Wilshire and Irving to the Blue Phalarope on the corner of Sunset and Cahuenga, Moxie to put the finishing touches to the choreography for that night's hot jazz take on *The Rite of Spring*, Abie to scope out the Phal for a telephone that might be usefully employed for dime-dropping purposes at some point in the future, so that any blame attached to Rusty McGrew's expiring in Old Sparky might accrue to a disgruntled employee of the Phal. Alas, dear Reader, no sooner do Moxie and Abie alight from their shared cab than they commence gazing upon one another in wild surmise, for the very sidewalk upon which they stand shudders in a manner conflatable with the impact of very many flat feet pounding along Sunset Boulevard toward the Blue Phal.

'Jings!' says Moxie. 'A raid!'

Whereupon, as the Reader will easily conceive, the conscientious legal counsel Abie Cohen advises Moxie La Roux to scarper lively, before taking to his heels as incontinently as did the infamous Dolon upon Ilium's plain; and thus is another opportunity for progress lost.

All of which, of course, must be considered an egregious breach of promise, not only because every narrative contains an implicit guarantee of progress, but because this particular narrative's subtitle explicitly states that our tale is *a Progress, embarked upon by a mixed company of gunsels, loogans, molls and knights from Hollywood to Tropico Springs*. Alas, your n. will not scruple to state that our tale is currently possessed of roughly as much progress as might be discovered in Bugs Dooley's motion picture adaptation of *The Pilgrim's Progress*, which, as the attentive Reader will undoubtedly recall, is so very little as to persuade any Esquimaux art critic wandering by Bugs' garret that Bugs is in fact an aspiring *avant-garde* painter currently working upon a canvas entitled *Ghost of Polar Bear Half-Glimpsed in Blizzard*.

Thus it is, and without further preamble, that we recommence our latest chapter with the raid aforementioned. To wit:

Chapter Thirteen

A raid on the Blue Phal. Rusty McGrew invokes the Lockean hypothesis enshrined in the Declaration of Independence.

It was afterwards bruited about as testament to the potency of the Blue Phal's 'tea' that imminent disaster inkled into the collective conscious of said speak's clientele only when Adele Fitzhalligon clambered onto the banquette table whirling her fox fur about her head like a shepherd boy limbering up to put a rock plumb spang where it might do a Philistine giant the least good, all the while whooping 'Hot socks! A raid!'

Howe'er, while it is undeniably true that a considerable fraction of the Phal's clientele is to a greater or lesser degree puggled, mithered or fully frizzled on the Phal's 'tea', your n. is ne'ertheless obliged to state that Rusty would be, at best, disingenuous in claiming that his tea is wholly responsible for the Phal's clientele being somehow caught unawares by a company of the LAPD's finest advancing with the quality of stealth generally associated with a herd of parched pachyderms scenting the first watering-hole for fifty miles, and whose rumbling, as they bear down upon the Phal in flat-footed concert, sends women and young children screaming into the night for fear the Pacific and North American tectonic plates have resumed their timeless joust.

For lo! it is also true that a secondary considerable fraction of the Phal's clientele, which fraction largely overlaps with the fraction of the first part, are engaged in the *hot-shoe shuffle*, which is the latest dance craze to sweep Hollywood and consists in the main of its practitioners stomping the floor as if their shoes are aflame and in need of violent extinguishment, the exuberance of which regularly drowns out both the thunder of fists pounding upon nightclub doors and the earliest tremors of tectonic grind, and which is, in fact, held responsible in some quarters for precipitating said disasters, with the entirely understandable consequence of the *hot-shoe shuffle* being banned in those Hollywood nightclubs managed by a citizen possessed of a strong social conscience and / or antennae keenly attuned to imminent disaster, natural or otherwise.

Unfortunately, as the attentive Reader will no doubt recall, Rusty is at this crucial juncture consumed with plotting Archie's untimely demise in the Old Mill Country Club's old mill; and, his blood being consequently up, and thus thrumming in his ears, he entirely fails to register the cacophonous drumming on the dancefloor, which pounding in turn masks the thunderous hammering on the Phal's doors. Thus we may regretfully conclude that it is to deflect attention from his negligence that Rusty might claim that his tea is the most sense-guddling *liquid asset* on the market; indeed, we can calibrate Rusty's hubris to the nth degree by noting how, as the LAPD's finest pour into the Phal in a veritable tsunami of blue serge, Rusty is heard to sing out, in paraphrase of the immortal Swift, how true genius may be recognised by the sheer quantity of the dunce-like confederacy besetting him on all sides, in response to which, from the balcony o'erlooking the dancefloor he has immediately established as a bridgehead, one Aloysius 'Bumbles' McGee is heard to riposte with an abridged version of Proverbs 16:18, i.e., *that pride goeth before destruction, and the haughty spirit before a fall*, there being naught more certain, nor more pleasing to Bumbles McGee, than that Rusty McGrew's stock has plummeted in a manner not unakin to Norwegian lemming o'er-leaping the precipice brink in the fatal clutch of suicidal ideation.

This narrative being more concerned with the genus *Homo sapiens* than that of *Lemmus lemmus*, and it being likely the case that the Reader has no personal experience of a police raid upon an unlicensed premises, your humble n. now turns away from the tragedy unfolding upon the far craggy fjord to observe more closely the rude spectacle unfolding in the Phal. For, and not to put too fine a point on it, the serge-clad warriors of justice go about their work in a business-like manner which suggests that, like Othello before them, *the tyrant custom hath made the flinty and steel couch of war their thrice-driven bed of down*; indeed, goaded e'er onwards by Bumbles McGee, the blue-clad Boys – armed with billy-clubs, bastinadoes and sundry similar tools of cranial despoilment – wade into the stampeding clientele in a decidedly robust variation on the *tête-à-tête* which generally attends such events, which usually amounts to little more than the Boys cheerily announcing 'Righty-o, tickety-tock!' and rhetorically inquiring as to whether said clientele have no homes to go to, the implicit jest in such queries being that the well-to-do citizenry are generally spoiled for choice in the matter of residences wherein which they may find refuge, solace and, if required, one final nightcap before ascending the wooden hill to Bedfordshire.

In the Blue Phalarope, howe'er, the air is thick with a Greek chorus of protest, outrage and pained yelpage filtering down from the rarefied heights of dudgeon as the Boys in Blue crunch teapots, smash windows and employ their knobkerries, yataghans *et al* to belabour the buttocks of fleeing citizenry. It is, in short, an horrific vista that perhaps only the immortal Breughel might do full justice, and thus your humble n., conscious as always of the delicate sensibilities of his Reader, employs the cinematic convention of *panning across the room*, to where we now observe Rusty McGrew, who has recently scrambled aboard the very same banquette as the fox fur-whirling Adele Fitzhalligon,[1] from which vantage point he is currently endeavouring to rally the troops.

'Now is the time,' halloos Rusty, 'for all stout men to rally round!'

1 While the modern definition of *banquette* is that is an upholstered bench, especially in a restaurant or nightclub, previous generations understood a *banquette* to be a raised step behind a rampart.

Alas, every stout man, which adjective encompasses those of a rotund, plump and corpulent stature (and thus accounts for yet another considerable overlapping fraction of the Phal's clientele) is otherwise engaged in unwittingly mimicking our tragic *Lemmus lemmus* as they decant themselves headfirst through the nearest window, almost all of which the federales, in their righteous fervour, have inadvertently rendered opportunities for egress by reducing the glass previously therein to smithereens, in consequence of which Rusty McGrew discovers himself so abandoned as to call to mind bereft Ariadne on some long-forgotten shore, still scanning the far horizon for the Theseus she believes will someday return to make good on his pre-coital sweet nothings.

A poignant scene, no doubt, although here your humble n. is obliged to remind the Reader that Rusty McGrew is not only a gangster, outlaw and bootie, but Irish to boot, and thus (*cf.* Dickens) a red-haired exemplar of the lowest order of anything, and is further such an accomplished spadassin that were he to feature in the LAPD's 'Most Wanted' calendar he would undoubtedly be designated April, which, as Mr T.S. Eliot stated as recently as last November's issue of *The Dial*, is the cruellest of all the year's dozen divisions.

And yet, as he stands above the wreckage of the Blue Phal, its dancefloor littered with Panama hats, feather boas, semi-precious gems, trampled refection and the ripped shreds of formerly gleaming silken fallal, your n. experiences a sympathetic pang for this erstwhile Titan of black market industry, who is brought so low as to be heard, e'en above the best efforts of the Hot Stomp Trio, who, being to a man hopped up on 'tea',[2] and thus blissfully unaware of their departing audience, are still giving it the full and

2 Whilst the vast majority of the Blue Phal's clientele have been *drinking* 'tea', the jazz musicians have been *smoking* 'tea', the 'tea' of the second part being slang for weed, reefer, and *mary-jane*, which latter term is derived from 'marijuana'. Your n. further notes the etymological incongruity of the 'j' being 'hard' in 'mary-jane' but rendered 'soft' in 'marijuana', a consequence of 'mary-jane' being an American English corruption of the original Mexican-Spanish word.

unexpurgated Gershwin – I say, the best efforts of the Hot Stomp Trio notwithstanding, Rusty may be heard to lament the egregious tergiversation of the until recently euphoric assemblage of actors, politicians, union bosses, sports stars, saxophone players *et al*, whom Rusty had until very recently considered a band of brothers taking up their cups of tea (in lieu of arms) against the tyranny of oppression, and specifically the despotic provision which the Member from Minnesota, Andrew Volstead, nailed through the heart of the Lockean hypothesis enshrined in the Declaration of Independence, *viz.*, the unalienable right to Life, Liberty and the pursuit of Happiness.

'O the tergiversation,' laments Rusty in tremulous register, 'the egregious tergiversation!'

To which Bumbles McGee is heard to bawl in riposte, 'When there is crime in society, there is no justice!'

Here your humble n. pauses in order to acknowledge that said retort might appear to the Reader an obliquely tangential response, at least on first reading. In point of fact, it masks a complexity that redounds handsomely to Bumbles McGee's credit, as will now be related. For Bumbles, being a canny student of both psychology and philosophy – indeed, he would have hardly ascended through the ranks of the LAPD were he not – I say, Bumbles understands that Rusty McGrew, in bewailing the egregious tergiversation of his erstwhile comrades, broaches the very topic that so concerned Socrates in the *Republic*, i.e., *the relation of justice to happiness*. Bumbles being not only a keen student of Greek philosophy, but a bit of a wag to boot, he considers it entirely appropriate to rebut Rusty's Socratic lament with Plato's contention that *the presence of crime equals the absence of justice*, which the Reader will doubtless agree is a whimsically humorous refutation in itself, but, moreo'er, one that embraces the secondary but no less plangently devastating punchline that, notwithstanding the fact that the *Republic* is composed of Socratic dialogue, said opus was conceived and executed by that scrivener *nonpareil*, Plato himself!

Alas, it is at this very moment that Bumbles McGee discovers himself undone, for his barb, being so sharply honed, not only pierces the metaphorical breast of Rusty McGrew but stuns the LAPD's serge-clad myrmidons into muted awe. Indeed, so brilliantly does Bumbles skewer Rusty's pretensions that his sally penetrates e'en the fog drifting through the tea-addled minds of the Hot Stomp Trio, so that they tail off in a diminuendo of poignantly questing bass semibreves, and the entire room falls silent and still, like unto frozen tableau, the consequent hush, by comparison with the tumult and alarums foregoing, being the very hiss of eternity's reckoning, until Archie, from under the banquette, where he has discovered a cup of tea still miraculously half-full, is heard to declare, 'Here's mud, old jade!'

Alas, dear Reader, an untimely interpolation into the silence (or hissing hush) of frozen tableau frequently constitutes a prelude to the frenzied alarums previously in play, so it should come as no surprise that Archie's impulsive toasting of Vanessa Hopgood has a galvanising effect on Bumbles McGee.

'Havoc!' sings out Bumbles in a monarch's voice, by which regal declaration he fully intends that the dogs of war be let slip, at which point Bumbles, like Brutus, pauses for any reply, and, like Brutus, receiveth none, it being the case that his serge-clad warriors have neither the time nor the inclination to engage in idle badinage, being elsewise engaged in bruiting taratantaras and surging forward to overrun the dancefloor-adjacent banquette in a manner conflatable with some considerable portion of the Zulu nation descending upon Rorke's Drift.

The fate of our Rorkian Few being therefore sealed, with imminent arrest and consequent public disgrace reconfiguring the destinies of all involved to a previously unimaginable degree, it behoves your n. to formally introduce their Instrument of Doom, aka Bumbles McGee, with the traditional pen sketch. To wit:

Height: 5'2"
Eyes: Green, of almond shape
Demeanour: Froward

Role:		Keeper and crucifier of his city's conscience

Thus it is that Rusty McGrew, having previously scrambled atop the banquette, now stares across the dancefloor to the balcony recently occupied as a bridgehead by said froward keeper and crucifier, and discovers himself gazing upon a nemesis *of mean and hungry look*, e'en if said descriptor is more poetic than strictly precise due to Bumbles' life-long devotion to the sugared doughnut – I say, Bumbles McGee's reputation, as Rusty knows only too well, is that of a fearless combination of Bulldog Drummond and C. Auguste Dupin, a man of Robespierrean resistance to external influence so ironclad as to be reputed bullet-proof, so that Rusty, atop the banquette, discovers himself lorn for the want of a carriage-mounted M1895 Gatling gun, if only to test the hypothesis.

Here, with the storm up and all upon the hazard (*cf.* the Bard), your humble n. reluctantly breaks in upon the action to provide the Reader with the barest sliver of salient pettifog concerning the progress of the knobkerrie-brandishing federales, which might appear to the impatient Reader to be erring a tad on the leisurely side, given that their assault upon the Rorkian Few commenced some half-dozen paragraphs past and has yet to result in so much as a busted Rorkian snoot.

The Reader perhaps conceiving, given Rusty McGrew's reputation as a maestro of the Chicago Piano, that the gendarmes' sluggardly advance amounts to discretion prevailing at the expense of valour, your n. is here obliged to refute such interpretation as an unmerited slur upon our serge-clad warriors. For lo! our doughty gendarmes are in fact a light brigade which, far from disrelishing the opportunity to engage with villains and render their skulls all riven in twain, requires only the syllable 'Charge!' to sally forth with considerable vim, and frequently, such being their enthusiastic commitment to rivening, without first pausing to inquire as to the direction intended by the sabre-waving rabble-rouser in the rear.

In truth, the delay currently attending the breaking of the serge-clad wave upon the rock of the Few's banquette is directly related to your humble n.'s negligence in failing to provide the Reader with an appreciation of the dimensions of the Blue Phalarope's dancefloor, which is roughly the size of a gridiron field and, moreo'er, slopes upwards in the direction of the bandstand, it being further the case that the exertions of those hoofers most exercised by *the hot-shoe shuffle* have left the dancefloor exceedingly pocked with divot, pothole and crevice. Thus the federales advance not at the post-gallop they and the Donnybrook-craving Reader might prefer, but in a style, and at a pace, not unakin to a band of Achaean brothers blundering across the Ileian plain up to their oxters in Trojan gore.

It being the case that it's *an ill wind that blaws naebody gude* (*cf.* Scott), we here take the opportunity provided by the gendarmes' plodding advance to insert a second sliver of salient pettifog, this concerning the fallacy currently beguiling Rusty McGrew, who, as he sings out 'You'll never take me alive, copper!' from atop the banquette, appears to be labouring under the misapprehension that the destruction wrought earlier that afternoon upon a disused warehouse in Bay City has precipitated Bumbles McGee's raid, as a consequence of which Rusty now discovers himself at the stake and bayed about with many enemies, with a trip to the hoosegow in the offing and hence, courtesy of a nasty jolt from Old Sparky, very likely to *sic transit* ye olde *gloria mundi*.

In point of fact, Bumbles' sortie was planned long in advance of Rusty's ascent to the pantheon of America's Most Wanted, for Bumbles is raiding the Phal for the purpose of seizing any and all income tax returns, receipts and balance sheets likely to be considered evidential proof in a court of law, when compared and contrasted with the contents of his bank accounts, that one Jasper Huxtable 'Rusty' McGrew is employing the Blue Phalarope as a *front* for a trade or business not entirely on the up-and-up, which activity is considered actionable under the legislative apparatus of the great state of California.

Thus, as we breathlessly return to the fray, we discover Rusty atop the banquette in rather less than full possession of the facts and preparing for rubbers in good earnest, i.e., swearing a sacred oath to sell himself dearly. Brandishing the double-barrelled Remington derringer of the calibre .41 rimfire short which Cordelia de Havilland craftily slipped him whilst your humble n. was divulging the salient pettifog above, Rusty draws himself up like unto a boy upon a burning deck and embarks, apropos the immortal Herrick, upon his valediction.

'Gather ye rosebuds while ye —'

'*Hsssst*,' hisses Adele Fitzhalligon from her vantage point beneath the banquette.

'Not now, Adele. I say, Gather ye rosebuds while —'

'The trapdoor!' insists Adele.

' — ye may, old time is still a-flying. Trapdoor?'

'There is a trapdoor,' says Adele, with one eye on the gendarmes, who are as near as a toucher into the baggage train despite Archie's best efforts, our knight of the realm being currently engaged in bowling googlies of empty teapots at the serge-clad ranks — 'I say,' says Adele, 'there is a trapdoor in the chorus dolls' dressing-room.'

'Ah,' says Rusty.

'Quite,' says Adele, who, as a freelance irregular in the Blue Phal's chorus line, has on occasion availed of said escape hatch in order to flee the overly familiar attentions of gentlemen stewed to the gills on strong tea, and has on yet other occasions, and for a nominal sum, opened said trapdoor to allow similarly fallen angels to regain the paradise of the Phal's hallowed precincts.

Your humble n. allowing that it may seem a significant strategical failing on Rusty McGrew's part that he appears oblivious to such a potentially vital point of secret ingress / egress to and from his own nightclub, your n. further proposes that said ignorance redounds handsomely to Rusty's credit, for Rusty is indeed intimately familiar with the network of tunnels, passages and shafts which honeycomb the Phal, they being designed for the express purpose of facilitating the subterfugial transportation of *liquid assets*. Howe'er, Rusty being a true *chevalier* in all matters pertaining to the delicately nurtured, he considers the chorus dolls' dressing-room not only off-limits but sacrosanct to a degree that would have satisfied e'en the priestesses charged with preserving the dignity of the Eleusinian Mysteries, and is thus blissfully ignorant of said dressing-room's structural anomalies.

Howe'er, Rusty McGrew is above all else a pragmatist, especially when in every way encircled, begirt and bayed about with enemies, and now reveals himself as a man considerably more decisive in war than in love by abandoning the immortal Herrick's bittersweet elegy on *tempus fugit* mid-lament.

'Then there shall we hie!' sings out Rusty. 'To the chorus dolls' dressing-room!'

'What *ho*!' halloos Archie, who is already having the night of his life, albeit Archie's inexpressible joy is shot through with an *aperçu* of regret, it being Archie's firm belief that this Night of Nights represents the apotheosis of all his ambitions and desires, and that, having achieved so much so young, the rest of his life will likely prove an anti-climactic disappointment precipitating a descent into an excess of port, incipient gout and premature dotage.

Meanwhile, Rusty has *o'er-leapt* the miniscule gap twixt banquette and stage and gone barrelling for the offstage egress, behind which lies the corridor leading to the chorus dolls' dressing-room, only to discover that, of the Rorkian Few until recently begirt, and despite Rusty's well-honed survival instincts, he is in fact bringing up the rear, Vanessa *et al* showing a clean pair of heels as they go tumbling *pêle-mêle* for sanctuary backstage with Adele leading the charge by a short head, in consequence of which Rusty finds himself dwelling briefly on how Vanessa's impressive scramola might prove an auspicious augury for their post-nuptial future, although not to the extent that he forbears to toss behind him jazz musicians (two), the drum kit and a double bass, the better to strew obstacles designed to frustrate the progress of those serge-clad myrmidons in hot pursuit.

The chorus dolls' dressing-room being subsequently gained, it is but the work of several moments, most of which are devoted to Bartley McGuffin's efforts to rouse Archie from a mid-season funk occasioned by the absence of any scantily clad *coryphées* – I say, it is with the Few but the work of several moments to make good their escape via the trapdoor previously advertised, which, once returned to its original position, lies entirely flush and thus invisible to the uninitiated eye, with the consequence that the Few sneak away into the Phal's subterranean honeycomb of passages and tunnels, said snucking masked by Bumbles McGee's muffled roars from overhead, which bellowing causes the classically inclined Cordelia de Havilland to note with her replacement gold pencil that said hollers are quixotically reminiscent of a minotaur shut out of a labyrinth of which he is entirely unaware, notwithstanding that said bawling, albeit muffled, is easily deciphered as LA's preeminent conscience-crucifier berating his serge-clad warriors on the theme of their inability to locate their lard-like rear padding with both hands and a compass, to which one warrior is heard to pithily respond with the old adage relating to the bad workman who blames his tools, causing Bumbles in turn to state that *tools* is the operative *mot juste*, which slander provokes audible dissent in the ranks, which grumbling precipitates in Bumbles McGee a choler that can only be described as *rash*, in the throes of which he swears a sacred oath to bring Rusty McGrew and his compadres to justice, *or he will know the reason why*.

There being little by way of penetrating insight into the human condition to be gained from observing a man in the throes of choleric rash, your n. now drifts ahead of the Rorkian Few, the better to observe Rusty emerging from his labyrinth in a manner not entirely unlike that of Theseus leading the Athenian youths to freedom, only to discover, lurking in the shadows on the corner of Sunset and Cahuenga, a certain Samuel L. Silverstein, who, having recently hied himself hence to the Blue Phalarope with all due haste, as advised by his legal counsel Abie Cohen, the better to be on hand lest Rusty McGrew discover himself compelled to take a noble knee in the presence of Vanessa Hopgood, and thus be conveniently situated to issue a forceful *nolle prosequi* in the matter of any banns being bruited – I say, Sammy now discovers himself confronted by the post-raid horrors of a tea-puggled clientele decanting itself headfirst through shattered windows, or clinging by finger-tip to second-floor windowsill, or being batoned up and down Sunset Boulevard by the serge-clad gendarmerie, all of which, as the Reader will readily conceive, has given Sammy L. pause for thought.

Indeed, it is while he is mid-pause, and still awaiting inspiration, that Sammy hears a somewhat hollow subterranean grating that suggests an especially heavy metal object being displaced, whereupon Sammy bends down and peers beneath the Pierce Arrow *coupé* behind which he is lurking and thereunder observes a manhole cover rising and being placed to one side, which activity is followed in short order by the appearance of *a big bushy head of curly red hair*, which rather wild mane is followed by a coiffure that is not only blonde, but fine-spun and bobbed like Irene Castle's, and fluffed into curls – in short, Sammy observes the entire Rorkian Few emerging from the honeycombed depths of the Blue Phalarope, whereupon the Few nip swiftly into the *coupé* and, with Rusty at the helm, ~~*peel out burning rubber*~~ depart the corner of Sunset and Cahuenga at the sedate pace you might expect of a veteran bootlegger experienced at journeying hither and yon without piquing the interest of motorcycle federales charged with enforcing the statutes pertaining to speed limitations.

And so we go, following in the wake of the departed Few, pausing only to note that Samuel L. Silverstein's eyes, which first commenced to boggle when he realised the identity of the citizen possessed of *the big bushy head of curly red hair*, have since grown e'er larger, and that the expression on his phiz, being that of a platypus stumbling across a mirror carelessly discarded by some Outback adventurer, is that of a man so stunned by his own accidental brilliance as to purse his lips into silent whistle, all of which has reconfigured his features so that they appear somewhat duckish, but not quite.

Which is to say, dear Reader, that Samuel L. Silverstein, motion picture mogul and *svengali nonpareil*, appears to have had an original idea.

And so, having stood upon the order of our going in order to note the foregoing, we now depart, casting anxious glances aloft, for lo! and as the Reader will readily conceive, a Hollywood motion picture mogul conjuring up an original idea is so unusual as to be considered wholly unnatural, and thus entirely likely – we have the Bard's word on't – to precipitate a huge eclipse of sun and moon, and cause th' affrighted globe to yawn at alteration.

O Sammy!

Chapter Fourteen

A brief digression on the legal status of crimes of the heart.
Edward 'Bugs' Dooley unmasked.

Our Second Act now commencing with some long overdue *progress*, as the Rorkian Few, crammed into Rusty's Pierce-Arrow, hie themselves to the Beverly Hills Motel, wherein Sir Archie has promised his fellow fugitives sanctuary and a stoup or two of Rhenish in his suite on the third floor, it now falls to your humble n. to declare that the Few are not only on the move but *on the lam*, and might thus be collectively described as *lammisters*. In consequence, it behoves your n. to clarify the likely upshot of Bumbles McGee's recently issued vow, when he cholerically yoked together Rusty McGrew and his *compadres*, in the process obliquely alluding to our narrative's sub-theme, which treats with *the law of unintended consequences*, or, in a word, Fate.

For lo! where but a few short pages ago the Few were merely guilty of *crimes of the heart*,[1] they are now designated *compadres*, which is to say fully-fledged outlaws in the eyes of the Law, which, the proverbial blindness of Justice notwithstanding, may be considered a quality of sight conflatable with that of far-seeing Apollo. In other words, and at the risk of descending into legalese, those of the Few explicitly guilty of assisting Rusty McGrew in his tactical withdrawal from the Blue Phalarope are now

1 This appears to diminish the importance of *crimes of the heart*, although the emotionally intelligent Reader will likely consider such crimes to be the very stuff of which tragedy is made. Strictly speaking, however, crimes involving the heart only qualify as illegal on those occasions when graverobbers plunder corpses and liberate said organs for the purpose of medical dissection, voodoo ceremony, cannibalism, pagan sacrifice, *&c.*

accountable under the heading of *aiding and abetting* our anti-hero in his flight from justice, and thus considered actionable as *accessories after the fact*.

The evidence is as follows:

Vanessa Hopgood, being Rusty McGrew's subterfugial troth-plight, is immediately designated a gangster's *moll;*[2]

Cordelia de Havilland was spotted supplying Rusty McGrew with the double-barrelled Remington derringer 'muff pistol' he brandished atop the banquette;

Adele Fitzhalligon was o'erheard providing Rusty McGrew with crucial intelligence pertaining to the dressing-room trapdoor;

Sir Archie was observed bowling teapot googlies at the serge-clad ranks in direct contravention of those legal provisions specifically designed to prevent the obstruction of justice;

Bartley McGuffin, despite refraining from offering advice, ordnance or succour, and partaking in Archie's last-ditch defence of the banquette only to the extent of cheering those googlies which resulted in a direct hit, is ne'ertheless *guilty by association*.

And so to the Beverly Hills Motel:

Your humble n. having slipped, wraithlike, into Archie's suite of rooms on the third floor, he now peeps through the crack between bathroom door and jamb at our merry band of scofflaws, who currently chaffer and coo like doves who have narrowly escaped a weasel's clutches by tunnelling out of dovecot by way of trapdoor, albeit said dissonant musicality is largely drowned out by Rusty McGrew adopting a Groton tenor as he communicates, by telephone, and employing nautical code, the full extent of the disaster at the Blue Phal to his most senior subaltern, Redser McGrew. To wit:

'It's all ahoo, Brother Mariner Two! The infernal swab raked us

2 A colloquial term denoting a woman of loose morals, and commonly deployed to describe a gangster's girlfriend, or partner-in-crime, 'moll' is derived from the notorious Fleet Street thief Moll Cutpurse, aka Mary Frith (1584-1659), from whom the immortal Defoe's heroine adopted her *nom-de-guerre* in *Moll Flanders* (1722).

aloft and boarded with all hands and laid on handsome. Spread every stitch of sail she'll bear and crack on like smoke and oakum, neglecting not to beat to quarters!'

'Rusty, dearest?' murmurs Vanessa as Rusty replaces the telephone receiver. 'We're in society now. Be so kind as to moderate your language.'

'It's my understanding,' says Adele Fitzhalligon, 'that Rusty is paraphrasing the immortal Tertullian, who was of the opinion, if you'll excuse my excessive italicisation, that *Qui fugiebat rursus proeliabitur*, i.e., *He who has fled will do battle again.* Which is to say, Rusty is departing the jurisdiction forthwith, and is prepared to defend his right to the pursuit of happiness with extreme prejudice, if necessary.'

'Thank you, Adele,' says Vanessa in a tone evocative of the Coleridgean frost performing its secret ministry, 'but I am deeply sensible of Rusty's meaning. I am concerned only that Sir Archibald remains abreast of events. Archie?'

'Wotcher, old harpsichord!' sings out Archie in distracted timbre, our noble knight being elsewise engaged in haranguing his batman Bartley McGuffin into drumming up a Balthazar of top fizz for the slaking of his guests' thirst, with the consequence that his persiflage is somewhat lacking in —

'Oh I *am* sorry,' says Cordelia de Havilland, it being the case that your humble n. was so intent on recording the facts as they pertain to our Fate-ravaged lammisters that he neglected to notice Cordelia hieing her way to the bathroom to powder her nose, whereupon, having stepped inside, she discovers that the facilities are already occupied by a craggily handsome gallant, who is now engaged in pressing his fingertips to the bathroom door's jamb as if assessing it for cracks and splintering resulting from a recent earthquake, if any such had occurred, which is by no means the case. 'I didn't realise,' says Cordelia as she commences reversing, 'that the bathroom was occupied.'

'Quite alright.'

Here, alas, Cordelia pauses in her reversing. 'If you don't mind my asking,' says she, 'who *are* you?'

'Just the, ah, you know. Room service.'

'Room service?' Here Cordelia advances again, shutting the bathroom door behind her and gazing upon our gallant in a manner not unakin to that of the Basilisk of Cyrene, as first reported by the immortal Pliny the Elder. 'Shouldn't you be wearing a uniform?'

'Not at all. An easy mistake to make, as it happens. We're rather informal here at the Beverly Hills Motel.'

'I see. And might one be so bold as to enquire as to what service, exactly, you are providing?'

'Oh, just a general tidy-up. Towels and so forth. You wouldn't believe how prickly people get when the soap isn't in the dish. May I be of any particular assistance, madam?'

'A little privacy would be most welcome, if such were possible.'

'Ah.'

'So I can powder my nose.'

'Of course.'

'Any time around now would be good.'

'That goes without saying.'

'And yet you remain.'

'Yes, well. Having entered the bathroom through the suite adjacent, and somehow contrived to lock the door, I would now be obliged to exit through Sir Archibald's suite, this in direct contravention of the Beverly Hills Motel policy that staff are never visible to guests.'

'But I have already seen you.'

'That is correct, madam. However, and technically speaking, you are the guest of a guest.'

'Very true.'

'Moreo'er, as Sir Archibald failed to register your presence at Reception, instead hustling his party up the back stairs more commonly employed for emergency exit in the case of fire, you are – again, a technical point – not actually here, at least according to the relevant statute legislation.'

'In which case,' observes Cordelia de Havilland, 'and legally speaking, it is impossible for me to see you.'

'Precisely.'

'Or, by way of corollary, for you to see me.'

'Quite so.'

'And thus we achieve impasse.'

'Or would, were either of us actually here. And now, if I may paraphrase the immortal Marvell, Time's wingèd chariot is hurrying near, and yonder all before us lie deserts of vast —'

'Not so ~~vast~~ fast. Don't I *know* you?'

'I don't think so, madam. I would undoubtedly have remembered meeting such a uniquely stunning —'

'The Blue Phal,' says Cordelia, with a rather nifty snap of her fingers. 'You were skulking around our banquette tapping a toe to the hot jazz.'

'Hardly, madam. I have been on duty since —'

'And you were wandering around the terrace of the Musso & Frank Grill earlier this afternoon, if I'm not very much mistaken. I wasn't aware,' says Cordelia, 'that they require much by way of soap in the dishes served on the terrace of the Musso & Frank Grill.'

'You are mistook, madam. It is simply the case that I have one of those faces which is easily confused with —'

Here, howe'er, Cordelia de Havilland, having rooted in her diamante Dior clutch, flourishes the notebook in which, being a bestselling and critically acclaimed author, she is frequently to be observed noting events of interest with her slim gold pencil; and, having silenced our mysterious gallant with said flourish, and leafed back a page or two, she now proceeds to read aloud some samples of same.

'*Scruffy bugger*,' says she. '*Jug ears. The eyes of a young marsupial recently dropped on its head. Face like a bletted medlar*.' Here she pauses. 'Shall I go on?'

'Bletted medlar?' says our gallant, who, as the Reader will readily conceive courtesy of Cordelia's jottings, is in fact Edward 'Bugs'

Dooley, whom your n. previously neglected to mention was also observing the doings and sayings of the Few through the very same crack between bathroom door and jamb as was your n., which belated revelation now obliges your humble n. to state that Bugs, having previously referred to the *garret* wherein he composed, is in fact living the high life on Samuel L. Silverstein's dime, it being Bugs' first order of business, on being commissioned to knock out a motion picture photoplay adapted from *The Pilgrim's Progress*, to take a suite at the Beverly Hills Motel and charge same to Silverstein Studios, Bugs being as one with Tristram Shandy in said worthy's opinion that *the periwig maketh the man*, providing, for the purpose of the foregoing, we might conflate a man's periwig with a luxurious third-floor suite furnished with Queen Anne bed and *escritoire*, upon which latter an aspiring scribe might place his Underwood. Indeed, had your n. e'er mastered the art of bilocation, which he has not, it was in said suite that Bugs Dooley might have been observed some minutes previously, Bugs having hightailed it from the Blue Phalarope in the moments previous to Bumbles McGee's raid clutching a sheaf of hastily scribbled notes gleaned from Toots 'Fata' Morgana, albeit our observing of Bugs would have amounted to a literary hill of beans, Bugs being at the time exclusively engaged in glancing in despair from blank page to hastily scribbled notes, and from scribbled notes to the one-page treatment for Act One he had dashed off earlier that afternoon, and hence, still despairing, back to the blank page again. Thus it was that Bugs, being wholly bereft of *mot juste*, and thus dwelling, as did immortal Aeschylus' Agamemnon, *twixt woe and woe*, discovered himself hearkening to the *pipes and timbrels* erupting in Sir Archie's adjacent suite, and, being as naturally curious as any writer, and, for that matter, as easily distracted, crept into the bathroom his suite shares with the adjacent suite and commenced peeking into Archie's rooms, in which activity Bugs was surprised by Cordelia de Havilland, who now, on being queried as to the precise definition of a bletted medlar as it applies to his physiognomy, delivers same.

'A bletted medlar,' says Cordelia, 'is a fruit softened after the ripening process, which renders it especially mushy.'

'A tad harsh, no?'

'Well, it's a note, a first impression in need of refinement, perhaps. But you cannot deny the essential accuracy.'

'Of the physical description? No. But that only leads me to believe you have encountered my twin brother, Herbert.'

'Twice,' says Cordelia, 'in the same evening?'

'Ah. I see I have neglected to mention Farquhar, the first-born triplet.'

'An implausible scenario,' says the de Havilland, who, as a bestselling and critically acclaimed author of such tomes as *For Whom the Belles Toll* and *A Man of Infinite Geste*, is preternaturally sensitive in the matter of narrative logic and credibility – 'I say, sir, an implausible scenario, not least because triplets do not generally jaunt around and about sporting an identical soup stain on the very same spot just below the half-Windsor knot in their ties. Such being irrefutably the case,' says she, snapping the elastic of her notebook to create an audible punctuation to the foregoing, 'we must now enquire as to the true identity of our jug-eared skulker. Or shall I alert our friend Rusty McGrew to the presence of a Bureau agent lurking in his bathroom?'[3]

'Sir Archibald's bathroom, technically speaking.'

'I imagine, in the heat of the moment, the distinction will be lost on Mr McGrew.'

The implicit threat in the foregoing passes by Bugs Dooley like the idle wind, which he respects no more than did Brutus in his prime; but when Cordelia renders her threat considerably more explicit by placing a forefinger against her temple and subsequently cocking her thumb as if it were the hammer of a pistol about to descend upon imaginary firing pin, Bugs discovers himself obliged

3 Colloquially known as 'the Bureau', the Bureau of Investigation was initially established in 1908 by President Theodore Roosevelt under the auspices of Napoleon Bonaparte's grandnephew, Attorney General Charles Bonaparte, in the wake of the assassination of President William McKinley (1843-1901), who was foully murdered by the Ohian anarchist Leon Czolgosz in Buffalo, NY.

to register his umbrage, if only on principle. 'Madam,' says he in severious tenor, 'you forget yourself!'

'Pardon me?'

'I said, *Ms de Havilland*, that you forget yourself.'

'I'm afraid you are sorely mistook, sir. I am Felicia Fortesque, confidante and boon companion to —'

'Tell it to the Marines, sister.'

There being no Marines present, Cordelia now states her intention to protest Bugs' erroneous familiarity in the strongest possible terms.

'Stand not upon your punctilios, madam!' says Bugs. 'Are you, or are you not, the bestselling and critically acclaimed author Cordelia de Havilland, currently masquerading as Felicia Fortesque in order to deceive Rusty McGrew and Vanessa Hopgood and thus plunder their Volstead-defying experiences for the purpose of researching your next opus?'

Does Cordelia colour, dear Reader? Does she blush, a hand flying to her breast to mask her confusion? She does not. For lo! said hand goes rooting in the diamante Dior clutch again, this time emerging with the double-barrelled Remington derringer of the calibre .41 rimfire short she had retrieved from Rusty McGrew just as soon as the Few were clear of the Phal, this according to Polonius' sage advice in the matter of borrowing and lending, and Cordelia being loath to lose either muff pistol or Rusty as a friend, or, as would very likely have been the case had Rusty neglected to return same, both.

'Lor!' says Bugs, who has quite failed to anticipate this contingency.

'Do you shudder?' says the de Havilland, advancing across the bathroom. 'Do you tremble in anticipation of your being imminently scragged?'

'Madam, I do not.'

'Then why do you quiver like a quail in Aspen?'

'Aspic, surely?'

'Ah,' says Cordelia, advancing another yard or three across the spacious bathroom, 'you would not contradict me had you ever been to Aspen for shooting season. Imagine, if you will, how quiveringly a quail might behave were it to fly down and perch upon the top branch of an aspen, a tree so notorious for its flimsy resistance to external pressures that it is classified *Populus tremuloides*, the Quaking Aspen.'

'Handsomely done,' says Bugs, who is only now belatedly realising that Cordelia de Havilland, being a bestselling and critically acclaimed novelist, might prove something of a useful ally in Bugs' interminable siege of the blank white page.

'Thank you,' says Cordelia, her miniature equalizer pointing directly at Bugs' beezer. 'But if you are not trembling at the prospect of your being imminently cooled off, why the localised shivering?'

'That's not so much me as the building in general.'

'The building?'

'My money's on an earthquake or a hot-shoe shuffle party in the basement. The Beverly Hills Motel being a reputable establishment,' says Bugs as the bathroom veers nor'-by-nor'-west and the ceiling caves in, 'I'd suggest it's the former. Blame it on the bellhop.'

Here, alas, your humble n. is obliged to intrude upon our narrative yet again, it being likely the case that the attentive Reader, having been informed only a few short pages ago that Bugs Dooley could be observed gazing forlornly at his Underwood and grasping in vain after e'en a single *mot juste*, might now wonder at Bugs' rather implausibly smooth expositionary reverie, and, further, find herself at a loss to understand how Bugs, who was until very recently closeted in his third-floor suite, might be *au fait* with topical events occurring at the tectonic level, all of which your n. reluctantly attributes to the presence of Cordelia de Havilland, who, in addition to her multi-faceted role as boon companion, *spy in the house of love* and bestselling and critically acclaimed author, must now also be considered Calliope's representative on earth, i.e.,

Bugs' muse.[4]

'Sir,' says the de Havilland, nimbly dodging a chunk of masonry before drawing herself up to her full height (5'10" in heels and cloche hat) and quivering to a quail-in-Aspen extent only partially attributable to the tiled floor giving a passable impression of a drunk blancmange going over Angel Falls, 'I simply refuse to believe that any bellhop has the capacity to engineer a natural disaster of this magnitude. What *is* the magnitude, by the way?'

'Roughly IX-point-two on the modified Mercalli scale.'

'Then it is ridiculous to suggest that any menial employed in the hospitality sector could —'

'You are mistook, madam. I allude specifically to the bellhop Barnaby Karlsson, who was partaking of a crafty gasper by the window on the second return as Sammy & Co. went biffing up the back stairs. Said party travelling at pace, and Barnaby being a minor character who was by no means foreshadowed, and was further shadowed by the floor-length velvet curtains he was lurking behind, he likely escaped your notice as you went pootling by lickety-split.'

'Yes?' says the de Havilland, neatly sidestepping a wayward two-by-four as it goes whizzing by close enough to bury a splinter in her marcelled 'do'. 'And?'

'Barnaby's is a pitiable case,' says Bugs, visibly warming to his theme, 'Barnaby being the first son of second-generation Swedish immigrants, whose father, Henrik, succumbed to a touch of lung not two years hence, Barnaby's father being a fireman and said touch of lung being a direct consequence of smoke inhalation suffered during those evening hours when he relieved the stress of his daytime endeavours by inhaling opiates by the pipeful in that labyrinth of sybaritic pleasure known collectively, to non-Asians, as Chinatown. As a result, Barnaby, despite his tender years, is his

4 This is surely a matter of conjecture. Calliope being the muse of epic poetry, and Bugs being engaged in writing a motion picture photoplay, it is equally likely that his particular muse might be Erato (love poetry), Melpomene (tragedy) or Euterpe (lyric poetry and flutes).

family's only breadwinner, and solely responsible for the welfare of his mother, three sisters, and a young brother who appears to have contracted polio, although the Karlsson family are so fiscally pressed that an authoritative diagnosis of same remains beyond their slender means.'

'All very tragic, of course, but I quite fail to —'

'Young Barnaby, madam, is entirely dependent on tips for his livelihood. Which is to say, Barnaby earns his potatoes by guiding the Beverly Hills Motel's residents to their rooms. And when a considerable smattering of said residents, and especially a citizenry that appears to Barnaby's eye to be particularly flush in the matter of potatoes, goes biffing up the back stairs and thus gypping Barnaby out of his natural entitlement, young Barnaby gets the hump.'

'Perfectly reasonable, and please remind me to bestow upon Barnaby a fin before we depart. But what I fail to understand is how a bellhop could —'

'Well, Barnaby stamped his foot.'

'And that caused an earthquake?'

'Don't be ridiculous,' says Bugs. 'The stamping caused a dime to slip out of the hole in the sole of Barnaby's shoe, which is where Barnaby keeps his tips, this because Barnaby's fellow bellhops are a larcenous crew such as a man wouldn't trust as far as he might toss a baby elephant up a spiral staircase. And it was when Barnaby gazed down upon the dime where it lay upon the carpet that he hit upon a wheeze.'

'Wheeze?'

'Or caper, if you prefer,' says Bugs, who has by now slipped into a veritable ecstasy of expositionary reverie. 'Barnaby, you see, and despite – or perhaps because of – his family's straitened circumstances, is in the habit of brightening the drab lives of his three sisters by treating them to a matinee picture show on the last Saturday of every month. Thus it was that Barnaby recognised the ineffably luminous star of the silver screen, Vanessa Hopgood, as she went shimmering up the back stairs. Further, Barnaby being understandably keen to advance his prospects, our young bellhop devotes his lunch hour not to throwing craps in the back alley, as do his less ambitious peers, but to reading the broadsheet blats left behind by the Beverly Hills Motel's guests, the better to remain abreast of the latest developments in politics, economics and international affairs that concern the largely middle-class readership of said blats. Rusty McGrew,' says Bugs, holding up a forefinger to forestall Cordelia's imminent interjection, 'being the very exemplar of the God-scourging wrath of God that constitutes said readership's worst nightmares, it was but the work of a moment with young Barnaby to realise that the party gone hotfooting it up the back stairs had much to hide, and that reward and tips aplenty might well shower down upon him from gendarmes and fourth estate alike if Barnaby was to give the old *focum* a rattling good *excitandum*, as it were.'

'So Barnaby took the dime laying upon the carpet …'

'… and dropped it. Correct. With the result that the Beverly Hills Motel now shudders to its foundations in consequence of a combination of tectonic joust and its being surrounded by a flat-footed company of Bumbles McGee's finest serge-clad Boys, whose previous ordnance of knobkerries *et al* have been replaced with rather more lethal examples of same, i.e., pistols, pineapples and Chicago Pianos of varying design, Bumbles being, if I may paraphrase the Bard, *fractious for redress* given his recent humiliation at the Blue Phalarope.'

'Hmmm,' says Cordelia.

'Your tone, madam, hints at incredulity.'

'Well, I find myself more than somewhat disconcerted,' says Cordelia, 'with the depth and breadth of your knowledge relating to recent events. Indeed, one might go so far as to say, if one were a bestselling author prone to lapse into trade-speak, that you appear to be possessed of a quality of first-person omniscient that can only be described as Victorian.'

'You are too kind, madam. Alas, I am but Dante being guided by Virgil, if for the purpose of comparison we might equate

Cordelia de Havilland with Virgil and yours truly with the callow scribe stumbling along in his wake.'

Here Cordelia finally colours, and blushes, and her hand flies to her breast, with the unfortunate consequence – said hand being the one gripping the double-barrelled Remington derringer 'muff pistol' – of sending a .41 calibre round skimming vertically past her aquiline nose to bury itself in the ceiling, thus dislodging a number of ceiling tiles, which now cascade down in a flurry of ceramic shards, splinters and dust.

Cordelia now finding herself so distracted by the necessity for picking splinters out of her marcelled 'do' that she neglects to satisfactorily proceed to the logical conclusion of the foregoing, it falls to your humble n. to confirm what the Reader has undoubtedly begun to suspect due to Bugs' apparently miraculous revelations pertaining to minor characters, tectonic activity and Bumbles McGee's strategic intentions, all of which implies that Bugs is possessed of what the Bard was once pleased to describe as *the poet's eye, in a fine frenzy rolling, glancing from heaven to Earth, from Earth to heaven*, and *an imagination which bodies forth the forms of things unknown, and gives to airy nothing a local habitation and a name* – I say, it would appear that Bugs Dooley is no ordinary author, if any author might be considered ordinary, but our Author, and that the origins of our narrative might be discovered in the brief treatment delivered by Bugs to Samuel L. Silverstein and George P. Dangleberry III early this afternoon on the terrace of the Musso & Frank Grill as an outline for his proposed motion picture adaptation of *The Pilgrim's Progress*, albeit, given Bugs' considerable issues with the immortal Bunyan's language, pacing and an over-dependence on religiously inspired allegory, an adaptation suitably tailored for a Jazz Age audience.

Here, it being akin to a schoolboy error for an Author to allow one of his characters to glimpse their Creator during the creative process, your n. begs the Reader's indulgence on behalf of Bugs, this on the basis that our tale is not only Bugs' maiden voyage into uncharted waters, but a first draft of same. Further, it is hoped that the Reader will not judge Bugs too harshly in the matter of the momentary lapse in concentration that allowed Cordelia to catch him unawares in the bathroom of Sir Archie's suite at the Beverly Hills Motel, for Bugs might be considered unlucky not to be discovered by Archie, say, or Adele Fitzhalligon, or any other character who might well have accepted Bugs' *bona fides* as an non-uniformed member of the Beverly Hills Motel's janitorial staff, but was instead discovered by Cordelia de Havilland, who possesses that sixth sense common to all bestselling and critically acclaimed novelists and which invariably alerts said scribes to any and all narrative anomalies that suggests they have *stepped through the looking-glass* into another writer's yarn.

'But the earthquake,' says Cordelia, who, having divested herself of all splinters and stowed the gat in the diamante Dior clutch whilst Bugs was waxing lyrical about his being possessed of a *poetical eye in fine frenzy rolling, &c.*, now returns to the fray. 'It's *your* doing?'

'Well, it would be immodest to claim *all* credit,' says Bugs. 'Truly, I am but a conduit through whom the celestial promptings flow to —'

'Gallop post o'er the particulars, sirrah! Did you or did you not precipitate an earthquake?'

'Well, with Bumbles and his myrmidons surrounding the Beverly Hills Motel, a ruse was required. A diversion, if you will, to allow Rusty and his fellow lammisters to access Archie's rented touring car and depart with all haste in the direction of the nearest sunset, lest our fugitives discover themselves clapped in irons and languishing in some inconvenient brig and our tale come screeching to an abrupt conclusion before the resolution desired, which is to say, with everyone just getting along.'

'Scandalous,' says Cordelia.

'Pardon me?'

'Well, it is rather a waste, is it not? Of resources, I mean. An entire earthquake of the magnitude of roughly IX-point-two on the modified Mercalli scale simply to facilitate a powdering out?

And that's before we consider the authorial morality of employing a *deus ex machina*.'

'Madam,' says Bugs, 'I fully accept your Aristarchian critique in the spirit it is intended. Furthermore, I applaud your Aristotelian rectitude in the matter of narrative purity. Howe'er, having peeked through the gap between what is left of the bathroom door and its splintered frame while you were delivering yourself of same, I am honour-bound to inform you that your erstwhile compadres have had it on their toes.'

'The coprolites!'

'Quite so. Shall we join them?'

'But how?'

'If you would be so kind as to take my hand, madam, I will endeavour to extricate us from our perilous position to one decidedly more advantageous to us both.'

'Like so?' says Cordelia, taking the hand now offered by Bugs.

'Just so,' says Bugs.

Here, and despite their imminent peril, your n. is obliged to pause in order to note the electrical charge which ensues when flesh presses flesh and sparks a smouldering chemistry between the parties of the first and second parts, if electricity might be considered a catalyst in a chemical reaction, which detail your n. will need to research further at a more propitious time in order to establish the facts to his own and the Reader's satisfaction, and especially if the Reader is more knowledgeable about the sciences than those citizens who read fiction to the exclusion of all else tend to be.

Further, your n. states that any Reader expecting Bugs Dooley to dematerialise into the aether like unto Creusa fading from Aeneas's sight into the insubstantial air is likely to be disappointed, for while a narrator may on occasion adopt the persona of an author, the corollary is by no means inverse. Which is to say that, while an author might, and particularly when employing the first-person narrative mode, seek to conflate the roles of author and narrator, the better to persuade the Reader of a tale's emotional and psychological verisimilitude, an author may be deplored a fribble of the first estate should she claim to have mastered the wraithlike drifting of any narrator worth his or her salt.

Thus, having taken Cordelia by the hand, and noted with some interest the electrical charge ensuing, Bugs Dooley stands not upon the order of his going from the collapsing bathroom, but hoists the de Havilland aloft and dumps her down the laundry chute situated between bath and bidet, then executes a passable forward dive with one-and-a-half pike as he plunges in her wake, thus departing the bathroom in the very instant before the ceiling, weakened by tremors, aftershocks and a wayward .41 calibre round, finally collapses in what Cordelia de Havilland or Bugs Dooley, being authors *in esse* and *in posse*, respectively, and were they still present and capable of observation and detailed articulation, might well have described as *a blazing conflagration*; but, as they are not, our *procès-verbal* here ceases, to be taken up again in Chapter Fifteen.

Chapter Fifteen

Archie misplaces his car keys. A further digression, in which is explored the difficulties involved in the striking of bulls' posteriors with banjos.

Alas, dear Reader, it would be paltering with the truth to declare that all went subsequently to plan, if by *plan* we might be understood to mean the hastily confected scheme Bugs doped out whilst travelling at pace down the laundry chute in the perpendicular style, and which might be condensed as follows: Bugs and Cordelia, newly liberated from the collapsing Beverly Hills Motel, sneak into the rumble seat of Archie's rented Locomobile Sportif just as the Rorkian Few make good their escape, leaving Bumbles McGee and his serge-clad myrmidons to no more productive an evening than they might derive from scratching their collective mazzard and shaking their fists at the sky in impotent fury.

Indeed, said ingenious ploy comes unhorsed at the first fence, despite Bugs engineering the perfect conditions for the Few's powdering out, i.e., a diversionary earthquake combined with the stationing of Archie's Sportif directly across the road from the Beverly Hills Motel and already facing north on the only stretch of asphalt within a one-mile radius not newly warped and deeply riven with miniature ravines.

Such being the case, the Reader may not easily conceive why the Few fail to skedaddle whilst subjecting Bumbles McGee to the old Bronx razoo. The matter is susceptible to ready explanation, it being the case that Archie, being so sick with the old incurable for

Vanessa Hopgood *as to have trouble locating carpet with the soles of his brogues*, has, in his hasty departure from Suite 301 of the Beverly Hills Motel, omitted to carry with him the Sportif's keys.

That the snide observation italicised in the foregoing comes courtesy of Bartley McGuffin's muttered aside to Adele Fitzhalligon suggests that Bartley, like the Player Queen, doth protest too much, for Archie tends to delegate to Bartley on all matters automotive, from such trifling concerns as ignition keys and insurance to the more pressing issues of bribing highway policemen sored up at the illegally rapid rate of the Sportif's progress, which abdication of responsibility is a necessary consequence of Archie being lit up like the Fourth of July from his breakfast mimosa onwards, and why Archie is generally to be discovered, whilst in transit, perched on his knees in the Sportif's rear seat with his face in the breeze and tongue a-loll.

Thus it is that, as Bugs and Cordelia arrive in the Sportif's dickie, the discourse prevailing might be best described as that of multiple citizens simultaneously embarked upon rancorous velitation, with Rusty particularly keen to establish whether it was Archie's intention all along to make minstrels of his fellow lammisters, which enquiry, Sir Archie being a true *chevalier*, and were his hands not elsewise engaged in vainly patting his pockets for absent keys, would likely have caused Archie to bite his thumb at Rusty McGrew, which would, in turn, have left Rusty with no option but to send his friends to wait upon Archie's and demand satisfaction.

Indeed, the mood inside the Sportif being conflatable with the disposition of Mr Ty Cobb on the occasion of the Georgia Peach waking up with a gin hangover on the morning after the Babe knocked a walk-off homer out of the park in the bottom of the 12th, your n. confesses himself somewhat relieved to execute the cinematic convention of *a reverse dolly* away from the Sportif, whereupon we *pan across the street* to where Jonjo McGubbins, aka one of the LAPD's most fearsome myrmidons, may be observed casting about for something very like the sight of a strolling doll who might be impressed by the dimensions of the impressive Chicago Piano cradled in Jonjo's arms, by which expedient does Jonjo belatedly observe the Few playing hunt-the-keys in the Sportif across the way.

'Here,' says Jonjo to his comrade-in-arms Reggie Blenkinsop, who is casting about for possibly the very same doll and likely for the very same reasons, albeit Reggie is casting sou'-west, 'ain't that Rusty yonder?'

'Well, I'll be,' says Reggie, although precisely what it is Reggie is about to declare himself is lost to posterity when Rusty, catching the collective eye of the staring Jonjo and Reggie, realises any hope of a subterfugial powder is currently steaming at pace for the source of the Swanee.

'We are had by the hip!' halloos Rusty in nautical timbre, and he outs with the old equalizer – i.e., prevails upon the recently arrived Cordelia de Havilland to once again loan him the Remington derringer of the calibre .41 rimfire short, along with any additional ammunition rattling around in her diamante clutch – and discharges both barrels in the general direction of Jonjo and Reggie without so much as an on-your-marks; and, boys being boys, and guns being guns, it is no time at all before the street is a perfect bedlam of *bang-bangs!*, *rat-a-tat-tats!*, *pe-ows!* and *ka-zings!* Indeed, the ferocity of the hail of fire laid down is such that the Sportif would have swiftly discovered itself perforated like unto jailhouse dartboard were Bumbles McGee's myrmidons not so keenly honed for action that, when the cry halloo went up, they paused not to enquire where away, but let fly in whatever direction they happened to be facing, hence the prevalence of ricochets, aka *pe-ows!* and *ka-zings!*, for Bumbles had previously ordered that the blazing Beverly Hills Motel be surrounded, in consequence of which most of his myrmidons commenced firing into billowing clouds of thick black smoke, and striking only solid concrete, the inevitable result of which was that most of the errant rounds redounded upon their fellow gendarmes, and not to their credit, which *friendly fire* is the cause of much swearing of coarse oaths, serge-clad warriors falling down mortally stricken, and a rapidly evaporating mutual regard in the ranks.

Meanwhile, Rusty being something of a Renaissance man, he simultaneously reloads his duke, reminds his fellow lammisters that now is the time for all good men to rally around, and glances aft to ensure no federales have snuck into the baggage train, which is how he belatedly comes to glimpse, through the billowing pall of thick black smoke swirling around and about, Bugs Dooley in the dickie.

'It is my firm belief, sir,' says Rusty, aiming the muff pistol at Bugs' beezer, 'that we have yet to be formally introduced.'

Your n. here assuming that the Reader has never found herself on the business end of a muff pistol, and particularly one being waggled in so menacingly a fashion by a bootie reputed crueller than Mezentius of Etruria scorning the gods in mid-April, he now implores the Reader to do all in her power to avoid said circumstance lest she discover herself discommoded, as is Bugs Dooley in the scenario under advisement, by a constriction of larynx and severe case of gummy tongue, and thus, finding herself unable to speak, in dire danger of being twice perforated with ordnance of the calibre .41 rimfire short.

'He's with me,' pipes up the de Havilland.

'Such is apparent to all,' says Rusty in snarling timbre. 'Alas, I remain entirely ignorant as to his identity, and thus concerned he may be a fifth columnist in the pay of Bumbles McGee.'

'Edward 'Bugs' Dooley, sir, at your disposal,' croaks Bugs, Cordelia's interjection having provided him with sufficient opportunity to work a little moisture in between tongue and roof of mouth.

'A motion picture photoplay writer,' clarifies the de Havilland, 'fresh in from Chicago, and a *bona fide* expert, as are all full-grown males from the Windy City, when it comes to the hot-wiring of engines which remain stubbornly cold and silent for the want of an ignition key.'

'Ah,' says Rusty, snapping off a brace of slugs in the general direction of the gendarmes lest they believe he is too busy in scouring the Sportif's interior for a white flag to keep up his end. 'Welcome aboard, Bugs. Come on up and take the tiller.'

Here the de Havilland plants an elbow in Bugs Dooley's ribs, an affectionate jab intended to convey a collegiate pleasure at his initiation into the Few. It is with a growing sense of dread, howe'er, that Bugs clambers out of the dickie into the Sportif's rear seat, so-sorrying and begging-your-pardon as he goes, for the Sportif, while undoubtedly one of the roomiest touring cars on the market, was never designed to allow unimpeded passage from stern to bow, and particularly when stuffed to the gunwales with loogans, chorus dolls, motion picture stars and sozzled aristocrats. Thus it is considerably more than the work of a moment – and yet, for all that, rather too soon for comfort – before Bugs finds himself hunched under the Sportif's hood and goggling in bemused fashion at a six-cylinder puzzle wrapped in an enigma, the sensation of dread now salted with considerable agitation as those enraged federales still standing, and one or two from a prone position, lay down *a withering hail of white-hot lead.*

Nervous to begin with, for Bugs, as is generally the case with authors, is predisposed to the solitary life, and thus uncomfortable with meeting too many new people all in one go, and especially when such citizens are fictional creations sprung, like unto Athena from the divine mazzard of Zeus, from Bugs' own synaptical cracklings – I say, Bugs is feeling a tad fretful as he contemplates the Sportif's six-cylinder engine, not least because Rusty McGrew's voice has grown hoarse with the effort of denouncing Bugs as a *prevaricating phonus bolonus* o'er the cacophonous racket generated by the gendarmes, the more excitable of whom have graduated from tossing lead to lobbing pineapples,[1] with the result that any man with his head beneath the hood of a Locomobile Sportif would be hard pressed to distinguish between localised explosions

1 A colloquial term, here deployed as slang for grenades rather than the $50 note, the otherwise admirable members of the LAPD not being renowned for any great enthusiasm when it comes to heaving cash money in the direction of the public.

and earthquake aftershocks, and particularly when his immediate locale is cavernous enough to serve as an echo chamber. Thus it is that, when he feels a hand upon his shoulder, Bugs ascends in the vertical style to rattle the old parietal off the underside of the hood and returns to *terra firma* seeing stars of such a multitude as to plunge Copernicus into a post-season funk.

'Bugs,' says the de Havilland – for lo! it is she – 'Rusty's of a mind to hand you the mitten. Crack on.'

'Absolutely,' says Bugs. 'No sooner said than done.'

'And yet,' says the de Havilland, after allowing a decent interval to elapse, during which Bumbles McGee can be heard bawling for the mortars to be brought up and Rusty McGrew declare himself fully persuaded in the matter of Bugs' inability to strike a bull's behind with a banjo – 'I say, and yet, here we still are.'

'Neatly observed, madam.'

'What seems to be the trouble?'

'Alas,' says Bugs, 'I am by no means familiar with the Locomobile Sportif's engine, this being a new-ish model and a six-cylinder beast.'

'I see,' says the de Havilland. 'But couldn't you just, you know …'

'I'm afraid not. These cylinder heads appear to be non-removable.'

'No, I mean,' and here the de Havilland tips Bugs the wink, '*you* know.'

'Ah,' says Bugs, as realisation belatedly dawns that the eyelash-batting refers to the earthquake he recently brewed up as diversionary ruse, by which Bugs is given to understand that Cordelia believes that any author, or Author, capable of rustling up a natural disaster of a magnitude roughly IX-point-two on the modified Mercalli scale should be able to make short work of hot-wiring a Locomobile Sportif, non-removable cylinder heads or no, which bloomer is largely a consequence of Cordelia being herself an author of epic sweeping romances, and thus rarely required to research such matters as tectonic activity and the hot-wiring of automobiles.

'I quite fail to understand,' says the de Havilland when Bugs puts her abreast of the foregoing, her tone sharp with just enough Coleridgean rime for Bugs to wonder if he shouldn't have accepted the mitten previously offered by Rusty McGrew in order to stave off frostbite, e'en if said mitten (singular, alas) was metaphorically intended. 'Are you seriously trying to tell me that a man who can rustle up an earthquake lacks the wherewithal to hot-wire a car?'

Bugs here conceiving that the electrically generated chemistry which previously sparked between he and Cordelia is in grievous danger of evaporating, if sparks might be said to evaporate, he now hastens to inform the de Havilland that knocking up a swift earthquake is considerably easier than, if he might employ Rusty's striking metaphor, the bashing of a bull's posterior with a banjo, for the latter depends heavily upon one's ability to persuade a steer to remain stationary, which is no mean feat, and particularly if any citizen has succumbed to the temptation (as some wag drawn to the vicinity of such exotic endeavour almost inevitably does) to pluck a string or two on said instrument, there being few sounds more likely to cause livestock to commence stampeding in emulation of the *Lemmus lemmus*, all of which must be taken under advisement, continues Bugs, e'en before we acknowledge the extent to which the circular-headed banjo is an object rather less than aerodynamically ideal when it comes to striking any target with any degree of accuracy, e'en if said target is as ample as a ruminant's posterior generally affords, with the caveat that said hindquarters tend to diminish in size the faster said ruminant is galumphing away from his banjo-wielding assailant. 'By contrast,' concludes Bugs, 'tectonic plates are so large and slow-moving that a diapered babe could manoeuvre them into adversarial conflict.'

'I am obliged to confess,' says the de Havilland, 'that I remain unclear as to how tormenting our bovine chums might be conflatable with hot-wiring a car.'

'Ah,' says Bugs. 'Well, hot-wiring a car, which involves frictionising two wires in order to create an ignitionary spark, is as tricky a scheme as the bull-and-banjo proposition, not least when any spark accruing may well pop a man in his iris, causing his already bruised parietal to encounter said automobile's hood in violent conjunction. And that, madam, is under circumstances we may describe as oojah-cum-spiff, as opposed to finding ourselves in circs closely resembling a re-enactment of Bull Run.'[2]

'Indeed,' says the de Havilland as a ricochet goes *pe-owing!* fore-and-aft through her marcelled coif. 'I've been meaning to broach that very topic.'

'Oh?'

'Some of us,' says she, jabbing a thumb in the direction of the Sportif's interior, 'and much as we hate to complain and so forth, being deeply sensible of the less than optimal conditions in which you are obliged to —'

'You appear to be standing upon your punctilios, madam.'

'Quite. Well, there have been murmurings, in fact I'd go so far as to say mutterings, about the quantity of potentially lethal ordnance buzzing about our ears, not to mention,' says she, poking a finger through the latest hole in her barnet, 'the occasional stray round which delivers a whole new centre parting.'

'Bally nuisance, what?'

'To say the very least,' says Cordelia. 'Which is why I was wondering, if it isn't too much trouble, if you could, you know ...'

'Ah,' says Bugs, as realisation glimmers toward matutinal awakening, 'I see. Sorry, old bean, but no can do. It's the plan, you see.'

'There's a plan?'

'There *was* a plan. The earthquake and so forth, and Rusty and the Rorkian Few engaged in tyre-smoking departure while Bumbles McGee and his serge-clad myrmidons shook their fists at the sky in impotent fury, *&c.* But then Archie forgot his keys and

2 The First Battle of Bull Run (July 21, 1861), which took place at Manassas in the early stages of the American Civil War, when Confederate forces comprehensively defeated their Union foes. Not to be confused with the Second Battle of Bull Run (August 28-30, 1862), also at Manassas, in which the Confederate forces again comprehensively defeated their Union foes.

the old scheme went awry and here we all are with *la vie* irrevocably *c'est*.'

'But I thought …'

'Speak up, old stick. Pineapples and whatnot going boom. Give the pipes a good airing.'

'Of course. It's just, well, *you* know.'

'Afraid not, old pipterino. The gist remains hieroglyphical, as it were.'

Now Cordelia de Havilland, as the Reader has no doubt already conceived, is a woman of many gifts, chief among them a talent for dissimulation to rival the combined efforts of all the Medici firm, so it should come as no surprise to learn that Cordelia is secreting a veritable mint of candles under her bushel (*cf.* Matthew 5:15), one of which now emerges, or so it seems to Bugs Dooley, as a lightning bolt, which is to say a right cross of the magnitude of roughly VII-point-four on the modified Mercalli scale, or, in layman's terms, sufficient to propel Al Panzer into the middle of next week.

It being the work of some several moments before Bugs subsequently peels himself off the asphalt and regains a more-or-less vertical footing in a manner the immortal Tennyson would likely have immediately identified as that of a man rising on the stepping-stones of his dead self to higher things, your n. here confirms that Bugs' recovery is by no means instantaneous. Indeed, the extent to which Bugs discovers himself possessed of a disorientating lively astonishment can be ascertained by the hallucination which presents itself o'er Cordelia's right shoulder, which apparition emerges from the thick black clouds of billowing smoke and takes the form of the genus *Ursus arctos horribilis*, i.e., grizzly bear, a rather impressive specimen about eight feet tall which has reared upon its hind legs the better to shamble across the street towards the Sportif with claws bared and jaws a-slaver.

'Lor!' says Bugs, said syllable being as much as he is capable of croaking before the de Havilland, not content with landing the aforementioned humdinger of a right cross, lays her hands on Bugs' shoulders and shakes him until his left tonsil winds up in the aural cavity of his right ear.

'Steady on, old brick,' says Bugs, albeit that, due to the unprecedented tonsil-ear rearrangement, his mild protestation may well have been couched in a more cutting tone than Bugs generally allows himself in the presence of a lady.

'Get! A! Grip!' bellows the de Havilland, punctuating each syllable with a smartly administered crack of palm to Bugs' left cheek. 'This is *your* story. If the old plan is scuppered, just make a new one, and preferably one in which I don't wind up on the sidewalk impersonating crushed pomegranate!'

'Roger that,' says Bugs, who is of the opinion, which the Reader likely shares, that Cordelia, despite resorting to brute force persuasion more often than he might prefer, is ne'ertheless displaying a rather impressive *sang-froid* at discovering herself a character in another author's yarn, which Bugs, and likely the Reader too, attributes to Cordelia's hard-earned experience of extricating her characters from a variety of dramatical scenarios in which they discover themselves in mortal peril. 'Howe'er,' continues Bugs, maintaining a watching brief on the grizz, which is still advancing, albeit in a curiously stiff fashion that suggests it has recently shipped a poker-shaped object up its fundament, 'it is nevertheless incontrovertible that if thrushes were wishes, beggars would eat birds.'

'Pardon me?'

'I make the point, old stickleback, that this is no longer my yarn, regardless of how we might desire the old circs to fall out contrary-wise. *My* tale is gone with the wind due to Archie forgetting his keys. Or not gone anywhere, with or without the assistance of favourable climactic conditions, if we're of a mind to be pedantic about it, which, from your squinted eye and clenching of fist, I can safely assume we're not. That's not to say,' Bugs hastens to add as Cordelia limbers up for another bout of pugilistic persiflage, 'that it might not become my story again.'

'How so?'

'Well, it would require a rather complex recalibration of —'

'Vast the punctilios, sirrah!'

'Fair enough. Basically, we need to catch up to where we're supposed to be and slip back into the original scheme.'

'We can do that?'

'In theory, certainly.'

'So what's the hold-up?'

'Well, these cylinder-heads appear to be non-removable, and unless we very quickly get the old Locomobile Sportif living up to the *mobile* element advertised in its title, ha-ha, we are likely to be soon overrun by Bumbles McGee's serge-clad hellions, providing yon grizz doesn't get us first.'

'Grizz?'

'I didn't mention the grizz?'

It is fervently hoped that the Reader is at this point fully persuaded of Cordelia's credentials, for said beazel is as redoubtable a Sheba as e'er strolled the leafy boulevards of Hollywood and environs, which is to say that your n. is of the opinion that Cordelia de Havilland is a bestselling and critically acclaimed author from whom the *Victory*'s beam, circa Trafalgar, could well have taken a correspondence course in the matter of stuff (stern). It being the case, howe'er, that e'en immortal Homer was prone to nod, your n. believes that Cordelia may be forgiven for momentarily falling out of character, it being the case that e'en the pillar formerly known as Lot's wife would likely have given vent to a decidedly salty oath had an *Ursa* (major) come rampaging up out of Sodom ablaze. Such now is the case with Cordelia, whose terrified shriek is not only entirely understandable in the context of human frailty and the survival instinct intrinsic to same, but has the unexpected benefit of so rattling Bugs Dooley's aural cavities that its effect on the previously errant tonsil is akin to that of a Sarn't-Major bawling a squaddie back into formation.

Howe'er, it is but the work of a moment for the momentary lapse to pass, as is a momentary lapse's wont, and Cordelia is soon returned to her more usual bobbish state. 'Bugs,' says she, adopting a tone specifically designed to remind Bugs that the word 'author' is derived from 'authority'.[3]

'Present and correct,' says Bugs.

'There's a grizzly bear crossing the road.'

'Bearing down on us, you might say, ha-ha.'

'It seems to be on wheels.'

'Do you say?' Being previously concerned only with the upper half of Old Smokey, which half boasts the aforementioned ursine claws and jaws a-slaver, Bugs now gives the lower half a good squint. 'Well, whaddya know? Castors, what?'

'It would appear,' says the de Havilland, 'that said grizz is in fact a stuffed animal requisitioned from the blazing lobby of the Beverly Hills Motel, and is currently being propelled in our direction by a number of serge-clad myrmidons using it for cover.'

'Damnably clever.'

'Quite. May I make a suggestion?'

'Have on, old *consigliere*, and spare not the horses.'

'Generally speaking, by which I mean always, the hot-wiring of a car takes place *inside* the automobile, and generally, by which I again mean always, in the vicinity of the steering column, where the wires which connect the ignition mechanism to the engine are to be found.'

'Ah.'

'Shall we adjourn inside?'

'That would probably be for the best.'

And so Bugs goes scrambling back inside the Locomobile Sportif and descends into the well wherein might be discovered the elusive wires which will, when brought together in suitably abrasive fashion, create the spark to set the Sportif's six cylinders a-roar, there to find Cordelia already *in situ* and generating the hoped-for spark with an impressively deft twitch, at which point

3 In fact, the word *author* is more likely derived from the Latin *augere*, i.e., to originate, to promote, which evolved into *auctor* in Old French and afterwards, being translated into 15th-century English, found itself conflated with *authentic*, in consequence of which it became synonymous for 'a person who invents or creates'.

the engine gives a rumble not unakin to that of tubercular pachyderm.

'Stab it and steer!' yodels the de Havilland from the depths, which is Rusty McGrew's cue to slot the Sportif into gear and *peel out with a tyre-smoking roar*, ~~leaving Bumbles McGee and assorted gendarmes to shake their fists at the sky in impotent fury, &c.~~, or would have been, had Bartley McGuffin remembered to gas up the Sportif the evening previous, which, alas, Bartley had not, Bartley at the time being elsewise engaged in ruminating upon his One True Work, which negligence, being the consequence of Bartley's pursuit of Art, Morality and Higher Purpose in the modest hope of enlightening the generations to come, may be considered a forgivable lapse by any Reader who wishes to be considered a *bona fide* citizen of the Republic of Letters.

That said, Bartley's inadvertent abnegation of the old feudal spirit, with the inevitable consequence of the Sportif's engine giving vent to a throaty cough and two backfires before conking out entirely, must also be considered in the context of our narrative's aspiration to be a tale of *progress*; further, Bartley's failure to gas up the Sportif results, as the Reader will undoubtedly conceive, in a discourse conducted in such salty Anglo-Saxon euphemisms as to make a mockery of our tale's philosophical proposition – i.e., *that the world might be a better place if only everyone would make a little more effort to get along* – which discourse has long since deteriorated to the point of Rusty McGrew declaring Bartley a jackanape *nonpareil* who fully deserves to be well tossed in a blanket, and calling for a show of hands in support of same, when lo! a Rolls Royce Silver Ghost comes a-purring up alongside, with none other than Samuel L. Silverstein at the helm.

'Ahoy-hoy!' sings out Sammy L. 'All aboard the Silverstein Ghost!'

The grateful Few standing not upon the order of their leaping from Sportif to Silver Ghost, but leaping as one, and thus pausing not to wonder how Samuel L. Silverstein comes a-purring up alongside their besieged Sportif just in the nick of time – Bumbles

McGee's myrmidons boarding the Sportif to starboard at the very moment the Few disembogue to port, said serge-clad warriors urged on by Bumbles' hoarsely bawled Yeatsian lament for the fallen, *viz.*, '*Did that play on words of mine send out / Certain men Rusty McGrew shot?*' – I say, the Few in their haste neglecting to clarify the hows and wherefores of Sammy L.'s transfiguration from motion picture mogul into knight in shining armour (albeit Sammy, as previously recorded, is garbed in the pongee sports shirt, well-tailored jodhpurs and leather puttees currently favoured by Hollywood's more sartorially inclined motion picture producers), your n. now reminds the Reader that Sammy was last observed outside the Blue Phalarope witnessing the Few's departure in the wake of the Phal being subjected to the myriad indignities of a raid, whereupon Sammy, despite being a Hollywood motion picture producer, conceived of an original idea, the details of which will be revealed in chapter the next, for Sammy L.'s Silver Ghost is currently trundling north out of Hollywood at a bone-shaking thirty miles per hour, pursued by castor-mounted bear, and your n. is loath to distract the Reader from the sight of what might well be considered, and not a moment too soon, to be the first meaningful instance of our pilgrims' *progress*.

Chapter Sixteen

Fresh calamities.

Rusty McGrew being a pimpernel *nonpareil* in the matter of extricating himself from circs of a parlous nature, it is the work of but several thousand moments before the Silver Ghost is purring along through the citrus-scented orange groves of rural California on a bearing nor'-nor'-east, *making like the waves towards the pebbled shore* (*cf.* the Bard) of Tropico Springs and Cordelia de Havilland's writing bolthole on the banks of Lake Tropico, whereupon, all going to Bugs' hastily confected Plan B, they will reconnect with the Few's destiny, i.e., the plot strand severed when Sir Archie left his car keys behind in Suite 301 of the Beverly Hills Motel, a disaster subsequently compounded by Archie's belated realisation that he has mistaken the car keys for Suite 301's room key, and will thus need to locate a post office in short order, the better to mail back the room key or face the appalling vista of being blackballed by the Californian Association of Motel Proprietors.

'Feeling peckish?' enquires the de Havilland.

'Moderately,' says Bugs, who is maintaining a watching brief on the rear-view mirror up front, wherein Rusty McGrew's hooded eyes are to be regularly observed darting daggers at our Author, for Rusty, having persuaded Sammy L. (a) that it is entirely demeaning for a mogul of Sammy's burnished reputation to be seen driving around and about *sans* chauffeur, and (b) that Rusty is a veteran of countless scramolas, has eased Sammy L. out of the driver's seat and is now to be discovered at the Silver Ghost's tiller.

'I don't think so,' says Cordelia as she goes rootling through the luncheon hamper lately discovered at her feet in the Ghost's dickie, this in consequence of Bugs enquiring as to whether bananas feature on ye olde bill of fayre. 'There's lobster, a cold chicken, tongue sandwiches, a nest of plovers' eggs, an insufficiency of Bollinger … yes,' says she, 'we have no bananas.'

'Pity.'

'Partial to a banana, are we?'

'Sunshine on the tongue, old *chef de partie*, a rich source of potassium and a marvellous source of slow-release energy. That said, the current passion for the Cavendish curve is based on the incontrovertible truth that there are few things less intimidating than a man with a banana in his hand, unless it's that very same man with a banana in both hands, and yours truly is currently keen to project an aura of biddable docility.'

'Why so?'

'Well,' says Bugs, 'unless I'm very much mistaken, Rusty McGrew is currently girding his loinal environs to take yours truly out for a good airing at his earliest convenience, which ventilation will very likely take the form of twin perforations of the mazzard administered by muff pistol at point blank range.'

'Surely not,' murmurs the de Havilland.

'See for yourself,' says Bugs, as the bushy-browed menace peeps from the reflective battlements once more. 'Well?'

'Eyes as cold,' confirms the de Havilland, 'as an Arctic hawk glimpsing a lone lemming limping toward the abyss.'

'Precisely.'

'Not to diminish the horrific prospect of your possible demise,' says the de Havilland, rootling again amidst the viands, 'but it occurs to me to wonder aloud about the extent to which your personal tragedy might impact upon those of us left behind.'

'Given your penchant for tightly plotted tales,' acknowledges Bugs, 'it was inevitable the foregoing would present itself for consideration.'

'Because,' continues Cordelia, 'and correct me if I'm wrong, but it seems to me as if your demise would very likely coincide with, and perhaps e'en precipitate, that of the Few at large.'

'Neatly grasped, old coffee bean.'

'In which case, and in *lieu* of bananas, a brace of chicken legs might answer.'

'Good thinking. Have on.'

The de Havilland being a woman with a prodigious capacity for fress, she now proceeds to treat the contents of the luncheon basket tolerably rough, while Bugs, being moderately peckish, as previously established, commences to gnaw upon one of the chicken legs Cordelia provides, thrusting the other aloft like unto Olympic torch whene'er the urge comes upon Rusty McGrew to *glut death's maw* (*cf.* Shelley, M.) with the blood of one Edward 'Bugs' Dooley. Thus they ride along the sunlit byways in companionable silence for some miles, the Ghost's engine emitting such a soporific rumble that, Cordelia and Bugs both being authors to a greater or lesser degree, respectively, they might easily have nodded off in post-prandial homage to immortal Homer were it not for the maw-glutting intentions of Rusty McGrew intruding upon Bugs' ataraxic bliss and the mewling yelps emerging from Sir Archie as he hangs out the window with tongue a-loll.

The conversation consequently finding itself in want of the raillery and badinage that generally persuades the Reader a narrative is proceeding in sprightly fashion, your n. here pauses to closely observe the Ghost's passengers, the better to consider the extent to which each of the Few's lives have been thrown out of kilter by circumstances they are helpless to control, thus entangling them in the cat's cradle woven by Fate, or, being precise, by that mischievously meddling one-third of the triad which collectively constitutes the Classical world's anthropomorphological conception of Fate, i.e., Atropos. To wit:

Up front, behind the wheel, Rusty McGrew discovers himself motoring along the citrus-scented byways of California as a direct consequence of his chosen profession of gangster, outlaw and Volstead-defying bootie, whose long and winding journey to this point may be traced all the way back to Rusty's ill-fated heist of

Dublin's GPO on the only weekend in that august building's history when it was occupied by revolutionary forces rebelling against 800 hundred years of colonial oppression.[1]

Also in the front rank, riding shotgun, is Samuel L. Silverstein, motion picture pioneer and Olympic-standard *svengali*, a man whose journey – i.e., from Ukrainian *shtetl* to Hollywood, albeit his recent apostasy suggests that his origins are not necessarily as Sammy has previously stated – is e'en longer and windier than that of Rusty McGrew, and whose critical flaw (providing our tale is to conclude in tragedy, as your humble n. supposes it will) may be sourced to those long, cold hungry nights when Sammy's *babushka* entertained young Sammy and his seventeen siblings with tales of hot and spicy food, the personification of which – i.e., the hot *tamale* Moxie La Roux – has left the adult Sammy so devoid of splosh as to oblige him to get into the ribs of the managing director of the Tropico Springs S&L, George P. Dangleberry III.

Between Sammy and Rusty sits Vanessa Hopgood, *paramour* to both and currently America's Darling™ and Hollywood's most shimmering star, but soon to be rendered professionally redundant due to the imminent splicing of cinematic sound and vision and a genetic heritage that has bestowed upon her a laugh akin to that of a buzzsaw giving vent to irrepressible ebullitions of mirth.

In the seat behind, albeit with his face in the breeze, we observe Sir Archibald l'Estrange-B'stard, a man heretofore happy to dally with chorus dolls in pursuit of temporary romantic relief but who, by dint of the chorus doll Adele Fitzhalligon's suggestion that they take refreshment upon the terrace of the Musso & Frank Grill, has recently discovered himself so enamoured of Vanessa Hopgood as to be grappled unto her soul with hoops of steel.

Alongside Archie we discover Adele Fitzhalligon, lately Archie's temporary intended, and who is in consequence suffering the

1 A conservative estimate. Indeed, were one to trace Ireland's colonial oppression all the way back to the first Viking raids (circa 795 AD), it might be more correctly stated that the rebels were seeking to undo more than a millennia's worth of unchecked aggression prosecuted by successive waves of Viking, Norman and English invaders.

existential angst experienced by those chorus dolls who have found themselves compared with the *Selenicereus grandiflorus*, i.e., the night-blooming cereus which blooms only once a year, and for one night only.

Adjacent to Adele, of course, is Bartley McGuffin, who, heedless of his father's warnings, pursued a qualification in Anglo-Irish literature at the lesser Dublin university, and in consequence finds himself employed as gentleman's gentleman to Sir Archibald l'Estrange-B'stard, and thus contractually bound to follow Archie where'er he goes, yea, e'en *on the lam*.

And so to the rumble seat, wherein, as previously noted, perches Cordelia de Havilland, a bestselling and critically acclaimed chronicler of reversals of fortune visited upon luckless heroines (i.e., *A Vicar to Call Her Own* and *All That Devon Allows*, among other tomes), who has *stepped through the looking-glass* to become herself a destiny-scourged lammister (and very likely a luckless heroine, if our tale, as supposed, falls out as tragedy).

Finally there is Bugs Dooley, the Author who has contrived to conjure into being the Few from *airy nothing*, but who is currently suffering the ignominy of discovering himself on the lam with his characters, i.e., motoring along the citrus-scented byways of California and entirely at the mercy of his tale's sub-theme (predestination as it pertains to the tormenting foibles of Fate, *&c.*) and utterly helpless, for the moment at least, to invest events with that quality of inevitability that generally persuades a Reader that a narrative is proceeding in sprightly fashion.

O Atropos!

'Bugs?' murmurs the de Havilland.

'Speak on, old Paracelsian peer.'[2]

2 Philippus Aureolus Theophrastus Bombastus von Hohenheim (1493-1541), who took the name Paracelsus later in life, was a Swiss-German philosopher, physician and occultist. He is credited as the founder of toxicology, and is believed to have influenced Carl Jung with his observation that some diseases have their roots in psychological conditions. He also named zinc ('zink'). In referring to Cordelia de Havilland as his 'Paracelsian peer', Bugs appears to be conflating Cordelia's vocation as a novelist with Paracelsus's theory (unproven) that humans could be created without mother or father, i.e., by alchemy.

'It occurs to me to wonder.'

'Always to be encouraged. Is there anything specific meandering around that perfectly proportioned noodle, or shall we simply cogitate mournfully on the pace at which the old *mundi's gloria* is *sic transiting*?'

'It's more to do with Tropico Springs.'

'Yes?'

'You may not remember, but I believe I recall it being mentioned in passing, perhaps as an afterthought, some miles back, that our ultimate destination is my writing bolthole in Tropico Springs.'

'The one on the lake. Correct and true.'

'Well, it's been a busy day, as we all know, with so much happening by way of alarums and excursions that I have quite worn out two slim gold pencils since first I observed you lurking on the terrace of the Musso & Frank Grill, which was, if memory serves, mid-afternoon, and yet here we are, some considerable number of hours later, with the sun so high in the sky that if I was asked to swear on a Bible as to the time of day, I would have to say mid-afternoon or risk perjuring myself before a jury of my peers.'

'I take your point. Continuity and so forth.'

'Actually, my point is – and I do appreciate that it's entirely possible it has simply slipped my mind – I mean, given, as I say, the extent to which we have all been o'ertaken by events – which is to say —'

'You appear, madam, to be suffering from a surfeit of aposiopesis. Pray tell, what ails thee?'

'Well, for the life of me I can't remember *ever* owning a property in Tropico Springs, on or off any lakes.'

'Ah. Fret not, old pipterino, for the *culpa* very much lies with yours truly there. But first things first, eh?'

'Golly,' says Archie from up front a moment later, 'it never ceases to amaze how quickly the sun sets in California. One minute you're riding along quite dazzled, the next you're breaking out the lanterns. If a man had recourse to lanterns, of course. Bartleby?'

'It appears that in our headlong flight from the Beverly Hills Motel under a hail of machine-gun fire, sir, we neglected to pack the lanterns.'

'Probably that grizz, what? Nothing like a charging bear to induce a spot of lantern-related amnesia.'

'Such has been my experience, sir.'

'Rusty?' says Vanessa. 'There's no lanterns.'

'What's that now?'

'Lanterns, Rusty. We're all out of lanterns.'

'Being strictly accurate, old termagant,' says Archie, 'there were never any lanterns to begin with.'

'We should probably start thinking about finding somewhere to stay for the night, Rusty,' says Vanessa. 'These backroads are far too dangerous after dark.'

The plunge into crepuscular gloom notwithstanding, Bugs could not fail to notice how the words *dangerous after dark* set a pair of coal-red orbs a-smoulder in the rear-view mirror, prompting Bugs to wonder, *vis-à-vis* Rusty but apropos the immortal Blake, *in what distant deeps or skies burnt the fire of thine eyes*.

'Calm yourself, Bugs,' says Cordelia in soothing register, by which the Reader is given to understand that Bugs' anxiety is so pronounced as to cause him to inadvertently wonder aloud about *tygers, tygers burning bright*. 'There are no tygers in the vicinity.'

'What about lynx?'

'As I understand it, there are no tygers, lynx, puma nor lions to be discovered in this part of California.'

'Dashed inconvenient,' says Archie. 'I do enjoy a good links.'

'There's a nice parkland course in Tropico Springs,' says Bugs. 'Set around the lake. Cordelia's pile backs onto the ninth green, as it happens.'

'No it *doesn't*,' hisses the de Havilland, tugging at Bugs' sleeve. 'I don't *own* a pile in Tropico Springs, and you're setting me up for a complete flat when we all arrive and tumble out of the Ghost to discover a big fat nothing where a pile, *my* pile, is supposed to be.'

'O ye of little faith. I refer you to Matthew 17.20, and the mustard seed of belief that may move mountains, yea verily.'

'If your intention is to conflate your authorship with a more divine quality of creativity,' says Cordelia, 'I am obliged to point out that, in all his many and varied adventures, Jesus never once confused room-keys and car-keys.'

'Not according to the canonical text, no. Perhaps in the apocrypha there may be found a parable —'

'And yet,' says Cordelia, riding roughshod o'er Bugs' efforts to divert her into scriptural conjecture, 'you would have me believe that a man who can engineer a Himalayan farrago out of so straightforward a worm-cast may be trusted in the considerably more complex business of real estate.'

'An entirely different proposition, old scepterino. For starters, there's —'

Alas, dear Reader, the Socratic *tête-à-tête* nicely brewing is now rudely interrupted by the Ghost veering sharply nor'-west and giving vent to a pronounced *bumpity-bump-bump*, a manoeuvre which results in the Few bouncing about the Ghost's interior like so many ping-pong balls engaged in unruly can-can and much sand being lodged between Bugs Dooley's teeth, which *twist*, being e'en more wholly unexpected than the conventional reversal of fortune tends to be, and thus disorientating not only for characters and Reader alike, but leaves your humble n. entirely at a loss as to how best he might proceed – I say, the Few's latest setback obliges us to conclude our current chapter, the better to draw breath, tend to any bumps and bruising, and perhaps e'en offer up a silent prayer that no fatalities have accrued amongst the minor characters as a consequence of Rusty's wilfully sharp veering off the public highway and into some undiscovered country which, on the evidence of the particulate recently deposited between Bugs' teeth, is likely some northern Californian equivalent of those *lone and level sands* observed by the immortal Shelley's traveller from an antique land, or might easily be so designated, given our pilgrims' similarity to travellers, and the frequency with which your n., and likely the Reader too, looks upon their works and despairs, if only

Hollywood might be considered an antique land, which, alas, it is not.

And so to Chapter Seventeen.

Chapter Seventeen

In which Rusty McGrew takes issue with Bugs Dooley's critique of the immortal Browning.

The darkness all round being of a decidedly Stygian hue, and your n.'s night-vision, alas, being nowhere as impressive as his facility for lip reading, it is some moments before he discerns in the gloom a flagpole with the number nine upon its flaccid ensign, at which point it becomes clear that Rusty has veered sharply onto a golf course, and hence struck a bunker, all of which renders pellucid the *bumpity-bump-bumping* and the teeth-lodging particulate aforementioned, and further persuades Archie to give vent to a 'View halloo!' and prevail mightily upon Bartley McGuffin to unscabbard his niblick post-haste, for a swift nine is in the offing.

Alas, in his excitement Archie has forgotten the old Scottish saw that there is *nicht as boggin* as a golf course by night,[1] and thus it is a rather moody Archie who thrusts his tongue into the breeze again as the Silver Ghost continues its rather turbulent passage.

'Is it just me,' enquires the de Havilland as Bugs hauls her back into the dickie on the occasion of her second failed back-flip out of same, 'or is there an extravagance of bunkers on this course?'

'I think he's aiming for them,' says Bugs. 'The idea being, or so I assume, to shake me loose from my spats and leave me spluttering in his dust. Or sand, as the case may be. Hold on, here's a dyke.'

The Silver Ghost clearing the foreshadowed dyke in a manner not entirely dissimilar to that of three-legged giraffe attempting

1 Old Scottish. *adj. naught as useless.*

Beecher's Brook, i.e., not at all, our pilgrims swiftly discover themselves crawling about spitting foliage.

'Bad luck, sir!' declares Archie. 'Ripping effort.'

'What the actual hell,' enquires Vanessa in a tone not unakin to a nasal cat gargling about six links of rusted hawser, 'was *that* all about?'

Her fellow Few being in broad agreement with the tone and content of Vanessa's request for clarification *vis-à-vis* Rusty's motives in departing an admittedly unpaved but perfectly serviceable country backroad for the decidedly more perilous environs of a golf course by night, Rusty now clears his throat and gives it the full and unabridged Zarathustra, the condensed version of which is as follows:

Many moons ago, holed up in a New Jersey motel to avoid any unpleasantness that might accrue in consequence of specious allegations made against his character in general and, in particular, his whereabouts on the fateful night a cadets' armoury was knocked off by persons unknown, Rusty hit upon the wheeze of absenting himself from the jurisdiction indefinitely, and set out sou'-sou'-west under cover of darkness, hop-scotching from one country club to another and hiding out each night in the bathroom facilities generally provided by the more upmarket country clubs at or near the 10th tee, country clubs being for the most part frequented by a clientele of an age when one's bladder becomes something of a 5-to-4 proposition with regard to leakage and said membership being in the main a class of ladies and gentlemen who see very little merit in amassing wealth sufficient to plunge Croesus into post-season funk if it means answering the call of nature with their peers, friends and rivals eavesdropping on the conversation.

'I'm afraid I don't follow,' says Vanessa, albeit in a manner suggestive of a rodent previously domiciled in mediaeval German village who finds herself abandoned to the rural wild, and, as the last piped note fades into nothingness like unto the tragic Echo of Ovid's telling, discovers herself no longer bewitched but increasingly bewildered and bothered. Which is to say, Vanessa *does* follow, but is experiencing more than a twinge of *follower's regret*, a variation on buyer's remorse common to those who belatedly realise that they might have been better served by a guide possessing map and compass as opposed to a *Zauberflöte*-tootler in technicolour motley.

'It's really quite simple,' says Adele Fitzhalligon. 'Rusty is a genius.'

This, as the Reader will easily conceive, is not only grist to Rusty's mill but a veritable cataract cascading upon his wheel, although his reaction to Adele's encomium – a mute preening – is ill-considered, in that it causes Vanessa to give vent to such spleen as would have required immediate corrective surgery were said emanations actual rather than proverbial.

'Gah!' says Vanessa in remonstrative timbre. 'You're a wrong gee, Rusty McGrew, and you'll always be a wrong gee. So you're going over big with a daffy frail with three left feet and a one-way ticket to Dannemora. Big deal, buster!'

'Now you're gone soupy,' says Rusty, pouring oil on troubled waters, although only if said waters are the *Schamayim* (שמים), i.e., the fiery outflow decanted, in the Hebrew tradition, from the Eternal Mind. Which is to say that Rusty's retort enflames rather than calms the situation, insulting as it does both Vanessa and Adele in equal measures, Vanessa by its dismissive tone and Adele in its alluding to the possibility that Vanessa might be considered 'soupy', i.e., of a mental capacity equal to a bowl of mulligatawny, for merely suggesting that Rusty might be going big for Adele Fitzhalligon.

'Cordelia, darling?' says Vanessa.

'Yes?'

'Be a sweetie and break out the Remington .41 rim fire short, would you?'

'Now can that jive!' snarls Rusty, for Rusty, in common with most men, labours under the delusion that jive, once uncanned, might be returned to source, whereas jive, as all women know, is the very *sine qua non* of genie escaped from bottle.

'If I may be so bold, ladies and gentlemen,' says Bartley

McGuffin, who, as the son of an Irish publican with political ambitions, has been mediating in fractious velitations since he was knee-high to a bottle of porter. 'I believe that when she refers to Mr McGrew's genius, Ms Fitzhalligon is simply suggesting that in utilising the 10th tee bathroom facilities for what is referred to in the trade as a *crash-pad*, Mr McGrew has lent the lie to the old Scottish saw that there is *nicht as boggin* as a golf course by night.'

'Ah,' says Vanessa.

'Precisely,' says Adele.

'Three cheers for Rusty!' sings out Archie. 'Hip-hip …'

Alas, Archie has sorely misjudged the mood, and the fruitless effort the Few subsequently expend upon searching the Ghost for the picnic basket Sammy is absolutely certain he packed improves the ambience by significantly less than the standard whit. Thus it is a hungry, silent and dispirited citizenry that eventually trudges into the lavabo adjacent to the 10th tee, which, the Few now numbering eight if we include Samuel L. Silverstein and Bugs Dooley, which we surely must, proves a rather cramped accommodation, with Archie blundering into the low-hanging chandelier on two separate occasions and Bartley having little by way of swivel-room behind the baby grand as he begins bashing out *My Melancholy Baby*, which poignant tune causes Sammy L. to commence ruminating on what the immortal Tennyson once described as *thoughts too deep for tears*, albeit Sammy, being of the sentimental disposition that is considered the fatal flaw of far too many Hollywood motion picture producers, now discovers that *his subdued eyes drop tears as fast as the Arabian trees their med'cinable gum.*

Happily, Sammy is by no means representative of our justice-fleeing pilgrims, for it is now, as they settle into the 10th tee lavabo, that the previously testy Few begin to display the first tentative signs of the solidarity which, your humble n. hopes, will be deployed to such devastating effect at the climax of our tale. Rusty, for example, wandering off in search of sustenance, returns with the contents of the frigidaire he has discovered in the lavabo's servants' quarters, while Adele lays to with paper and kindling, and soon has a log fire blazing in the grate. Archie being something of a bloodhound in the matter of Scotch-and-swish, it is the work of but a moment before he is dispensing highballs from the rosewood cabinet. Thus it is that the lavabo is transformed into a salon answering to the description *cosy* rather than *cramped* in less time than it might take a verbally dextrous observer to say 'scat', especially as Bartley has laid off the hot jazz to treat the assemblage to a more sophisticated noodling, i.e., a selection of nocturnes by Schubert, Field and Chopin. Indeed, so deeply *delphic* is the prevailing *phila* that Bugs Dooley finds himself moved to aver, in murmuring aside to the de Havilland, that God is in his heaven and all is right with the world.

'Do you speak, sir?' says Rusty.

'Only in murmuring aside, old sport. Naught for the citizenry at large to concern itself with.'

The McGrew brow knits. 'Do you dare, sir, *in mixed company,* sir, to end your sentence with a preposition left suggestively a-dangle?'

'Such was never my intention, good sir,' says Bugs. 'I was merely noting, in barely audible fashion, how, in contradistinction with the Few's recent mood of generalised discontent, larks and snails now seem to be upon the wing and the thorn, respectively.'

'Wot larks!' pip-pips Archie, who is by now in executive session with a bottle of 12-year-old Glenmorangie and sufficiently sniftered to be game for a little equivoque.

'Vast the larks,' snarls Rusty. 'Tell me more about these snails on thorns.'

'Indeed I shall,' says Bugs, settling himself in his armchair with a posset of highball to hand, 'e'en though, the verbal evidence of your enquiry notwithstanding, your froward demeanour leads me to believe that you have little or no interest in clarifying the immortal Browning's imagery. Moreo'er, I note with interest that your request for clarification was combined with a glance at the crossed claymores hanging above the hearth that could only be described as *meaningful*, which leads me to believe you are deliberately misconstruing Browning's intent, which posits the theory that a snail upon a thorn is symbolic of universal harmony, it being the case that the best place a gastropod mollusc could possibly find itself on a spring morn is reclining on a barb high among the foliage and basking in the sun, whereas you, sir, interpret the poet to mean that said escargot was *impaled* upon spike, a conclusion born of intentional misreading, a pitiful lack of classical education, or a psychology so brutalised by Fate's whims as to lead a man to instinctively extrapolate the worst possible conclusion from e'en the most benign of scenarios.'

'It would not be entirely untrue,' concedes Rusty, 'to state that one had a rather rough run of it during one's formative years growing up in the inner-city tenements of Dublin's Buckingham Street.'

'Taking said alternatives in the order named,' says Bugs, 'we now address ourselves to the possibility of your intentionally misreading the immortal Browning's intention, for it has been my experience, during my close reading of the works of the bestselling and critically acclaimed author Cordelia de Havilland, that there is frequently to be discovered a sub-textual conflict between what a character *says* and what she *means*, and vice versa.'

'And did you arrive at any conclusion at all,' enquires Cordelia once she has recovered from the brief swoon that generally afflicts authors whose work has been subjected to a close reading, which momentary fainting puzzles the assembled citizenry somewhat, they still labouring under the misapprehension that Cordelia is in fact Vanessa's confidante Felicia Fortesque – 'I say, did you arrive at any conclusion at all in the matter of this apparently counter-intuitive mode of communication?'

Bugs had, and then some. 'The first thing that must be said in defence of Cordelia de Havilland,' says he, 'or indeed any author who employs sub-textual conflict as a means of disorientating the Reader as to the true intentions of her characters, is that, as the scholars have long since established, Homer nods. Which is to say, drowsy authors are prone to making errors, particularly when they have been up half the night with a colicky infant, which experience is one of the very few commonalities shared by scribes of all nations and styles. Moreo'er, Homer was blind, and this in a time when braille was not so widely available as in our more enlightened era. Indeed, given that he was both sightless and borderline narcoleptic, it may be regarded as something of a miracle that Homer e'er managed to put quill to parchment at all,[2] let alone compose the twin epics of *Iliad* and *Odyssey*. Ne'ertheless, while Homer may not always have said what he meant, or meant what he said, the gist was generally as pellucid as his beloved *wine-dark seas*, his admittedly crude and frequently non-existent rhyme notwithstanding, albeit said critique is offered with the caveat that the Father of Literature was Greek, and may well have been let down badly, in the matter of shoddy rhyme, by his translators.'

'Poetry and comedy,' says Bartley, 'are equally ill-served by translation,' by which interjection does Bartley divest himself of roughly 90% of all he learned whilst earning a 2:2 in Anglo-Irish literature from the lesser Dublin university.

'Having established, then,' continues Bugs, 'that an author may be betrayed into inadvertently misdirecting the Reader by his or her physical infirmities, we are further obliged to acknowledge that there are times when the author simply gets it wrong, the recently foreshadowed Browning being a case in point, and specifically his howler in the poem *Pippa Passes*, when the poet deploys the word *twat* in the mistaken belief that the word refers to a nun's wimple as opposed to an erogenous unmentionable.[3] The fact that *Pippa Passes* was published in 1841, with *twat* in currency as low slang as early as the seventeenth century, suggests that Browning led an uncommonly sheltered boyhood, or that he had sampled a tincture of his wife's laudanum before taking up his quill on that fateful day, and on all subsequent days devoted to the revision of said text. At this point, of course, we remind ourselves that the quality of mercy

2 It is very likely that Homer, being his era's Titan of dactylic hexameter, was sufficiently wealthy as to employ a scrivener for the actually quilling, i.e., the tidying up of commas and periods, &c.

3 *Twat*, n. derived from the Old Norse *thveit*, meaning *forest clearing*.

is not strained, and paraphrase the immortal Pope in noting that, while it is the very essence of humanity to err, forgiveness elevates us into the pantheon wherein we achieve divinity.'

Here, alas, Rusty McGrew deliberately and maliciously misinterprets Bugs Dooley's literary critique as a verbal assault on his character, said alleged denigration taking the form of Bugs employing a vulgarity pertaining to a lady's undercarriage to describe and thus belittle Rusty's virile masculinity.

'A twat, am I?' snarls Rusty as he wrenches a claymore from its bracket above the fireplace, in the process giving Bugs pause for thought *vis-à-vis* the immortal Chekov's advice on ordnance left hanging upon hearths, said pause being largely filled with the making of a mental note to the effect that, in future, no weapon of any shape or fashion, nor any ornament nor bric-a-brac that might at a moment's notice be adapted to violent ends, should be found in any room likely to be visited by one Rusty McGrew, who is currently bellowing, 'I'll give *you* twat!'

'Biologically impossible, old *épée*-wrangler,' says Archie. 'Rather the other way around, as it were. Although,' he concedes on consideration, 'that wouldn't work either, Bugs being of the male genus and so forth.'

'You are mistook, sir,' says Bugs as Rusty warms up with some deep knee-bends and a wristy two-handed swipe of the claymore reminiscent of a seasoned pro playing a baffy out of thick rough. 'I was merely employing the immortal Browning's *faux pas* in the matter of nun's wimple to illustrate how e'en the best of us might discover ourselves unintentionally guilty of causing offence where none is intended.'

'Ah,' says Rusty in conciliatory timbre. 'I see.'

Alas, it is at this very moment, said juncture being of the kind best characterised as *better late than never*, that Cordelia de Havilland now stands forth, the better to insert herself between Bugs and the McGrew, Cordelia being anxious that Bugs not discover himself fatally impaled upon claymore and thus obliged to enter a *nolle prosequi* as regards our tale and all in it, and especially one Cordelia de Havilland.

'Put up thy swords!' sings out our bestselling and critically acclaimed author, presumably for dramatic purposes, it being rather the nub of the matter that Bugs is entirely without sword, a fact apparent to all, e'en Sir Archie, whose singular devotion to the Glenmorangie has left him seeing double. 'If you want to get to Bugs,' she now informs Rusty, 'you'll have to go through me first!'

A noble sentiment, as the Reader will doubtlessly agree, and especially given Rusty's reputation as a latter-day Clausus of the blood of the Sabines, who was a great army in himself, *&c.*, although, the point of the claymore being surprisingly honed for (a) broadsword and (b) lavabo gimcrack, Cordelia's declaration is nowhere as reassuring for Bugs as it might have been, Bugs being of the opinion that the de Havilland is a sylph-ish frail who might benefit from a steak dinner or six if she plans on making a career of martyring herself as human shield.

For lo! Rusty reacts to the de Havilland's words as e'en the most callow Reader might expect, i.e., like a Russian poet receiving a glove plumb spang in the kisser; which is to say, the McGrew brow knits.

'Sir,' says he, addressing Bugs at a volume likely to have plunged Stentor into a post-season funk, 'I will be sending my friend directly to wait upon yours,' which civilised declaration of hostilities is rather undermined by Rusty's subsequent waggling of the claymore clutched in his right hand, by which Bugs is given to understand that said ordnance is in fact the chum alluded to, and that Rusty's intention is to test to the utmost Bugs' hypothesis *vis-à-vis* universal harmony by impaling our Author upon the claymore-shaped thorn in the approved Chekhovian manner, whereupon Bugs, concluding that the quality of mercy is so strained as to twang like a banjo protesting at being ill-used upon bovine rump, now dangles at pace for the Great Outdoors, said departure being so rapid and unexpected that your n. is caught quite unawares and thrown into fluster and must thus conclude this chapter in unexpectedly abrupt fashion.

Chapter Eighteen

Wherein Vanessa Hopgood takes issue with those suitors who stand idly by and allow a maiden's honour be besmirched by Yahoo.

But stay! the Reader may well sing out at this crucial juncture, and hence wonder aloud as to whether, on the occasion of a tale's Author dangling at pace for the Great Outdoors and thus abandoning his characters to fend for themselves, a country club lavabo thronged with peevish lammisters might not find itself plunged into a rather misshapen chaos of ~~well-seeming~~ sored up forms aimlessly wandering around and about for want of motive or purpose, o'er which existential horror your n. would be obliged to draw the proverbial veil.

Your humble n., however, having previously sworn a sacred vow to treat the truth as an unpalterable quantity (or, if he has not, he does so now) – I say, your n. is here compelled to deliver some *verum* that is not only inconvenient but possibly heretical, which is that characters who discover themselves abandoned or neglected by their Creator do not necessarily descend into disarray and debauched anarchy, and nor is it inevitable that they grow witless and dull, stumbling about in meaningless torpor as if consigned to some purgatorial limbo, it being the case that the vast majority of characters go about their daily business entirely unaware that an external agency is guiding their every gesture and crafting each syllable that passes their lips; further, and by way of corollary, many of those characters who *are* aware of the external agency care significantly less than an embryonic mote for said agency's expectations, needs or desires in the matter of credible narrative progression, instead behaving as they themselves see fit and trusting to luck, Fate or coincidence to iron out any wrinkles arising from their heedless *que sera*.

So it is that Bugs Dooley's dangling at pace for the Great Outdoors has little or no impact upon the Few he leaves behind, as will now be related, commencing at the very moment when Samuel L. Silverstein, amidst all the pipes and tabors attending Bugs' departure, observes the quietly admiring gaze Vanessa bestows upon Rusty McGrew – for what woman, truly, can resist a broadsword-wielding *chevalier* who refuses to allow discourse in mixed company to descend into the coarse bruiting about of euphemisms pertaining to *a forest clearing*? – I say, Sammy, being as intuitive as to *the Slawkenbergian involutions of a woman's heart* (*cf.* Sterne) as Hollywood motion picture producers tend to be, discovers that he is now obliged to obstruct any and all woo pitched by Rusty, this to maximise Moxie La Roux's chances of employing love's filaments to lasso her one true intended, which happy event, according to Abie Cohen's scheme as previously sketched out, will result, on the occasion of our freshly minted Public Enemy Number Nine subsequently perishing in the tender embrace of Old Sparky, with Sammy escorting Moxie down the aisle with carnation in buttonhole and thus, in one fell swoop, reclaiming the last few several millions he recently delivered unto said hot *tamale* courtesy of conferring upon her power of attorney o'er his finances, in the process clarifying his status *vis-à-vis* American citizenship with the Department of Labour.

Such being the case, and Sammy being a man disinclined to stand upon his punctilios, he now wastes no time in denouncing Rusty McGrew as not only red-haired Irish (and thus of the lowest of all possible orders) but a Volstead-defying bootie who, in common with the immortal Fielding's dastardly creation Fireblood, believes there is no better pastime than blowing a man's brains out.

'What's that, Sammy?' sings out Rusty, who quite fails to detect the sinister nuance in Sammy's opening salvo due to Bartley

McGuffin's energetic rendition of Liszt's *Fantasy and Fugue on the Theme of B-A-C-H*, and who now brandishes his claymore broadsword to encourage Sammy to halloo lively, which unorthodox employment of Chekhovian ordnance causes Sammy to blench more than somewhat and discover that his punctilios might well suffice for Reason's monument were he to stand on same for the foreseeable future.

'Oh,' says Sammy, hallooing in Cape Horn voice, 'I was just wondering if being a pirate king is, as Messrs Gilbert and Sullivan aver, truly a glorious thing.'

'As to that,' halloos Rusty in retort, 'I am naught but a slave of duty. But I'm more concerned for you, Sammy? How *is* every little thing?'

'Tolerably fine,' acknowledges Sammy, 'although I have yet to discover myself in any situation wherein a freshet of fizz wouldn't improve the mood considerably.'

'Might a Scotch-and-swish answer?' says Archie.

'It might,' concedes Sammy, bowing low and extending the courtly leg to the ladies present, i.e., Vanessa Hopgood and Adele Fitzhalligon, it being the case that Cordelia de Havilland has recently dangled for the Great Outdoors in pursuit of Bugs Dooley (more of which anon).

'What news of *Daddy's Girl*?' halloos Rusty as Sammy avails himself of a refreshing quaff of Archie's decoction, said italicised foregoing a reference to Vanessa's forthcoming motion picture, which, being directed by Erich von Stroheim, with jewellery by Tiffany, is eagerly anticipated as the forthcoming season's hottest ticket, although here your humble n. is obliged to disregard any answer Sammy might make (which would, after all, contain little but the conjecture and magical thinking that generally attends any optimistic foretelling of the future, Sammy being unlikely to divest himself of Cassandraic prophecies in the presence of said motion picture's shimmering star, e'en if the early word is that Vanessa and Erich were embattled from the very first day of the shoot, when Erich was obliged to bar Roman Navarro from the set, Roman being a raconteur of some note and thus guilty of causing Vanessa to chortle more than somewhat, which in turn caused the lions to panic and trample down their temporary corral, with tragic consequences for a best boy, key grip and the set's Venezuelan catering manager) – I say, your n., being conscious as always of the Reader's needs and wants, now directs the Reader's attention away from the idle chit-chat between Rusty McGrew and Samuel L. Silverstein, and invites her instead to note that a rather chilly silence has descended upon the couch situated before the lavabo's blazing log fire, it being the case that Vanessa has declined to acknowledge the courtly leg recently offered by Sammy L., instead elevating her aquiline nose five degrees north and delivering herself of a delicate sniff, by which means Vanessa leaves any interested party in no doubt that she would, on discovering herself yet again bound to railway sleepers, albeit in real life as opposed to on the set of *Daddy's Girl*, much prefer to be pummelled unto oblivion by steam locomotive than be rescued by one *Samuel L. Stinkerstein.*

That said, and bearing in mind Vanessa is a motion picture actress wholly dependent upon gesture and nuance if she wants her act to go over big, the Reader will easily conceive that her sniff, despite the delicacy of its sentiment, is delivered with considerable vim, in consequence of which Sammy now discovers himself experiencing precisely the quality of dismay that attended Sancho Panza's belated discovery that knights-errant were not only out of fashion, but that books of chivalry were full of nothing but folly and fiction, whereupon Sammy, operating according to the precedent established by the Lady Caroline Lamb, who believed that *Truth is what one thinks at the moment*, declares himself so ensnared in a crisis of infatuation that were he a maharajah he would be obliged to strangle himself with one of Vanessa's silk stockings, before bruiting his intention to pay Vanessa Hopgood the highest compliment any man could make her, just as soon as said America's Darling™ might be shrived according to the statute legislation pertaining to same, if any such applies, but certainly no later than noon on the following day.

Naturally, Sammy bruits forth in the stated fashion whilst maintaining a watching brief on Rusty McGrew and his claymore broadsword, for no man travels the long and winding road from Ukrainian *shtetl* to the rarefied heights of Hollywood who is not all the while possessed of a preternatural awareness that he may at any moment be set about by brisk, gamesome fellows bent on trampling his puddings. Alas, Sammy has here grievously miscalculated in the matter of Vanessa Hopgood's swain, being entirely ignorant of Rusty McGrew's recent adoption of the prevarication principle practised by the cat i' the adage due to his temporary inability to legally secure a diamond ring worthy of his one true intended, in consequence of which Rusty discovers himself entirely ill-equipped to leap once more unto the breach wherein Vanessa's honour might best be defended against the unwelcome parping of ~~Purcell's~~ Clarke's *Trumpet Voluntary*; further, Sammy being elsewise engaged at the time auditioning *ingénues* for his forthcoming croquet musical epic *Oh! My Wicked Wicket Ways*, our banns-bruiting mogul is utterly bereft in the matter of intelligence pertaining to previously related events at the Musso & Frank Grill and, in particular, Sir Archie's particular veneration for Vanessa's rare endowments.

Thus it is that Sammy discovers himself starting like a guilty thing upon an especially fearful summons when Archie, with a throaty 'Forsooth!', wrenches the second claymore from above the hearth and swiftly embarks upon a program of deep knee-bends and loinage girding whilst flourishing the claymore in a manner to warm e'en the most steppe-chilled Chekhovian cockles.

'I caution you, sir,' says Archie, 'against proceeding to descant in a manner not entirely advantageous to Ms Hopgood's reputation, for such might warrant rather more than a bust in the snoot!'

'Do you threaten me, sir,' says Sammy, emboldened by the effects of Archie's legendarily heavy hand in the pouring of Scotch-and-swish, 'with rather more than a bust in the snoot, sir?'

'I do, sir!' says Archie, who is himself preternaturally emboldened by his intimate association with the bottle of 12-year-old Glenmorangie.

'And are you aware, sir,' says Sammy, 'that you seek to defend the reputation of a lady who is my officially designated *fiancée* according to all the reputable blats?'

'Crumbs!' says Archie, who has, alas, become more rather than less blootered on bathtub hooch since last he was reminded of said crucial snippet of intelligence pertaining to Vanessa's impending nuptial mirth. And, there being few revelations more likely to cause a prospective swain's claymore broadsword to droop than the belated realisation that his one true intended has elsewhere pledged her troth, Archie, being a true and spruce *chevalier*, discovers himself obliged to issue multiple *mea culpas* for inadvertently pitching woo at a lady previously promised, it being the case, as previously related, that Archie has no desire to see his legacy conflated with that of the immortal Cervantes' notorious innkeeper, who boasted of doing wrongs in abundance.

'Sir,' says Sammy, 'I accept your apology and hereby put away the glove by which I proposed to issue challenge to your honour. Is there any more Scotch-and-swish at all?'

Indeed there is, and there matters might well have rested, and the evening evolved into a convivial gathering of wine and song and a rueful reminiscing on a theme of misunderstandings in love, were it not for Vanessa Hopgood taking understandable umbrage at the gentlemen of the party making claim and counter-claim upon her troth, all of which puts Vanessa in mind of *women being bought and sold like any other vendible thing*, Vanessa being, as the more sophisticated Hollywood actresses tend to be, a devotee of the works of the immortal Dickens. Such being the case, Vanessa now proceeds to confound the prospective conviviality by stating in no uncertain terms, but terms which are vividly illustrated and decanted in strident tones, that she refuses to accept any apology issued in conjunction with an apology to Samuel L. Silverstein, it being Vanessa's considered opinion that Sammy L. is a wretch, a mook and a cigar-chomping Yahoo, and that no good could possibly come of any woman whose suitors (plural) stand idly by and allow her honour be besmirched by its association with said

Yahoo, if by Yahoo she might be understood to allude to Swiftian satire, which is very much her intention.

Here, alas, our scene comes grinding to a halt, it being the case that Rusty McGrew remains bereft of diamond ring, and thus honour-bound to prevaricate like unto the cat i' the adage, whilst Sir Archie endeavours to persuade Samuel L. Silverstein to accept his retraction of the general apology he has recently issued, the better to issue a specific apology crafted for Vanessa's ears only, with Sammy refusing to accept said retraction on principle, and further cautioning Archie that, were he to pursue his current course of action, his reputation as spruce *chevalier* would discover itself in dire peril of being tainted by allegation that Archie's word, freely given, can no longer be considered his bond.

Said impasse doing little, or so your humble n. imagines, to persuade the Reader that our narrative is proceeding in sprightly fashion, we now take our leave of the country club lavabo and drift, wraithlike, for the Great Outdoors, wherein will be discovered, in chapter the next, Cordelia de Havilland and Edward 'Bugs' Dooley discoursing at some length on the existential crisis invariably experienced by bestselling and critically acclaimed authors who belatedly discover themselves a character in a fellow scribe's tome.

Chapter Nineteen

In which Cordelia de Havilland is warmly pressed to enter into collaboration with her Creator, Bugs Dooley.

The Great Outdoors being surpassingly large, and, by some inexplicably bizarre quirk of physics, e'en larger after dark, the Reader may well experience a degree of lively astonishment at how quickly Cordelia de Havilland locates Bugs Dooley lurking nor'-west of the ninth green, although the matter is susceptible to a ready explanation, for it is now that time of night, if we might plunder the immortal Dickens' oeuvre yet again, *when e'en sound appears to slumber, and profligacy and riot have staggered home to dream*, into which quiet Bugs, assuming that the faint rustling of Cordelia's approach is that of Rusty McGrew bearing down upon his prey with hanger at noon, now squawks a pitiable prayer ('Lawks a mercy!').

'And there didst mighty Achilles languish in his tent,' says Cordelia, having confirmed for Bugs that she is in fact alone, albeit never lonely, 'eating out his heart and longing for the sound and fury of battle.'

'More pothole bunker than tent,' says Bugs from the sandy depths, 'if we're being strictly literal. And less of the sound and fury, if you don't mind. I'm pretty sure I heard Rusty in the copse over yonder and limbering up for wanton slaughter by felling a spruce.'

'Unless I'm very much mistook,' says Cordelia, 'you appear to be confusing a homicidal gangster with the rabbit I saw just now bolting into the undergrowth at my approach.'

'You're sure?'

'Fear not, old strategic withdrawer. Rusty is currently paralysed by prevarication, and was last observed muttering in pyretic timbre about diamonds the size of infant pachyderms' tusks.' Here the de Havilland shuffles a little to the right, which manoeuvre situates the moon at her back, at which point she holds up her hands in order that a brace of glasses and a jeroboam of the old fizzy shampoo might be observed in silhouette. 'Won't you join me for a restorative?'

It being something of an unshakeable principle with Bugs Dooley to never refuse a glass of pop from a pretty girl, no matter the threat to life and limb, he wearily rakes the bunker and clambers out, joining the de Havilland where she reclines against the bole of a spruce on the edge of the aforementioned copse.

'It behoves me,' says Bugs as the de Havilland pours the fizz, 'to commend your impressive *sang-froid*.'

'*Skål*,' says Cordelia, hoisting her Bolly-brimmed bumper.

'I mean to say, if they were handing out prizes for the brave smile and stiff upper lip, you'd be first in line for a ribbon. Given the circs and so forth.'

'Circs?'

'Well, discovering yourself a fictional character, and then forced to defend your Creator against the bloodthirsty predations of a claymore-wielding gunsel. Not quite the kind of sketch to have a girl whistling *Lillibullero*, is it?'

Here your n. reluctantly interpolates to note that Cordelia's being nowhere as perturbed as the Reader might expect at discovering herself a character rather than flesh-and-blood citizen is largely due to the style and content of Cordelia's own novels, wherein the astonishing plot twist and outrageous reversal of fortune are not only frequent but *de rigueur*, a good example being *A Galaxy for Cuddles O'Shaughnessy*, Cordelia's very own homage to the works of Jules Verne, in which young Cuddles, fleeing the Irish potato famine, discovers herself elevated from crust-stealing scullery maid to venerated empress of the known universe.

'The situation is by no means ideal,' acknowledges the de

Havilland, having reflected and considered, 'not least because I am myself an author, and there is a certain ironic sting in finding myself the biter bit.'

'Poacher turned gamekeeper, what? No, wait – poacher turned poachee?'

'The main difficulty,' continues Cordelia, 'is in deciding whether I find myself in a tragedy, which is to say underdeveloped comedy, or a comedy in which the tragic elements are yet to be made fully manifest. One always likes to have an inkling one way or another, if only to ensure one is wearing the correct shoes.'

'Indubitably.'

'For example, I can't help but notice that you're wearing brogues, which suggests tragedy, brogues being entirely unsuitable for the nimble work of nipping through french windows and rushing in and out of boudoirs and so on.'

'Or pothole bunkers, what?'

'Or, for that matter, pothole bunkers. Bugs,' says the de Havilland, gazing earnestly upon her Creator, 'you do *have* a plan, don't you?'

'Plan?'

'A scheme, as it were. It wouldn't have to be an actual plot *per se*. Just a generalised idea as to how matters will turn out for the best.'

'Fear not on that score, old Paracelsian chum.'

'Don't get me wrong. There are few things more bracing, if I might wax Quixotic for a moment, than wantonly thrusting the arms up to the elbows in adventures. But what I'm hoping for, if I may be so bold, is some tiny comfort that this is all first draft material, to be knocked into shape once you get a firmer grasp on your characters' needs, wants and desires.'

'Ship-shape and Bristol fashion, what?'

'Well, precisely.'

'Sheet out, trim the sails and set a course for the Isles of the Blest, posting sharp-eyed Palinurus in the bow.'

Reassured on this point, the de Havilland settles back against the bole and sips on her fizzy joy. 'Is that your usual process?' says she.

'Process?'

'Method. Routine. The old *modus operandi*.'

'Ah. The process.'

'You do *have* a process, don't you?'

'Oh, absolutely. Never leave home without one.'

'Bugs,' says the de Havilland after a gravid moment or two has passed, 'may I ask a delicate question?'

'Have on, old confidante. Ask and it shall be answered.'

'This wouldn't happen to be your very *first* attempt at writing a story, would it?'

'Good question, and well put. I'm glad you asked me that.'

'Well, is it?'

'Yes.'

'By which I am given to understand, and correct me if I'm wrong,' says the de Havilland in a tone such as might be imagined emanating from a pterodactyl experiencing a twinge of old war wound, 'that you don't actually have a process.'

'Not a process that might be recognised as such, no. That said, I would here refer you to the writings of Mr James Joyce, who recently stated that a man of genius makes no mistakes, and that any apparent errors are in fact volitional and the very portals of discovery.'

'Right. You perceive yourself a genius, then?'

'Oh, absolutely, albeit only if we dispense with the most recent definition of same, and instead cleave to its original meaning, which was derived from the Latin *gignere*, and which was popularly understood, circa the sixteenth century, to mean *the attendant spirit present from one's birth*.'

'I see.'

'More fizz?'

'I think not, Bugs. I appear to have a headache coming on.'

'Probably for the best.' In truth, the de Havilland is as white as any whipt syllabub, and displaying three of the four symptoms associated with a bad case of the botts. 'Can't have you squiffy at the old Underwood, eh?'

'Pardon me?'

'Well,' says Bugs, who is feeling considerably embiggened after sluicing down his freshet of fizz, 'you know what they say about the Chinese, how they have the same word for crisis and opportunity, which strikes me as carelessly economical, or possibly a consequence of confusion – or conflation, perhaps – arising from the use of squiggles where alphabetic letters might answer more handsomely, but there you are, a civilisation four thousand years old, they seem to have managed pretty well, wouldn't you say? Confucius and so forth.'[1]

'I'm not sure I follow,' says Cordelia, albeit she employs the very same tenor employed by Vanessa Hopgood when our shimmering goddess recently expressed a modicum of followers' regret.

'Well, the Chinese, as I was saying, mix up their crises and opportunities. Which brings me to a little proposition.'

'I'm really not in the mood, Bugs.'

'No, but listen. What I need right now is a mentor, a Palinurian visionary to point the way, as it were. And here's you, the bestselling author of *Tender is the Knight* and *Do Not Go Gently, Good Knight*, among other titles, reclining upon the very same bole as I.'

'You're suggesting we collaborate?'

'Synergy, old co-conspirator. You bring the process, and a quantity of slim gold pencils, and maybe e'en a plot, if such can be rustled up without too much frogging of the persp-damp'd brow. I'll toss in the vim.'

'I see,' says the de Havilland, who has been for some moments now patting her pockets with the increasingly desperate air of a sporting aficionado informed by the crackly tannoy at Saratoga Springs that the heavily backed favourite which romped home eighteen lengths clear in the 2.15 has been disqualified after a

1 Alas for Bugs' scheme, the Chinese word for 'crisis' – in simplified Chinese 危机, or more traditionally 危機 – is not a conflation of the characters signifying 'danger' and 'opportunity', it being the case that neither 机 nor 機 denote 'opportunity'.

steward's enquiry instigated when said favourite not only failed to stop running but subsequently cleared the winner's enclosure without breaking stride, making a retrospective virtue of said aficionado putting her chemise on the thousand pounds worth of future kibble that placed second at 10-1, or would have, if only she hadn't torn up her ticket in a fit of pique, as is generally the first instinct of a woman who loses her best silk on an alleged cast-iron plunger. 'I say, Bugs?'

'Speak on, old word-wrangler.'

'I appear to have left my muff pistol in the lavabo. Be a sweetie and run inside for it, would you?'

'No fear, old gunsel. And put Rusty McGuillotine in a snit again? No, I think not.'

'In which case,' says Cordelia, in resigned timbre, 'I am obliged to point out that your proposition o'erlooks a rather crucial detail. Those novels of mine you reference, and many more besides, may well have gone to number one with a bullet, and been critically acclaimed in the broadsheet reviews, but I have no recollection of writing them.'

'Retrospective writers' block?'

'I'm afraid not. It is because I am not a bestselling author, as per memo, but a character thus designated. Which is to say that, while I may give the impression of having led a long and critically acclaimed life to date, being shortlisted for a number of important prizes and lauded in the Parisian salons, the fact of the matter is that I simply didn't exist before you first spotted me on the terrace of the Musso & Frank Grill.'

'So what you're saying is …'

'I am very much afraid, Bugs, that I have no more experience of process than you.'

'*Quelle horreur*!'

Here concludes our current chapter, it being the case that our failed co-conspirators discover themselves gazing into the abyss as the abyss stares back, as is its wont, with the consequence – an abyss being notorious for not keeping up its end when it comes to dialogue, mere echoes being a poor substitute for the cut-and-thrust of Socratic persiflage – that there will be very little worth reporting for the foreseeable future from the environs of the spruce copse fringing the ninth green nor'-west of the lavabo.

And so we hie our way hence, if by hence we might be understood to mean the following morn, it being now grown late and our lammisters likely to grow vexed and fractious for want of repose and consequently commence behaving in a manner best described, as might a mother gazing indulgently upon colicky infant, as *not quite themselves*, which is to say our plucky Few may well begin *acting out of character*, a development to cause e'en the most sanguine of narrators to quail in anticipation of unexpected segues and *non sequiturs*, for said characters, i.e., pilgrims, are already diverted out of their intended *progress* and are currently advancing like those sages who *perne in a gyre*, or, less poetically rendered, in a manner conflatable with the apparently aimless circling flight of the honey-buzzard.[2]

And so, in preparation for our next chapter, wherein will commence the third and final act of our tale, your n. now takes his leave of the Few, in the hope that all will soon ascend the proverbial wooden hill to Bedfordshire, the better to be rested and refreshed for the morrow's adventures.

2 This is by no means the canonical interpretation of 'perne in a gyre'. However, the narrator may also be referring to the Few's facility for adjusting to circumstance, for which Dr. Andrew Perne, Dean of Ely (1519-1589), was notorious, and particularly when said adjusting was likely to boost Dr. Perne's prospects.

Chapter Twenty

In which Rusty McGrew discovers that Tropico Springs is by no means thronged with what Mr Barry Lyndon was once pleased to describe as 'gallant votaries of fortune'.

'Zooks!' sings out Rusty McGrew in a tone as morose as might be expected from a citizen who emerges from a country club lavabo early one morning to discover the fuel tank of his fellow lammister's Rolls Royce Silver Ghost punctured by what Rusty can only assume was a stray round shipped during the altercation outside the Beverly Hills Motel on the evening previous, it being the case that the serge-clad myrmidons operating under the aegis of Bumbles McGee were as liable to be confused with sharp-shooters as Clara Bow with a stand of flamingos, and thus unlikely to score a deliberate hit on the fuel tank, if such was e'er their ambition, it being far more probable that the object of their fusilladous intent was one Jasper Huxtable 'Rusty' McGrew.

Indeed, so woe-ish is Rusty's general demeanour that it is no exaggeration to state that it would have wrung tears from Heaven's eyes were it not for the intervention of Bugs Dooley and Cordelia de Havilland, who now hurriedly enter stage right brushing leaves and twig fragments from their garb, by which means will the Reader conceive that Bugs and Cordelia have spent the entire night, unchaperoned, in the copse of spruce fringing the ninth green nor'-west of the lavabo.

'But stay! what's amiss?' cries the de Havilland upon noting Rusty's air of Keatsian gloom.

Rusty being a man of few words, it is but a matter of moments before Bugs and Cordelia are abreast of the intelligence that the Ghost is possessed of a punctured fuel tank, which unexpected circumstance, continues Rusty, rather punctures in its turn the Few's ambition to progress to Tropico Springs by means other than ambulatory, whereupon Cordelia gives Bugs a nudge with her elbow, by means of which Bugs is given to understand that Cordelia believes him responsible for the latest unforeseen impediment to our pilgrims' progress, and thus obliged to rectify same by drifting, wraithlike, back in time to redraft the scene wherein said round was shipped, it being the case that, as the bestselling and critically acclaimed writer of such tomes as *An Igloo to Call Her Own* and *The Peacock Sings of Peacock Things*, Cordelia understands better than most that writing is, in fact, rewriting.

Alas, dear Reader, Bugs Dooley is but a neophyte scribe, and has yet to experience *that particular grief of so floodgate and o'erbearing a nature that it engluts and swallows other sorrows, and is still itself* that is the woe a writer tends to be englutted by when, having inadvertently steered his characters wrong, he fails to immediately return to the fault's origin and remedy same, but instead ploughs e'er onward, convinced of his capacity to rectify any and all errors without recourse to redraft, much in the manner of immortal Carlyle's Novel-wright, who, upon taking the anonymous advice that he should *write on, worthy Brother, even as thou canst, even as it is given thee*, invariably discovers himself *the Foolishest of existing mortals*, i.e., a Novel-wright with nary a Reader to lend *a long ear* to his fictitious Biography.

'I have it!' sings out Bugs, who, being an author, or more precisely an Author, entirely lacks your humble n.'s capacity for wraithlike drifting back in time. 'This,' says Bugs, gesturing at the tank-punctured Ghost, 'is a blessing in disguise.'

'A blessing, you say?' says Rusty in a timbre which might easily be conflated with the spectacle that greeted good King Wenceslas on his first looking out on the Feast of Stephen, which is to say that said tenor is deep and crisp and even, and tinged with potentially cruel frost.

'But of course,' says Bugs. 'The gendarmes will be on the prowl for a Silver Ghost, and preferably one stuffed with gunsels, chorus dolls, Hollywood superstars and soused aristocrats. Indeed,' says he, 'were any impartial observer on hand to critique our headlong flight from justice, said observer might consider it a little *too* convenient that we are now obliged, courtesy of a random and erroneously aimed round, *of which we are only belatedly made aware*, to stash the Ghost in the nearest dyke, old mill or pothole bunker, and steal another flivver.'

'Now stow that gammon!' says Rusty, said retort being in fact a significant abbreviation of Rusty's actual response, the gist of which pertains to the traditional absence of pinchable flivvers in the vicinity of country club lavabos, this in consequence of said lavabos being geographically incompatible with such infrastructure as a flivver might generally require, i.e., roads, albeit Rusty's discourse was of a *vers libre* so profanely blasphemous as to outfoul the proverbial blacksmith's oxter, and is here elided in order to spare the more sensitive Reader any blushes still held in reserve after the shocking revelation that the unwed Bugs Dooley and Cordelia de Havilland spent the entirety of the night previous in nocturnal proximity, and without chaperone.

Indeed, Rusty's invective is so prolonged and coarse that your humble n. has no choice but to acknowledge his origins in the notoriously wicked lower classes, and thus designate him our tragedy's villain, e'en if, in so doing, we discover ourselves transgressing against Lord Henry Home Kames' opinion as stated in the magisterial tome *Subjects best suited to tragedy*, wherein, as the attentive Reader will undoubtedly recall, Lord Kames declares that the misfortunes of a wicked person ought not to be represented.

And yet, villain or no, and e'en as his Bugs Dooley-directed broadside turns the early morning air blue, your n. here admits to experiencing a sympathetic twinge on behalf of our latter-day Mezentius, it being entirely understandable that Rusty might be more than somewhat sored up at accompanying the Few as they lurch from pillar to post, for, while a pillar might be a truly splendid place to tarry, with larks flitting about o'erhead, it is Rusty's bitter experience that a post tends to be a miserable billet of thorns unadorned by molluscs of any shape or stripe.

Thus it is that Rusty now concludes his diatribe by alluding to the brace of broadswords recently returned to their brackets above the hearth within the lavabo, and announces a burning desire to employ one of same in discovering whether the bile-secreting organ of the miserable specimen currently wibbling on about stealing non-existent flivvers is as pigeon-liverish as he, Rusty McGrew, suspects.

Indeed, it is while Rusty is enquiring as to whether Bugs wishes to engage in honourable *seppuku* or subject himself to ritual disembowelling at the claymore-clutching hands of one Rusty McGrew that Bartley McGuffin, and not for the first time, saves the day by inserting himself into this particular nick in time, providing we acknowledge that the *day* in question is figurative as opposed to the period of twenty-four hours artificially imposed on the diurnal cycle, which, being a fictional construct, is impossible to save, hoard or otherwise preserve, and that *time*, being a quantity both invisible and imaginary, is equally impossible to nick, gouge or in any other way notch.

'What ho!' halloos Bartley from the cockpit of a rather spiffing low-slung black Lincoln sedan, albeit Bartley, having discovered scarf and goggles in the glove compartment, is unrecognisable as a gentleman's gentleman and instead bears a striking resemblance to one Toad of Toad Hall.

'How now!' says Archie, as he wanders out of the lavabo with a posset of breakfast mimosa in hand. 'What news?'

Bartley now divesting himself of scarf and goggles, and debouching from the Lincoln sedan, he informs the assemblage that he had risen early, as is his wont, to prepare Sir Archie's breakfast mimosas, whereupon, having snuck outside for a crafty gasper in order to enjoy the pink-fingered dawn already gilding the low hills on the far shore of the lake which laps not far from the lavabo's front portico, Bartley scented the unmistakable aroma of gas recently escaped from a punctured fuel tank. Further investigation beneath the chassis of the Silver Ghost persuading Bartley that alternative transport would be required in short order, Sir Archie being a gentleman who believes that walking is only e'er appropriate when being frequently spoiled in the manner wittily alluded to by the contemporary novelist Mr Harry Leon Wilson, i.e., during a round of golf, Bartley took himself off in wandering quest of replacement flivver, and shortly thereafter encountered a rather frizzled gentleman with a top hat tilted rakishly above his right eye who was snoring gently in the passenger seat of a pleasingly low-slung black Lincoln sedan in the parking lot between the country club's clubhouse and first tee, with whom Bartley instigated a rather one-sided dialogue, given said party's ongoing slumber, albeit Bartley received the distinct impression, on requesting the temporary use of said Lincoln sedan, that the dozing citizen snored acquiescingly, at which point Bartley assisted the gentleman from his chariot and conveyed him safely to an adjacent bench, relieved him of his ignition keys, and returned with all speed from whence he came, pausing only to don scarf and goggles lest any highway policeman note his unorthodox traversing of golf course in low-slung sedan and conclude that Bartley was by no means of the class of buffle-headed clowns who tend to make up the membership of exclusive country clubs, but was in fact a servitor engaged in larcenous endeavour.

'Stout work, Bartleby,' toasts Archie, who, like the immortal Cervantes' Anselmo, has a disconcerting tendency to rejoice o'er dissembled impostures that bear away the opinion of truth. 'Remind me to slip you a sawbuck at some point in the near future.'

'You are too kind, sir.'

'We have the weather gauge!' bellows Rusty, who, your n. is now obliged to note, is by some distance more decisive in crises than he is in matters of the heart. 'Let out reefs and carry on!'

Thus it is but a matter of a considerable number of moments – Vanessa Hopgood, in particular, being unwilling to be observed abroad in daylight swathed in anything less than tippity-top shimmer – before the Few find themselves back on the road again, weary pilgrims crammed into a low-slung black Lincoln sedan on their ne'er-ending *progress*, bound for a destination known only to Fate,[1] or one-third of the anthropomorphological conception of Fate to be exact, the capricious Atropos if we are to name and shame, into whose eternally spinning hands the Few now commit their hopes and dreams, albeit the most recent addition to the ranks of the increasingly numerous Few, Samuel L. Silverstein to be precise, is offered no choice in the matter, Sammy having been abandoned, still dreaming, in a Marmon speedster parked alongside the copse of spruce adjacent to the lavabo (more of which anon), for Sammy is a man who likes to sleep late, as is the prerogative of the Hollywood motion picture mogul, and has recently proved himself a rather disruptive presence in casting covetous glances at his *fiancée* Vanessa Hopgood, refusing to allow Sir Archie to retract his general apology, and remarking at length and in mysterious fashion on the uncanny similarity between the big bushy heads of curly red hair sported by both Rusty McGrew and George P. Dangleberry III, which latter conversational gambit, the Few being unacquainted with the aforementioned Mr Dangleberry III, was considered by all present as gallimaufry verging on hurlothrumbo.

And so our pilgrims return, as aforesaid, to their long and weary *progress*, albeit your n. is almost immediately obliged to acknowledge that said progress will be nowhere near as ne'er-ending as he may have led the Reader to believe, for no sooner has Rusty McGrew manoeuvred the low-slung sedan around the spruce copse, negotiated the knotty rough beyond and subsequently gained a paved road, than our pilgrims pass a sign bearing the legend 'Tropico Springs Country Club', which intelligence causes the ex-chorus doll Adele Fitzhalligon to give vent to a theory-positing murmur in querying register.

'What's that, old beazel?' says Archie. 'Didn't quite catch the *sine*

1 That is, Tropico Springs.

qua non there, what with your murmuring and the windows being rolled down and the Lincoln sedan being possessed of a pleasingly throaty roar at full throttle.'

'Oh,' says Adele, 'I was merely wondering aloud as to whether, now that we have left behind the Tropico Springs Country Club, the hamlet of Tropico Springs itself might not follow with all the inevitability of Robespierrean winter.'

Indeed, the theory is hardly posited before its proof is confirmed by an informative city limit sign, which reads 'Welcome to Tropico Springs! The Biggest Little Town in the World! Elev: 4,505. Pop. 1280.', which sight is cheered to the rafters by our weary pilgrims, if by rafters we might be understood to mean the horizontal rods spanning the interior roof of the Lincoln sedan, which is very much our intention.[2]

Curiously, given that he was until recently so sored up as to threaten to visit involuntary *seppuku* on Bugs Dooley, none cheers so lustily as Rusty McGrew, who, as the low-slung sedan rolls through downtown Tropico Springs, discovers the serried ranks of a choir invisible delivering multiple *Hosannas!* in his heart, in consequence of which the bolt reverses out of Rusty's previously troubled soul at a rate of knots.

In order that the Reader might fully understand why, your n. here reminds the Reader that Rusty, being an outlaw, gangster and Volstead-defying bootie, is a citizen whose horizons have until now been bounded by mean streets, back alleys, gin-joints and speaks, all of which amount to a hanging garden of Babylonian design by comparison with the rat-infested open sewer that comprised the inner-city tenement on Dublin's Buckingham Street where the young Rusty was first thrown back on his own resources.[3]

2 It appears that the narrator here employs the first-person plural (i.e., 'if by rafters *we* might understood to mean'; 'which is very much *our* intention') to illustrate the extent to which the relationship between Reader and Narrator is so symbiotic as to be considered that of an indivisibly singular entity.

3 Readers interested in the conditions pertaining in Dublin's inner-city tenements during Rusty's youth are directed to James Plunkett's *Strumpet City*, although said direction should not be construed as a recommendation, particularly for any Reader

Thus it is that Rusty stares around and about in mild surmise as he motors through downtown Tropico Springs, it being the case that Tropico Springs might without exaggeration be described as the very essence of semi-tropical dream-oasis to the weary traveller who has traversed antres vast and deserts idle. The bright desert sun twinkles upon white stucco and red-tiled roofs, flickering into rainbows where it encounters fountains at play. Swimming pools can be glimpsed glittering behind high hedges like so many diamonds loosely strung, and time itself seems to doze in the torpid air. Tall palms line wide boulevards, water runs with a kind of glistening glee, and the lawns are so lush, Rusty notes approvingly, as to radiate the quality of green-ish glow that likely emanated from Madame Curie as, sipping upon the first of her Friday night's well-earned martinis, she reflected on another good week's work.

'It's quiet,' observes Vanessa as she stretches and yawns in the sedan's shotgun seat.

'It is,' agrees Rusty.

'Would you go so far as to say *too* quiet?'

'They do say it's possible,' says Rusty, as his choir invisible gives voice to the concluding movement of Beethoven's *Ninth*, 'to have too much of a good thing.'

'I take it you are referring to the immortal Weber,' says Vanessa, 'whose considered opinion of Tropico Springs would very likely be that *every prospect pleases, and only man is vile.* Take all those bums stooging around, for example. One or two, okay, can give a place a bit of colour. But this joint is infested.'

'Looks like it,' says Rusty.

'It's a shame.'

'I couldn't agree more.'

Here, alas, your humble n. is obliged to add *barefaced liar* to the dismal litany that comprises Rusty McGrew's rap sheet, it being the case that Rusty's internal choir is at this very moment turning a collective hand-spring whilst yodelling *Hoopla!* To understand

with delicate sensibilities in the matter of corpses being gnawed by rats the size of regulation footballs, *&c.*

why, it should be noted that the foregoing dialogue is the first of its kind to occur between Rusty and Vanessa since Rusty wrenched claymore from chimney breast the previous evening, with the consequence that Rusty is keen to promote a tone of bonhomie, e'en if such involves lying through his teeth, i.e., concurring with Vanessa that a plethora of bums stooging around is a shame.

Further, we must more closely observe the phenomenon Vanessa so offhandedly dismisses as *bums stooging around*, i.e., the men to be seen on every corner gazing blankly at walls, or standing at crosswalks staring up into the flawless blue desert sky, or otherwise wandering aimlessly along palm-lined boulevards scuffing stones and kicking cans with eyes glazed and hands stuffed in pockets, their shoulders hunched in what might easily be construed by the casual observer as the physical manifestation of apathy, ennui and soul-shrivelling *weltzschmerz*.

Among all the failings his many detractors lay at the feet of Rusty McGrew, howe'er, that of casual observer is notable by its absence, and the reason why Rusty is now tapping a toe to Handel's *Hallelujah Chorus* is because Rusty, much in the way deep calls unto deep, perceives in the sightless and shambling meandering of its menfolk the symptoms of a town sickened to its very soul for the want of a venue wherein might gather gentlemen conflatable with those colleagues of Mr Barry Lyndon who were far advanced in the science of every kind of profligacy, but especially ~~gambolling~~ gambling.

'Let's blow this dusty joint,' says Vanessa.

Alas, Rusty's inner ear is by now tuned entirely to the choir invisible as it calls, Siren-like, to his entrepreneurial spirit by repeatedly trilling through a truncated variation on the scales, *viz.*, the old *do-re-mi*.

For lo! where Vanessa sees only a quiet burg populated almost entirely by bums stooging around, Rusty has visions of a new Shangri-La, it being the case that Rusty has long since harboured a secret ambition, unbeknownst to all but his confidante Bendix McGroarke, which is to shake off Hollywood's tinsel and start afresh, far from the provocations and persecutions of Bumbles McGee; and where better than the somnolent spa town of Tropico Springs high in the Sierras, where the pine-scented air itself sparkles with the promise of bumper-throttling fizz. 'If Tropico Springs ain't my gold-paved El Dorado,' muses Rusty in the secret quiet of his conscience, 'the very Platonic ideal of a home-from-home for those outlaws, gangsters and booties who find themselves on the lam and happy to pay a premium for some home cooking and a little dice on the side, then my name ain't Jasper Huxtable 'Rusty' McGrew,' which, as the attentive Reader will undoubtedly recall, it very much is.

'Cordelia?' says Rusty.

'Yes?'

'Where's this lakeside writing bolthole of yours?'

'Not entirely sure, being honest. Bugs?'

'Head for the lake, Rusty. Then pootle around a bit until you come to where the country club's ninth green abuts the lakeside aforementioned.'

'Roger that. Although …'

'Yes?'

'I don't suppose there's a more roundabout route, one involving multiple sharp turns and blind corners, by which we might possibly shake off the mustard-yellow Marmon speedster that has been doggedly trailing us e'er since we passed the city limits?'

'Who, Sammy?' enquires Bugs.

'It's *Sammy* in the speedster?'

'Well, it was, until he just now pulled in at the Snoqualmie Hotel and disembarked, before beckoning authoritatively at a uniformed flunkey.'

'Ah,' says Rusty, and he ins with the gat, i.e., muff pistol,[4] he had previously removed from an inner pocket preparatory to ventilating the pilot of the Marmon speedster had said citizen

4 Here the Reader is advised to intuit, in all further instances of Rusty or Cordelia brandishing the Remington derringer, that the brandisher has either recently borrowed or retrieved same.

attempted, with daring slalom and squeal of brakes, to o'ertake the Lincoln sedan and strive to perforate the Lincoln and the citizens therein with Chicago Piano broadside. Having stowed the gat, he now peers into the rear-view mirror in the eye-narrowing manner of Caesar spotting a sheet-draped citizen of lean and hungry look. 'Bugs?' says he.

'Rusty?'

'You'll forgive me for saying so, I'm sure, but you appear to be surprisingly well informed on Sammy's movements.'

'Yes?'

'So well informed, in fact,' says Rusty, and he outs with the gat again, 'as to lead a citizen predisposed to detecting perfidy where none exists to wonder whether you and Sammy aren't in cahoots.'

'On a point of clarification, are you pondering on whether Sammy and I *are* or *are not* in cahoots?'

'The former, chiefly.'

'Ah. In that case, old gunsel, fear not. It is simply the case that I spent the night huddled against the bole of a spruce in the copse nor'-west of the ninth green, this lest you found yourself unsettled in a strange bed and unable to nod off, and possessed of an excess of vim and in need of working off same by way of decapitation, involuntary *seppuku* or suchlike extravagance, in consequence of which I found my slumbers disturbed by one Samuel L. Silverstein, who, fearing your nocturnal wanderings in verisimilar fashion, crept away from the lavabo and filched a mustard-yellow Marmon speedster from the country club parking lot, which he then proceeded to park adjacent to the very same spruce copse wherein I reclined upon my bole, albeit Sammy slept poorly, the speedster being a fine automobile in many respects but bearing little by way of resemblance to the interior of a Pullman sleeper, and, Sammy being plagued by bad dreams, night terrors and a propensity for talking in his sleep, I subsequently discovered that Sammy is in Dutch with the authorities as regards his legal status as a US citizen, and is in consequence currently in self-imposed exile from Hollywood, which exile he intends to sit out at the Snoqualmie

Hotel in Tropico Springs, an establishment that maintains a tab on Sammy's account, their not knowing the day nor the hour when Sammy might arrive with a chorus doll, cigarette girl or *ingénue* in tow, said tab being crucial to Sammy's current scheme, he being for nonce financially embarrassed due to the wily machinations of one Moxie La Roux, of whom I know naught but that she is, according to Sammy's half-muttered fever-dream, the hottest of *tamales* and Sammy's one true intended.'

'Well, why didn't you just say so?' says Rusty in peeved register, and he ins with the gat again and commences pootling for the lake.

The subsequent journey containing little of narrative interest, with only Archie's plaintive queries ('Are we there yet?') to provide any diversion, and there being naught to see around and about but assorted mountain-tops, i.e., three silent pinnacles of aged snow, thro' the clefts of which can be seen the yellow down border'd with palm, and many a winding vale and meadow set with slender galingale, or Eurasian sedge, all of which bears a striking resemblance to a Tennysonian landscape carved out of *the airy nothing* – I say, there being little of note to delay us, we now proceed swiftly to the Few's arrival at Cordelia's bolthole, a modest three-storey hacienda in white stucco and roseate tile with wraparound veranda o'erlooking the lake and backing on to the ninth green of the Tropico Springs Country Club, as per invoice.

'What *ho*,' breathes Archie reverently. 'Top hole, m'dear.'

'This little thing?' murmurs the de Havilland as the Few detrain from the low-slung sedan. 'I'd almost forgotten it was here.'

'Bring up the bags, Bartleby,' states Archie as he bounds forth in the direction of the ninth green.

'Of course, sir,' says Bartley, there being in fact no bags, the Few's departure from the Beverly Hills Motel being so precipitate that Bartley had discovered himself, as previously reported, so pressed for time that he had quite failed to pack so much as a single lantern or, indeed, niblick.

'Is there a telephone?' enquires Rusty of Cordelia, Rusty being an entrepreneur with a blacksmith's verve coursing through his veins, and thus keen to strike whilst the iron is still hot, said striking being for the most part literal and mainly the province of his subalterns Foxy, Carrots and Redser, who have been known to cut up rough on those occasions when Rusty blurs the lines of demarcation by engaging in some unauthorised busting of snoots attached to persons reluctant or otherwise unwilling to validate Rusty's singular interpretation of free-market economics, a philosophy indebted to Rusty's childhood devouring of Adam Smith's *The Wealth of Nations* in his Buckingham Street tenement as he staved off hunger's pangs by consuming said opus one page at a time.[5]

'Again, not entirely sure,' says the de Havilland. 'Bugs?'

'There's a telephone in the library,' says Bugs, prompting Rusty to stand not, *&c.*, but immediately depart in the direction indicated without so much as a *totsiens*.

'Bugs?' murmurs the de Havilland. 'A quiet word?'

Our tale having now advanced to a semi-crucial juncture with the arrival of the Few in Tropico Springs, but temporarily hung a-fire for the want of sundry antagonistic characters (i.e., Bumbles McGee, the Siblings McGrew and possibly e'en Moxie La Roux) to provide the pip-squeezing tension that makes such a pleasurable release of explosive climax, and there being few more pleasing prospects than a lakeside perambulation in the company of an attractive young woman, Bugs immediately acquiesces to the de Havilland's suggestion that they walk out together, without chaperone.

The circs, it should be noted, are far from ideal, it being the case that lakeside vegetation provides little by way of fauna wherein might be discovered thorns and snails thereon, and that any larks encountered in the High Sierras are likely to be found in captivity and thus significantly duller in spirit than those that flit wild upon

5 It bears no comparison with the burning down of the Royal Library of Alexandria, of course; and yet there is a tragedy of sorts to be discovered in the fact that, between the years of 1904 and 1911, the Buckingham Street Library found itself entirely denuded as starving tenement children went through the stacks like so many locusts.

the wing. E'en so, the sun is shining, a cooling zephyr is ruffling the lake's azure, and it is Bugs Dooley's private contention that if God is not currently in His heaven, He has at least had the foresight to leave a competent minion at the wheel.

Alas, his companion is displaying all the *joi de vivre* of Lady Macbeth struggling with the ramifications of a surfeit of gin.

'You appear troubled,' says Bugs, who never could see a damsel's brow wrung with pain and anguish without feeling obliged to oil on the ministering angel salve. 'Prithee, shrive thy soul and confess what ails thee.'

'The house,' says the de Havilland, 'is fabulous.'

'You're welcome.'

'Especially as it didn't exist until just before we arrived.'

'Ah,' says Bugs, surprised to find himself on the defensive, but alert to the accusatory note in the de Havilland's otherwise dulcet tone, 'a bracing pre-prandial debate on the subjective nature of the universe. Nothing like it to whet the appetite. If a tree, for example, falls in the —'

'I mean to say,' says Cordelia, 'that this morning I was so certain I owned no author's bolthole in Tropico Springs that the very idea of same wouldn't even occur. And yet here I am, only a few short hours later, wondering what the property tax might be on a three-storey lakeside domicile with wraparound veranda.'

'As I understand it, that depends upon usage. If you're resident for more than six months in any given tax year, then you —'

'Actually,' says the de Havilland, 'my concerns are more rooted in the fact that your magicking up a house out of thin air appears to confirm that you are, as advertised, our *bona fide* Author.'

'Well, modesty precludes and so forth. Indeed, if I might paraphrase our old Paracelsian peer Cervantes, it is my study to deserve and avoid applause, it being the —'

'I mean,' continues Cordelia in dogged register, 'the earthquake at the Beverly Hills Motel might well have been a happy coincidence, and you, in claiming responsibility, and generally swanning about aligning yourself with such worthies as Mr James

Joyce, a raving lunatic to be humoured lest you do yourself a damage.'

'Ah, but isn't it to a certain degree true, old page-botherer, that all scribes are raving lunatics to be humoured lest they —'

'Howe'er,' says the de Havilland, 'the lakeside domicile seals it. Further, it becomes pellucidly clear, once we factor in the extent to which the Few discovers itself in narrative disarray, that your ambition wildly exceeds your grasp.'

'Harsh, I think. But probably fair.'

'In point of fact,' continues Cordelia, 'one might e'en be persuaded to believe you have yet to read an entire novel.'

'They are very long,' says Bugs.

'Long?'

'Novels, yes. They do tend to err on the verbose side, at least when compared with a motion picture photoplay.'

At this point, and possibly in tandem with the committed Reader, Cordelia de Havilland blanches and colours a shade of green not unakin to that of seasick frog. 'Please don't tell me,' she gasps, 'that you're a *photoplay* writer.'

'Not quite.'

Here the de Havilland swallows hard and places a knuckle to her lips. 'A photoplay *doctor*?' she whispers.

'Almost.'

'But surely you're not … I mean, it can't be that you are …'

It being easier for a camel to reverse through the eye of a needle than for a woman of delicate sensibilities to form the foul words required, it now falls to Bugs Dooley to confirm the de Havilland's worst suspicions.

'Technically speaking,' says he, 'and until such time as I conclude my first commission, I'm a photoplay reader.'

There now follows a brief hiatus, during which Cordelia de Havilland executes a half-pike reverse in the direction of the proverbial fainting couch, although Bugs, being a veteran of Hollywood cocktail parties (albeit as a waiter) and thus anticipating this very manoeuvre, is already advancing as she falls, catching her neatly in the crook of his left arm and passing under her nose the smelling salts he carries for just such occasions.

'Oh Bugs,' says the de Havilland on reverting to even keel. 'How *could* you?'

'A man has to eat.'

'Couldn't you just eat the scripts?'

'I tried. It seems they've been laminating the pages ever since the Buckingham Street Library farrago.'

'But how does a man progress from reading photoplays,' says the de Havilland with a shudder, 'to writing a full-length narrative yarn?'

'Ah, therein lies the rub.' Here Bugs indicates a nearby bench, situated for the convenience of lakeside strollers, and observes that it might be the ideal venue for a brace of weary travellers to take their ease, especially as one half of the sketch is suffering the post-swoon staggers. 'It's the writers' strike, you see,' says he, once Cordelia is in no further danger of tottering into the lake. 'Writers, as you well know, are of the noblest breed, all for one and so forth, and every scribe from Hollywood to Bangalore refuses to pass the picket. And not just the photoplay writers. Novelists, playwrights, biographers, they're all out. I'd imagine the poets would've joined too, had anyone thought to ask them. Although one never really knows with poets, does one?'

'Stick to the point, Bugs.'

Here Bugs relates the salient garniture pertaining to his transfiguration from photoplay reader to aspiring motion picture scribe, omitting no detail, not e'en his titanic struggle to cut *The Pilgrim's Progress* down to a manageable length. 'I've tried everything,' says Bugs, 'including using a smaller typewriter. But nothing seems to work.'

'I see,' says Cordelia in hollow timbre. 'And the fact that we are in California as opposed to the immortal Bunyan's rather dystopian vision of Merrie Olde England?'

'That's *my* wheeze. I figured a Jazz Age version would be more likely to play in Boise, Idaho. I mean, I don't know if you've ever tried to read *The Pilgrim's Progress*. I'd tried three different copies before I realised it's supposed to be like that.'

'Am I to understand that you are abridging the *Progress* without having read it?'

'Not in its entirety, no.'

'And would my mental health suffer a fatal setback were I to enquire as to exactly how much of it you *have* read?'

'Right now, and given that you're post-swoon, I'd have to say yes.'

There now falls upon our party of two a silence that could not accurately be described as comfortable. Indeed, as they gaze out upon the azure lake dotted with the tiny white triangles of pleasure craft skimming to and fro, the de Havilland is noticeably prone to jactitation, to the point where the ever-considerate Bugs is moved to enquire as to whether she is being besieged by a colony of red ants.

'I'm curious about this writers' strike,' says Cordelia by way of reply. 'How come I haven't heard of it?'

'That's likely because, as previously discussed, you're a character playing the part of an author as opposed to the kitemarked article.'

'According to you.'

'Say again?'

'What I'm getting at, and at the risk of waxing excessively philosophical, is the question of what truly matters.'

'Well, family, I suppose. And your health. They do say that if you don't have your health, you have —'

'I mean, is it more important that I am a character, or that that character is an author? For the purpose of the story.'

'The latter, obviously.'

'So we can say, for the sake of argument, that I am in fact an author.'

'Absolutely.'

'And our narrative is, according to your own testimony, your maiden voyage, as it were.'

'With its fair share of icebergs, what?'

'Indeed. In fact, I would go so far as to say that so perilously haphazard a journey strongly resembles the idle jottings of an author as they rough out a first draft, unconcerned for the nonce with narrative plausibility and the thematic complexities underpinning the traditional three-act structure.'

'Well,' concedes Bugs, 'I've had a lot on, what with getting shot up by Bumbles McGee's *federales* and suchlike. Not easy, this writing lark, e'en under optimum conditions, and being pursued by stuffed grizzlies and threatened with disembowelment would put Willa Cather off her game.'

'No doubt,' murmurs the de Havilland. 'Bugs, would you mind terribly if I were to ask you a deeply personal question?'

'Have on, toots.'

'I ask it with the greatest respect, of course, and couch it in the context of my being a critically acclaimed and bestselling author of such titles as *Fly, Unfledged Dunnock!* and *Madeleine Remembers*, among others, and you, no offence intended, an aspiring scribe to cause Amanda McKittrick Ros to keel over clutching the ribs of her whalebone corset in a vain bid to prevent her split sides from leaking all o'er the parlour floor.'[6]

'Duly noted.'

'Well, has it occurred to you that, rather than being the guiding hand behind this surprisingly inelegant universe, you might instead be an embryonic character in a very rough draft of a story currently being worked out in a more obscure corner of a real writer's subconscious, said scribe being, for the sake of argument, yours truly?'

'Can't say that it has. Do you think it should?'

'It might be no harm to consider the possibility. At least that way you can abdicate all responsibility for any failings that might accrue were the tale to be subsequently critiqued for its want of

6 Described by the *Oxford Companion to Irish Literature* as 'uniquely dreadful', novelist and poet Amanda McKittrick Ros (1860-1939) is currently regarded as the ultimate purveyor of unfashionably prolix prose. Her poem *Visiting Westminster Abbey* begins: 'Holy Moses! Take a look! / Flesh decayed in every nook!' It is to be hoped that future generations will be both kinder and wiser in their assessment of her oeuvre.

the smooth inevitability that generally attends good fiction.'

'Cracking good wheeze!'

'You're welcome. The prospect doesn't cause you to experience any kind of debilitating existential angst?'

'Not that I've noticed. Then again, it's early days.'

'It is.'

'I should also point out that I'm experiencing dire pre-prandial pangs, which might well be masking more nuanced concerns.'

'They certainly would.'

'If I'm still experiencing the old gut-gnawing after the port and cigars, that would probably indicate a more deep-seated anxiety.'

'Very likely.'

'Providing it's not the old incurable.'

'Pardon me?'

'Well, consider the symptoms. The gut-gnawing, the cricked neck from constant craning in vain search of lark upon wing, and an irresistible yearn to drop to one knee and pitch woo.'

'Please don't.'

'Ah,' says Bugs, 'but if your theory holds water, and I am in fact an embryonic character in the previously referenced obscure corner of your subconscious, then it must surely be the case that I am your secret heart's desire.'

Here, having paused to consider said prospect, Cordelia informs Bugs that, if such does in fact transpire to be the case, her stated wish is to be roasted in sulfur and washed in steep-down gulfs of liquid fire.

'The troth wants,' says Bugs, 'what the troth wants.'

'You seem to presume, sir,' says Cordelia, 'that the troth always knows what's best for itself.'

'You allege otherwise?'

'Sir, I do.'

'Madam, I hereby refute your contentious allegation.'

'Ah, but can you rebut it?'

'Ah, but I can.'

'Can't.

‘Can too.’

It being the case that the unseemly bickering of young lovers very rarely results in dialogue of a morally instructive stripe, and especially when both parties are in dispute as to who, or whom, exerts a God-like power o’er the other, we now take our leave of Cordelia and Bugs and drift, wraithlike, back to the lakeside villa’s library, wherein will be discovered Adele Fitzhalligon engaged in the act of subterfugial perfidy our narrative requires if its protagonists (i.e., the Few) are to be discovered in frictional contradistinction with its antagonists (i.e., Bumbles McGee, the Brothers McGrew and, possibly, Moxie La Roux).

To the library!

Chapter Twenty-One

In which Adele Fitzhalligon proposes dropping multiple dimes. Rusty McGrew is revealed, in true tragical fashion, as the instrument of his own downfall.

Alas, dear Reader, we arrive at Cordelia's three-storey hacienda to discover the forlorn figure of Vanessa Hopgood upon the wraparound veranda, who, alone and wrapped for comfort in fur pelisse, rocks back and forth in wicker loveseat, her mien very much that of a woman who has drunk pottle-deep of a distemp'ring draught, if by said imbibing we might be understood to mean Vanessa's recently o'erhearing Bugs Dooley speak of Moxie La Roux, the hottest of *tamales* and allegedly the one true intended of Vanessa's official beau, Samuel L. Silverstein, whose wily machinations have rendered Hollywood's premier *svengali* so financially embarrassed that he is obliged, *sin Dios, sin vergüenza*, to live on credit at the Snoqualmie Hotel, which, in Vanessa's considered opinion, is knavery of such low toby that it cannot be sufficiently deplored.

There being naught we can do for Vanessa at this juncture, it being considered poor *ton* for a narrator to adopt the persona of ministering angel when pain and anguish wring a character's brow, we drift onwards, across the veranda and through the orangery and into the dim corridor beyond, just in time to see Rusty McGrew exit the library and Adele Fitzhalligon enter, Adele remarking insouciantly as she goes by that she has a hankering for some Emily Dickinson, to which Rusty, otherwise absorbed in strategy, replies with a grunt, an understandable but fatal negligence, for had Rusty paused but a moment to wish Adele well in her endeavours, or e'en to express a preference for Longfellow's lyricism over Dickinson's tautly strung stanzas, he may well have noted Adele's suppressed glee, and perhaps wondered at the presence, suppressed or otherwise, of an emotion generally to be observed sprinting in the direction of the nearest gin-mill when the words 'Emily' and 'Dickinson' are conjunctively deployed.

But for a nail the kingdom was lost! For had Rusty paused for just that very moment he would surely have recognised Adele's expression of suppressed glee for what it is, *viz.*, the barely contained satisfaction of the chorus doll scorned who is proposing to drop dimes left, right and centre as she advances upon library telephone, albeit Adele subsequently discovers that the telephone is of the domestic variety as opposed to its commercial equivalent, and thus requires no dimes, whereupon Adele gives vent to a self-mocking chuckle and silently chides herself for being, on occasion, naught but a buffle-headed fribble.

Howe'er, it will no doubt be noted by the attentive Reader that Adele's intention is to drop dimes plural, and that said plurality would likely amount to a minimum of three, i.e., *left, right and centre*, in consequence of which the Reader might well find herself experiencing no small degree of perplexity, given that the phrase is more commonly deployed with reference to the dime singular, e.g., *Despite informing Rusty McGrew she was entering the library in search of a volume of Emily Dickinson's poetry, Adele did so in order to drop a dime.*

Such, of course, is susceptible to ready explanation when we consider the earning potential of a chorus doll in Hollywood. Indeed, it is a matter of record that a chorus doll's wage is a pitiful specimen of remuneration, and scarcely sufficient to keep e'en the most frugal hoofer in Bulgarian fizz, which crude economic philosophy reasons that hungry chorus dolls are more inclined to kick it up a storm, the better to secure tips from the spifflicated gents in the stalls. Thus it is that a private room is generally made available backstage for the purpose of providing the more enterprising chorus doll with an opportunity to augment her meagre earnings, wherein any gentleman sufficiently squiffed might, for a mutually agreed fee, lay his head upon accommodating lap while he weeps about the e'er-expanding lacuna of misunderstanding between he and his wife, with he, Crusoe-like, stranded on one island, and she, Girl Friday, marooned on her own lonely shore.

Such, then, are the legal earning opportunities available to Hollywood's chorus dolls, although Adele Fitzhalligon, as previously related, has devised an additional wheeze, in which she propels herself beyond the footlights by way of stumbling pirouette, and thus reverses the backstage conventions by launching herself into accommodating lap, whereupon Adele, having established to her satisfaction that the twin sturdy bulges poking her fleshy rump suggest that her gentleman of choice is possessed of a well-stocked wallet and the inclination to open same, is eventually persuaded, once the shock at learning that he is a doctor has subsided to pleasant surprise, to allow her chosen gentleman accompany her to the nearest private venue, the better to ensure no bones are broken.

A further option, of course, which is available those chorus dolls willing to risk being aspersed as *a monstrous regimen of women*, is the dropping of dimes on those gentlemen who, on entering the precincts of a nightclub, immediately forget everything their mothers taught them about the *chivalrye* and *curteisye* expected of *verray parfit gentil knights*, and who instead engage in crude badinage, low foppery and much waggling of pizzles, it being Adele's experience that waggled pizzles, much like Hamlet's sorrows, come not as single spies but by the battalion-load, and that newspaper editors and the public they court have an insatiable appetite for whimsy relating to the public waggling of pizzles attached to gentlemen of the married variety, providing they are rich or famous, and preferably both.

Here, lest the Reader believe the foregoing is non-salient pettifog, your n. reminds the Reader that Adele Fitzhalligon discovers herself at this point in her career a chorus line veteran, and a woman for whom time is a tide not only disinclined to wait, but already on the ebb. It being unchivalrous, of course, to allude to a lady's age or veteran status in any context, your humble n. begs the Reader's indulgence by protesting that he does so in order to garner sympathy on Adele's behalf, who might otherwise be perceived by the more sensitive Reader as the gold-digging equivalent of Judas Iscariot, had said traitorous wretch betrayed his One True Lord for pieces of gold as opposed to silver.

Indeed, the more emotionally sensitive Reader may well be wondering if, amid all the motley assemblage of gunsels, loogans, molls and knights thronging our *comédie larmoyante*, Adele Fitzhalligon may not be your n.'s secret favourite, his Flaubertian *c'est moi* as it were, and that a fondness for Adele might be colouring his account of her dismal behaviour, which appears to be largely modelled on the thinking of the vaudevillian philosopher Fanny Brice, the redoubtable Fanny being entirely persuaded that *wrong is for other people*. For lo! it is indubitably the case that Adele, believing herself possessed of free will and ignorant of her status as a fictional character, advances upon the library telephone suppressing a glee incompatible with any sense of guilt or regret at her actions, thus causing the more morally incorruptible Readers to tut disapprovingly at what must be considered Adele's unseemly delight in executing a perfidious ~~*fate*~~ *fait accompli*.

Ne'ertheless, your n. contends that no Reader who has observed at first-hand the soul-shrivelling sight of a veteran chorus doll with a rapidly deteriorating high-kick extension straining to achieve 90°N, only to fall short at 67°NW, could fail to experience the heartfelt pang which eventually comes to us all, and which the reformer and martyr John Bradford best expressed, upon witnessing the execution of a group of prisoners, as *There but for the grace of God goes John Bradford*.

By way of mitigation, your n. here points out that Adele is, like her infamous predecessor Judas, a predestinate, which is to say a pawn doomed to act in treacherous fashion in order to chivvy a story along, in which function she might be considered an unwitting narrative fulcrum, i.e., a poorly disguised *deus ex machina*, Bugs Dooley having recently boxed his characters into Tropico Springs without sparing sufficient thought as to how to engineer his tale's conclusion in the absence of the Few's Hollywood-based antagonists, with the result that Adele is now obliged to shoulder the Rocinantic burden of dropping multiple dimes on the Few, the very rarely happy Few, that band of brothers and sisters with whom Adele has soldiered in the metaphorical Agincourts of the Blue Phalarope and the Beverly Hills Motel, by which dime-dropping will she reveal the Few's whereabouts not only to the world at large but, crucially, for the purpose of our narrative's eagerly anticipated explosive climax, to Bumbles McGee, the Siblings McGrew, Moxie La Roux, sundry G-Men, and very likely the IRS too.

Having established, then, that any infamy accruing from her actions is derived entirely from the failings of her creator, Bugs Dooley, we return to the library wherein the blameless Adele pauses with her hand upon the telephone as she considers her strategy, for Adele discovers herself possessed of so many juicy tidbits relating to citizens whose foibles and idiosyncrasies are of a matter of pressing public interest as might be considered the dime-dropping equivalent of an embarrassment of riches.

Which is to say, Adele might drop a dime on Sir Archibald l'Estrange-B'stard, the American public being inordinately intrigued by the prospect of permanently soused English (or, at a pinch, Anglo-Irish) aristocrats crisscrossing California in pursuit of elusive motion picture goddesses. She might also blow the whistle on Cordelia de Havilland, despite the public being generally disinterested in authors, e'en those responsible for such critically acclaimed and bestselling tomes *A Pirate Called Prudence* and *A Rumour of Warmth*, for Cordelia's habit of toting a concealed double-barrelled Remington derringer of the calibre .41 rimfire short would likely stimulate a heated debate on the intended scope of the Second Amendment. And then there's Vanessa Hopgood, the most shimmering star in Hollywood's firmament and America's Darling™, who is currently consorting with a gangster, and thus a moll, and whose behaviour of late is likely to be construed as aiding and abetting, for said gangster, as the Reader will easily conceive, is Rusty McGrew, the criminal mastermind behind Cecil B. DeMille's suddenly discovering himself possessed of sufficient extras to begin shooting his long-gestating epic *Genghis Khan: The World Must Go*, albeit Adele here discovers herself reluctant to trigger a libel suit unnecessarily, given that said mass round-up of disposable extras would likely be interpreted as strategic self-defence by any reasonably objective jury of Rusty's peers.

Having decided to begin with Vanessa, Adele now lifts the telephone receiver and requests of the operator a connection to her favourite newshound, and responds to the peremptory bark down the line as follows: 'Madame Blavatsky speaking.'

'Adele? Baby! Who is it this time, Pickford?'

There are moments in time which, crackling with the intensity inherent in their epoch-making potential, seem to defy the universal laws and expand beyond the confines of the dictionary definition of a moment (i.e., n. *a very brief period of time*), and thus become a moment of considerable moment, such as the immediate aftermath of the great Alexander's expiring in Babylon, aged only 33, in 323 BC; or Young Tom Norris, aged only 18, stroking home golf's first recorded hole-in-one at Prestwick's old eighth hole in 1868 (or, some say, 1869); and, e'en allowing that the aforementioned crackling is in fact static on the line, Adele ne'ertheless experiences the ineffable frisson that generally attends a moment of some moment, although, Adele being something of a naif in the business of momentous moments, she first interprets said frisson as a touch of heartburn, before belatedly acknowledging that any mild internal scalding might well be self-recrimination whispering through the secret quiet of her conscience.

All of which suggests that the elongated moment of the foregoing might well be considered what the immortal Bacon once declared the *instantia crucis*, for Adele suddenly repents of her intended perfidy, and hangs up the telephone; and with that single gesture lays to rest not only the receiver in its cradle but the impossible burden of her troubled conscience, a matter of not inconsiderable import in the matter of Adele's eventual redemption, e'en if we accept, as we must, that the receiver itself weighs less than two ounces and that the putting down of same was largely underwritten by gravity.

'How now! what noise?' sings out the Reader, or so your n. presumes and subsequently interprets as a query relating to Bumbles McGee, Moxie La Roux, the IRS and a smattering of G-Men, *et al*, who are currently run aground in the narrative backwater of Hollywood and must now be considered, plot-wise, as returned to shelf, which in turn suggests that our tale is doomed to conclude with something of a whimper rather than the more traditional bang associated with explosive climax.

But stay, dear Reader, and be so kind as to recall that Adele Fitzhalligon, on entering the library with multiple dimes clutched in her palm, passed Rusty McGrew *on his way out*.

Further, the Reader is advised to hark back to the previous chapter, and specifically the momentous moment when Rusty first observed Tropico Springs' thwarted votaries of fortune stooging around like bums, their shoulders hunched in what might have been construed as the physical manifestation of apathy, *ennuyé* and soul-shrivelling *weltzschmerz*, but which Rusty immediately identified as the absence of those classic symptoms which tend to identify the thwarted gambler, i.e., the dicer's involuntary wrist-shimmy, the card sharp's unconscious tugging of earlobe, the glazed eyes of the roulette player with no spinning wheel to gaze upon. Such being the case, Rusty leaped to the only possible conclusion: that said votaries were self-medicating against the torture of being deprived of the reckless delirium that has provided the working man with a bulwark against life's tedium for generations without reckoning, and that their strangely pale faces – their dark pale faces – bespoke what the late, lamented Lord Tennyson was first to diagnose as *the mild-eyed melancholy of the lotos-eater.*

Rusty subsequently finding himself alone in a library at last (Rusty, of course, being barred from every public library in Christendom on foot of the Buckingham Street Library farrago), he swiftly went to the Geography section of Cordelia's well-stocked stacks, whereupon he quickly discovered, in Farquhar T. Rondelay's magisterial tome *O Tropico Springs, I Sing Of Thee!*, that, in our little-known corner of nor'-east California, 'the High Sierras' is considered as much a state of mind as a geographical designation, it being the case that the local climate is such as to render Tropico Springs and its adjacent plains equivalent to the poppy fields of Afghanistan, if for 'poppy' we may substitute the word 'lotos', said climate being determined by the singularly distinctive landscape wherein Tropico Springs is located, and which, as the attentive Reader will undoubtedly recall from our previous chapter, is composed of assorted mountain-tops, i.e., *three silent pinnacles of aged snow, thro' the clefts of which could be seen the yellow down border'd with palm, and many a winding vale and meadow set with slender galingale*, all of which, as the well-read Reader will undoubtedly recall, is the precise topography mapped out by Lord Tennyson in his epic poem *The Lotos-eaters*, and which now confirmed Rusty in his initial suspicions.

In consequence, Rusty swiftly concluded that the prospect of perpetual beds of amaranth and moly beneath a heaven dark and holy might be calculated at short odds if a body of entrepreneurial young men were to relocate to the High Sierras and, harking back to a Cervantic Golden Age, wherein the fatal words of *mine* and *thine* were distinctions unknown, cut out the middle-man and establish themselves, collectively, as the lotos kingpin, it being Rusty's belief that Tropico Springs would prove an ideally sleepy desert oasis wherein any frazzled lammisters might discover, to paraphrase Lord Tennyson, *a sweet music that softer falls than petals from blown roses on the grass*, which music is a hallucinatory by-product of the intoxicating combination of eating the lotos day by day whilst watching ripples crisp upon the beach, a state of affairs likely to prove hugely beneficial in the matter of ducats and doubloons pouring into the coffers of Hollywood Fruit Import-Export, Inc.

Returning Mr Rondelay's tome to the shelf, Rusty wasted no time in employing the library telephone to urge the operator to connect him with the offices of Hollywood Fruit Import-Export, Inc., Los Angeles, whereupon the following conversation took place:

Telephone: *Brrring-bring, brrring-bring, brrring—*

Redser: 'Hollywood Fruit Import-Export, Inc. How may I direct your call?'

Rusty: 'Brother Mariner One, reporting for duty.'

Redser: 'Where away, Brother Mariner One?'

Rusty: 'Tropico Springs.'

Redser: 'The dusty spa burg in the High Sierras which offers little prospect of commercial opportunity, e'en to a singularly efficient body of entrepreneurial young men not o'erly concerned with observing the laws, statutes and stifling conventions of civilised society?'

Rusty: '*Au contraire*, Brother Mariner Two. Pack the coffers. I repeat, coffers *plural*.'

Redser: [audible gulp] 'Plural?'

Rusty: 'One word, Brother Mariner Two: lotos.'

Redser: 'Blooming?'

Rusty: 'Below barren peak *and* by every winding creek.'

Redser: 'Criminy.'

Rusty: 'We might need to bust a few snoots first.'

Redser: 'Roger that.'

Rusty: 'But then it's beds of amaranth and moly beneath a heaven dark and holy.'

Redser: '*Holy* moly, you say?'

Rusty: 'Your ears have heard true. Let out the reefs, Brother Mariner Two. We have the weather gauge.'

Redser: 'Aye-aye, Brother Mariner One.'
Telephone: *Brrrrrrrrrrrrrrrrr* …

Thus it is revealed that, having urged the Brothers McGrew to northward ho! for Tropico Springs and spare not the horsepower, Rusty McGrew might be considered guilty of o'erweening ambition, i.e., his desire to establish a cushy billet at Tropico Springs, and thus becomes the instrument of his own downfall, as is frequently the case in the better class of tragical hero, the ancient tragedians being fully aware that audience *schadenfreude* is immeasurably enhanced by the knowledge that the skull-fondling blowhard prancing about onstage is undone by specific character flaws as opposed to the slings and arrows of pitiless Fate, not least because Fate is blind and thus erratic in its aim, and as likely to skewer an innocent audience member as any reckless libertine prating beneath the proscenium.

And so we return to Adele Fitzhalligon in the library as she, ably assisted by gravity, puts the telephone receiver where it can do no harm, much to the relief of her supporters, chief among them your humble n., who firmly believes Adele to be as magnificent as any half-dozen Ambersons. And so, with Adele's character not only preserved but enhanced, we now depart Cordelia de Havilland's three-storey hacienda to join the Rorkian Few in the restaurant to be discovered in the Snoqualmie Hotel in Tropico Springs, wherein the Few may be observed in best bib and tucker and Sunday spats, quaffing copious bumpers of fizz and feasting upon broiled lobster, as will be related in the next chapter, along with much juicy stuff concerning Vanessa Hopgood's apostrophizing Samuel L. Silverstein with frantic vehemence as she endeavours to winkle out the truth pertaining to his alleged dalliance with the Mexican-born *ingénue* Moxie La Roux.

And so we go.

Chapter Twenty-Two

Wherein Vanessa Hopgood demands satisfaction of Samuel L. Silverstein on the first misty morning to present itself as ideal for the purpose.

Our latest chapter now commencing with Adele Fitzhalligon bustling in late to the dining room of the Snoqualmie Hotel, her arrival and inner glow of redemption going largely unnoticed by the Few who are already at table, your n. now states that Adele's recent redemption will have no significant bearing on the events immediately following, and that her arrival is noted only in order that the *mise-en-scène* is complete in every respect and to ensure the attentive Reader will not be distracted by the nagging query, 'Whither Adele?'

'Jeez,' mutters Adele, 'who died?', for lo! the dining room of the Snoqualmie is by no means a joint that could be described as jumping, its ambience being what an intrepid explorer might as a rule expect to encounter in a ransacked necropolis around midnight on the dark side of the moon.

All rules requiring an exception if they are to be considered provable, we turn now to the table under the central chandelier, whereat the mood might best be described as *bonhomic*, it being occupied by the roistering Few and groaning – albeit metaphorically, for it is constructed of stout oak – under the weight of steak, lobster, caviar, *foie gras* and Dom P '21, which latter, being dished out by the posset, may be considered in part accountable for the revels, high jinks and excellent foppery which are the order of the day, or late evening if we are to be precise.

Indeed, the gaiety may be considered remarkable, given that it is only a few short hours since Rusty McGrew was offering Bugs Dooley the honourable option of *seppuku* to be conducted with ordnance acquired in the approved Chekhovian manner.

'How *is* every little thing, Bugs?' Rusty now yodels at Bugs, who, the generalised gaiety and Olympic-standard foppery notwithstanding, is taking no chances, and has stationed himself at the opposite end of the table from Rusty, the walls of the Snoqualmie Hotel restaurant being liberally adorned with tomahawks, spears and similar *memento mori* commemorating the Native American tribe wiped out in order that Tropico Springs be built upon its sacred burial grounds.

'Tolerably fine!' yodels Bugs in reply, brandishing an entire lobster to confirm the sentiment lest his riposte be drowned out by the babble of badinage, the volume of which is commensurate with that of a crop-duster with dicky throttle, for while conversations characterised as *simpatico* tend to murmur along in the lower frequencies, the Few are for the most part conversing at cross-purposes, as we discover when we employ the cinematic convention of *zooming in* to focus on the scrivener Bartley McGuffin, who has glommed onto the bestselling and critically acclaimed author Cordelia de Havilland and is pouring into her shell-like the entirety of the first chapter of his One True Work, begging the boon of a tip or two that might knock the corners off said Work and transform it from a rather square-ish ugly duckling into an elegantly aerodynamic swan, so to speak, and failing miserably to interpret Cordelia's gnomic utterances to the effect that *authors are in fact characters*, and *there being no point in penning so much as a word, no point at all*, all of which leaves Bartley wondering if Cordelia hasn't been poisoned recently by a surfeit of Kierkegaard.

Meanwhile, Vanessa and Archie fare no better, as Vanessa attempts to persuade Archie to avail of the Tropico Springs Golf & Country Club early-bird special (a post-dawn tee with breakfast or brunch thrown in), which would free up Vanessa for a spot of afternoon shopping, while Archie, for his part, is so sniftered on Dom P that he has abandoned all words but the one most vital to his cause, and is thus repeatedly bellowing the word 'Woo!' at Vanessa's finely honed features from a distance of no more than eighteen inches.

The absence of murmurous *simpatico* notwithstanding, the mood at table is ne'ertheless, as previously related, *bonhomic*, so your n. can only assume it is fickle Atropos who now causes Vanessa to avert her finely honed features from Archie's latest 'Woo!' by the exact number of degrees (seven) that allows her to glimpse, through the narrow gap formed by Corinthian pillar and Native American totem pole, one Samuel L. Silverstein at table in the far corner of the dining room adjacent to the kitchen doors, which table is the Snoqualmie's equivalent of *purdah* and reserved for those long-standing customers who are temporarily residing in said establishment *sin Dios, sin vergüenza.*

'Excuse me for just the teensiest of moments,' says Vanessa as she rises like the fabled rocketing pheasant and sets a course for Sammy's table, whereupon your n., sensing impending *imbroglio*, hastens in her wake.

'How's the duck?' says Vanessa as she arrives some minutes later at Sammy's table, Vanessa being obliged in the interim to sign multiple autographs, kiss three separate babies and sing *Happy Birthday* to the Tropico Springs Rotary Club, which is celebrating the first year of its inauguration. Alas, Sammy was so immersed in his pecuniary sorrows as to be entirely oblivious to the kerfuffle caused by Vanessa's progress, with the result that her sudden appearance at his table, shimmering like foam-born Aphrodite but bristling as if possessed of the combined rage of all three of Aphrodite's sisters,[1] causes Sammy to sway back in his seat, feint to the left and then deliver a haymaker with his right, it being the case that Vanessa's employment of the word 'duck' has led Sammy to believe he has been unwittingly cast as the straight man in a

1 Aphrodite was born when some drops of blood fell into the sea in the wake of Cronus castrating his father, Uranus. Other drops of blood fell on the earth, from which sprang the Erinyes, or Furies.

sketch and would, on replying with an entirely understandable 'Pardon me?' to Vanessa's query, for Sammy is in fact dining on roast peacock – I say, Sammy believes he will discover himself on the wrong end of a bust in the snoot and subsequently advised that his 'duck', or facility for evading a bust in the snoot, has been found wanting.

Happily, Vanessa had only the year previous starred in *Fists of Steel, Heart of Gold*, a motion picture biopic of Elizabeth Wilkinson, Clerkenwell's very own European Champion of women's bare-knuckle brawling and a notorious figure e'en by the standards of Georgian London, so it is with Vanessa but the work of a soft-shoe shuffle to step neatly out of range of Sammy's rather wayward haymaker, which, if we are to be entirely fair to Sammy, was executed whilst Sammy was still dazzled by Vanessa's unexpectedly shimmering arrival, in which condition Sammy might be considered to be punching blind, it being the case that Sammy, whilst no one's idea of a *preux chevalier*, would never, under normal circumstances, aim a haymaker, or any other kind of violence, in the direction of a lady, it being further the case that Vanessa, in enquiring 'How's the duck?', was channelling all three of the aforementioned Erinyes, designated by the immortal Virgil as Megaera ('jealous rage'), Tisiphone ('vengeful destruction') and Alecto ('endless'), with the consequence that Vanessa's tone was so harsh as to be unrecognisable as that of Sammy's official betrothed, Vanessa's tone being generally considered rather soothingly melodic providing she remembers to omit any chuckle, giggle or titter from her delivery.

Having executed the evasive soft-shoe shuffle aforementioned, Vanessa now proceeds to get in amongst Sammy with no little vim, her heart swoln with a quality of wrath not unakin to that of noble Mycetes contemplating the notoriously thievish villain Tamburlaine.

'Corks!' says Sammy as he reels hither and yon in consequence of Vanessa's expertly delivered jab. 'Madam, you appear to have lit ten thousand candles out of my left eyebrow.'

'There's plenty more where that came from, buster,' says Vanessa. 'What's this I'm hearing about your being in dispute with the immigration authorities?'

'A simple misunderstanding,' says Sammy in amelioratory register. 'Naught for you to worry your pretty little head about. Ow!'

Having fetched Sammy a right-cross which your n. is obliged to report Sammy fully deserves, it being the case that his amelioratory register occupied a frequency betwixt patronising and condescending, Vanessa now announces that in the matter of simple misunderstanding she is more than amply provided, by which Vanessa wishes to be understood to mean, if your n. might be so bold as to interpret on her behalf, that Sammy had better move on swiftly from bland generalisations to diamond-honed specifics lest he discover his right eyebrow also ablaze with the light of ten thousand candles.

'It would appear,' says Sammy, getting down to cases, 'that some tittle-disbursing sneak has dropped a dime pertaining to the legality of my relationship to Uncle Samuel.'

'Ah,' says Vanessa, who has until now, and understandably, given the heightened emotional intensity of the moment, quite forgotten that it was she who dropped the offending dime on her employer and *fiancé*, Samuel L. Silverstein.

'Vanessa,' sings out Sammy, 'I am so desolate as to roll in ashes!'

'Metaphorically, one assumes,' says Vanessa, 'it being the case that you are currently putting away roast peacock like a man possessed.'

'A man needs to eat.'

'Indeed. And drink, apparently. Do my eyes deceive me, or is that a Mouton Rothschild '73?'

'Being scrupulously pedantic,' says Sammy, 'it's a '79.'

'I see. Celebrating the year of Moxie's birth, are we?' says Vanessa, by which clever segue she not only raises the spectre of the allegedly hot *tamale* who has caused Vanessa's *fiancé* to unilaterally repledge his troth, but casts barbed aspersion upon her rival's age.

'Moxie, you say?' says Sammy. 'Madam, you are grievously mistook if you believe for one moment that I might —'

'I have it on good authority,' says Vanessa, 'that one Moxie La Roux is not only the hottest of *tamales* but the wench responsible, via sundry wily machinations, for your finding yourself living *sin Dios, sin vergüenza*.'

'Rings not so much as a single bell, old screen sizzler. Sorry.'

'Sammy,' says Vanessa, seizing upon Sammy's musical motif, 'is Moxie La Roux, or is she not, the Mexican-born *ingénue* who has drowned out the poignant strains of Clarke's *Trumpet Voluntary* with a more vibrant strumpetry in the mariachi style?'

'No, she is not,' says Sammy with a quiet but impressively dignified conviction, although here, alas, your n. is obliged to note that Sammy would have been better served had he paid more attention to his choice of words than the manner of their delivery.

'Aha!' says Vanessa.

'Aha?' says Sammy

'If my ears don't deceive me,' says Vanessa, who seems to believe herself plagued by sensory organs prone to treachery, 'you have answered by way of a double negative, by which I am given to understand that my initial query is answered in the affirmative.'

'You are again grievously mistook, madam. I simply employed the second negative to emphasise the extent to which the original syllable is to be understood as the very last word on the matter.'

'How *dare* you, sir?' cries a visibly shaken Vanessa, for Vanessa has always known that Sammy is no one's idea of a true *chevalier*, but has never once suspected that his want of gallantry might be so absolute as to persuade him that he might, whilst discoursing with a lady in the throes of conference harsh, expect to have the last word. 'Sir,' says she in trembling register, 'you are quite the most unpleasant species of toad ever to crawl out from under a harrow. I shall send my friends to wait upon yours, whereupon they will issue my demand for satisfaction on the first misty morn to present itself as ideal for the purpose.'

Here, finding herself ill-provided for in the matter of gloves, full evening dress being the exception rather than the rule in the Snoqualmie's dining room, Vanessa fetches Sammy a bare-knuckle right cross & uppercut combo, the better to confirm the seriousness of her declaration of intent.

'You're calling me out?' says Sammy when he has finally concluded his latest bout of reeling hither and yon.

'Most certainly,' says Vanessa.

'But *I* can't fight a duel with a woman.'

'Why not?'

'What if you win?'

'Not *if*, sirrah, but *when*.'

'Point taken,' says Sammy, 'although the general thrust of the query remains unaltered.'

'Well,' says Vanessa, considering, 'I guess you'll pass beyond the veil into the treasury of life e'erlasting from whence unstrained mercy droppeth like the gentle rain.'

'Just as I suspected,' says Sammy, albeit the attentive Reader, detecting the faintest quiver in said delivery, will easily conceive that Sammy has observed a vision streaking across his inner eye in which Sammy observes himself at some future point deep in conversation with the shade of the deceased Achilles and finding himself in broad agreement with said hero's contention that while death before dishonour has a snappy ring, and is factually correct for those whose greatest joy in life is the compiling of dictionaries, it is ne'ertheless an objective truth that the combination of dishonour and sufficient oxygen is infinitely superior to any state in which a dearth of oxygen is the prevailing condition. In consequence, Sammy now issues a ~~fulsome~~ full apology to Vanessa Hopgood for any inconvenience she might experience as a consequence of his ungallant want of biddability, for he discovers himself entirely unable to oblige her in the matter of the satisfaction sought, which horrid intelligence causes Vanessa to take a turn at reeling hither and yon as she seeks a fainting couch in the immediate vicinity, for Sammy's ungallant want of biddability, as the Reader will easily conceive, is ungentlemanly conduct to leave pizzle-waggling in the ha'penny place.

Alas, the Snoqualmie's dining room being found wanting in the matter of fainting couches, Vanessa finally concludes that she has no choice but to remain vertical, whereupon she draws herself up to her full height and demands that Sammy explain how he suddenly finds himself simultaneously defying the laws of both biology and physics in revealing a spine composed of a yellow streak a mile wide.

'Actually, it's you I'm thinking of,' says Sammy in earnest register.

'Oh?' says Vanessa.

'Well,' says Sammy, 'if it were to be the case, hypothetically speaking, that I was to find myself fatally punctured whilst temporarily thrown back on my own resources due to the allegedly wily machinations of a Mexican-born *ingénue* —'

'Aha!'

'I pause here, my one true intended, to fetch as deep a groan as did Parson Adams when he groaned for faithless Leonora, and further remind you that, having prefaced the foregoing with the phrase *hypothetically speaking*, we are currently wandering in the realms of the future conditional, wherein anything said, alleged or implied, or e'en baldly stated, is considered inadmissible in a court of law.'

'Duly noted. Have on.'

'Thank you. I say, my great fear is not that I should perish at the hand of my one true troth-pledge, but that I would do so in parlous financial circumstances which might, at some later date, and possibly in the very court of law previously alluded to, be construed as *intestate*, leaving my current *fiancée* in legal limbo and obliged to issue a writ of replevin in order to recoup any last few several millions of mine which may or may not have embezzled by an *ingénue* who may or may not be Mexican-born.'

'I see. Solutions?'

'Well, Abie reckons the obvious first step is that we marry with all haste.'

'Abie?' says Vanessa. 'Can this possibly be true?'

'It is,' says Abie Cohen, who has in the last hour come panting hot-foot to Tropico Springs on being summoned by a pink flimsy detailing the considerable quantity of Sammy's woes, and whose qualification for the status of *verray parfit gentil knight* might be measured by his willingness to dine in purdah with his client Samuel L. Silverstein e'en though Abie is himself financially solvent, albeit for the nonce, for Abie's resources are intimately bound up in those very resources Sammy finds himself temporarily thrown back upon, which largely explains Abie's gallant biddability. 'May I be the first to wish you *mazel tov*?'

'But once we're married, old legal equerry – what then?'

'You might, madam, being caught up in the spirit of the nuptial festivities, withdraw your demand for satisfaction, citing the crucial lack of glove on the occasion of your challenge being issued.'

'I might. On the off-chance, howe'er, that a touch of *sparagmos* inflicted upon one Samuel L. Silverstein remains my most o'erpowering urge in the wake of said nuptial mirth, is there any alternative to my entering a rather anti-climactic *nolle prosequi*?'

'It being the case, madam,' says Abie, having dabbed at the corners of his mouth with his napkin, 'that your blood, once up, will require more than gravity to restore it to equanimity, I propose that you transfer your demand for satisfaction to the unnamed Mexican-born *ingénue* whose peculation may or may not be wholly responsible for the farrago in which you discover yourselves.'

'Tempting,' says Vanessa. 'And where might she be discovered, this lewd minx to whom you allude?'

'Ah me,' says Sammy. 'They seek her here, they seek her —'

Here Abie cuts across his client's recitative to state that Moxie's exact whereabouts are so obscure as to plunge the entire body of the Pinkerton National Detective Agency into the most perplexing torment of doubt. 'Howe'er,' says Abie, glancing from Sammy to Vanessa with a gaze that is surely the very quintessence of keenness, 'there is more than one way to skin a cat.'

'Not sure why we might need even one cat-skinning dodge, old legal eagle,' says Sammy, 'unless it be the case that, in alluding to the feline motif, you're suggesting Moxie is possessed of a familiar, by which tenuous allegation she might be branded a witch, and thus considered burnable under some obscure statute buried in the legislation of the great state of California.'

Abie Cohen being an aspiring *chevalier*, and squeamish to boot, he now recoils in horror at the prospect of consigning any woman to the flames, let alone a woman he privately considers to be the *ingénue* equivalent of Shakespeare, who, according to the immortal Dryden, left no praise for any who came after.

'Not quite,' murmurs Abie. 'In point of fact, it is my contention that were Samuel L. Silverstein and Vanessa Hopgood to announce their intention to marry no later than noon on the morrow, or sooner if both might be shrived in so short a time, then it is a cast-iron plunger that Moxie will attempt to assassinate one or both of the happy couple.'

'At which point,' says Vanessa, 'one or both of the happy couple might assassinate the Mexican-born *ingénue.*'

'Or,' says Abie, who is as squeamish at the prospect of assassinating women as he is at consigning them to the flames, or, for that matter, any other method of foreshortening their three-score-and-ten in a fashion that might be considered a Jazz Age attempt to out-Herod Herod – 'I say,' says Abie, 'you might simply abduct Moxie and hold her *incognito* until such time as she reveals the whereabouts of Mr Silverstein's last few several millions.'

'At which point,' says Vanessa, 'we give her the old what-for.'

'That's one option, certainly,' says Abie. 'Howe'er, and for what it's worth, my opinion on the matter of —'

'What ho, Sammy!' sings out Rusty McGrew as he wanders by aiming for the kitchen doors.

'Hullo, Rusty. Fancy seeing you here. What noise?'

'Oh, I've just noticed that the Snoqualmie's menu makes no mention whatsoever of Baked Alaska,' says Rusty, 'so I'm making it my mission to enquire of the chef as to whether he might be so kind as to whip up a sample of same, it being the case that Vanessa here is especially partial to a slab of extravagant meringue.'

'*C'est le petit Jésus en culotte de velours*,' confirms Vanessa.[2]

'Rather fond of Baked Alaska myself,' says Sammy. 'Abie?'

'I wouldn't say no.'

'Tell the chef to toss another dozen eggs into the meringue mix, Rusty.'

'Roger that. Oh, and Sammy?'

'Rusty?'

'You seem to be a man who knows his way around Tropico Springs. I don't suppose you'd know where I might locate a jewellers still open at this hour of the evening?'

'As a matter of fact, I do. Would you prefer me to issue directions or, more conveniently, accompany you on your idiosyncratic endeavour to visit a jewellery emporium at such a late hour?'

'The latter, preferably.'

'But of course. Vanessa? Would you mind terribly if I were to rally round to Rusty's party?'

Alas for Vanessa, she now discovers herself rendered speechless at the prospect of her *fiancé*, Samuel L. Silverstein, proposing to assist her secret paramour Rusty McGrew in the latter's attempt to purchase what Vanessa can only assume is an engagement ring possessed of a diamond no smaller than a mammoth's molar, and thus discovers that, contrary to the unwritten laws of chivalry, Sammy is in fact destined to have the last word.

Vanessa now indicating by way of terse nod that Sammy has her express permission to accompany Rusty in his quest to secure both Baked Alaska and engagement ring, our unlikely pair, being in theory bitter rivals for the hand of Vanessa Hopgood, now depart the Snoqualmie's dining room, with your n. in as hot a pursuit as the business of wraithlike drifting allows, for your humble n. possesses, as any self-respecting narrator must, a sixth sense for impending *imbroglio*, and furthermore suspects that Rusty, in

2 French argot, which roughly translates as *It's the baby Jesus in velvet shorts*, or, in plain Anglo-Saxon parlance, the *bee's knees* (or *bees' knees*).

embarking on his stated mission of persuading the chef to rustle up a swift Baked Alaska, does so according to a motive that will likely reveal itself as ulterior, the truth of which (and, indeed, that of Samuel L. Silverstein's rather surprising display of gallant biddability), and the consequences thereof, will be revealed in the following chapter.

Chapter Twenty-Three

In which George P. Dangleberry III is belatedly elevated from minor to major character.

It being rather the done thing that two gentlemen, both alike in dignity, and being rivals for the same fair lady's hand, must eventually hie themselves hence to some damp heath upon a preferably misty dawn, there to break new mutiny from ancient grudge and engage in doings beyond all remedy, your n. is ne'ertheless obliged to begin our latest chapter by stating that Rusty McGrew and Samuel L. Silverstein are currently long odds to engage in same, not least because they are insufficiently *preux* to qualify as gentlemen, each being a *Spark*, if we might paraphrase the immortal Fielding, who is by no means of the *Herculean* Race, e'en if both, as they emerge from the dining room into a long, quiet corridor, now commence discoursing in the gentlemanly style as they ramble along, side by side, with hands clasped behind their backs.

'Settling in comfortably, Rusty?' enquires Sammy.

'Tolerably well, Sammy, thank you. Say, was that the mayor I glimpsed dashing into the kitchen just now?'

'The busboy laden down with tray, methinks,' says Sammy. 'But might I understand from your somewhat hallucinatory conflation of menial and elected public official that you are inordinately keen to encounter one or more of Tropico Springs' most prominent citizens?'

Here Rusty confirms Sammy's contention by stating that he is indeed anxious to be introduced, and as swiftly as possible, to any and all Chief Kahunas, Big Bwanas and Top Bananas to be discovered within the city limits.

'Say no more,' says Sammy. 'And would this be before or after you achieve your previously stated ambition of visiting a jewellery emporium?'

'Before, preferably.'

'I see,' says Sammy, with that very air of barely suppressed glee which Rusty, had he paused upon departing Cordelia's library to engage in literary critique with Adele Fitzhalligon, would have immediately recognised as the physiological manifestation of a citizen engaged in subterfugial perfidy. 'As it happens,' says Sammy, 'the biggest bwana in all of Tropico Springs is very likely on the premises, for George P. Dangleberry III is not only the managing director of the Tropico Springs S&L but the manager of the Snoqualmie Hotel to boot.'

So saying, Sammy now leads Rusty down the corridor which is, as previously referenced, both long and quiet, and thus raises the spectre of temporary *longueur*, which your humble n. now bridges by confirming the suspicion which the Reader very likely harbours, which is that Sammy and Rusty recently departed the dining room of the Snoqualmie Hotel with motives that were not only at odds with their stated intent, but motives which are, in fact, separate but identical, i.e., a burning ambition to see Rusty introduced to Tropico Springs' Grand Poobah, George P. Dangleberry III. Moreo'er, neither man entertains the slightest thought for the fair lady who might be supposed to have rendered them rivals in love, i.e., Vanessa Hopgood, who, back in the dining room, is very likely displaying the outward signs of tizzy as she wonders how best she might juggle the necessity of marrying Sammy L., this in order to lure the Mexican-born spadassin Moxie La Roux into the open, with the very strong probability of Rusty McGrew returning from his perambulation around Tropico Springs to present her with an engagement ring possessed of a diamond no smaller than orangutan's knuckle.

O Vanessa!

Lest the Reader begin to suspect that your n.'s speculation as to Vanessa's tizzy quotient is an attempt to divert attention away from his recent assertion that he possesses a Cassandraic sixth sense – for Sammy and Rusty are no closer to commencing their anticipated two-man Donnybrook than they were when first they embarked upon their perambulation down the long, quiet corridor – I say, your n. is here obliged to state that while every narrator is possessed of an uncanny facility for detecting impending *imbroglio*, no narrator can state with certainty that an *imbroglio* foreshadowed is the *imbroglio* that will eventually fall out, it being generally the case that the latter, or least expected *imbroglio*, once revealed, will be understood by the Reader to represent a narrative *twist*, i.e., that unexpected and frequently counter-intuitive development which generally results in a *reversal of fortune* for one or more characters.

Indeed, the ongoing courtly discourse between Rusty and Sammy ('Gosh, this really is a long, quiet corridor, Sammy.' 'Not sure I've ever seen a longer and quieter one, dear heart.' *&c.*) suggests that the pivot upon which our third act will twist and (likely) reverse is not the Sammy-Rusty dust-up keenly anticipated by Reader and narrator alike, but the George P. Dangleberry III just now alluded to by Sammy L., whom we last encountered upon the terrace of the Musso & Frank Grill, when George P. was subject to that very quality of frantic importunity which admits no denial as Sammy beseeched George to finance his latest motion picture wheeze.[1] George being at the time designated the managing director of a rural Savings & Loan, and thus a minor character, as all financiers, regardless of any and all blandishments suggesting otherwise, tend to be regarded in Hollywood, he was by no means then entitled to the traditional pen sketch, which your n. now hastens to provide. To wit:

1 In point of fact, George P. Dangleberry III was afterwards briefly observed in taking part in croquet tourney at Sammy's palatial stucco mansion in the Moorish style on the corner of Wilshire and Irving.

Height:	5'3"
Eyes:	Iron-grey
Role:	Financier
Facial features:	Oddly reminiscent of battered Norman helmet
Hair:	A big bushy head of curly-red

But stay! sings out the attentive Reader, who, being well read in the Classics, and thus wholly unaccustomed to previously minor characters belatedly assuming a more significant role in the latter stages of a final Act, might now wonder aloud as to whether George P. Dangleberry III's transubstantiation from minor to major character is not, in fact, the most egregious example of *deus ex machina* she has e'er had the misfortune to witness. The concern redounds considerably to the Reader's credit, although, in mitigation, your n. now reminds the Reader of the original idea conceived by Samuel L. Silverstein outside the Blue Phalarope as the Rorkian Few made good their escape from the Phal via subterranean passageways leading to a manhole on Sunset Boulevard, which originality, being wholly unnatural to a Hollywood motion picture producer, eventually yielded a huge eclipse of sun and moon, and caused th' affrighted globe to yawn at alteration, and thus, as the Reader has no doubt long since suspected, and despite Bugs Dooley's self-deluding claims to the contrary, precipitated the localised tremors which allowed the Few to make good their escape from the Beverly Hills Motel and left Bumbles McGee shaking his fist at the sky in impotent fury.

Here, reasoning closely, your n. reveals the minute details of Sammy's diabolical scheme to introduce Rusty McGrew to George P. Dangleberry III, which is largely predicated on Sammy's observing that the first citizen to emerge from the manhole was possessed of *facial features oddly reminiscent of battered Norman helmet* and *a big bushy head of curly red hair*, and his lively astonishment at the very idea of a respected financier lowering himself to such depths as to require a manhole to make good his escape. On subsequently realising, when the citizen had fully emerged, and had risen to his full height of 6'3", that he had momentarily mistaken the notorious gangster Rusty McGrew for George P. Dangleberry III, Sammy immediately conceived of a scheme in which Rusty would impersonate his vertically challenged *doppelgänger* as the managing director of the Tropico Springs S&L, thus allowing Sammy to loot said venerable institution of every last rixdaler and moidore within, and thus finance his latest motion picture wheeze without being obliged to negotiate compound interest, back-end percentage and associate producer credit.

Thus it is, as the Reader will readily conceive, that Samuel L. Silverstein is in rather bobbish mid-season form as he indicates that Rusty should now veer hard right, abandoning the long, quiet corridor and entering the Snoqualmie's kitchen, which short-cut to George P.'s office Sammy has previously employed when moved to lodge an official complaint about the deplorable quality of service offered to a Hollywood motion picture mogul on the rare occasion of said worthy being obliged to dine on credit, whereupon Rusty, who is first through the swinging doors, claps peepers upon the Snoqualmie's head chef.

'Hullo,' says Rusty. 'Mind if we cut through?'

'By all means!' sings out the head chef, who, his title notwithstanding, is currently the kitchen's solitary employee and more than somewhat flushed of cheek, it being the case that the entirety of his staff called in sick earlier that very evening, leading the head chef to brood on the distinct possibility that his staff are elsewhere celebrating the sous chef's birthday, it being the case that the sous chef had a week previously requested the night off but proved somewhat elusive as regards the reason for same. 'But don't feel any obligation to scurry through apologetically whilst avoiding eye contact,' sings out the head chef. 'Should the spirit move you to dally awhile, and perhaps engage in some idle chit-chat as to whether the mulligatawny requires another bay leaf if it is to be considered just as mother makes it, then please feel free,' which friendly overture causes Rusty to reflect that here was a chef who would very likely have responded with a cheery *Huzzah!* had Rusty broached the topic of whipping up an off-menu Baked Alaska, the attentive Reader no doubt noting the crucial *had* in the foregoing that confirms your n. in his suspicions that Rusty's private intentions in the matter of Baked Alaska were never as publicly stated, said *had* being suggestive of a past tense future conditional, which combination rarely concludes in satisfactory fashion in the matter of the action mooted.

The Reader, of course, will readily conceive of the psychology that has prompted Rusty to deceive his fellow lammisters in the matter of Baked Alaska, for Rusty, while at table, found himself beguiling the time by glancing around and about in surreptitious fashion, his gaze now falling upon the listless vacancy of a man who sits hunched o'er his roast peacock, hands uselessly cupped for the want of a brace of die as their owner – alas! only in his mind's eye – rolls a boxcar; or now noting the man who, nodding absently as his betrothed waxes lyrical about the exquisitely tender veal, detects in the random arrangement of four green peas on his plate a possible flush, needing only one more pea (green) to scoop the pot; or, roving further afield, the corpulent gentleman dining alone who contemplates the revolving cheese plate and who, seeing not the glistening wedges of Brie, Wensleydale and Roquefort but the exhilarating blur of roulette's wheel of chance, visibly plunges, mood-wise, to full fathom five.

For lo! everywhere he looked Rusty encountered naught but that glassy-eyed stare more usually associated with Jimmy the Schnook on the fateful evening when, perusing the library of Frankie One-Punch as he waited for Frankie to knot his cravat in the Osbaldeston style, Jimmy stumbled across the dictionary definition of 'schnook', albeit the glassy-eyed stare indigenous to the Snoqualmie's dining room confirmed for Rusty his diagnosis of that sickness which rots the sporting man from the inside out when there is neither wager nor hope of same on the horizon.

Is it any wonder, then, that Rusty found himself so chock-a-block with treasons, stratagems and spoils as to be considered a man who hath no music in himself? No, dear Reader, it is not; and, it being something of a convention e'er since the fateful day Cain established his fearful precedent that any man possessed of a bosom heaving with treasons and stratagems must out with same or perish from o'erstrained heart, Rusty made his excuses and took his leave of the Few, ostensibly to enquire about the possibility of the chef confecting a Baked Alaska for dessert, but in reality to seek out the Snoqualmie's manager with a view to exchanging pleasantries before getting down to cases *vis-à-vis* the inauguration of a covert gaming establishment on the premises, and perhaps e'en, all going well, sounding out said worthy as to the strengths and weaknesses of Tropico Springs' current lotos kingpin.

'Am I thus given to understand,' says the head chef to Sammy L. as we return from our expositionary reverie to the Snoqualmie's kitchen, 'that the quality of the steak is virtually irrelevant in Hollywood, and that it's far better a dinner of herbs where love is than a stalled ox and hatred therewith?'

'Better, certainly,' says Sammy. 'Although best, of course, is the entire stalled ox equally seasoned with herbs and fond regard.'

'Well, I never!'

Sammy and Rusty now departing the kitchen possessed of that gentle glow that tends to accrue when a man avails of an unexpected opportunity to do a little good, they discover, directly across the plushly carpeted corridor, a door bearing the legend *George P. Dangleberry III: Manager.* Here Sammy pauses, tappity-taps on the door, then ushers Rusty on ahead.

Here your n. reminds the Reader that Rusty McGrew only ascended to the pantheon of America's Most Wanted late yesterday afternoon, and further states that Rusty, while notorious in the precincts of Hollywood and Greater Los Angeles, is something of an urban phenomenon, and thus – as might be divined from his dining unmolested in the Snoqualmie's restaurant – not immediately identifiable in the High Sierras as the terror of six city police departments and all right-thinking Republican voters everywhere. Thus it is that Rusty, an unusually modest god-scorning wrath of God by the standards of same, is as a matter of courtesy preparing to announce himself as he enters George P.'s inner penetralium; and yet, as the door snicks shut behind Sammy, Rusty's *pourparlers* wither away unvoiced, leaving in their unspoken wake a quality of profound silence that could not have been more paradoxically deafening were Rusty in fact a Danish prince announcing his imminent expiration.

It is not the lavish extravagance of George P.'s furnishings that renders him mute, although to Rusty's eyes the office is opulent on a papal scale. Nor is it the portrait of George P. Dangleberry III dominating the rear wall, which is roughly three times larger than life and depicts George as Henry V at Agincourt, visor up and left foot propped on the headless torso of a vanquished foe, the reins of his warhorse gripped in his right hand, which scene has rendered stronger men than Rusty McGrew so weak at the spleen as to pre-empt conversational overtures until such time as tongue and larynx might be trusted to combine in a manner not to be confused with raucous hilarity. Nor, indeed, is it a desire to leave unscored that veneer of civilisation which requires a man to refrain from busting the proverbial gut when confronted with another's ludicrously aspirational self-perception that causes Rusty to gawp in speechless *homage* to the hush that generally attends the untimely demise of Danish prince.

For lo! Rusty McGrew is experiencing the dumbfounding awe that tends to get in amongst a man on his first clapping peepers upon a *gänger* that can only be described as his *doppel*.

'You!' says Rusty on finally recovering the power of speech, albeit said power was of a wattage sufficient to generate only the bare syllable recorded.

'You!' says George P. Dangleberry III, who, despite being every bit as passionately bemused as Rusty at the unheralded appearance of his ominously identical twin, is more renowned at the Tropico Springs Golf & Country Club (TSGCC) for his forehand smash than quick-witted badinage, and so contents himself with the conversational equivalent of a solid base-line return designed to force his opponent into developing a new line of attack.

'But you're *me*!' says Rusty in the despairing timbre of a man suddenly confronted by his *fetch* in the early evening.[2]

Here your n. is obliged to state that George P. Dangleberry III is by disposition the mildest of men, his Highland Scots ancestry notwithstanding; and yet, no man transcends his lowly origins to become hotel manager, managing director of the Tropico Springs S&L *and* honorary vice-president of the TSGCC who is not possessed of the inner steel of a moderately sized skyscraper.

'How *dare* you, sir?' he now declaims in the stentorian tenor that has brought many a TSGCC acting secretary to the very brink of resignation. 'It should be patently obvious to even the most myopic of identity-usurping dullards that you, sir, are in fact *me*.'

'How now!' snarls Rusty. 'I'm the *gänger*, and you're the *doppel*.'

'Calumny!' sings out George P., who hadn't hauled himself up by the bootstraps from a youth spent picking buffalo chips on the prairie to become Tropico Springs' biggest bwana so that his reputation might be traduced by an admittedly handsome but certainly uninvited representative of the shallower end of that stagnant soup composed of the great unwashed, i.e., the *hoi polloi*.

'Don't you calumny me,' ripostes Rusty. 'I'll calumny *you*.'

'You wouldn't dare.'

'Try me.'

'Sir,' says George P., who, a disposition as mild as the proverbial westering zephyr at sunset on any given Friday evening in June notwithstanding, is most definitely not the kind of havering cove to leave untried a challenger who so blatantly demands a trying – 'I say, sir, I am reliably informed that the forecast for tomorrow's dawn is misty, and for the want of a glove I hereby give verbal notice of my intent to do you down in an illegal but entirely honourable fashion. Do you choose pistols or sabres, sir?'

2 In Irish folklore, the *fetch* is a supernatural double, roughly equivalent to the German *doppelgänger*. The *fetch* is generally considered an ill omen portending imminent doom, although only if encountered in the evening, being instead, if glimpsed in the morning, a harbinger of a long and happy life.

'All going well,' says Rusty, who in the matter of ordnance had never knowingly brought a knife to a gunfight, 'I'll be toting a carriage-mounted M1895 Gatling Gun.'

'Pardon me?'

'Ah,' says Samuel L. Silverstein, standing forth, 'I only now belatedly realise that I have neglected to make the necessary introductions. You see before you, friend George, none other than Jasper Huxtable McGrew, although it is perhaps the case that Mr McGrew's reputation is more fearsomely preceded by his *nom de guerre*, Rusty.'

It would be no exaggeration to state, dear Reader, that the silence which subsequently pertains could not have been more profound if Sammy had announced the simultaneous demise of twin heirs to the Danish throne. Indeed, it is a silence so complete that, when it is finally broken, George P.'s gulp is that of a pirate's parrot who has just copped a musket ball in a manner later described in the captain's log as *tragically, the full and irreparable beakage*.

'*The* Rusty McGrew?' he whispers.

'In the flesh,' confirms Rusty, 'currently backing and filling but with the weather gauge very much in the offing.'

'Is that a yes?'

'It is.'

'Cripes.'

His Highland Scots ancestry and a well-earned reputation as a non-havering cove notwithstanding, George P. Dangleberry III is only rarely a man to confuse courage with suicidal foolhardiness. Thus it is that, confronted by a man who is reputed the Jazz Age incarnation of the Bard's Coriolanus in his propensity for carrying before him noise and leaving behind only tears, George finds himself somewhat jellied in his quaking, which is to say that his inner structure retains the very same quantity of steel required to shore up a moderately sized skyscraper, albeit one built upon the tectonic fault-line known as the Pacific Ring of Fire and which currently finds itself at the epicentre of an earthquake clocking in at roughly IX-point-seven on the modified Mercalli scale.

'Ho!' sings out Rusty, who is possessed of a nose that can sniff out a jellied quaking at fifty yards.

Alas, dear Reader, it gives your narrator no pleasure to relate that it is this 'Ho!' that sets the seal upon George P. Dangleberry's fate; or, to be precise, George P.'s response to said 'Ho!', which can only be described as an unbecomingly prickly bridling in a man of George P.'s rank and status.

To understand why Rusty's apparently innocuous ejaculation should so fatally discommode a man who, having risen from humble bedesman to assume the mutually beneficial positions of hotel manager, S&L managing director *and* honorary vice-president of the TSGCC, and who should in theory represent the Platonic ideal of equanimity in the face of non-vulgar single-syllable provocation, we are now obliged to drift, wraithlike, back in time to the Texan Panhandle and a homestead far removed from Tropico Springs, where we encounter a tow-headed boy who is barefoot and wearing patched dungarees as he picks buffalo chips on the prairie, said chips intended to provide the evening's fuel for a meagre fire that will prevent Little Georgie and his widowed mother Myrtle from freezing to death, and who, trudging home engulfed in a stink of buffalo dung with his knapsack half-empty, crests a rise to observe two gentlemen a-horse and gazing westwards, where Myrtle, silhouetted against the sinking sun, is engaged in tending her vegetable patch. The joy leaping salmon-like in Little Georgie's bosom is only to be fully understood if we now reveal that one of the gentlemen a-horse is the Widower McCoy, a rancher possessed of fifty thousand acres, a considerable smattering of longhorn steers and a quantity of family fortune referred to in the social pages as *fair*, and thus a man, according to local scuttlebutt, in want of a wife, which was why Little Georgie's hopes soared like a lark upon the wing and Georgie began glancing about the barren prairie for thorns and snails thereon, only for said hopes to be dashed by a casual utterance emanating from the Widower McCoy as he observed Myrtle tilling her vegetable patch, said utterance being, ''Tis pity she's a hoer,' which Georgie instinctively understood to mean that the Widower McCoy had no issue with the tool his mother was wielding *per se*, but was instead sneering at the sight of a potential wife tilling the soil, the implication being that the Widower McCoy, being as close as the Texan Panhandle might muster in the matter of gentry, considered the Widow Dangleberry a woman only fit to pull chair to table below the salt, which slight was sufficient cause for a hope-dashed Georgie to avenge Myrtle's honour by drawing from his knapsack his deceased father's Colt Peacemaker and pop a couple of slugs plumb spang between the shoulder blades of the Widower McCoy, and then, dead men being in no position to tell any tales before a jury of Little Georgie's peers, slot a brace into the Widower McCoy's companion (the Widower McCoy's foreman, Jeremiah von Bingen) for good measure.

Thus it is that, as we now return to our tale, George P. Dangleberry III's mien is very much that of the hot-brained Barry Lyndon proposing to avail of that rough-and-ready law which is of great convenience to persons desirous of expeditious justice.

'Do you *Hoe!* me, sir?' says George P, who has, alas, mistook Rusty's 'Ho!' for 'Hoe!'

'I do *Ho!* you, sir.'

'I advise caution, sir.'

'Ho-ho-*ho*!' says Rusty, who, on being challenged to consider the respective merits of discretion and valour, opts to present himself as a sociopathic Saint Nick.

Now George P. Dangleberry III is, as previously noted, the Platonic ideal of mild-mannered equanimity, as befits a man of his class, status and not inconsiderable achievements. Ne'ertheless, he is first and foremost a man, and few men worthy of the nomenclature, and especially those erroneously confusing 'Ho!' with 'Hoe!', will sit idly by whilst an identity-usurping *doppelgänger* gives tongue to a lusty 'Ho-ho-*ho*!' with a blithe indifference for the consequences.

Courage, of course, is not the absence of jellied quaking; nay, it is the willingness to descend into the Valley of Death despite the quivering limb, the spongy knee, and the tum that has without notice been leased out as a sanctuary for uncommonly agitated butterflies. Confronted by the legendarily homicidal Rusty McGrew in top-notch 'Ho!'-bruiting form, George P. Dangleberry III's inner steel may well have been impersonating a strawberry blancmange embarked upon furious rumba; howe'er, it is with the ghostly 'Hoots!' of his long entombed Highland Scots progenitors echoing in his ears that George P. takes a deep breath, pushes back his chair, and stands.

'Sir,' says George in a tone of such gravitas as to cause the shade of Pitt the Elder to weep bitter tears of unfulfilled potential for as much of eternity as remains to him, 'you have disgraced yourself again.'

'Hm,' says Rusty.

'Do you 'Hm' me, sir?'

'Hm.'

The Reader likely now wondering why Rusty has so swiftly abandoned the rather provocative syllable 'Ho!' for the infinitely more restrained 'Hm', your humble n. now urges the Reader to recall that Rusty had cause to lapse into a prince-demised hush on the occasion of his entry into George P. Dangleberry's office, but that said silence was not precipitated by the enormous portrait depicting George as Henry V and giving it the full *Et voila!* in respect of decapitated Frenchies. Indeed, given George P.'s reputation as Tropico Springs' Top Banana, Chief Kahuna and Big Bwana all rolled into one, the portrait seemed entirely apposite to Rusty, e'en if Rusty, if sorely pressed, would have been obliged to state that his preference in the matter of portraiture tends to lean towards the geometric distortions of the Post-Impressionists, or, at a pinch, the dramatically strident brushwork of the Fauvists.

Crucially, howe'er, George P. Dangleberry III was sitting down at the moment of Rusty's ingress; and it is only now, as George rises in umbrage-taking outrage, that Rusty is in a position to fully compare and contrast the reality and the aspiration as he gazes anew upon the jauntily canted visor, the snorting warhorse, and the thumb held aloft by the victorious Henry. Howe'er, it is the generously exaggerated dimensions that cause Rusty to goggle more than somewhat, the portrait being roughly three times larger than life and the flesh-and-blood George P. being no taller in pin-striped vest and spats than he was in patched dungarees, i.e., 5'3" or thereabouts in Cuban heels, which is why the word *Preposterous!* soars unbidden to Rusty's tongue, only to discover his tongue already snarled in his larynx due to said larynx being independently engaged in venting a belly-busting guffaw, with the result that Rusty experiences the odd sensation of gargling a minimum of two coconuts, the audible consequence of which is the surprisingly restrained 'Hm' which has provoked George P.'s ire.

'Have a care how you 'Hm' me, sir,' says George P., 'or I will have thee hymned!', by which the Reader is given to understand that George's dander is so far up as to risk perishing in the rarefied atmosphere of courage previously unsuspected, for George's *Hm / Hymn* word-play alludes to the future funeral arrangements of one Rusty McGrew if said *provocateur* persists in what George P. has misinterpreted, yet again, as an egregiously monosyllabic provocation.

Alas, dear Reader, George P. is on this point, as elsewhere, grievously mistook, it being very much the case that Rusty McGrew has always been possessed of a quiet admiration for any man with the guts to oppose him, and especially when Rusty's jelly-quaking nose has already detected said guts in an advanced state of butterfly-churned ferment. Which is to say that Rusty, rather than giving George the high hat, as George erroneously supposes, discovers himself decidedly impressed with the cut of George P.'s jib, particularly as George is now engaged in a little backing and filling himself, his blue peter proudly fluttering as he prepares to hoist sail and swoop down, goose-winged, upon the one-man crime wave feared and abhorred by a minimum of six Californian police departments and all right-thinking Republican voters everywhere.

Sadly, the die is cast when Rusty, in attempting to verbalise same, can only muster a somewhat strangulated 'Hm'; and the attentive Reader will no doubt nod sagely at the irony of an inadvertently cast dice setting the seal upon the velitation foregoing, for it was to establish a mutually beneficial gaming establishment in the Snoqualmie's back rooms that Rusty first set out in quest of Tropico Springs' very own *Señor Fromage*.

'In which case, sir,' says George P. as he draws himself up his full 5'3" in Cuban heels, 'I shall see you on the 10th tee at dawn on the morrow, misty conditions or no, leaving it to your sense of honour, sir, as to whether you tote along the aforementioned carriage-mounted Gatling, for I, sir, choose sabres.'

There being little more to be said on the matter, and Rusty's probable contribution of yet another 'Hm' being likely to pour oil on waters already aflame, Rusty simply bows his head to indicate his understanding and acquiescence, and, with a terse nod to George P. and Sammy L., departs George's office, leaving behind such a silence that any casual bystander might assume he had just announced, during Lenten matins in a Copenhagen monastery, the tragic news that the entire lineage to the Danish throne, extending to three generations, has violently perished.

'Say, George,' says Sammy after allowing a decent interval to elapse. 'How *is* every little thing?'

'Oh, as to that,' says George in morose timbre, 'I discover myself cast down more than somewhat.'

'Entirely understandable,' says Sammy, 'given that you've just had the traditionally disconcerting experience of meeting your *doppelgänger*, or *fetch*.'

'I'm afraid it's rather more complex than that.'

'Oh?'

'Well,' says George, pouring a brace of Glenmorangie highballs, and handing one across to Sammy, 'for a moment there, during my recent verbal skirmishing with the notorious gangster Rusty McGrew, I believed that we had recognised in one another sufficient commonality to allow for an unlikely bond to form, which might e'en have developed into a mutual agreement to impersonate one another, Rusty to enjoy a well-earned break from terrorising a plurality of Californian police departments and Republican voters everywhere, and I, in turn, to give free rein to my Scots Highland ancestry and indulge in a latent instinct for carnage and gore, and perhaps e'en, if Rusty's associates were agreeable, the daubing of our faces with streaks of blue woad.'

'Sounds delightful,' says Sammy L. 'In fact, there's likely a motion picture in it, providing you somehow manage to survive the morrow. You'll be in need of a second, I take it?'

'I will.'

'Might I offer my services?'

'Would you?'

'Certainly, old sport. Nothing could make me happier than providing psychological comfort to an old friend in need, and ensuring both pistols are correctly loaded, or that neither blade is tipped with poison, and so forth.'

'You really are too kind, Sammy.'

'Think nothing of it,' says Sammy, reaching into his breast pocket and extracting a boilerplate contract, upon which, on the dotted line inserted for such contingencies, he now scrawls *The Pilgrim's Progress*. 'Think instead of attending to your affairs, lest it be the case that you are not Rusty's *doppelgänger*, or *fetch*, but he yours, and thus not only the harbinger but the instrument of your inevitable doom.'

Here, having first commented favourably on Sammy's pragmatism, George P. pauses before appending his signature to the proffered contract, and enquires of Sammy as to whether he has anyone in mind for the role of public notary, it being George P.'s understanding that such is required to bear witness to the fact that George is by no means being subjected to undue stress, or being otherwise prevailed upon in cruel and unusual manner, to legally copper-fasten the Tropico Springs S&L's obligation to finance Sammy's latest motion picture wheeze, *The Pilgrim's Progress*.

'Certainly,' says Sammy. 'Just ring through to the dining room there, and ask for Abie Cohen to join us just as soon as he has paid the bill, Abie being not only Silverstein Studio's in-house legal counsel but a public notary on the side.'

George being agreeable, he now reaches for the telephone on his desk, which alerts your n. to imminent *longueur*, for Abie, once reached by telephone, will be obliged to first request his bill, and then pay same, before embarking down the *antres vast* of the long, quiet corridor that leads to the Snoqualmie's foyer, Abie being unaware that he might cut through the kitchen as a shortcut – I say, a *longueur* of interminable duration now looming, your n. concludes our current chapter, pausing only to echo George P.'s disappointment in the matter of Rusty and George failing to mutually hatch a scheme in which each *doppelgänger* might impersonate the other, for such might well have provided humorous diversion for any Reader familiar with the Classical comedies, wherein confused identities provide the source material for much by way of japes, *espièglerie*, and existential commentary on Nature *vs* Nurture in the forming of character.

Alas, it is not to be, and as your n. drifts away, wraithlike, from George P.'s office in the Snoqualmie Hotel, his only consolation is that the events foregoing serve to confirm the crucial importance of our tale's philosophical proposition, i.e., that *the world might be a better place if only everyone would make a little more effort to get along.*

Chapter Twenty-Four

In which the elusive Moxie La Roux makes good on our obligation to honour the foreshadowing alluded to in Chapter Twenty-Two.

As Rusty McGrew wends his way back to the Few's table in the Snoqualmie's dining room, his brow as frogged as any Hussar's regimentals as he strains to devise an explanation which might plausibly reconcile his twin promises of Baked Alaska and engagement ring with the noticeable absence of same, whilst simultaneously cogitating on how best to broach the topic of his somehow managing to wangle himself into a duel at a time when the desired low profile might have been more handsomely answered by a non-conflict resolution, your n. avails of the opportunity provided by Rusty's dawdling – Rusty, requiring thinking time, having decided to forego the kitchen as a shortcut, and take the long way round – I say, your n. now reflects upon the irony of our tale discovering itself potentially stymied only a few short chapters ago, when its expected explosive climax hung a-fire due to the Few being on the lam in Tropico Springs whilst their foes, adversaries and mortal enemies – in a word, antagonists – lay marooned in the narrative backwater of Hollywood for the want of intelligence that might reveal to them the whereabouts of the Few.

The future, alas, being a realm beyond the remit of e'en those narrators endowed with the acutest sense of impending *imbroglio*, your n. had no way of knowing that Rusty would discover himself called out by George P. Dangleberry III, nor that Vanessa Hopgood might similarly issue Samuel L. Silverstein with a demand for satisfaction, nor that Vanessa and Sammy, on the advice of Abie Cohen, might instead make good on their engagement of convenience by announcing their intention to marry no later than noon on the morrow, the better to flush out any Mexican-born *ingénues* who might subsequently act according to the old saw which states that *a stitch in time saves nine*, i.e., that a swift assassination now, or no later than noon on the morrow, would likely prevent inordinate amounts of mazooma being frittered away in a court of law should the widowed Vanessa Hopgood issue a writ of replevin in the matter of her deceased husband's mysteriously missing millions.

Thus it is that your humble n. now discovers himself echoing the angels in paradise who, on being beseeched by Dante to explain the nature of their hauntingly plaintive song, declared that *they only longed for what they already had*, by which means is the Reader informed that, had your n. only possessed the wisdom of paradisiacal angels, which resembles to an uncanny degree the far-seeing omniscience of Apollo, or at a pinch the Victorian-era author, he would have understood that our tale was already possessed of the potential for explosive climax, or, indeed, multiple examples of same.

Alas, dear Reader, of all sad words of tongue or pen, the saddest are these: 'It might have been!' For, our tale having long since foreshadowed the arrival of the Siblings McGrew in Tropico Springs, said trio being lured by Rusty's scarcely credible promise of lotos blooming below barren peak *and* winding creek, we now discover ourselves obliged to drift, wraithlike, sou'-west across the great state of California to the environs of Hollywood, where we alight outside the offices of Hollywood Fruit Import-Export, Inc., there to note the unexpected presence of the renowned tough Chancer McGurk, who skulks in lurking fashion in the shrubbery which sprouts midway between the front door of Hollywood Fruit Import-Export and the sidewalk where a LaSalle Coupé sits with engine idling, the better to facilitate a tyre-screeching getaway if Chancer is stumbled upon, discovered or otherwise unmasked in his intelligence-gathering expedition.

Chancer being not only a renowned tough, but infamous as a recidivist perpetrator of *foul crimes that no darkness can ever hide, no oblivion can wash away, nor any power on earth remove* (*cf.* Sophocles), the Reader will easily conceive that he is a citizen of notably pockmarked phiz, with the crass habits of wearing Sunday spats every day of the week, squirting chaw without regard to the whereabouts of the spittoon, and inserting unnecessarily sneering *sees* into his discourse to achieve a vaguely intimidating effect. Which is to say, were we to now accost Chancer as to his motives for skulking in shrubbery, he would likely respond by loosing a mahogany stream of liquid chaw in any direction but that of his Sunday spats and say, 'I'm here, *see*, to see what I can see, *see*?'

It being the case, howe'er, that it is only in the less persuasive tales that we encounter characters who are wholly good or entirely bad, your n. here notes that while he is known to the authorities as a Sophoclean bad 'un, Chancer McGurk is a surprisingly nimble and genteel character during those Friday night tango lessons which represent for Chancer a whimsical interlude from the daily grind of sapping loan defaulters in dark alleyways, and during which Chancer might e'en be said to possess the instincts of the *verray parfit gentil knight* who would undoubtedly recoil in horror at the prospect of a lady being reneged upon by a gentleman who, in so reneging, has proved himself neither gentle nor a man, but a scullion of base instincts.

Thus any Reader who finds her sensitivities discommoded by the dishonourable intentions of Samuel L. Silverstein and / or Rusty McGrew as they pertain to Moxie La Roux and Vanessa Hopgood, respectively, will easily conceive of the motive behind Chancer McGurk's skulking in the shrubbery adjacent to the entrance to Hollywood Fruit Import-Export, Inc., for Chancer, at the behest of his Friday night tango partner Moxie La Roux, is maintaining close watch on Redser, Carrots and Foxy McGrew, Moxie being no man's fool and, having cogitated mightily upon the whereabouts of her one true intended, i.e., Jasper Huxtable

McGrew, in the wake of her magnificently dramatic exit from Sammy L.'s palatial stucco mansion on the corner of Wilshire and Irving, rapidly came to the conclusion that keeping an eye on the Siblings McGrew would likely shed light on the vexing conundrum of Rusty's mysterious disappearance, the Siblings McGrew sharing in one respect an unexpected trait with the dandelion upon closely mown lawn, which is to say that dandelions, in a manner not unakin to Adele Fitzhalligon's experience of waggled pizzles, come not as solitary spies but by the —

But stay! There comes a throaty *brum-a-brum-BRUM!* from the garage adjacent to Hollywood Fruit Import-Export, Inc. which entirely rends your n.'s expositionary reverie, which discord is shortly followed by a Buick Roadmaster fairly bristling with red-headed McGrews shooting forth with copious discharge of oily smoke, whereupon, having narrowly avoided bashing in the LaSalle Coupé's front bumper, the Roadmaster pulls a sharp right and burns rubber in the general direction of nor'-east.

Chancer McGurk being as light on his feet as the Reader might expect of a tango devotee, it is with Chancer the work of a moment before he is installed behind the wheel of the idling LaSalle, whereupon he shoots off in hot pursuit of the Buick Roadmaster in a manner befitting a particularly diligent *gentil knight* of the automobile age, and especially one who has been promised a hefty chunk of boodle for services rendered to one Moxie La Roux, who – lo! – is now discovered in the Coupé's passenger seat and urging on Chancer with a verve previously reserved for Spartan mothers sending out their first-born sons to be slaughtered for the honour and glory of Lacedaemon.

Thus, alas, is set in train the events that will lead to our tragical climax. For just as the moth is drawn to the flame, the Siblings McGrew, hailed by the Siren song of Brother Mariner One, are so dazzled by the prospect of filthy lucre to be scooped up in handfuls from the gold-paved streets of Tropico Springs that they have quite neglected to check the shrubbery for possible skulkers, the upshot of which is that Moxie and Chancer are now on their tail, which sequence might easily be deciphered by the attentive Reader to mean that the Siblings McGrew will fetch up at Tropico Springs with Chancer and Moxie in their wake and spoiling for broils at almost precisely the same time (i.e., dawn-ish) as Rusty McGrew strides onto the 10th tee of the TSGCC to contend with his freshly hatched mortal foe and *doppelgänger*, George P. Dangleberry III.

But stay! What's this? Can it be possibly be a Stutz Bearcat rumbling off in hot pursuit of the hotly pursuing Chancer McGurk, with said Bearcat being piloted by the redoubtable Bumbles McGee? It can; moreo'er, it is!

For Bumbles, being the Platonic ideal of no man's fool, has in verisimilar fashion to Moxie La Roux instituted surveillance on the Siblings McGrew, the better to divine the whereabouts of that pimpernel *nonpareil*, Rusty McGrew; and who now, by peeling out in surprisingly indiscreet rubber-scorching manner, makes good on your n.'s recent promise that events have been *set in train*, the Reader being no doubt aware that a train is generally composed of multiple carriages, and that the invisibly linked Buick-LaSalle procession would scarcely warrant the nomenclature for any profit-oriented transport company, whereas the Buick-LaSalle-Stutz triptych, being comprised of three distinct carriages, as it were, may now be accurately described as a train.

And so, with said events *set in train*, and our obligation to foreshadowing duly executed, we gird our loins for another wraithlike drifting across the great state of California, noting only as we go that as our three-ship flotilla spreads sail, bound for Tropico Springs, there is to be observed in its wake a veritable armada of automobiles, said vehicles variously piloted by IRS agents and sundry G-Men, all of whom have been independently operating, as the Reader has no doubt already conceived, according to the immortal Juvenal's time-honoured principle, i.e., *Quis custodiet ipsos custodes*?

The scene thus set, it remains only for your n. to sigh heavily, and shudder in anticipation of the cataclysmic blood-letting to come, the details of which will be revealed in chapter the next, providing our motley citizenry behave in a manner commensurate with character already established and all falls out as presumed, of which, alas, we have no guarantee.

Chapter Twenty-Five

In which our explosively tragical climax is nipped in the bud by the belated arrival of Jonathan Law, i.e., Bumbles McGee, the IRS and sundry G-Men.

'Bugs?' says Cordelia de Havilland as Author and author, respectively, amble down the dewy sward of the TSGCC's ninth fairway in the pre-dawn mistiness on the following morn a half-niblick or so behind their fellow Few, who are currently engaged in murmuring disputation, for the non-appearance of the promised Baked Alaska the night previous still rankles with some, and notably Sir Archie, who is more partial than most to a wedge of *frou-frou* pie. Meanwhile, Vanessa Hopgood, in antimonial undertone, cautions Rusty McGrew against pursuing his intended course, it being rarely the case that the reputation of an America's Darling™ is burnished by her ring-side presence at the scene of lethal joust, unless it be on the set of a Cecil B. DeMille epic; while of the crude Anglo-Saxon epithets employed by Adele Fitzhalligon as she describes for Bartley McGuffin her displeasure at being roused a good six hours prior to noon it is best to recount naught and draw the proverbial veil, or else adopt Bartley McGuffin's tactic of fixing in the mind a far horizon and nodding every 30 seconds or so, the better to approximate the conversational courtesies required of a man when a woman finds herself in a state of dudgeon so high as to warrant a prudent dudgeon's strapping on of precautionary parachute.

Thus, dear Reader, it is a rancorous Few which finds itself bound for the 10th tee, upon which, vaguely discerned through the faint mist of early dawn, Samuel L. Silverstein and George P. Dangleberry III await with a brace of sharply honed sabres.

'Speak on, old Paracelsian peer,' chirps Bugs, who is unique in his revelling in the pre-dawn *flânerie*, largely because his patent leather footwear is entirely unsuitable for dew-soaked sward, with the result that his toes are sloshing about like a pair of tiny schools of fish in his Argyll socks, a sensation which is proving most enjoyably ticklish.

'I've been thinking,' says Cordelia.

'Another critically acclaimed bestselling tome in the works, old page-botherer?'

'In a manner of speaking, yes.'

'And there's a wrinkle or two in the wheeze you're hoping to iron out by running it up the mast in the presence of a fellow scribe to ascertain whether he is more likely to salute or deliver a broadside raking it stem to stern?'

'If you wouldn't mind.'

'Not in the least, old quill-tickler. Have on.'

'Well,' says the de Havilland, 'it's a story about an impossibly beautiful young woman —'

'Vanessa Hopgood?'

' — whose role in life it is to play confidante to a motion picture goddess who might very easily be conflated with one Vanessa Hopgood.'

'Ah.'

'Howe'er, it soon transpires that the impossibly beautiful young woman is in fact *a spy in the house of love*, a veritable Mata Hari commissioned by the motion picture star's jealous beau to maintain subterfugial tabs on said goddess.'

'Good wheeze!'

'But that's not all.'

'Not by a long shot?'

'Not, as you suggest, by a shot that is indeed significantly longer than previous events might have led us to believe was likely.'

'Corks!'

'It is further revealed that the impossibly beautiful young woman —'

'Has she a name at all, this fine girl who, if I might paraphrase Squire Thornhill, is worth all the priestcraft in the nation?'

'Well, the name Dame Ophelia Montefiore sprang to mind last night whilst we waited in vain for the Baked Alaska. Too much, do you think?'

'Not in the slightest. Rather a ring to it, what?'

'I think so, yes. Anyway, Ophelia is further revealed to be the critically acclaimed and bestselling author of titles such as *A Duet for Kazoo* and *April's Cicada Sings But Once*, who is merely pretending to serve as confidante to America's Darling™ in order to garner material for her latest opus, which is set in the murky world of Volstead-defying bootlegging, gangsterism and generalised lawlessness.'

'Ruddy marvellous.'

'But that's not all.'

'No?'

'Ophelia meets a fellow author, a man whom she believes —'

'Handsome, is he? This scribe, I mean.'

'Not conventionally, no.'

'I see. Then it's his indifference that proves a very magnet which attracts the dauntless iron of our Calista's soul?'

'Not noticeably.'

'Right.'

'Anyway, it seems that this fellow author —'

'What's he called, this bland gink notable only for a surprising absence of memorable physiognomic features and character-establishing quirks?'

'Numps.'

'Numps?'

'Numps. Anyway, the gist is that Numps is not so much a fellow author as The Author, if you follow my significant capitalisation.'

'I see.'

'You do?'

'Not so much a novel, this latest parchment-scrawling wheeze of yours, but a memoir.'

'Precisely.'

'Albeit with names changed to protect the guilty.'

'It seems only fair.'

'So how does it end?'

'Well, this is not only the crux but the very nub of the matter.'

'The nub, eh?'

'Bugs,' says Cordelia, pausing abruptly and taking Bugs' hands in hers and gazing into his eyes with the steely intensity of an impoverished foundry worker assessing the merits of the metal tent he has built with foundry scraps and off-cuts for his newly pregnant wife-to-be, 'it's the very Platonic ideal of the nub. In fact, if I was to say it was the *sine qua non* of nubbishness, I would not be —'

'Say no more,' says Bugs, 'for no more needs to be said.'

'You'll do it, then?'

'Do what?'

'Give me a happy ending.'

'Absolutely, old termagant. Just say the word.'

'I just did.'

'Ah.'

'What you have to understand,' says the de Havilland, 'is that my ambitions were always modest. And, were it the case that I had risen through life's ranks from humble beginnings to become confidante to a motion picture goddess *and nothing more*, such would likely have sufficed.' Here Cordelia sighs heavily and places a tremulous hand upon bosom. 'But ah me, oh my!'

'Touch of heartburn, old stick?'

'Untune that string,' says the de Havilland, inadvertently quoting Avon's Finest, 'and hark! what discord follows.'

'I don't follow. What discord?'

'Don't you see, Bugs? You have taken me to the mountain top and allowed me gaze down upon the valley-shaped paradise of being a bestselling *and* critically acclaimed author with a writing bolthole on the lake at Tropico Springs, a position I am loath to relinquish providing I can manage the taxes on a three-storey hacienda in white stucco and roseate tile with a panoramic view of the TSGCC's ninth green.'

'I see. Discord indeed, and all for the want of a solitary lute-string correctly tuned.'

'Therein lies the nub.'

'The crux.'

'The very gist. Bugs,' says the de Havilland, fixing Bugs with the steely intensity of any newly pregnant wife-to-be gazing keenly upon the metal tent constructed overnight by her poverty-stricken beau from foundry scraps and off-cuts, 'if there is any way of maintaining the *status quo*, I would likely be grateful to the person who has so maintained said *quo*.'

'*Likely* be grateful?'

'The probability is in the realm of distinct.'

'Cor!' says Bugs, as his soul invokes the twin immortals of Dante and Chaucer in its rising and rapturously going towards the concavity of the eighth sphere, *&c*. 'But Cordelia,' says he as the plaguy rub hoves into view to blemish the eighth sphere's until recently perfect concavity, 'can you truly wish to be considered an impossibly beautiful bestselling author for all eternity —'

'And critically acclaimed.'

' — I say, an impossibly beautiful bestselling *and* critically acclaimed author for all eternity, *even if it's not true*?'

To this Cordelia responds with the full and unvarnished John 18.38, i.e., '*Quid est veritas?*'

'Not sure I'm entirely *au fait* with the essence of your admirably terse riposte just then, old bean.'

'Who cares if it's *true*?' says the de Havilland. 'What matters is how it *feels*.'

'A good point, and well made.'

'Thank you.'

'And Numps?'

'Numps?'

'I'm just wondering,' says Bugs, 'where old Numps-a-Daisy

might figure in this paradisiacal valley you're currently gazing down upon from the proverbially craggy peak.'

'Oh,' says Cordelia, pointing by way of diversional sleight-of-hand into the middle distance, wherein can be discerned the 10th tee previously alluded to, 'might that be the infamous George P. Dangleberry III I see before me?'

It might; indeed, it is!

Here your humble n. takes this opportunity to pause and pay tribute to the courage of George P. Dangleberry III, and further record that George P., his *mentis* not only shipshape but in impressively Bristolian *compos*, and with a full foreknowledge of Rusty McGrew's fearsome reputation as a god-scorning wrath of God – I say, George P., having earlier kissed farewell to his wife and three children as they slumbered in their blissful ease, now stands upon the 10th tee as solitary as any lonely pine, this providing we o'erlook, for the purpose of poignant poetical allusion, the stolid presence of his second, Samuel L. Silverstein.

Moreo'er, it is clear from the Alpine up-jut of the Dangleberry chin that George P. is possessed of a deficit of daunt, e'en if the more observant Reader might discern in his narrowed eyes and pursed lips an expression suggestive of a man deploring his ineluctable fate and experiencing a fleeting regret for lost opportunities for pleasure, aye, and perhaps e'en reform; but of visible clues as to jellied quaking, or tum-trapped butterflies a-churn, there is none.

It is not, howe'er, George P.'s heroic pose that now causes the Few to mill about all a-flap and cooing. For lo! the expression of ineluctable deploring upon George P.'s phiz is insufficient to obscure the fact that, their respective heights notwithstanding, George P. Dangleberry III is the very mirror image of the Few's champion Rusty McGrew, for Rusty, on returning to the Few's table the night before, having determined to distract Vanessa from the notable absence of any and all diamond rings by *hear ye*-ing the following morning's coming attractions, and being further distracted in deflecting queries as to the whereabouts of the promised Baked Alaska – I say, Rusty has quite neglected to mention that George P. Dangleberry III is his very own *doppelgänger*, or *fetch*.

Thus Vanessa can be heard to bewail the fact that she is *always the last to know*, whilst Archie, still a tad squiffed from downing three jeroboams of fizz in *lieu* of the promised Baked Alaska, loudly requests that the combatants adopt the time-honoured uniforms of shirts *vs.* skins in order that his wager not go on red rather than black, so to speak. Meanwhile, Bartley McGuffin, classically educated in the lesser Dublin university, can be heard to note, darkly, the ominous consequences that tend to accrue, historically speaking, when a *gänger* chooses to thwart, let alone skewer with sharply honed sabre, his supernatural *doppel*, which consequences are, to the best of Bartley's recollection, that '*Sick Earth convulsive groans from shore to shore / And Nature shuddering feels the horrid roar*,' which intelligence, and subsequent quoting of the immortal Falconer, represents the remaining 10% of everything Bartley learned in the lesser Dublin university.

Indeed, the hubbub grows so cacophonous that it is with some relief, tinged with trepidation, that your n. now observes Samuel L. Silverstein standing forth to commence the pre-duel conventions, which begin with Sammy clearing his throat and enquiring as to whether an apology to the upstanding pillar of his community George P. Dangleberry III might be forthcoming from the red-haired Irish galoot Rusty McGrew, and whether, in its theoretical absence, both gentlemen's honour might be satisfied by each man shooting wide, which suggestion, given the heightened emotions roiling in his breast, is perceived by Rusty as an unconscionable slur on his marksmanship and results in Rusty challenging Sammy to a duel on the first misty dawn to present itself for the purpose, this providing Rusty survives the best efforts of George P. Dangleberry III, which contretemps might have been entirely avoided had Sammy only taken a moment to confirm that the weapons of choice are sabres rather than pistols.

Alas, dear Reader, it is at this juncture that the low rumbling your n. has until now omitted to mention, but which is presumed by the citizenry gathered about the 10th tee to be the pathetically fallacious drumroll of a thunderstorm announcing its imminent arrival – I say, there now comes a low rumbling which subsequently erupts into the throaty *brum-a-brum-BRUM!* of a Buick Roadmaster careering around the copse of spruce and bumpity-bumping across the ninth green, much to the outrage of Sir Archie, who is heard to wailingly wonder aloud as to whether or not there is nothing sacred anymore, albeit the close conjunction of double negative deployed by Archie leaves his potential supporters – chief among them Vanessa Hopgood and Bartley McGuffin, ardent disciples of the noble Scottish art both – flummoxed to such a degree that neither is entirely comfortable with advancing an aye or a nay.

Meanwhile, the Buick, having screeched to a halt at the 10th tee, swiftly disgorges a small stampede of red-haired McGrews, all of whom are *up and doing with a heart for any fate*, i.e., spoiling for broils. Indeed, being a corps so well drilled as likely to cause King Leonidas himself to dampen his *chitōn* in involuntary appreciation, it is but the work of a moment before all three of Rusty's callow lieutenants are getting in amongst George P. Dangleberry III and lashing him about with cudgels, knobkerries and suchlike tools of chastisement, it being George P.'s great misfortune that on this misty dawn in particular the Siblings believe they have a point to prove to Rusty in the matter of demarcation, i.e., that when it comes to the bashing of mazzards and busting of snoots, the responsibility for same devolves to Rusty's subalterns Redser, Carrots and Foxy, either individually or, as in the case under preferment, collectively. Moreo'er, the Siblings are acutely aware that the sleepy burg of Tropico Springs represents virgin territory in respect of bootlegging, gambling and generalised outlawry, and that it is thus incumbent upon them, on the occasion of establishing a new fiefdom, to put their best foot forward, this according to the principle implicit in the immortal Voltaire's *pour encourager les autres.*

Indeed, so ferocious is the Siblings' assault that it takes the combined efforts of Rusty, Bugs and Sammy L. to persuade them that the impending duel is an extra-curricular joust designed to satisfy a personal point of honour, which is precisely why it is taking place outside of business hours, at which point the Siblings offer their sincerest apologies to the prone George P. Dangleberry III and withdraw to the sidelines, there to lay side-bets with Archie on the eventual outcome of the bout, albeit at significantly reduced odds than they might have obtained before their ill-advised intervention.

Hardly have Bugs and Sammy hauled George P. vertical, howe'er, when another *brum-a-brum-BRUM!* is to be heard, said brummage presaging the arrival of a LaSalle Coupé piloted by the renowned tough Chancer McGurk, from the passenger seat of which now springs Moxie La Roux, who wastes only such time as is required to ensure, via the rear-view mirror, that all is surely as God intended before leaping forth into the fray and stating in no uncertain terms that if the old saw be true, i.e., that a stitch in time saves nine, then she, Moxie La Roux, might be considered the very Needle of Destiny!

At which point, and as the Reader will easily conceive, Samuel L. Silverstein starts like a very guilty thing upon a fearful summons issued by Mexican-born *ingénue*.

'Moxie!' sings out Sammy, 'put up thy hanger, for the engagement of Vanessa Hopgood and I was always one of convenience, and our proposed ratifying of the treaty no later than noon today naught but a cunning wheeze to flush out any mercurial hot *tamales* who might be harbouring the murderous impulse in their cold, black hearts.'

'Tchah!' says Moxie, who, having delivered said withering syllable in Sammy's direction, now turns to face Vanessa directly. 'It is my considered opinion, madam,' says Moxie, 'that you are affianced to a gapeseed of the first estate, and you're welcome to him. In the matter of *the frail craft of love*, Rusty McGrew is my very stay and anchor, unless it be the case that said *craft* is not noun but verb, in which case I rephrase my declaration of unswerving affection to further clarify that Rusty and I will carefully craft a love that is as frail as any reed, and thus likely to bend before the world's tempests, yet never break.'

'Golly!' says Rusty, who is, alas, as susceptible as any Irish-born male to the blandishments of an Iberian-descended *ingénue* as is the Chevalier O'Keefe to all sorts and conditions of women.

'Madam,' says Vanessa with admirable restraint, 'I hereby commend your aspiring to those *three difficult Ingredients* the immortal Fielding considers vital to every Comic Writer, by which is meant that in Works of the Comic kind, *the main End or Scope be at once amiable, ridiculous and natural,*[1] and further applaud your vain attempt to compensate for your lack of natural amiability by going big on ridiculous.'

'Ridiculous *this*,' says Moxie, and, so saying, launches herself upon Rusty McGrew whilst declaring the unswerving affection aforementioned, which very likely would, in time, and with a patience gently spiced with kind words and good deeds, have matured into that *love* which, as Mr Barry Lyndon had good reason to believe, is formed on purpose out of all the prettiest soft vowels and consonants in the language.

Alas, dear Reader, Moxie being something of a *naïf* in the matter of the misty dawn broil, she has in her haste thrown herself upon Rusty McGrew's sword-arm; and while the Reader will no doubt be relieved to discover that Moxie narrowly avoids impaling herself upon Rusty's sharply honed sabre, her impeding of same results in George P. Dangleberry III immediately issuing a *nolle prosequi* in the matter of imminent duel lest any innocent bystanders discover themselves prinked in the process, whereupon, and much to his dismay, your n. is obliged to state that our tale's potentially explosive climax discovers itself rendered something of a damp ~~squid~~ squib.

But stay! No sooner has Moxie La Roux glommed on to Rusty McGrew like unto Mexican-born limpet than Vanessa Hopgood

1 See the Preface to *David Simple* (1744) by Sarah Fielding, second edition.

finds herself possessed of the green-eyed monster which doth mock the meat it feeds upon, by way of which allusion, as the Reader is undoubtedly aware, the Bard was referring to those cats who toy with their prey before delivering the *coup de grâce*, and which your n. now employs in his turn to allude to the feline grace employed by Vanessa as she springs upon Moxie's undefended rear and, having established a firm grip on Moxie's stylish *chignon*, drags our *ingénue* backwards off the 10th tee, whereupon Archie and the Siblings McGrew open a book on the Hopgood-La Roux undercard, with Vanessa at 6-4 and Moxie, her hot-blooded Latin temperament considered something of a fatal flaw in the cold heat of battle, going to post at evens.

'Now hold on just one cotton-pickin' nonce!' declares Samuel L. Silverstein in stentorian timbre, whose desire to see Vanessa vanquish Moxie, or Moxie dispatch Vanessa, is trumped only by his more pressing need to have Rusty scrag George P., or George P. so terminally puncture Rusty as to warrant said red-haired bootie peppered for this world, albeit Sammy's words descend upon deaf ears like so many proverbial trees falling in the forest, for his potential audience – the embattled Vanessa and Moxie excepted – is by now all agog to discover the pilot of the latest automobile to come *brum-a-brum-BRUM!*-ing up the ninth fairway, a mystery susceptible to ready explanation by the attentive Reader, who is no doubt keenly anticipating the arrival of a Stutz Bearcat with Bumbles McGee at the tiller.

Here, alas, your n. is obliged to state that the low rumbling which presages Bumbles McGee's arrival upon the 10th tee is by no means a low rumbling singular, but a rumbling evocative of multiple automobiles *brum-a-brum-BRUM!*-ing up the ninth fairway, which crucial detail your humble n. has carelessly omitted due to his being distracted by the unpropitious aspect of Vanessa and Moxie engaged in mutual drubbing. Thus it is that Bumbles McGee's Stutz Bearcat hoves into sight around the copse of spruce at the head of a small convoy of G-Men and IRS agents, a sight to instil terror in e'en the most law-abiding of hearts, and which certainly renders the citizenry gathered about the 10th tee a frozen tableau as they gaze in horror upon the sight of motorised Horsemen of the Apocalypse swooping down goose-winged across the ninth green with the weather gauge at their back.

Indeed, it is likely that a rout on a par with that of the Persians at Gaugamela would have subsequently accrued had the terrible spell not been broken by that most faithful of sentinels, Adele Fitzhalligon, who, having first delivered herself of a throaty 'Hot diggity!', now advises all and sundry to 'Run like buggery, it's the filth!', upon which shrieking stimulus the 10th tee citizenry scatters lively, scarpering for the 10th tee lavabo, it being true that no one loves a G-Man or IRS agent, nay, not e'en their children.

To the lavabo!

Chapter Twenty-Six

Concerning certain particulars relating to the Few finding themselves besieged yet again.

In truth, dear Reader, the scattering and scarpering aforementioned is contrived largely for dramatical purpose, for the rate of advance evinced by the company of G-Men and IRS agents, despite all their *brum-a-brum-BRUM!*-ing, might easily be conflated with that of a group of especially indolent young sloths on their way to school with no homework done and no dog to blame for eating same, sloths being yet to evolve to the point whereby they might domesticate other species. For lo! by the time the G-Men and IRS agents come screeching to a halt and debouch from their vehicles, and confer as to the whereabouts of the *persons of interest*, and conclude that the 10th tee lavabo is the only possible sanctuary to which the Few might have fled, and, neither side wishing to step on the toes of their federal peers, hastily negotiate the lines of demarcation *vis-à-vis* their respective responsibilities – I say, by the time the G-Men and IRS agents finally get around to training their mortars and howitzers, respectively, on the lavabo, the Few, their number swelled by sundry McGrews, a La Roux and George P. Dangleberry III, have long since barricaded themselves inside and sworn a collective oath to sell themselves dearly.

'You'll never take us alive, copper!' sings out Redser from behind a sandbagged window, which unilateral mission statement causes Samuel L. Silverstein to quibble somewhat, and remind the assemblage of the opinion of the shade of deceased Achilles on the topic of sufficient oxygen being the best possible thing in all possible worlds, to which cavilling Foxy might have been heard to make sharp retort were it not for a dull *crump!* which drowns out Foxy's salty reply, said *crump!*, along with a subsequent spattering of sod, pebble and shrapnel against the lavabo's gable end, being the explosive consequence of the G-Men's first sighter, which gouges a brand new pothole bunker roughly twenty yards nor'-east of the lavabo.

Loud and shrill are the shrieks of terror which now fill the lavabo, until Cordelia de Havilland, discovering herself unable to concentrate on her note-taking, and having twice misspelled *crump!*, calls upon Adele Fitzhalligon to administer a bust upon Sammy's snoot, purely for medicinal purposes. The tactic being a success, and silence again descending upon the lavabo, Bartley's tinkling of the baby grand's ivories notwithstanding, Sir Archie now tosses back the last of his Scotch-and-swish, clears his throat and announces that, in common with Sammy L., he too believes he might have been a tad hasty in agreeing to sell himself dearly, for Archie has recently discovered he has much to live for, not least of which is his depthless admiration for the vast majority of Vanessa Hopgood's particular endowments and a burning desire to live long enough to see said admiration reciprocated, and preferably before an ordained minister, or, in the worst case scenario, the captain of any floating vessel.

'With bells on!' sings out Sammy, e'er hopeful that an excess of fervour might compensate for a want of eloquence.

'Now can that jive!' snarls Rusty McGrew. 'If anyone's going to be waiting for Vanessa at the top of the aisle whilst a lone trumpeter parps out the plaintive strains of Clarke's *Trumpet Voluntary*, it'll be me, Jasper Huxtable McGrew, or *I'll know the reason why*.'

Here the Few look expectantly to Vanessa, who, being the most shimmering star in all of Hollywood's firmament, knows a cue when she hears it, e'en when otherwise engaged in interminable drubbing of a Mexican-born rival in love. First fetching Moxie a conclusive one in the snoot, and thereafter tenderly laying her former rival down upon the smaller of the lavabo's fainting couches, Vanessa now stands forth to where the spotlight would likely have shone had the lavabo been possessed of such, and spake as follows.

'It being apparently the case, Rusty,' says she in a tone which the Reader will surely interpret as the very quintessence of tremulous poignancy, 'that you desire to know the reason why you will wait in vain at the top of the aisle whilst a lone trumpeter parps out the plaintive strains of Clarke's *Trumpet Voluntary*, I am obliged to record that I find myself in an invidious position not unakin to that of Penelope as she considered the merits of her various suitors, none of whom were her absent husband, Odysseus.'

At this point a gasp is heard to issue from our Rorkian Few, it being entirely likely that Vanessa, if she is to carry her classical allusion through to its logical conclusion, is about to announce that she is already married to a wandering hero who will appear at our narrative's climax in a manner strongly reminiscent of a divinely persecuted *deus ex machina*.

The Reader no doubt concurring with Aristotle *vis-à-vis* plausible narrative development, said immortal being of the opinion, as expressed in the *Poetics*, that, in structure as in character, the poet *must always seek what is either necessary or probable*, and thus very likely finding herself in agreement with the immortal Nietzsche as he wonders, rhetorically, where metaphysical consolation might be found once the *deus ex machina* is employed – I say, the Reader will be as relieved as your n. to discover that Vanessa merely alludes to Penelope by way of preamble, and now gets down to cases by citing the sad tale of Marcella, rich William's daughter, as recounted by the immortal Cervantes in *Don Quixote*.

'Gather ye round,' says Vanessa, 'and hear ye true, for I am about to conflate my experience of being wooed by multiple suitors with that of Marcella, rich William's daughter, in a parable that may or may not fall out as entirely apt by its conclusion.'

'Ripper!' says Archie, who is already sitting cross-legged, eyes shining and utterly enthralled, at Vanessa's foot.

Alas, said syllables are the last to be heard for some considerable number of moments, for Vanessa begins waxing lyrical at the very instant the G-Men and IRS agents belatedly realise they have sent over their initial sighter without first issuing an ultimatum – e.g., 'Come out with your hands up, or else!' – which oversight, your n. now hastens to state, is largely a consequence of the hurried negotiations conducted to ascertain their respective responsibilities, and is certainly not to be understood as a wilful disregard for protocol – I say, having inadvertently acted without due regard for the conventions, the G-Men and IRS agents now decide to go all in, and proceed to mortar all hell out of the lavabo and its immediate environs, the better to leave no witnesses to their ungallant departure from the traditions of siege warfare, this according to the immortal Seneca's dictum *Per scelus semper tutum est sceleribus iter.*[1]

Thus Vanessa's speech is largely drowned out by a variety of *crumps!* and *ka-booms!*, which percussive effects are augmented by the *pee-ow!* and *wing-ding!* of shrapnel ricochet upon gable end and tiled roof, although, being as previously noted a lip-reader of no little skill, your n. here clarifies that Vanessa now recounts the unhappy experience of the aforementioned Marcella, who, discovering herself blamed for the suicide of Chrysostom, whose love for Marcella went unrequited, refutes the charges laid by Chrysostom's friends by stating that she is in no way obliged to love simply because she is loved, it being her prerogative to live as she desires, on her own terms, and regardless of others' needs and wants, it being the case, Vanessa concludes, that if any man might consider her a tigress or a basilisk for withholding her affections, they would do well to avoid her as a dangerous thing.

'Bravo!' sings out Archie when Vanessa's lips cease moving. 'Encore, I say! More!'

Alas, just as Vanessa is girding herself for the rigours of curtain call, and searching her memory for Helen's final speech to Paris, the lavabo heaves roughly three feet to the right and tilts at an

1 Quoted by Hieronimo in Kyd's *The Spanish Tragedy* (1592). Roughly translated, it means 'The safe way for crimes is through further crimes.'

alarming angle, which violence causes Cordelia's very last slim gold pencil to snap between her fingers and results in Cordelia flashing a reproachful glare at Bugs Dooley, whom she believes has attempted, in his Author's arrogance, to waft the lavabo aloft and away, with entirely predictable consequences.

'Not I!' sings out Bugs from beneath the lavabo's larger fainting couch, Bugs being as previously noted our tale's Author and thus as skilled a lip-reader as any narrator.

'Then who?' says Cordelia, whose lip-reading skills are legendary.

'I'd imagine it's the combined efforts of the G-Men and IRS agents,' says Bugs, 'with their incessant bombardment of the lavabo resulting in tremors causing a minor earthquake, it being the case that the Tropico Springs Golf and Country Club was zoned as unsafe for the building of human habitation due to its straddling a fault line running sou'-west from the High Sierras all the way through to Venice Beach, the lavabo being allowed as an exception, it being a building in which citizens were unlikely to spend any significant amount of time.'

'I see.'

'Hot diggity!' sings out Adele Fitzhalligon into the sudden silence, the G-Men and IRS agents having just that instant discovered the barrels of their mortars and howitzers, respectively, are so red-hot as to affect the accuracy of their missiles, and have agreed a temporary cessation of their unilateral hostilities. 'A trapdoor!'

'... ye rosebuds while ye may,' says Rusty, 'old time is still a-flying. Trapdoor, you say?'

For lo! according to the principle *it's an ill wind that blaws naebody any gude* (*cf.* Scott), the tremor-causing bombardment which resulted in minor earthquake and the lavabo's shifting three feet to the right and tilting at an alarming angle has revealed not only a trapdoor beneath the smaller of the lavabo's fainting couches, but a tunnel to boot, which discovery will likely be adjudged by the discerning Reader a consequence of expertly sketched foreshadowing designed to promote narrative symmetry, the sight of a trapdoor leading to a tunnel likely reminding the attentive Reader of the Few's escape from the Blue Phalarope at the conclusion of Act One, or, should the Reader prove excessively cynical and/or unusually devoted to the works of Aristotle and Nietzsche, a development to be denounced as the laughably strained contrivance of *deus ex machina*, albeit, and regardless of any corset-busting mirth it might provoke, a development considerably more *ridiculous* than it is *amiable* or *natural*, and thus by no means Comic Writing of the first water.

'But why would a country club lavabo require a trapdoor and tunnel?' enquires Abie Cohen, who, being a legal eagle, is understandably wary of any loophole that presents itself in so miraculous a fashion.

'I can only imagine,' says Bugs as he takes his place in the queue, the Few already taking turns at dropping through the trapdoor into the tunnel below, 'that it was considered essential so that the menials who service the lavabo – cleaning staff and suchlike – are never observed abroad on the golf course by the well-heeled members, who might easily be distracted whilst putting for par by the sight of a base-born non-national scuttling across the close-mown sward with replacement toilet-rolls piled high in their arms.'

'I see,' says Abie as he hoists the still groggy Moxie La Roux onto his shoulders in a lawyer's approximation of fireman's lift, Abie being an aspiring *verray parfit gentil knight* and thus adamant that no man, nor Mexican-born *ingénue*, should be left behind. 'And any idea, at all, of where the tunnel might lead?'

'Again, I can only surmise,' says Bugs, 'but if my initial speculation proves correct, then the tunnel will likely emerge – or, being strictly pedantic, those using the tunnel will likely emerge – in the vicinity of the kitchen area to the rear of the clubhouse, whereupon, were they to sneak around the corner of the clubhouse, they would likely be confronted by a parking lot wherein might be discovered a multiplicity of automobiles which could be usefully stolen for the purpose of powdering out.'

'I wish it to be read into the record,' says Abie, 'that I condone no part of the larcenous portion of your conjecture.'

'Duly noted,' says Bugs as he drops into the tunnel.

Abie Cohen's subsequent departure leaving the 10th tee lavabo quite empty, and your n. having discovered himself possessed of a hitherto unsuspected mild claustrophobia on the occasion of the Few's escape from the Blue Phalarope – I say, your n. being unwilling to pursue the Few into the dark tunnel, we now drift outside in wraithlike fashion, where we discover a ruined and smoking landscape, the previously verdant 10th tee and environs now a blasted heath pocked with craters, one of which eventually reveals itself as the pothole bunker previously occupied by Bugs Dooley on the occasion of his taking refuge from a claymore-wielding Rusty McGrew, and which now hosts a somewhat deafened Bumbles McGee, who proves himself no help whatsoever – Bumbles, alas, being by no means a proficient lip-reader – to the IRS agents and G-Men who come a-wandering by in search of any survivors who might require swift dispatch courtesy of the traditional *coup de grâce* behind the ear.

The G-Men and IRS agents now entering into conclave, and concluding that the unprecedented issue of tunnels uncovered in country club lavabos is a matter of jurisdiction to be decided by their respective superiors back in Los Angeles, and especially when the likely upshot of any federal agent descending into dark tunnel in pursuit of a plurality of McGrews would be his entombment therein – I say, the G-Men and IRS agents now depart the 10th tee at a considerably swifter pace than they arrived, *brum-a-brum-BRUM!*-ing away down the ninth fairway on a bearing sou'-west, until all is once more as it once was, the destruction wrought by a combined mortar-howitzer bombardment of the lavabo and its environs notwithstanding; and, as the last wisps of mist and sulphurous fumes drift away, Bumbles McGee finds himself enveloped in the pristine quiet found only on the 10th tee of the better class of a country club as the sun peeps o'er the horizon and the chilly digits of pink-fingered dawn yield to the warm embrace of golden morn.

And so we take our leave of Bumbles McGee where he stands upon the freshly cratered 10th tee with lips pursed and hands on hips, gazing out at the far horizon like unto Ariadne on her lonely shore; and, so far as we know, he stands there gazing still.

Chapter Twenty-Seven

In which our pilgrims' Progress concludes with many unexpected happy e'er afters.

And so, dear Reader, we come to our final chapter, wherein our weary pilgrims, having traversed *antres vast* from Hollywood, aka the City of Destruction, to the Celestial City of Tropico Springs, finally emerge from their metaphorical dark tunnel, via a trapdoor behind the trash cans adjacent to the kitchen's rear entrance, into the sunlit uplands of the parking lot behind the TSGCC clubhouse, whereupon, as is generally the case with a fractious citizenry that has passed through the flames to discover itself fired in the kiln of adversity o'ercome, the Few now commence clapping each other upon the back and chortling at their scarcely plausible narrow escape, and reminding one another of how ridiculously petty were the peeves which previously caused pilgrim to set about pilgrim with claymore broadsword, teapot, and suchlike instruments of cranial despoilment.

Alas, dear Reader, the merriment is by no means universal. For lo! one of our weary pilgrims discovers himself as solitary as Crusoe, who had no one to look upon him and see that he was solitary, albeit your n., being possessed of what might be considered a Dickensian quality of Victorian-era authorial omniscience, now calls to the Reader's attention the tragical sight of Bugs Dooley stooging about with eyes downcast and shoulders so bowed as to suggest he is experiencing roughly 90% of the sorrows that beset Young Werther at his lowest ebb.

'Oh?' says Cordelia de Havilland, when Bugs sidles up to same to paraphrase the immortal Kyd in informing her that *his woes are of such weight as to weary the earth*, whilst *his exclaims are such as to surcharge the air with ceaseless plaints*. 'Why so?'

'Well,' says Bugs, 'it's just, here we all are cheering ourselves to the rafters, or rather we would, were we not in fact outdoors, and were there any rafters we might aim our —'

'The point, Bugs, is well made.'

'What I mean to say,' says Bugs, 'it's that it's dawn, and bliss it certainly is to be alive, and no one could dispute that to be young, or young-ish, or at the very least on the sunny side of middle-age, is very —'

'Eschew the ambages, Bugs,' interpolates Cordelia, causing our Author to again lapse into aposiopesis. 'What is it that you *really* want to bewray?'

'It's the tragical *denouement*,' concedes Bugs in forlorn timbre.

'Yes?'

'I wot not how.'

'You wot not how?'

'Precisely,' says Bugs.

'Pray explain yourself, sir.'

'Might I quote the immortal Sterne for the purpose of same?'

'You may.'

'Thank you. I refer, of course, to Tristram's self-effacing estimation of his prowess as a recently minted scribe, which is to say that I am, like Tristram, but just set up in the business, so know little about it — but, in my opinion, to write a book is for all the world like humming a song — be but in tune with yourself, madam, 'tis no matter how high or how low you take it.'

'Sounds about right,' says Cordelia.

'But madam, I am by no means in tune with myself!'

'Your lute is unstrung?'

'But that's it! That's it in a nutshell! My very lute has come unstrung, as if … as if …'

'You are entirely stumped as to the discord to follow?'

'Exactly!'

'I see,' says Cordelia. 'And might one enquire, author to Author, as to whether you find yourself sorely deficient only in the matter of conclusions that echo the predestined doom of *Tragedia cothurnata*,[1] or entirely at a loss in the matter of any kind of ending at all.'

'Both, really,' says Bugs. 'Although, if warmly pressed, I would be obliged to plump for the latter,' whereupon, having confessed the torment which has haunted the secret quiet of his conscience e'er since he falsely took credit for the minor earthquake at the Beverly Hills Motel, Bugs now lets loose a flood of tears shed as salty confirmation of what the immortal Cervantes was once pleased to describe as *the undissembled testimony of his passion*.

'And am I to understand,' says Cordelia, as she glances around and about, Cordelia being understandably reluctant to gaze upon her Creator as he snuffles up the rhinorrhoea that is the inevitable consequence of a man who discovers himself at the mercy of an undissembled testimony of passion – 'I say, am I to understand that you confide in yours truly in her capacity as a bestselling and critically acclaimed author?'

'I do,' snuffles Bugs.

'I see,' says Cordelia. 'The logical conclusion, of course, is that you are about to propose a collaboration between Author and author, although I am loath to leap to said conclusion lest I discover myself persecuted by those gods who tend to take umbrage when mere mortals presume to ignore the lines of demarcation so fiercely defended by divinities with little else to do than meddle in human affairs.'

'As your Author,' says Bugs in doleful timbre, 'I hereby swear a sacred oath to defend you against the lesser divinities previously invoked in the telling of this tale, up to and including any union officials who might take exception to your strike-breaking collaboration.'

'Can I have that in writing?'

1 The most serious form of tragedy in ancient Athens, and generally performed by an actor, or actors, wearing buskins, i.e., calf- or knee-length boots of leather or cloth.

'Of course.'

'And the royalties?'

'Eh?'

'Momma de Havilland didn't raise any fools to work for free, Bugs. I'm thinking a seventy-thirty split.'

'In whose favour?'

Here Cordelia informs Bugs that his answer is to be discovered not so much in the question but in the questioning, it being a curious quirk of financial negotiations that enquiries as to the exact distribution of a split are invariably made by the party at the sharp end of same.

'But madam,' says Bugs, his expression almost exactly that of an elderly mole contemplating the taking up of arms against a sea of troubles, 'I am our tale's Creator, and might thus be conflated with that singular scribe identified in John 1:1 as the very beginning who was the Word.'

'There's no denying,' concedes Cordelia, 'that you've done much of the spadework. But it is my understanding that Aristotle, in the *Poetics*, is quite firm on the absolute necessity of a tale being possessed of a beginning, a middle *and* an end, which latter in particular seems to be causing you a spot of bother.'

'Gah!'

'Are we agreed?'

Bugs now stating aloud the time-honoured mantra of authors everywhere, which is that thirty per cent of something is a far, far better thing than one hundred per cent of naught, Cordelia now graciously acquiesces to Bugs' formal request that she devise a satisfactorily plausible conclusion to his yarn, 'providing,' continues Cordelia, 'I might be allowed to tweak the tragical aspect somewhat, for I am the bestselling and critically acclaimed author of epic romance fiction, and thus more *au fait*, when it comes to *denouement*, with sunsets and miraculously reconciled lovers riding off into same than, say, mothers inadvertently ripping their sons asunder whilst maddened by divinely-inspired frenzy.'

'Right,' says Bugs in dubious register, glancing around at the ragged band of pilgrims currently milling about the TSGCC's parking lot. 'And said shot is on the board, you believe, without recourse to the dread contrivance of *deus ex machina*?'

'Oh, absolutely. In fact, our scarcely plausible escape from the bombarded lavabo suggests that happy e'er afters are not only possible, but probable. Take Vanessa and Moxie, for example. Shall we lip-read their *tête-à-tête*, which, e'en from this remove, appears to be more than somewhat harmoniously sororal?'

Bugs and Cordelia now resting their respective gazes upon Vanessa and Moxie, we discover that said ladies' parley advertises the warmest possible mutual regard. To wit:

'What, this old thing?' says Moxie, patting her chignon in absent-minded fashion. 'Why, I had almost forgotten it was there.'

'Well,' says Vanessa, 'scraping back your hair as severely as all that certainly emphasises the extent to which, if I might quote the immortal Webster, your bright eyes carry a quiver of darts sharper than sun-beams.'

'Too, too kind,' murmurs Moxie. 'As to the recent misunderstanding concerning yours truly and your *fiancé* Samuel L. Silverstein, during which I might easily have been accused of loving not wisely, nor much, it behoves me to state that my behaviour was such that it could not be sufficiently deplored.'

'Think nothing of it,' says Vanessa, 'for Sammy and I were only e'er affianced as a ruse to deceive the great unwashed of the motion picture-going public. Thus my plotting to lure you out of hiding, the better to have you turned off or immured in the deepest cell of the nearest nunnery, was entirely ill-conceived, in consequence of which I discover myself obliged to issue an unconditional apology, and to make restitution conflatable with that *limitless reparation* Agamemnon was belatedly moved to offer Achilles, albeit with the caveat that said *limitless* is by no means to be interpreted literally.'

'Oh?' says Moxie.

'You can have Sammy,' says Vanessa, 'in exchange for fifty per cent of his paltry few several millions.'

'You are far too generous, madam,' says Moxie. 'In fact, I insist that *you* have Sammy, providing I might be guaranteed a ten per cent finder's fee on said paltry few several millions.'

'Your noble instinct for self-sacrifice redounds handsomely to your credit,' says Vanessa. 'Alas, I must insist that you deprive yourself not of our beloved Sammy.'

'And I, madam,' says Moxie, 'having first established that my only concern is that you beguile the course of e'erlasting time under green myrtle trees and cypress shades in the company of said mogul, must insist that *you* take our beloved Knight of the Burning Pestle.'

'It being only a matter of time,' says Cordelia to Bugs, by which means does she recall Bugs' gaze from the lips of Vanessa and Moxie to her own comely features – 'I say, it being only a matter of time before Moxie and Vanessa hatch a scheme wherein neither takes Sammy, and further agree to split his paltry few several millions down the middle …'

'Gramercy!' says Bugs. '*They're giving themselves their very own happy e'er afters!*'

'Quite.'

'It's almost as if,' says Bugs in the ecstatic tenor of the previously desolate Author who belatedly detects the glimmerings of a plausible conclusion to his yarn, 'the transcendentalist abolitionist Mr Theodore Parker was correct in his contention that while the moral arc of the universe may be long, it bends inexorably toward justice.'

'Indeed,' says Cordelia. 'Another example of same might be divined in the *pourparlers* ongoing between Bartley McGuffin and Samuel L. Silverstein, as Bartley pitches the gist of his One True Work and Sammy laps it up as avidly as any motion picture mogul potentially plunged into penury by writers' strike being propositioned by an unpublished scribe who has yet to secure representation.'

'And, oh Cordelia!' sings out Bugs. 'Mark ye the eyelashes being batted at Sammy L. by the adjacent Adele Fitzhalligon, who appears to have o'erheard Moxie and Vanessa straining verbal nerve and sinew to divest themselves of said imminently impoverished mogul, and in consequence schemes, providing I have correctly interpreted the notoriously opaque semaphore of come-hithery, to provide Sammy's soon-to-be bruised ego with salve sufficient to restore him to bobbish mid-season form.'

'Aye,' says Cordelia. 'And mark ye in your turn, good sir, the lascivious wink lavished by Sammy upon Adele, which, unless I sorely misconstrue same, is the very quality of non-verbal persiflage employed by Spanish sailors on those occasions when they discover themselves in ports which are not Spanish.'

'Gosh,' says Bugs, 'happy e'er afters are busting out all over, such that any bystander might remark upon how *the world might be a better place if only everyone would make a little more effort to get along.*'

'But stay!' says Cordelia. 'We have yet to consider Rusty McGrew and George P. Dangleberry III, who only a short chapter or so ago stood on the very brink of mutual annihilation, but are now so joyously infused by philadelphic sentiment as to be rustling up a wheeze by which each *gänger* will *doppel* the other, i.e., Rusty to assume the duties of managing sundry institutions around and about Tropico Springs, George to give free rein to the homicidal tendencies of his Highland Scots ancestry as he goes around and about the speaks and deadfalls of Hollywood daubed in blue woad.'

'Wot larks!' sings out Bugs.

'Shall we sidle up to their company, the better to eavesdrop upon their conversation?'

'I don't see why not,' says Bugs in companionable timbre, 'for it is entirely unlikely, at this late stage in the proceedings, that all our happy e'er afters might discover themselves undone by a wholly unexpected reversal of fortune derived from the kind of improbable misunderstanding that tends to set the music hall comedy apart from the more serious narrative forms.'

Indeed, dear Reader, it would appear that Bugs has hit the nail plumb spang where it might do the most good, for, as we join Rusty and George P., said worthies are going around and about the TSGCC parking lot with arms linked and engaged in an intricate two-part harmony which, from the references to Rugby's cleverness and Harrow's making more row, appears to be the *Eton Boating Song*.

'But we'll row for ever,' yodel George and Rusty in philadelphic orison, 'steady from stroke to bow, and nothing in life shall sever, the chain that is round us now!'

'Well said, old pilgrim!' sings out Rusty as our duo, tired but happy, wend their way to a halt, by which are we given to understand that George P. has been inducted into our happy Few, his recent cudgelling at the hands of the Siblings McGrew serving as his initiatory rite, and thus —

'Ho!' sings out George P. in the unmistakable tenor of a man grown wholly Byronic, his brain *a whirling gulf of phrenesy and flame*, in consequence of which he now levels a quivering forefinger at Bartley McGuffin, who, alas, can be observed discovered lurking beneath the steering column of a nearby Cadillac V-63 Touring Car. 'What the *deuce*,' demands George, 'does that man think he's about?'

'The matter,' sings out Sammy L., 'is susceptible to ready explanation, it being the case that the Few require a getaway flivver in order to abscond from the TSGCC with all possible haste, in consequence of which Bartley is being kind enough to hot-wire yon Cadillac at my request, Bartley being an unusually biddable menial and, further, a potential employee of Silverstein Studios who is obliged to undergo some frivolous initiation rite if he is to be fully accepted as one of the boys.'

'Hot-wire the automobile of a TSGCC member?' says George in strangulated register. 'This, sir, will not stand!'

'Whoa there, pardner,' says Rusty in soothing timbre, patting his diminutive *doppelgänger* on the shoulder. 'Cast your mind back and recall, if you will, that I'm the honorary vice-president of the TSGCC now. And if I think Bartley should hot-wire a member's flivver, then hot-wire a flivver is exactly what that admirably biddable menial will do.'

Alas, dear Reader, George P. Dangleberry III is, as the attentive Reader will likely recall, a man who pays nit-pickish attention to detail in the matter of contractual obligations. Thus it is that, with his verbal agreement with Rusty yet to be ratified by public notary, and the responsibility for TSGCC members' automobiles still technically in his care, George P. now commences to discourse on a theme first identified by the immortal Aeschylus as *the darkly streaming gore of civic broils*, by which means does George announce his intention to spit any biddable servitors exceeding their remit upon the Sword of Justice, 'an example of which,' continues George, brandishing the sabre he has been clutching e'er since he first met with Rusty McGrew ~~in the lists~~ upon the TSGCC's 10th tee, 'I now flourish in a manner likely to chill the very marrow of any biddable servitor who attempts to hot-wire a flivver for which they do not possess the appropriate documentation.'

'Alas for you, good sir,' says Rusty, flourishing his own sabre, 'I am by no means a biddable menial, but renowned as so notoriously fearsome that I would, like Laertes or the dastardly ruffians who laid low Saint Thomas à Becket, cut a man's throat in church.'

'In which case,' says George, 'I am obliged to state that you, sir, are a boggart, and it is as a boggart thou shalt meet thy Maker!'

Here, as the Reader will be pleased to note, Bugs Dooley stands forth and reminds our quarrelsome gentlemen that *the world might be a better place if only everyone would make a little more effort to get along*, whereupon, turning as one, our gentlemen inform Bugs that he runs the grievous risk of discovering himself as undone as any Elizabethan playwright in Deptford tavern who is determined to haggle o'er the bill. It is at this point, alas, that murmurs of discontent can be heard issuing from the cheap seats, which grumbles are largely generated by the Siblings McGrew and relate to the poor showing of both parties in the matter of *going to*, although in truth the loudest complaint issues from Sir Archie, who, his wager long since laid, and with an early-bird tee already booked for 9.30am, is keen to see the main players get stuck in and commence the slashing, skewering and woundings generally associated with sabre-related entertainment.

So it is that, in order to move things along at a pace sufficient to allow for goodly prinking, *&c.*, and get the losing corpse decently buried in a convenient pothole bunker, and the ninth green restored to its pristine state before his two-ball rolls around to same circa 11.30am or thereabouts – I say, Archie now sings out, 'Hoi, Rusty? I believe yon Dangleberry chap just called you a queynt.'[2]

Here the McGrew brow knits.

'A queynt, eh?' says Rusty, who, lacking a classical education and finding himself at something of a loss as to the etymological nuances, but deciphering from Archie's tone that he is being egregiously cozened, falls back upon the time-honoured response of 'No, *you're* a queynt,' to which George P. Dangleberry has no other option but to flash back with, 'Takes one to know one!', at which point the pelters come thick and fast.

'Fatherlasher!' says Rusty.

'Coxcomb!' says George P.

'Caitiff!' retorts Rusty.

'Cankered grandam!' bellows George, displaying an impressive knowledge of one of the Bard's lesser-known dramas,[3] which has the added bonus of casting aspersions on Rusty's masculinity, which matter Rusty wastes no time in bringing to the attention of George P.

'Fie, sir!' says George P. 'I cast the aspersion singular, sir!'

'Ah,' says Rusty, finding himself undone yet again by his want of classical education, and fervently wishing George P. would confine his pejorative allusions to Rusty's sole literary experience, i.e., the copy of Adam Smith's *The Wealth of Nations* consumed in the stacks of the Buckingham Street Library. Chafing at George

2 Middle English. Also, *cwointe*, *queinte*, *wheinte* and *koweinte*. In the works of Chaucer, 'queynt' might be understood to mean 'clever', 'strange' or 'ingenious'. Victorian dictionaries, however, defined 'queynt' as 'the female pudenda'.

3 *King John*. Shakespearean scholars have yet to pin down the exact date of its writing, although it appears to come between *Richard II* and *Henry IV, Part I*, despite being neither a sequel to the former nor a prequel to the latter.

P.'s goads, Rusty experiences the frustration that eventually comes to every autodidact when he runs up against the limits of his learning, whereupon, with his blood already up, and his warrior's instinct thrumming to the atavistic drumbeat of Archie's 'Fight-fight-*fight*!', Rusty gives vent to a full-blooded 'Have at thee, varlet!' and makes a pass at George's waistcoat which, had it taken effect, would, if we might paraphrase the immortal Dickens, have let a little more merriment out than could have been easily replaced in a month or two.

Thus is battle finally joined, George being forced to deflect Rusty's initial *prise-de-fer* with a desperate parry whilst bemoaning his opponent's infamy in plunging straight into combat without so much as an *En garde!*, to which Rusty, segueing deftly from *prise-de-fer* to *attack-au-fer*, responds that any fool knows *Have at thee!* is *lingua franca* for *En garde!*, and that any further linguistic *splitting of hairs* would see George P.'s gizzard skewered upon Rusty's blade *lickety-split*, pun intended.

'Do you pun, sir?' enquires George P., who, despite being recently well cudgelled by the Siblings McGrew, has the advantage of home ground in the TSGCC parking lot, and thus nips smartly around a low shrubbery before grasping sabre hilt in both hands and cleaving down upon Rusty's skull like unto Hephaistos taking axe to Zeus's mazzard on the occasion of the birth of Divine Athena.

'I do pun, sir,' says Rusty, who, having reverse-somersaulted away from George P.'s potentially lethal swipe, tosses his sabre from right hand to left before embarking upon an outrageous *flèche* which concludes with his poking the tip of his sabre into the right cheek of George P.'s posterior, causing George P. to rise three feet vertically and emit a screech like unto a *Megascops asio* (i.e., screech owl) being poked in the rear end with a sharply honed object.

Here Rusty pauses to draw breath, and declares that George P. Dangleberry III is no more than *Life*.

'Eh?' says George P., having returned to *terra firma* and reassured himself that the only significant aperture in his posterior was the one he'd borne into the world.

'I say, sir,' says Rusty, 'that thou art *Life*, by which I mean you are naught but a walking shadow, a poor player that struts his hour upon the stage and then is heard no more.'

'*Touché*,' says George P., delivering a terse bow that involves touching sabre blade to forehead. 'Ne'er have I heard a tale more handsomely told by an idiot, so full of sound and fury, and signifying less.'

'Nerts to you, sister!' retorts Rusty as he lunges in with a horizontal slash designed to decapitate George P. Dangleberry III, an assault so furious, albeit so neatly repelled, that the foes suddenly find themselves *pede pes et cuspide cuspis*, i.e., inextricably embroiled, cheek to cheek and close as wax, with neither one able to gain the purchase or leverage required to strike the fatal bust in the snoot.

'Do you yield, sir?' gasps George P.

'I yield not, sir!' declares Rusty.

'Might you yield at some point in the near future, sir?'

'Possible but unlikely, sir!' sings out Rusty.

A stalemate now accruing, with neither man willing to uncle or otherwise bend the knee, and a stalemate being the dreaded narrative *longueur* by any other name, your n. now looks to the citizenry gathered in the TSGCC parking lot for some noble soul who might break the impasse by declaring the Rusty-George bout an honourable draw, whereupon each man might withdraw from the field with blue peter still proudly a-flutter, having first shook the other's hand in a firm grip betokening mutual respect and admiration. Alas, dear Reader, it is as your n. glances around that he observes Sammy L. and his legal counsel Abie Cohen colloguing in urgent undertone, the gist of which, courtesy of your n.'s remarkable facility for lip-reading, runs as follows:

'Looks like a stalemate, Abie.'

'A veritable two-man Passchendaele, Mr Silverstein.'

'Solutions?'

'Well,' says Abie, opening his alligator-skin briefcase and extracting the brown-spotted banana within, 'it will require one of the combatants to prove himself the bigger man, albeit metaphorically speaking, for Mr McGrew is visibly taller than Mr Dangleberry III – I say, we require Mr McGrew to now acknowledge Mr Dangleberry's courage and skill in fighting him to a standstill, which will then allow Mr Dangleberry, in his turn, to state that Mr McGrew, being a warrior of uncommon —'

'Abie?'

'Mr Silverstein?'

'You do understand, Abie, that it is essential that one or other of Rusty or George passes beyond the veil.'

'Alas,' says Abie, munching upon banana, 'I was unaware of said necessity. Pray elucidate.'

'Well, if Rusty scrags George, we're copacetic as regards the financing of our latest motion picture wheeze, i.e., *The Pilgrim's Progress*. Although …'

'Yes?'

'I do wonder, Abie, if we shouldn't take a long, hard look at that pesky apostrophe tucked away in *The P's P* title, there being considerably more than one pilgrim involved in our proposed Jazz Age variation on the tale.'

'Indeed,' says Abie. 'It wouldn't be the first time a potentially profitable motion picture discovered itself scuppered as a consequence of wandering apostrophe. I'm told the New England audience, especially, is very particular about its punctuation.'

'Stick it down on the agenda for the next meeting.'

'Duly noted.'

'Now where was I?'

'I believe you were about to outline the benefits that would likely accrue should Mr Dangleberry cool off Mr McGrew.'

'Thank you, Abie. Should Rusty go the way of all flesh, then yours truly, once I have converted to the Church of Jesus Christ of Latter-day Saints, or Mormonism, will discover myself free to marry both Vanessa *and* Moxie.'

Abie discovering himself incensed at Sammy L.'s latest proposed apostasy, which seems to Abie to broach any number of taboos pertaining to the conventions espoused by Judaism, the chivalric code and basic common sense, he now demurs in vehement register, i.e., by stating, in a disbelieving tenor that fairly quavers with the barely suppressed violence of delicate sensibilities scandalised, that he believes himself audibly mistook, for it seems to Abie as if Sammy L. Silverstein has just now stated his intention to embark, with *malice prepense*, upon polygamy.

'Quite the wheeze, eh?' says Sammy. 'Can't imagine why it didn't occur to me before. Say, Abie? What's the absolute upper limit when it comes to the particular brand of polygamy practised by the good burghers of Utah?'

Alas for Sammy, Abie Cohen is so outraged by said *svengali*'s latest apostatic revelation that he now leaps into the fray bent on rendering the result of same null and void by slapping Rusty's face with the brown-spotted banana skin, thus blinding Rusty with an excess of phloem and – were Abie living in a Panglossian world wherein everything is for the best in the best of all possible worlds – obliging George P. Dangleberry III to metaphorically beat his sabre into miniature ploughshare.

O Abie! Would that he had employed the brown-spotted banana skin to blind himself with an excess of phloem! For, as Rusty goes reeling around and about the TSGCC parking lot bewailing an excess of phloem where it might do the least good, Abie is now obliged to bear witness to the most egregious example of unchivalrous knavery e'er prosecuted in the lists, as George P., in hot pursuit of said bootlegger, deploys his sabre in a horizontal swiping designed to decapitate his bootlegging foe.

Now George, as the Reader will undoubtedly recall, is not a man to be trifled with when possessed of Colt Peacemaker and presented with the broad target of a man's back as he sits ahorse and sneers at a woman's choice of gardening tool. Alas for George, he is by no means as proficient a spadassin with sabre as he is with Colt Peacemaker; indeed, George's only previous experience of decapitation has been slicing the top off his boiled egg before dipping his bread soldiers into the ~~yoke~~ yolk. Further, George has, in the heat of battle, misremembered that he is attempting to decapitate his very own *doppelgänger*, which is to say, a man with features strangely reminiscent of Norman helmet. Thus it is that George's horizontal swipe, in connecting squarely with Rusty's forehead, merely glances off with a dull clang, and entirely fails to cleave Rusty's mazzard in the desired fashion.

'I am largely undone!' sings out Rusty as he keels o'er into the dust and the claret fairly flows, causing Redser to echo the immortal Lord Brooke, and not without a certain bitterness, in observing that *if Nature did not take delight in blood, She would have made more easie wayes to good*. Prophetic words! For no sooner have they departed Redser's lips than Bumbles McGee, having long since grown weary of his Ariadne-ish gazing upon far horizon, and having motored his Stutz Bearcat around from the 10th tee to the TSGCC clubhouse in the hope of prevailing upon the head chef to rustle up sufficient steak and eggs to fortify him for the long and lonely journey back to Los Angeles, now springs lightly from said Bearcat to advise all present to lay down their weapons and come out with their hands up, Bumbles being a stickler for tradition and thus prepared to o'erlook for the nonce that all present are, in fact, already outside.

'Oi, copper!' sings out Carrots, adopting a Cockney accent for the purpose of disguise. 'Ain't you about two parasangs removed from your jurisdiction?'

Here Bumbles acknowledges that Carrots raises a valid legal point, but further suggests that Carrots is confusing Bumbles' public and private personas, it being the case that the *animus* existing between Bumbles and Rusty since the farrago at the Blue Phalarope has transformed Bumbles' pursuit of said god-scorning wrath of God from a professional concern into a personal obsession, as a consequence of which Bumbles has travelled to Tropico Springs on his own dime in order to make a citizen's arrest.

'Fair enough,' sings out Carrots, albeit his words are drowned out by a pained yelpage emanating from Rusty McGrew, for

George P., observing his foe stretched in the dust and still blinded by an excess of phloem, and sensing an opportunity that might never come around again, has inserted the sharply honed point of his sabre into Rusty's left buttock.

O Reader! Mark ye now the sequel! For it is by this very act of arrant knavery that George P. Dangleberry III discovers himself hoist on a petard of his own devising!

'Sir,' says Bumbles to George in a register so stentorian that it drowns out the boos of the citizens foregathered, 'I must trouble you for your sword.'

Thus does Bumbles erroneously prosecute the citizen's arrest that is his own private obsession, this largely on foot of Rusty lying prone in the parking lot with his phiz so obscured by a mask of bloody phloem as to be quite unrecognisable as a gods-scorning terror recently ascended to ninth in the pantheon of America's Most Wanted, whereas George P. Dangleberry III is not only Rusty's *doppelgänger*, but by his actions the dictionary definition of *arrant knave*, i.e., a base scullion who would skewer a man's buttock from behind when his guard is down and his sight obscured by an excess of phloem.

It is entirely probable, of course, that Bumbles McGee would have swiftly realised his error once Rusty McGrew was hauled vertical and the discrepancy in height between he and George P. Dangleberry III revealed, at which point some conscientious bystander would, no doubt, have stepped in to clarify the identification and confirm Bumbles' suspicions. Unfortunately for George P. and his future prospects of liberty, his back-shooting (or buttock-stabbing) instincts have caused the citizenry foregathered to consider him an honorary Irishman, i.e., the lowest order of anything, and thus fully deserving of this latest mischief inflicted by fickle Atropos. Meanwhile, Bumbles is too busy clapping George in bilboes and shushing his prisoner's vehement protests to assist in the hauling vertical of Rusty McGrew, in consequence of which our incorruptible combination of Bulldog Drummond and C. Auguste Dupin now perpetrates the scaliest of bloomers in tossing the shackled George into the back of the Stutz Bearcat and departing the TSGCC parking lot, with a throaty *brum-a-brum-BRUM!*, on a bearing sou'-west.

'Hm,' says Bugs as he observes the Siblings McGrew shoulder the blood-drenched Rusty around and about the TSGCC parking lot whilst bawling out a rather coarse three-part harmony, i.e., '*O multum dilecte Deo, recti soror est victoria juris!*'

'Is there a problem?' says Cordelia de Havilland.

Here Bugs reluctantly states that he is uncomfortable with the irony of the Siblings hailing Rusty as *one much beloved of God* when said bootie is in fact renowned as an exemplar of that havoc-wreaking cruelty identified by the immortal Eliot as the essential tragical flaw in Coriolanus and other heroes of that kidney. Further, states Bugs, he has all along been labouring under the impression that the villain of the piece, long since identified as one Jasper Huxtable 'Rusty' McGrew, would belatedly experience a comeuppance decidedly more significant than that of prink'd buttock, which fall from grace would serve to accentuate the happy e'er afters of his less morally bankrupt peers in the Few.

'Being honest,' says Bugs in morose timbre as he observes Redser McGrew going about dispensing possets of celebratory fizz from silver salver, thus causing those of the Few in possession of sweaty nightcaps to toss same aloft in a paroxysm of unbridled glee, 'I'm not entirely sure that our *progress* hasn't been a complete frost, for it seems to me as if none of the Few has actually learned anything, or matured, or changed in any noticeable way.'

'They are, of course, bound by their common revulsion of George P.'s buttock-stabbing,' murmurs Cordelia as she accepts a posset of fizz from Redser, 'and might thus be considered to be *all getting along*.'

'There's that, I suppose,' says Bugs, accepting a posset in his turn.

'And everyone seems to have fashioned their very own happy e'er after.'

'Well, yes,' says Bugs. 'Although a purist might contend that their happy e'er afters are precisely those they were already pursuing when they were first conjured into being on the terrace of the Musso & Frank Grill.'

'I do take your point,' says Cordelia, for whom any reminder of her fictional status remains something of a sore point, 'although I would further remind you of the response offered by the Lady Piccarda to Dante when said immortal enquired as to whether the Lady Piccarda's disembodied soul might not prefer to be more handsomely rewarded by God.'

'Which was?' says Bugs, making a mental note to bump Dante's *Inferno* to the summit of his to-be-read pile.

'The Lady Piccarda, encountered on lowest sphere of Paradise, informs Dante that *we only long for what we already have.*'

'I see,' says Bugs, making a mental note to eschew both the *Inferno* and the *Purgatorio* and go straight to the *Paradiso*. 'No thirst for greater blessedness, you say?'

'None.'

'Nor e'en the faintest of wistful longings after a higher sphere?'

'Zilch.'

'Right. And you're suggesting we might accept same as a precedent?'

'Well, if it was good enough for Dante …'

'A fair point, and well made.'

Thus it's a mightily reassured Bugs who now turns to contemplate the Few, the finally happy Few, as said pilgrims engage in fizz-quaffing revel, which scene, although pleasant to observe, as is generally the case when an Author gazes upon a tired but happy citizenry exuding mellow bonhomie and nicely sniftered fellowship, ne'ertheless strikes something of the jarring note with Bugs, said wassail being more appropriate to the City of Destruction than the Celestial City, which wrinkle in his scheme Bugs now decides to o'erlook for the nonce, and probably until the following morn, it being the case, according to the bestselling and critically acclaimed Cordelia de Havilland, that writing is in fact rewriting, and that Cordelia, having claimed 70% of the royalty split, will be contractually obliged to undertake said rewrite.

'I say,' says Bugs, experiencing those tingles peculiar to the Author who has just now realised that someone else will be wrangling his or her redraft, which sensation, fully realised, is a warming glow which turns handsprings whilst yodelling 'Hoopla!' — 'I say, where's Archie got to?'

'The first tee, I'd imagine,' says Cordelia. 'He had an early-bird special booked for 9.30am.'

'So he had.' Here Bugs raises his posset of celebratory fizz. 'Well, here's mud in your eye.'

'*Skål*,' says Cordelia.

Epilogue

Wherein is illustrated our narrative's philosophical proposition, i.e., that the world might be a better place if only everyone would make a little more effort to get along.

It being the most literary of conventions (*cf.* the *Poetics*) that any tale worth the telling must come to an end, and preferably with an *Epilogue*, we now drift, wraithlike, to the environs of the TSGCC's first tee, where we discover – it now being 9.28am – Sir Archie and his gentleman's gentleman Bartley McGuffin limbering up for their early-bird special whilst gazing in wide-eyed wonder at the prospect of a lush green course stretching unto the far horizon, a sight marred only by the pair of old duffers on the first fairway who, from their erratic swings, appear to have confused the fundamentals of the noble Scottish art with the hoeing of root vegetables.

Ne'ertheless, the course is, as stated, lush and green; moreo'er, the day is bright, sunny and warm, which latter is observed by Archie and Bartley as sharply contradistinctive when compared with the grey and e'er-louring skies of their otherwise beloved County Donegal in the Free State of Ireland.

'I say, Bartleby!'

'Sir?'

'I mean to say!'

'Ah,' says Bartley, belatedly catching his Young Master's drift. 'Indeed, sir.'

'Wot larks, eh?'

'I would go so far as to say larks abounding, sir.'

'In Xanadu did Kubla Khan a stately pleasure-dome decree, what?'

'Although,' says Bartley in murmuring approval, 'I'd hazard that e'en Xanadu could not boast of such forgiving greens.'

'Are they truly as forgiving as all that?'

'I have it on good authority, sir, i.e., that of the clubhouse pro, that the greens are so forgiving as to be designated the full and unexpurgated Luke 23:34.'

'Jolly good show. Shall we resist the urge to wander more, Bartleby?'

'The spirit urges the affirmative, sir, and yet the flesh quails at the prospect of your making good on the ill-advised challenge issued to both Mr McGrew *and* Mr Silverstein before we departed the parking lot just now, said battles to be joined on the next misty morn to present itself as suitably swathed in vaporous haze and inspired by your desire to secure the hand of Ms Hopgood in marriage, this despite Ms Hopgood's recent moving oration on the theme of her steely determination to rebuff any and all woo pitched in her direction for the foreseeable future, the better to live her life on her own terms, and in her own way.'

'I see. Something of a wrinkle in the old ointment, eh?'

'Somewhat, sir, and especially given the fearsome reputation of Mr McGrew, of whom it is alleged, if I may quote the immortal Milton …'

'Have on, Bartleby. You can never have enough Milton, I say.'

'Indeed, sir. Well, they do say Mr McGrew is a latter-day Moloch, which is to say *a horrid king besmear'd with the blood of human sacrifice and parents' tears*.'

'Horrid, you say?'

'Such is his reputation, sir. Although …'

'Yes?'

'It is worth considering, sir, that the climate in California being what it is, and particularly here in the High Sierras, misty morns are in rather short supply.'

'Oh?'

'Indeed, I am reliably informed that entire years may pass without so much, if I might paraphrase the immortal Dryden, as a subtil dew to be observed either soaring or settling.'

'Dryden, you say?'

'Indeed, sir.'

'And this Dryden's the goods?'

'He considered Shakespeare a Homer to Ben Jonson's Virgil, sir.'

'Ruddy infallible, then.'

'As close as may be achieved, sir, without tip-toeing into the realms of blasphemy in the matter of papal dependability on matters doctrinal.'

'Right. So we stick around?'

'Those greens do appear to be rather forgiving.'

'But all the while keeping a weather-eye on the old barometer.'

'Naturally.'

'Should we take out membership?'

'No point in tempting fate unnecessarily, sir.'

'True for you. Here, those old farts have finally hit a ball. Debouche the brassies and tee us up.'

'Very good, sir.'

And there we leave them, Archie and Bartley, as they one after the other rip a brassie down the middle of the lush green fairway and get a sweet bounce and henceforth *a nice little run* that leaves them only a long niblick from the forgiving first green, both men shining examples of this narrative's philosophical proposition, i.e., that *the world might be a better place if only everyone would make a little more effort to get along.*

Acknowledgements

No man is an island, *&c.*, and very few books are written without the invisible but invaluable contribution of those who lend their kind words, advice, support and encouragement. I would like to thank Elizabeth Reapy, Gavin Burke, Shay Bagnall, Paul Whittington, Anthony and Claire Quinn, Jonathan Williams, Emma Warnock, David Torrans, Rory Jeffers, John McFetridge, Adrian McKinty, Ben O'Reilly, Peter McEvoy, Aileen McGloin and – last but not least – my co-conspirator, Lily Burke.